C

By Steven Dunne

The Reaper
The Disciple
Deity
The Unquiet Grave
A Killing Moon
Death Do Us Part

www.stevendunne.co.uk

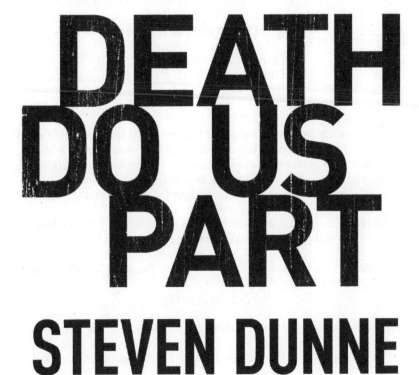

DEATH DO US PART

STEVEN DUNNE

headline

First published in 2016 by
HEADLINE PUBLISHING GROUP

1

Cataloguing in Publication Data is available from the British Library

ISBN 978 1 4722 1494 2

Typeset in Hoefler by Avon DataSet Ltd, Bidford-on-Avon, Warwickshire

Printed and bound by CPI Group (UK) Ltd, Croydon, CR0 4YY

HEADLINE PUBLISHING GROUP
An Hachette UK Company
Carmelite House
50 Victoria Embankment
London EC4Y 0DZ

www.headline.co.uk
www.hachette.co.uk

For Keith and Christine

Acknowledgements

Love and thanks to my wife Carmel for her support and encouragement. To Jeff Fountain for his editorial comments that are always to the point and insightful. Also to Keith Perch for his help with my website.

My vast team at Headline whose skills have contributed so much to the DI Brook series, chiefly my indispensable editor Vicki Mellor and publicity maestro Elizabeth Masters.

A special mention for my guides through the ins and outs of British policing. Thank you Steven Matthewman, Myles Lound and Joseph McDonald for your invaluable advice on various aspects of procedure.

Thanks to my agent, David Grossman, for continuing to believe in me and using his expertise to promote the series around the world.

A warm embrace for my favourite book chain, Waterstones, for the passionate and knowledgeable staff who have welcomed me so often through their doors to peddle my wares. A special mention for the hardworking staff in my local stores in Derby, Burton-on-Trent, Loughborough, Chesterfield and Nottingham, especially Dan Donson, Glenys Cooper, Matthew Brigg and Dawn Godfrey Jones, to name just a few of the friendly faces who've helped me to reach fans of the series in the East Midlands.

Finally a massive thank you to Tracy Fenton at The Book Club (TBC) for championing my work and introducing DI Brook to a whole new audience of enthusiastic fans at TBC. Special mention must go to super fans Sharon Bairden, Helen Boyce, Timea Cassara, Lynda Deutrom, Alexina Golding, Amanda Oughton, Susan Hunter. I wish I could list you all but you know who you are.

And finally, hello to Jason Isaacs.

One

October

REARDON THOROGOOD GRIPPED THE DOOR handle and tried to turn it, but her palm slipped on the cold metal. She stared at the blood on her trembling fingers, unable to remember what it was, who it belonged to, how it had got there. Instinctively she went to wipe the sticky mess on her clothes, but remembered she wasn't wearing any.

'It's okay. It's okay,' she panted, trying to accept the lie. 'You're alive. You're alive.' Her eyes flicked round the room, sliding past the bleeding carcass lying half on, half off the bed, knees on the floor, naked to the ankles, his jeans bunched and crumpled like a concertina. His face was to one side, eyes glazed and open.

She ran to pick up her mobile, lying broken apart on the floor, and tried to piece it together, but it wouldn't respond after its violent collision with the wall.

Closing her eyes, she sucked in a deep, calming breath before stepping over JJ's long legs and padding into the bathroom to run cold water over her hands. She dried herself

I

on a damp bath towel, blood smears staining the pale yellow cotton. Her blood or JJ's? She couldn't be sure.

Catching sight of her battered face in the mirror, she recoiled in horror at the stranger staring back. Her mouth was bloodied and swollen, her nose leaking a mixture of snot and blood, her left eye bruised and beginning to close. Wet hair trailed across her shoulders, mopping up some of the arterial blood spatter from JJ's neck. Using the bloodied towel, she wiped more splashes of red from the top of her breasts and shoulders before dropping it into the bath, the draught causing some of the tea lights burning around the porcelain ledge to gutter.

Unable to look at her disfigured face, she moved across to the wardrobe to find clothes. She yanked at the doors, but they wouldn't budge with JJ's massive feet blocking them. She stooped to move them but withdrew her hand, reluctant to touch his still-warm body, momentarily transfixed by the trickle of blood that had rolled down his muscular thigh to collect in the well at the back of his knee. His shocked face glared at her, the frozen expression still trying to make sense of the sharp pain in his neck as the knife was drawn across his throat.

'What the fuck, JJ!' she mumbled, feebly kicking his thigh, remembering the blows inflicted on her by the ex-boyfriend from her school years, long since discarded in her teens.

With a clench of fists to dispel the shaking in her hands, she composed herself. Luke Coulson was still out there roaming the house. Another old schoolmate, though him she barely knew. Luke had been the quiet one, awkward even – nobody invited him to parties or pubs as teenagers dipped toes into adulthood.

Her brother Ray knew him better, had kicked around with both Luke and JJ all through primary school and beyond.

How long ago? Seventeen years since that first day of primary school. She remembered it like yesterday.

Ray, a year older, had been ordered to walk his sister to her first day. He was annoyed at Mum and Dad for weeks after, and she remembered how he chivvied her along the country lanes, impatient to be there so he could cut the umbilical and play football with his mates.

JJ had been in her form, though, had marched in that first day like he owned the place, the only new kid not cowed with fear on that first step towards distant maturity. Even at five years old, JJ wasn't scared of the teachers, with their big rooms and bigger voices.

Reardon stared at his lifeless corpse, baffled that she could ever have imagined herself in love with him. It hadn't ended well.

JJ had started drinking in local pubs at fifteen, where he'd found his one true love. Alcohol. From that time onwards he was regularly drunk, and when JJ drank, he resorted to his fists. With his height and power, plenty of people had felt the weight of his destructive anger. And though he had never actually hit her during their courtship, there was the occasional push and shove. Towards the end his manner was rarely less than aggressive, and the one time he'd threatened to slap her was all the reason she'd needed to dump her 'bit of rough'.

By the time the police got to know him, his life was already turning sour, leaving school at sixteen with no qualifications and few prospects. Reardon had stayed on for A levels followed by university, and as their paths diverged, they lost touch with each other.

Ray had kept tabs on him, though, and it was no surprise when he reported that JJ had slipped seamlessly into a life of petty crime, picking up a two-year sentence for burglary and assault when he was eighteen.

She closed her eyes to the gore but opened them immediately. Concentrate. Luke was still out there – and he had a knife.

You have to leave. Looking around, she discounted the clothes she'd been wearing when JJ had burst into her bedroom – the T-shirt and skimpy shorts lay in tatters on the floor, torn to shreds in his powerful hands.

Instead, she picked up JJ's sweatshirt, discarded gleefully not ten minutes ago, and pulled it over her head. It reeked of his body odour and she had a flashback to him grinding his teeth as he struggled to pacify her, his breath reeking of cheap brandy and cigarettes, his underarms damp and pungent.

She found sensible cotton knickers in a drawer and stepped into them, being careful not to overbalance, then pulled them delicately over her thighs.

Padding barefoot to the door, she opened it and moved warily into the corridor, closing the bedroom door behind her. She crept along on the thick wool carpet towards the kitchen, placing her bare feet carefully to avoid the trail of bloody footprints coming in the opposite direction, trying to tamp down visions about their source. Everything felt so unreal, so incongruous in the deep quiet of a Monday lunchtime in the Derbyshire countryside.

As she moved, she barely noticed the sonorous tick of the grandfather clock in the entrance hall until it struck twelve thirty and she leapt out of her skin, pushing herself back against the wall to regain her breath.

Twelve thirty? Is that all? Hard to believe JJ had burst into her room only twenty minutes before – a lifetime seemed to have passed since then.

She glanced up at the security camera at the end of the hall. The ever-present red dot was gone, the camera switched off. At that same moment, she saw the door on her right and tried the handle. It opened, so she bolted inside, closing the door behind her then flicking on the light in the tiny, windowless cupboard of a space, an ideal location for the farm's security control room.

It was Ray who'd insisted his parents put in cameras after several outhouses had been broken into. In fact he had personally oversaw their installation. But now the bank of closed-circuit monitors was dark. Reardon sat at the console and examined the controls. The system's master switch had been turned to 'Off', so she pushed it back up and pressed the reboot button. The drone of waking machinery was immediate.

'Come on, come on.' She looked anxiously behind her, waiting for the monitors to spring to life, expecting Luke to rush in at any moment and investigate what seemed to her a deafening noise. Finally the monitors flickered into life and she clicked urgently at the control button, maximising the camera feed throughout the one-storey house, room by room. Living room, sitting and dining rooms, corridors leading to the other bedrooms of the sprawling bungalow. There was no sign of life. 'Where are you?'

Finally she loaded the kitchen camera and for a second was forced to turn her head away. She looked again at the grainy image of her father lying draped over her mother's contorted body, dark stains covering his neck and back. Both appeared lifeless.

Panting, she scrolled through the other cameras again but found no sign of the prowling Luke. She checked the front and back doors, which seemed clear, the drive too. Ray's silver Porsche wasn't there. Only her father's Range Rover stood on the gravel.

She turned off the security suite light before opening the door, putting her eye to the crack. The hall was still clear, so she skittered to the front entrance, looking all about her, senses supercharged.

She glanced up at the entrance camera, red light now winking at her. 'Ray?' she mimed softly towards the lens as though he might see her. 'Where are you?' Torn between flight and fright, she opened the heavy front door, allowing the sharp autumn air to sweep in from the grounds, damp and soothing. A couple of large leaves tumbled on to the welcome mat, sucked in by the draught.

With a deep breath, Reardon stepped barefoot across the threshold on to the chilled stone flags beyond. On the point of fleeing, her eye alighted on the closed kitchen doors. She hesitated.

What if Mum and Dad are alive? She couldn't just leave. Not without knowing. She took a moment to gather her nerve and approached the ranch-style double doors. After pressing an ear to the lacquered wood, she turned the handle and stepped inside.

Unlike the black-and-white world of the security monitor, the tableau that greeted her literally dripped with colour. The floor was awash with blood, some pooling beneath her parents' heads, some smeared into a slithering pattern where her father had crawled across the terracotta tiles to reach his dying wife. His arms enfolded her and his head sagged next to hers, their cheeks touching.

Reardon closed her eyes, forcing out a tear, which rolled down her cheek. She wiped it away and inched closer. To her bare feet, the floor seemed hot to the touch, and the bloody footprints of killer and victims were already drying to a stain.

Reardon spied her mother's orange Crocs at the edge of the scarlet pool, so she slipped them on to her feet and crept towards her parents through the coagulating blood. She knelt in the warm, sticky liquid, holding the back of her hand to her mouth, the smell of death, feisty and invasive, assaulting her nostrils.

She pressed fingers against her father's wrist then her mother's. Neither had a pulse. She held her hand to her mum's mouth and nose but could feel no breath, then withdrew it when she noticed it trembling.

Finally she knelt by her father, leaning in to listen for sounds of breathing. Her long hair trailed in the blood. No sign of life. Her parents were dead.

She leaned back on her haunches, kissed her fingers and pressed them to both her parents' lips in turn. Her eye was caught by the phone on the wall, and she rose to her feet to hold the receiver against her ear, leaning an arm against the adjacent thermostat to support her bruised forehead, seemingly on the point of collapse. The landline was as dead as her parents.

Blindly she pushed the bloodied handset in the vague direction of the cradle. She missed and tried again. Again she missed and the receiver fell to earth, the cord dangling in space, twisting and jerking like a bungee jumper. Now she covered her face with both hands, her shoulders shuddering with emotion, slumping against the wall in an effort to hold herself upright.

Turning, she spotted her mother's handbag on the kitchen table and hurried over to it, emptying the contents on to the pitted wooden surface. She scoured the debris and plucked the elderly mobile from among the junk her mum habitually kept in her bag – mints, empty lipsticks, cheap mascara and eyeliner. Her thumb trembled as she pushed at the buttons.

'Come on, come on.' A warning noise from the phone. The battery was flat. Reardon hurled the device at a wall, screaming then immediately putting a hand over her mouth when she realised she might be heard.

Trying to think, she remembered the Range Rover sitting on the drive and sifted through the detritus on the table for the keys. They weren't there. Looking round, she moved across to the French windows, peering out over the rear of the farm, at the mature lawn, the brick outhouses and beyond, the rolling fields across to Findern and safety. She tried the handle but the doors were locked and the keys weren't there. Worse, Sargent wasn't stomping around on the lawn or pawing at the glass for a walk or a ball to chase. She closed her eyes. *Please God, let Sargent be okay.*

Turning back, her eye alighted on the unblinking scrutiny of the wall-mounted camera. 'Where are you, Ray?' she pleaded at the lens as though it could answer. 'Help me!' She re-traced her steps to the hall, gaze averted from the savagery, and dashing out towards the front door ran straight into the burly figure of Luke Coulson.

She screamed and pushed herself away, raising her arms in a defensive stance, eyes widening in fear.

Luke was short and a little dumpy, but powerful through the shoulders. His nose was studded with blackheads and his hair was greasy and pushed back from his pockmarked face.

Reardon tried not to stare at the bloodied butcher's knife in his reddened hand.

His clothes, strangely, were free of blood, and she realised he was wearing some of her father's – corduroys and a checked shirt – which were a little baggy on him. Simultaneously she registered the plastic bag in his other hand, bulging with the bloody clothing he'd been wearing as he'd pulled the knife across JJ's throat. The bag handles were tied in a tight knot but blood had accumulated in one corner and was dripping on to the floor through the plastic.

'Hello, Reardon,' Luke said shyly, his eyes running up and down her long, slim legs, smiling at first before a look of dismay distorted his features when he saw her swollen face. He held out a hand, but she shrank back. 'You're hurt,' he said, the speech impediment that had limited his verbal contributions at school pronounced in the deathly quiet of the farm.

'Yes, I'm fucking hurt,' she spat, finding some useful anger. She was shocked at her thick voice, as though she'd had gas at the dentist, and blood and saliva sprayed from her damaged mouth. 'Where's Sargent?'

'Your dog? JJ gave him some meat. I don't know what was in it. I think he's all right.' Reardon inched to her left for a clear sight of the door, but Luke was alert. 'Where are you going?'

'I have to leave,' she said warily, not taking her eyes from him. Freedom was just yards away.

Luke dropped his gaze to the bloodied Crocs on her feet. 'You've seen them.' Reardon gulped and dipped her head, unable to speak. 'I'm sorry,' he mumbled, smiling to reassure her. 'They were nice.' He glanced up at the security camera then back at Reardon. 'But your dad shouldn't have shouted. He shouldn't have chased me.'

'What?' said Reardon, dumbfounded.

'He didn't give me much choice,' said Luke. Dismayed at her shocked expression, he smiled again, trying to affect levity. 'I had to borrow some of his clothes. I hope you don't mind.'

Baffled, she shook her head. 'What have you done with Ray?' she said, sounding out the words as though teaching a language.

'Your brother? Nuffin'.'

'He was here,' said Reardon. 'But now his car's gone.'

Luke grinned. 'Then it's just you and me.'

'What have you done with him?' she said more forcefully.

Luke's face contorted in anger. 'I just told you.'

Reardon swallowed, glancing gimlet-eyed at the knife. She held out her hands to pacify. 'Please put the knife down.'

'Knife?' Luke looked enquiringly at her then in surprise at the weapon in his bloodstained hand. His expression darkened. 'I didn't want to. I had no choice. You shouldn't have let JJ do that. He doesn't love you.'

Reardon trembled at Luke's sudden animation, realising she wouldn't have the strength to outrun him. Thinking weakness might rile him further, she tried to rustle up some aggression. 'Look at my face, Luke. I *didn't* let him. He made me.'

Luke stared, and a smile of understanding slowly creased his features. 'He made you. He hit you.'

'Yes, he hit me.'

'Then you don't love him.'

'Of course I don't fucking love him,' she snapped, holding back the tears.

'But he was your boyfriend,' insisted Luke.

'A lifetime ago. But I don't love him now. Why do you think he hit me?'

'I didn't realise . . .'

'Tell me where my brother is.'

'I haven't seen him,' insisted Luke, irritation catching in his voice. 'Why do you keep asking?'

'Because I'm worried about him.' She glanced at the front door, but her path was still blocked, then back towards the kitchen, where her parents lay butchered. She was trapped. She had to get past Luke and on to the drive. 'His car's gone.'

'Car?'

'The silver Porsche.'

'Sweet ride,' nodded Luke. He pulled a cotton bag from his belt and rummaged around. She saw her father and mother's watches and rings and a wad of cash. A second later, he held out the Range Rover's key fob. 'These were in your mum's handbag.'

'They're for the Ranger Rover,' said Reardon softly.

'I would've preferred the Porsche,' said Luke sulkily.

'Can I have those then?' asked Reardon, nodding at the key fob.

Luke shook his head. 'Think I'm gonna need 'em.' His lip wobbled and he seemed suddenly close to tears. 'I'm in trouble, ain't I?'

Reardon tried to think of an answer that wouldn't end up with Luke stabbing her.

'Ain't I?' he screamed.

She jumped out of her skin and nodded, her speech ragged and breathless. 'Yes, Luke. You're in trouble.'

She braced herself for the consequences of her admission, but suddenly Luke's anger dissipated and his eyes sparkled. 'You remember my name.'

'What?'

'You remember me,' grinned Luke. 'From school.'

Reardon hesitated. 'Of course I remember you. You're JJ's friend. You were in Ray's year.'

'I was in *your* year,' he snarled, tightening his grip on the knife.

'Yes. I remember now,' panted Reardon, holding out her hands in self-defence. She scrambled to get her wits back. 'It's just you seemed so much older.'

Luke's grin reappeared. 'Older?'

'Much older,' said Reardon, breathless at the deceit. 'I'm surprised.'

'You noticed me at school, then.'

'Of course.'

Luke's expression hardened. 'That's funny, because whenever I was near you, you acted like I weren't there.'

'I . . . it wasn't deliberate, Luke.' She cast around for a palliative. 'But you were very quiet. You never spoke to me either.'

Luke looked at the floor, nodding. 'I couldn't. I daren't.' He gestured at his mouth. 'Not with this.' He looked sheepishly at his feet. 'I love you, Reardon. From the first minute I saw you. You were beautiful.' He looked her up and down. 'You still are!'

'I didn't know,' said Reardon, trying to load sympathy into her voice.

'You must of.'

'I didn't, I swear. You . . . you should have told me.'

'Yeah?' scoffed Luke. 'And have people laughing their arses off at me like JJ done. He wet himself. Said you was popular. Reardon's clever and fit, he said. A girl like her wouldn't never look at a freak like you, he said. Not without pissing herself.'

'I wouldn't have laughed.'

'You *did* laugh,' said Luke, his eyes burning into her. 'JJ told Ray I loved you. He said Ray laughed. And next day Ray told JJ he told you and that you laughed so hard you were almost sick . . .'

'It's not true.'

'He told JJ to tell me you said I was a fucking loser.' Luke raised the knife and Reardon took a sidestep that moved her closer to the front door, her hands held in front, palms open.

'Ray never said anything, Luke. You have to believe me. Is that why you're here now? To pay me back for something that didn't happen?'

'I . . . it was JJ's idea. You did the same to him.'

'It's not true.'

'Said you treated him like shit and he wanted to talk to you, tell you how he felt.'

'He was lying, Luke. He didn't want to tell me anything. He wanted to hurt me. Look!' she exclaimed, gesturing at her face.

Luke looked shamefaced at the floor. 'When he was hurting you, I felt bad.'

'I know.'

'I couldn't just stand there,' he continued, encouraged. 'I had to stop him.'

'You did a good thing, Luke,' she said, slow and clear. With a sudden inspiration, she added, 'You saved me.'

A shy smile invaded Luke's features. 'I did, didn't I? That's because I love you.'

'I know that. Now.' She paused, trying to smile. 'But if you really love me, Luke, you'll let me go.'

'You didn't laugh at me?'

'Never. You and Ray were just kids. He never said a word

about you. He was taking the piss. That's what teenage boys do. Now please put the knife down.'

Luke dropped the knife and the tension in Reardon's shoulders eased a notch. 'I wouldn't have hurt you, Reardon. Promise.'

'I know.' Breathing easier, Reardon moved slowly to the door. 'I'm leaving now.'

Luke's eyes filled with tears. 'You're afraid of me.'

'No. It's just . . .'

'You are! And that's not what I wanted. Is it because of what I done to JJ?'

'No, I—'

'I had to. I'm not like him. You have to believe that.'

Reardon swallowed hard as he opened his arms and advanced on her. She couldn't bring herself to move closer, but it didn't matter as he stepped in to her and pushed his face into her neck, sighing like a well-fed puppy. He stank of fear and sweat and blood. She felt his hot breath on her neck as his hands pressed on her shoulder blades, pulling her body to him. She eyed the knife, but it was out of reach. Instead she laid a hand on his broad back, tilting her head away. He moved his mouth over her ear to speak.

She pulled away and stared at him, her eyes fixed on his beseeching expression. Finally, she nodded. 'Of course I will.'

'No sign of life,' mumbled DC Kevin Drinkwater, lowering binoculars as he crouched on the drive in front of the farm.

'The Thorogood girl said it was a massacre.' Detective Sergeant Rachel Caskey narrowed her eyes, hand subconsciously held to the pendant under her shirt. 'She mentioned a dog.'

Drinkwater flicked at his radio and put the question out there. A voice crackled on the radio.

'They've found the dog,' relayed Drinkwater. 'Seems to be breathing. Looks like it's been drugged.'

'That's bad,' said Caskey.

'Sarge?'

'Drugs smack of planning, and planning is bad. A random is one thing . . .' Caskey turned to the heavily padded uniformed sergeant in a baseball cap on his haunches a few feet away. 'What do you reckon, Tink?'

'Looks quiet,' said Authorised Firearms Officer Ellis Tinkerman. 'And no vehicles. The bird may have flown.'

'The victim said there was a Range Rover and maybe a Porsche,' said Drinkwater. 'We put them out on the wire. No hits yet.'

'Then my team had better saddle up,' murmured Tinkerman. He thumbed the radio on his epaulette. 'This is Bronze Commander . . .'

'Shouldn't we wait for the chopper?' said Caskey.

'Where is it?'

'About ten minutes out of Bradford.'

Tinkerman considered. 'That's too long.' He thumbed at his radio again, giving the signal. 'Be quick and small,' he added, raising his large frame into a crouching position – harder than it looked in his uncomfortable-looking garb of black combat trousers, heavy-duty black boots and black flak jacket – then broke into a trot, the carbine nestled easily under his right arm. Similarly dressed firearms officers stood in unison around the farmhouse and advanced from all directions on the property, each making haste without quite running but all hunched to present the smallest target.

Three officers arrived at the front door while others disappeared behind the building. At the front, one of the AFOs waited with the enforcer ram, while another had his hand poised on the handle. When the door opened, he pushed it back and the second AFO put down the ram and disappeared into the murk beyond, looking first left, then right, gun held high against his cheek. Tinkerman and the other officer fell in behind, their weapons poised, glancing all about as they entered the building.

Caskey and Drinkwater crouched to wait, ears cocked for gunfire, but all they heard was the word *Clear* shouted at short intervals, so they moved slowly towards the farmhouse.

'Sounds like he's in the wind, guv,' said Drinkwater.

'Then let's hope he has a plan,' said Caskey.

'Guv?'

'A spree killer with nowhere to run is a dangerous animal.'

'He's had a few hours' start. Could be anywhere.'

Caskey nodded faintly and flicked at her mobile, then held it to her ear. 'Still no answer from DI Ford,' she cursed.

'Maybe he's . . .' Drinkwater hesitated before tailing off, wishing he hadn't started the sentence.

Caskey gave him an admonishing glare before coming to a decision. 'Get someone round to his house, Kev. Pick him up.'

'Guv,' he acknowledged, turning to comply.

Caskey's radio crackled. *We're all clear. Three down, all dead.* She fired off an acknowledgement before setting off towards the farmhouse.

'That's an awful lot of claret,' said Tinkerman, staring at the intertwined bodies of Monty and Patricia Thorogood from the edge of the blood pool. Caskey was equally saucer-eyed, unable to reply.

'Just a bit,' replied Drinkwater, eyes also glued to the carnage.

'Tap an artery like that and there's no way back,' said Tinkerman, indicating Reardon's mother. 'Looks like the husband was trying to protect her from the perp.'

'True love,' quipped Drinkwater.

'Sorry, did I make a joke?' retorted Tinkerman. Drinkwater reddened.

'Go check if there's any news on the Range Rover, Kev,' said Caskey. Drinkwater shuffled past the pool of blood, heading for the front door.

'You okay, Rachel?'

Caskey blinked and turned to face Tinkerman. 'Whatever he did, it wasn't enough to save her.'

'At least he tried.'

Caskey nodded. 'That's something. Anything in the grounds?'

Tinkerman answered his radio, on the move. 'We've checked the perimeter.' He turned at the door with a further glance down at the entwined bodies. 'The site's secure. The other deceased is in one of the bedrooms. Blood trail all the way from here. Looks like one of the perps did the parents first, then went for the daughter only to find she was already taken.'

'And a difference of opinion ensued,' observed Caskey.

'Boyfriend?'

'Not according to the Thorogood girl. Both were perps.'

'So one perp killed the other perp over her,' nodded Tinkerman. 'No honour amongst rapists. I don't envy you clearing this lot up, Rachel. You should ditch CID and get back to shooting bad guys. Life's a lot simpler in Armed Response.'

'Life is never simple,' said Caskey, trying to force out a smile.

'Copy that,' said Tinkerman. 'Outside if you need us.'

'Guv!' said DC Drinkwater, hurrying in. 'Traffic pulled over the Range Rover on the M25. Provisional ID on our suspect. They've got him.'

Caskey looked at her watch. 'M25 – he didn't hang about. Any trouble?'

Drinkwater shook his head. 'Meek as a mouse.'

'Chalk one up to the Black Rats. What happened?'

'A patrol spotted the car parked at South Mimms and staked it out. Seemed the guy was off buying fizzy drinks and Mars bars and walked straight into their arms.'

'Outstanding.'

'It gets better,' said Drinkwater. 'He had clothes in a bag in the boot to dump but hadn't got round to it. Blood caked all over them. Plus he had inscribed watches, gold coins and cash. It's a slam dunk.'

Caskey's smile was slight but enduring. 'Good enough. This'll be a nice win for the guv'nor. Get the tape up, Kev, and scramble a SOCO team, stat.'

Two

Thirteen months later

'DON'T BE AFRAID, EDITH!'

Edith Gibson stirred from her slumber, grateful for the brief nap. Ever since her husband's health had started to deteriorate, she'd been short of rest. Taking forty winks when she could grab them was the only way to get through the day. Bert's heart disease caused problems with blood circulation in the legs, so at night she had to lie awake listening to his constant fidgeting as he looked for a position to ease his discomfort. On occasion, he was able to ignore the pain that came to him in bed, and when his jabbering and moaning stopped, Edith could steal a few hours' sleep, but those nights were rare.

When she did sleep, she dreamed of her grandchildren, Michael and Jessie – now teenagers – growing tall in the sunshine of Western Australia.

Bert, the lightest of sleepers, said he sometimes heard her call out their names in the night. He even said he once saw her cupping her arms as though holding one of the twins as a baby, the way she'd held them at the airport that last time, before she and Bert bade a tearful farewell to their son and daughter-in-law and the two oblivious infants.

They'd received photographs, of course. Pete and Jeanie had been scrupulous in the first few years, sending snaps of Michael and Jessie enjoying their new life thousands of miles from their heartbroken grandparents – eating huge shrimps from the barbecue or playing in the small backyard pool of their new home in Perth.

But these became more infrequent with the advent of digital photography and Bert's reluctance to own a computer.

'What do we want one of those for?' he'd said.

'So Pete can send pictures of Michael and Jessie,' she'd reply. 'And there's something called Skype, Bert. It allows you to speak in person and we could see them on the screen while we talk.'

'Must cost a fortune.'

'It's free.'

'Aye, well. If he wants to send pictures, he can post them.'

And that had been that. Since then, she'd had to wait until the once-a-year package at Christmas to see images of their grandchildren.

'Edith,' said the voice.

She opened her eyes and licked her lips, still able to taste the alcohol in her mouth. 'I'm thirsty.'

'Here.' She straightened up to drink the glass of water and saw Bert stirring in the chair next to her.

'Are you all right?' he croaked, his voice strained.

'What happened?' she asked.

'You had a little sleep,' said the voice. A hand took the glass of water from her.

'Did I? Wouldn't that have been the best time?'

'Course not. Defeats the object. The music's ready. The photographs, too.'

Edith looked down at the framed photograph on her lap. It was of her son and daughter-in-law with Michael and Jessie when they were little. She smiled and stroked the image with her liver-spotted hand. 'This one's my favourite.' She looked up earnestly. 'Can we hold hands?'

'I'd be upset if you didn't.'

Edith rested her hand on the arm of the chair and Bert covered it with his own shaking one. He tried to speak and lift himself out of the chair, but his face twisted with the effort.

'No,' he whispered, sinking back on to the foam cushions. 'This isn't right.'

'Calm yourself, Bert,' said Edith. A second later, the soft violins of Barber's *Adagio* filled the room with solemn lament. 'This is your favourite.'

Bert began to agitate more vigorously. 'No, stop . . .'

Edith squeezed his hand. 'Settle down, Bert, there's no time.'

'But Mother . . .'

'No, Bert. For once just stop fussing. And do your tie up.'

'But . . .'

'Your tie, Bert. You want to look smart.' She watched him fiddle with shaking hands, forcing the knot further into his gnarled old neck. She smiled at his efforts and a tear fell. He finished tightening the tie and returned his hand to hers.

'How do I look?'

'Like my handsome boy.' He grinned at this, false teeth shifting in his jaw. 'Remember the first time we met, Bert?'

Bert's mouth creased in recollection. 'Schott's dance hall. Just after the war.'

'That's it, my love,' said Edith. 'Do you remember our first dance?'

His face softened with a love that didn't need to be expressed. 'A bossa nova.'

'It was.' Edith chuckled. 'And remember how you cut in on Reggie Kane?'

'That ten-bob millionaire. He could barely keep his hands off yer, pinching yer backside like that, the slimy bugger.'

'I know,' giggled Edith. 'My bottom was bruised for weeks.'

The intensity of the strings heightened.

'I love you, Bert.'

'Love you, Edith.'

Their tender gaze was distracted by a mechanical click, and a pair of muted explosions accompanied the flash of ignition as the bullets tore into them. The two old people looked vaguely startled, then lay back with a sigh of escaping breath.

Three

Tuesday 1 November

DI DAMEN BROOK SIPPED HIS FOURTH tea of the day as the rain beat down outside his cottage. From the kitchen table, his daughter's opened pack of cigarettes caught his eye, butts lined up like a row of handsome guardsmen. But, having emptied the ashtray, the lingering smell of stale tobacco doused any yearning he might harbour to reopen the door on his addiction. He closed the packet and dropped it in a drawer.

The three empty wine bottles, however, he left on the kitchen table, determined to deploy them as a conversation starter. In the three nights of her visit, he and Terri had got through nine bottles of wine, and Brook knew for certain that he'd consumed no more than four glasses in total.

After draining his tea, he slipped the blanket from his shoulders and padded to the door to look out beyond the porch to the early-morning blackness beyond. There was little to be seen beyond the dry-stone wall at the other side of the steep little back road that wound its way up from the centre of the village to his cottage.

Low cloud covered Hartington, and though Brook wasn't averse to yomping for hours in the rain, he knew Terri wouldn't be so keen, even assuming she woke from her slumbers any time soon.

Brook glanced at his watch. Nearly seven o'clock. He'd normally be out on his regular morning walk by now. In summer, between cases, that would involve a quick six miles following the banks of the Dove, turning off at the Manifold Valley stream then back to his cottage on the high roads along Reynards Lane. In the winter, nothing so fancy, and if he was on a case he might be pushed to get around the duck pond and back.

He washed up and made another tea, taking his first sip as the letter box rattled. A moment later he dropped the bills on the table and examined the cheap envelope forwarded from his PO box.

It wasn't the familiar writing that caused him a flutter of anxiety but the thickness of the envelope. As part of an inducement to force a confession from a beaten opponent, and to bring closure to the families of victims, Brook had made a promise to play postal chess with an incarcerated serial killer, Edward Mullen. Too wary to provide an address, either electronic or geographic, he had insisted the games be conducted by letter, and only then with the filter of a post office box.

But today, squeezing the envelope, he could feel it contained more than the habitual slip of cheap notepaper detailing a next move and an additional series of provisional moves dependent on Brook's anticipated response. Very occasionally there'd been a line or two of text having a sly dig at the underhanded way Brook had ensnared his prey, but nothing too bitter. Unusually, Mullen was perfectly at ease, having swapped a house he dared not leave and couldn't maintain for a secure prison cell and three squares a day.

Mullen was an unprepossessing soul – meek and mild-mannered with a gentle but tortured intelligence – and to look at him it was difficult to accept that he was the Pied Piper, a serial killer who had abducted children and buried them alive in a home-made packing crate.

The children were abducted over the course of decades and died a slow and agonising death, no one around to hear their plaintive sobs for help. But Mullen didn't kill for kicks. He killed for company. For himself, yes, but also for a childhood friend who had died young at the hands of his own sister. For a while he'd scratched out a living as a medium and claimed, when caught, that he could see the ghosts of murder victims, clinging to their killers. Thus, each dead child represented eternal companionship for Mullen, and he was content to rot in Wakefield Prison with his coterie of young victims by his side.

But today was different.

Brook held an ear to the living room door. Terri was still snoring gently on the couch so he made his way to the tiny office, where a small square table supported a computer and a chessboard, the pieces scattered in mid-struggle.

He sat with his tea and opened the envelope, the note with his opponent's next move falling to the floor. He left it there while he opened out the two sheets of A4.

Inspector Brook,

I hope the screw that checks the outgoing mail has become so used to the routine of our little diversion that they'll pay no mind to my monthly missive and allow these thoughts to reach you unmolested.

Forgive the presumption, but I didn't know who else to approach. It has been a couple of years since you put me in here, and living out my days in blissful seclusion from other inmates has left me plenty of time for reflection – when I'm not busy with my entourage of friends and acquaintance from across the divide, you understand. How is your little band of other-worldly companions, by the way? Do you think of them near you, reaching out to you in the dark from beyond the grave for reason and comfort? Do they rob you of your sleep?

I digress. From our many (mostly enjoyable) conversations, I was convinced – despite your expressed cynicism and the deceitful way you outflanked me – of your moral probity and desire to get to the truth of a case. For that reason, I thought I'd lay out something that happened to me a month ago and which may interest you.

In my section of the isolation block up here in Wakefield, as you may or may not be aware, there are four cells – mine and three others. As far as I can tell, two of them are used on an occasional basis to inflict solitary confinement on the dolts who can't seem to accept their situation. A few days of sobbing and wailing and some sporadic rowdiness usually gives way to deeper introspection, at which point they are deemed calm enough to be moved back into general pop.

At other times the temporary inhabitants of IB are those in immediate danger of reprisal after they've stolen drugs or fags or been the object of sexual violence from another inmate. These cons tend to be much quieter, and though they are understandably not keen to draw attention to themselves, I can usually pick up their self-pitying snuffling. (Really, the amount of grief caused by sex and drugs in this place is baffling, since inmates are theoretically helpless to acquire either. V. tedious.)

Now I want to be clear that the dullards cooling their heels in IB wouldn't normally be of interest to me despite their occasional requests for conversation and a sympathetic ear. I prefer my own company, as you know, and have never yet been minded to answer entreaties from neighbouring cells.

However, this changed recently when I discovered that the third cell in the block, one I assumed to have been empty since my arrival, is in fact occupied and has been for several months. This was a surprise, because every time I'd been escorted to the yard for my solo perambulation, the door to Cell 3 had been closed and the grille steadfastly shut. I did wonder why, when the other two cells are invariably left open to freshen the air for the next resident.

Well, now I know. The cell was occupied all along, and yet, oddly, I'd never heard a peep from its inmate, never a groan or a scream in the night, no face pressed to the grille seeking the solace of companionship craved by every other deadbeat who lands in IB.

About a month ago, at the hour of my sky gazing, I was on the way to the yard when I noticed for the first time that the cell door was open, I assumed for cleaning.

But when I paused to glance inside, I saw a young man sitting cross-legged on the floor. His eyes were closed almost in meditation and he paid me no attention.

Nor was he interested in the prison guards, who I now realised were tossing his cell, which they're prone to do from time to time in the block. God knows what they expect to find when we have limited access to the rest of the inmates, but I suppose they have their procedures.

I was able to stop and watch for only a second before my own guard moved me on, but as I turned to continue to the yard, the young man opened his eyes and stared back at me. His gaze was cold and dead, and to my surprise, I recognised him. It was Luke Coulson.

Doubtless you know the name, even though I know it wasn't your case. I followed the trial with great interest earlier in the year – I still have the press cuttings – because Black Oak Farm is near Findern, a village where I liked to walk as a teenager when my family first moved to Derby. You'll remember Coulson was convicted of murder and conspiracy to commit rape and murder at the farm. The owner, Monty Thorogood, and his wife Patricia were killed with a butcher knife and their daughter Reardon beaten and sexually assaulted before she escaped to raise the alarm.

At his trial, his brief suggested that Coulson went along to the farm at the suggestion of Jonathan Jemson, a former boyfriend of Reardon and an old school friend who had a history of petty crime. According to counsel, Jemson told Coulson they were going to the farm to burglarise the safe on behalf of Ray Thorogood, Reardon's wayward and debt-ridden brother, a young man who had apparently argued with his parents on numerous occasions about money.

Well, you know the upshot. Coulson was convicted

of murdering Reardon's parents, as well as his co-conspirator, Jonathan Jemson, after which he ransacked the house for as much cash and jewellery as he could find before making his escape in the family Range Rover. After he was caught the same day, investigations began to lay bare the full extent of Ray Thorogood's plan to murder his family and inherit the family fortune.

According to text messages sent between Jemson and Ray, Coulson was to be recruited as a plausible fall guy to be blamed for the slaughter of the Thorogood family. The fact that he'd had a schoolboy crush on Reardon was the carrot to get him to the farm. For the plan to succeed, Jemson was supposed to dispatch the parents and then Ray's sister. Coulson had to die at the scene and Jemson would make it appear that he died from injuries sustained in a struggle with Reardon but only after he'd struck the fatal blow against the poor girl.

Then Jemson would set an 'accidental' fire, destroying any evidence of his presence, before escaping, leaving the dead Coulson to shoulder the blame as an obsessed lone killer. Ray would inherit a fortune and subsequently compensate Jemson from the proceeds.

A brilliant conceit in many ways, but one the jury didn't completely buy into. It didn't help that Coulson refused to testify on his own behalf, even though his brief argued that his client was in fact Reardon's saviour. According to his version, Coulson walked in on Jemson in the commission of a rape and as a result became so enraged that he murdered Jemson to save Reardon from harm.

Of course the prosecution could point to the fact that Coulson was already covered in blood when he killed Jemson, having just savagely murdered Mr and Mrs Thorogood. Failing to mount a defence, or even deny his guilt, Coulson was duly convicted of all three murders.

A fascinating tale of slaughter and mayhem, the kind you usually hear about in America, taking place in sleepy Derbyshire. Three people dead, a young girl sexually assaulted and traumatised and a feckless brother on the run in Spain, if the papers are to be believed.

You're probably wondering what this has to do with me. Do you remember my gift? Of course you do. All those child murderers I brought to justice, their accumulated victims standing beside them, reaching out from an unquiet grave to demand answers. I see the baggage a killer carries with him through life, Inspector. I see my friend Billy with the new companions I harvested for him. I see his murdering sister, ageless, always by his side with her own coterie of demons, and the company is a great comfort when I wake.

You're shaking your head, aren't you? Perhaps you've forgotten how easily I could identify your own special companion, stranded in purgatory, waiting for you to explain yourself. Would you like to know who haunts Luke Coulson? Don't pretend you're not interested. Let me waste no more of your valuable time – the official account of the murders is completely wrong. Your DI Ford, who let me slip through his fingers, has triumphed again. Luke didn't kill the Thorogoods. He did kill Jemson, of that there is no doubt, but he didn't slay the mother and father because they're not with him, bound to him in eternity looking for an explanation for the violence done to them. Somebody else killed the Thorogoods, Inspector, and it appears they've got away with it.

So why am I telling you all this? I hear you ask. Because you're the Great Detective, Brook. I know you care about justice and can't rest until you have all the answers, and the mere thought of you enduring all that angst and torment pleases me enormously. I look forward to when you're finally in the cell next to mine and you can tell me all about it.

Well there you are. A mystery befitting your talents – something for you to get your teeth into and hopefully distract you from our little tussles. My latest move is enclosed and you know where we are if you want to talk further. I won't hold my breath. I'm sure there'll be plenty of office politics to prevent you poking your nose into a colleague's case. From the little I saw of DI Ford, his arrogance and conceit were in direct contrast to his talents as a detective. The least you should do is come and talk to Coulson and try to winkle out his version of events. I know from personal experience how good you are at getting people to talk.

And if you do happen by, bring a bottle of you know what. The warden may not like our little arrangement but he's never threatened to dishonour it thus far. Sweet dreams.

Edward

Brook's mobile began to vibrate and he was happy to toss the pages on the table. It was Detective Sergeant John Noble.

Brook hesitated. 'I'm on leave, John.'

'Enjoying yourself?'

'Very much,' lied Brook.

'How's Terri?'

'She's fine,' he lied again. 'She asked after you.'

'Oh?'

'I told her you were fine.'

'Not sure you've got this small talk thing off pat yet.'

'And on that note,' prompted Brook.

Noble hesitated. 'Two more bodies. Similar scene to last month's double homicide in Breadsall. Shot through the heart.'

'Where?'

'Boulton Moor. Eastern edge of the city, near the A50 link road.'

'I know where it is. What of it?'

'Don't you want to know details?'

'If it's the same as last month, I'm assuming it's a gay couple, tied up and killed in their home,' answered Brook.

'So you *have* been following it.'

'There was something on the radio.' Brook looked towards the darkened lounge. No hint of Terri stirring. 'Why are you ringing me, John? If there's a clear link to the Breadsall killings, that's Frank Ford's case. Not mine and not yours.'

There was a pause at the other end of the line.

'The thing is, Ford is four weeks from retirement.'

'By my calculation, that still makes him a serving officer.'

'That's just it,' said Noble. 'If we're looking at a series, Frank will have to hand it off, so the Chief Super is standing him down. He wants you on it from the get-go.' Brook winced

32

but didn't react. Noble often teased him over his aversion to transatlantic vocabulary. 'He says you're his go-to guy.'

Brook sighed. 'And is Chief Superintendent Charlton American?'

'Feel free to ask him.'

'How sure are you about the MO?'

A hesitation. 'Certain.'

'You don't sound certain.'

Noble hesitated again. 'Method is close but there's a difference in victimology. The latest couple had been married for over fifty years.'

'Fifty years?' exclaimed Brook. 'Last month's victims were gay men, John.'

Noble sighed. 'I know. Look, Read and Smee were added to Frank's team while we were quiet. They think the method is almost identical.'

'Think? Almost?'

'Charlton wants you on board,' said Noble decisively. 'The thing is, Ford lost the plot last month and went overboard looking for a gay sex killer when a sexual motive wasn't indicated. Caused a lot of bad feeling in some circles. Well, you can imagine.' He fell silent, a tactic he'd learned from Brook, waiting out witnesses who would eventually start babbling to fill the awkward silence.

Brook blew out a long breath. 'Do you know how long it took to get my daughter to visit?'

'Is there a prize for guessing?' replied Noble.

'John . . .'

'Look, your leave is over in a few days. I've told the Chief Super I can run the day-to-day until then, but he wants you down as SIO and I knew you wouldn't want your name on it without taking a look.' While Brook searched for the excuse his daughter would need, Noble waited a beat before playing his final card. 'I can call Ford. He could be here in four hours.'

Brook emitted his one-note laugh. Ford's reluctance to drag himself to a crime scene outside office hours was legendary in Derby CID. 'Address?'

Four

THE RAIN BEGAN TO FALL as Brook turned off the ring road on to the A6 towards Boulton Moor, a small outpost at the south-eastern extremity of Derby. Beyond the clump of houses clinging to the city boundary were green fields, cleaved only by the A6, heading to the A50 out to the airport and the M1 in the east and Stoke in the west.

Brook turned on to Shardlow Lane, with its small estate of tidy modern houses and bungalows. His creaky BMW didn't have satnav so he held the directions in his left hand but crumpled them on to the passenger seat when he saw the first squad car blocking the approach to a short cul-de-sac. Swathes of police tape were still being unravelled, cordoning off the whole street to allow room for police vehicles, scientific support cars and an ambulance.

As Brook pulled up, he saw DS Rachel Caskey on her way back to her car, face like thunder. Spotting Brook, she glared in his direction, appearing to mutter something before angling her walk towards the BMW. Brook pretended not to notice and pressed his ID to the driver's window. Fortunately the uniformed constable was already lifting the tape so Brook drove on and manoeuvred his battered car next to Dr Higginbottom's sleek Mercedes.

He glanced across at the murder house. A middle-aged man was leaning against a chunky SUV, his face ashen, eyes locked into a thousand-yard stare. DS Rob Morton stood next to him, prompting him with questions, jotting down mumbled answers into a notebook, trying to load sympathy into his probing expression. A second later, Morton snapped his notebook closed and touched the man on the arm, guiding him towards DC Smee and a nearby patrol car.

Another citizen's thoughts forever scarred by sudden and inexplicable violence.

Brook stepped from his car and headed for the small semi-detached redbrick. Scene-of-crime officers in protective suits and blue gloves walked back and forth along the front path of a tiny garden through an open door, carrying equipment in and bagged exhibits out.

'I hope you're happy, Inspector.'

Brook turned to see Caskey advancing towards him. She was medium height, a little younger than Noble, wearing an expensive suit and cream gabardine. Brook stared impassively into her brown eyes. 'Sergeant?' he said, enunciating clearly. He wasn't a great believer in hierarchy, but when confrontation reared its head, he found it a useful ally.

Caskey hesitated, appearing to sense that a confrontation with a senior detective wasn't the best career move. When she spoke, her voice was controlled, making the point, no more. 'I wondered if you were happy about taking over DI Ford's case.' Brook prompted her with an eyebrow. 'Sir.'

'Two people are dead, Sergeant. How happy should I be?'

She hesitated. 'This'll finish him, you know.'

Brook held Caskey's gaze. He'd heard good things since

her transfer from Kent a couple of years before. 'Lucky him.'

Caskey considered another remark but apparently thought better of it, turning without further ado and trudging silently back to her car. On the way she glanced at the small knot of onlookers gathering at the edge of the tape and was held for a second. Brook followed her gaze to a burly, well-built man in his late thirties dressed in tatty, paint-stained fatigues and combat jacket. The man noticed Caskey looking, lowered his head and began to move away. Caskey hesitated, then apparently came to a decision. She glanced back at the murder house before ducking into her car and driving away.

Out of the corner of his eye, Brook watched the man in the fatigues pause before returning to the tape, shoulders hunched over against the drizzle, hands buried deep in pockets. He made a mental note, then turned to run a practised eye over the crime scene, the front yard gravelled for low maintenance, the modern front door made of generic uPVC for the same reason. A grey plastic wheelie bin sat on the pavement outside the property.

'Sir.' DC Anka Banach held out a protective suit and overshoes.

'Angie,' replied Brook, taking off his jacket to toss in the car and pulling on the oversized suit with difficulty. 'What have we got?'

'Victims are Albert and Edith Gibson, married pensioners, both late seventies, both shot to death.'

Brook sensed something unsaid. 'That it?'

'DS Noble said not to give impressions before you'd clocked the scene.'

'You're on probation. Call it on-the-job training.'

Banach sighed. 'It's a strange one. They're just sitting there like they're watching TV, two frail pensioners in a Derby suburb shot through the heart, execution-style. It doesn't make sense.'

'Any sign of a struggle?'

'None.'

'Robbery?'

'Nothing obvious. The whole thing seems excessive.'

Brook pulled on the overshoes and stood, panting from the effort. 'You'd be happier if they'd been beaten with a crowbar and their house ransacked.'

'No, but at least we'd know we're looking for a local addict or a burglar with a short fuse.' She shrugged. 'It jars, that's all.'

'How much violent death have you seen?' said Brook.

'Apart from Animal Farm last year, not a lot. My share of stiffs on the beat, obviously, especially the elderly, sealed in their homes until a neighbour realises the curtains have been closed for weeks.'

'I used to hate those,' said Brook, staring sightlessly at his own past and all too plausible future. 'My first year in west London, there was an old couple. The husband had died but his wife wouldn't leave him. She just sat with him holding his hand – not eating or drinking, literally willing herself to death rather than face life without him.' He nodded at the house. 'They smartly dressed?'

'They are,' nodded Banach, impressed. 'Clutching photographs of loved ones on their laps.'

'Then they made some kind of peace with the world. Maybe they had health problems.'

'It's not a murder-suicide.'

'Pity. At least that way they'd be making their own choices.'

'That's very harsh,' replied Banach.

'Is it? You see as many bodies as I have, Angie, you realise that any kind of choice about how your life ends is like winning the lottery.'

'Well, it's definitely murder. For one thing, the weapon's gone, and—'

'That's plenty, Angie,' smiled Brook. 'Leave me *some* work to do.' Looking beyond her, he scoured the throng of local bystanders watching from beyond the tape. The young chatted excitedly, filming and taking pictures; the old were sombre and uneasy – their natural state. The man Caskey had spotted stood out, staring hard at the house, concentration unwavering. 'How's the canvass going?'

'See no evil, hear no evil,' replied Banach.

'Keep at it. See if anyone gives off the vibe. And keep an eye on those hanging off the perimeter, particularly the guy with the zombie stare at two o'clock.'

She glanced briefly at the onlooker, then back at Brook. 'Fatigues? Got him.'

'If this is part of a series . . .'

Banach nodded. 'Serials like to inflate their sense of superiority by watching us chasing our tails.'

'You've been reading books,' teased Brook.

'Can't support your goddaughter on a DC's salary.'

'And how is the lovely Katja?' beamed Brook.

'I've got pictures, if you'd like.'

'You know me so well,' he replied, marching quickly towards the house.

Brook stood with Noble at the edge of the brightly decorated room, applying a eucalyptus gel under his nostrils. He stared unblinking at the elderly couple, seated in adjacent armchairs, torsos stiffened by death, hands and arms linked as much as pain had allowed, heads almost touching in an unintended declaration of affection. Their necks and faces were starting to bloat from decomposition, mouths slackened and eyes milky from the post-mortem breakdown of potassium in the red blood cells. What skin Brook could see was white from blood loss but with a tinge of yellow and green. This, and the ripening smell, suggested the Gibsons had lain undiscovered for at least a couple of days, probably longer.

And Banach was right. The pair had dressed smartly, Mr Gibson wearing shirt and tie, his wife a bright floral dress, their ensemble ruined only by the blood, now bone dry on their clothes.

Scene-of-crime officers drifted in and out of his vision, oblivious to spectators as they did their work without fuss, ticking off their allotted tasks until Dr Higginbottom, the police surgeon, had finished his examination and they could swarm back round the victims, filming and photographing the corpses before bagging hands and heads.

'Restraints?' asked Brook softly.

'Not when we got here, and there are no marks or bruises to suggest any,' said Noble. 'They wouldn't have needed much restraining.'

'Any clue on make of gun?'

Noble shook his head. 'None. The entry wounds don't look exotic, though, and if it's the same as Breadsall, we're looking at a standard semi-automatic. Maybe a Sig or a Glock,' he added, before Brook could ask.

'I'll take your word for it. Entry?'

'No signs of a break-in. We're assuming front door access for now. It was unlocked, the key still in the lock.'

'So they let the killer in,' nodded Brook.

'Unless they kept their door unlocked and he just marched in, but the son says they were security-conscious.'

'Someone they knew, then, or a neighbour with a grudge and access to a gun,' said Brook. 'Easy enough to check. Any known villains or ex-military in the neighbourhood?'

'Cooper's doing background. But they wouldn't let in a neighbour they didn't get on with, would they?'

'Easy enough to insist with a weapon,' said Brook. He looked at the Gibsons, dressed in their cheap finery, and frowned. 'But this is no grudge killing. Too clinical. Whoever did this didn't hate them, and if I had to decide right now, I'd say he probably didn't even know them.'

'Which makes access more problematic,' nodded Noble. 'Unless he's faking officialdom. Some random con artist holding a cereal-packet sheriff's badge. Or maybe council, utilities, postman.'

'I doubt the killer called during daylight hours.'

'And a con artist would be robbing the place,' nodded Noble.

'No sign of that?'

'Nope. There's even an envelope full of cash in the bedroom.' He hesitated.

'Go on.'

'I had a quick scan of the main points from the Breadsall killing.'

'And?'

'The post-mortem found the killer used handcuffs. Once the victims were secured, they were tied with rope and the cuffs removed,' said Noble.

'It's not hard to get access to police kit these days,'

concluded Brook. Noble shrugged. 'Any similar bruising on Mr and Mrs Gibson's wrists?'

'Nothing,' said Noble. 'It would be showing by now.'

'Remind me about the Breadsall vics,' said Brook.

'They were younger. Both male. Not spring chickens, but a lot fitter. The Gibsons would have been easier to handle.'

'Any hints from Higginbottom on time of death?' asked Brook.

'No, but it smells like three days to me.'

'Which would put it at the weekend,' said Brook. 'What about relatives?'

'Just their son,' said Noble. 'He owns the property, found the bodies first thing this morning.'

'I saw him outside. He looked convincingly shocked. Anything in the rest of the house?'

'No sign of forced doors or windows, no drawers and wardrobes tipped out – the place is untouched.'

'You mentioned cash.'

'Four hundred pounds in twenties.'

'Nice round figure.'

'There's some jewellery in the bedroom, watches too, though it's mostly tinsel.' He looked at Brook. 'There is one weird thing, in the kitchen.'

Brook stood at the Belfast sink and stared at the tray on the work surface. Two empty champagne flutes stood next to a half-finished bottle. He leaned in to sniff at the dregs. 'Vintage champagne.'

'You're a champagne expert now.'

'It says so on the bottle,' replied Brook, before catching Noble's grin. 'Very funny.'

'So what do you think – a celebration of some kind?'

'Looks like it. But was it for the victims?' Brook noticed the third flute, washed and upturned on the drainer. 'Or the killer?'

'Could have been opened before the attack.'

'Three glasses, two Gibsons,' said Brook.

'So maybe all three raised a glass before the deed.'

Brook raised an eyebrow. 'Last month?'

'Nothing about champagne in the reports I read,' replied Noble.

'Bag the glasses for the labs in Hucknall, John. Maybe the killer didn't wash his flute as thoroughly as he should.'

Noble gestured to one of the SOCOs. 'Okay, Col.'

While Col bagged the washed glass and labelled the bag, Brook moved to a calendar on the back of the kitchen door. With a gloved hand, he examined the sparse entries for October beneath a wide-eyed tabby kitten, before checking September and August in turn. He read each handwritten entry then leafed forward to November. 'Nothing here except doctor's appointments. Wedding anniversary end of August, no birthdays.'

'There wouldn't be. The dates are months away,' said Noble. 'Their birth certificates are upstairs in a drawer. Marriage, too.'

'No cause for champagne on there. They might have been celebrating absent friends or relatives.'

'Or something unofficial, something not on the calendar, like the anniversary of their first meeting.'

'Possible,' said Brook. 'But that's expensive fizz.'

'And apart from half a bottle of sherry, not another drop of alcohol in the house,' said Noble. 'I'm betting the killer brought it. Maybe the glasses as well.'

Brook's eye was caught by a small board sporting four cup hooks, one of which held a padlock key. The back door was locked, with the key in the lock. 'This key was in the lock when we arrived?'

'Same as the front,' said Noble. 'But the front door was unlocked when the son arrived.'

'According to him.' Noble shrugged his agreement. 'He has his own key?'

'He owns the property, so yes,' said Noble. 'Didn't need to use it, though.'

'And he walked in on his parents shot to death,' said Brook.

'Right. He had the stare on him, but he held up well enough,' answered Noble. 'He was able to answer questions, and at some length.' Brook shot him an enquiring glance. 'Just saying.'

'It's not the son,' declared Brook. They returned to the lounge and Brook noticed a SOCO dropping a remote control into an evidence bag. He turned to Noble for an explanation.

'I was coming to that,' said Noble gravely. 'Gibson Junior said music was playing when he walked in.'

'He turned it off?' asked Brook.

'So he says. Natural enough.'

Brook's mouth tightened. 'What kind of music?'

'Classical.' Noble was tentative with his next utterance. 'Reminded me of the Reaper. The music, the element of celebration at the kill.'

Brook nodded at the Gibsons. 'The Reaper only killed petty criminals and their offspring, and he preferred a scalpel to a gun.'

'*Prefers* a scalpel,' said Noble, trying to catch Brook's eye. 'He's still out there, remember.'

'As you say,' replied Brook, turning away. 'But it's not the Reaper. He left messages for us. In blood.'

Noble shrugged. 'His last recorded kill was in Derby.'

'Fine,' said Brook. 'Check with the neighbours, see if the Gibsons were a public nuisance and get Cooper to check if they have form.'

Noble strode away, reaching for his radio. 'Angie. Get the canvass to ask specifically if the Gibsons were problem neighbours, any antisocial activity or small-scale offending, the sort that might not be reported to us.' Her response crackled. 'I don't know. Disputes about parking a car, cutting a hedge or late-night noise. You know the drill.'

Five

HIGGINBOTTOM SNAPPED HIS BAG CLOSED and stepped away from the two corpses, glancing at Brook before leaving the room. Brook accepted the invitation and followed the doctor towards the relative cheer of the street.

Back in the cold pale light, Noble wandered over, rummaging under his protective suit for his cigarettes, lighting up as the three men came to a halt at Higginbottom's car.

'Good to see you, Brook.'

'Doctor,' acknowledged Brook. 'How long?'

'Judging from rigor and lividity, between forty-eight and seventy-two hours.'

'Sometime at the weekend,' nodded Brook. 'Big window.'

'It is what it is,' said Higginbottom. 'And at least it would have been quick. Dead in seconds. No obvious molestation. Not much more to say.'

Brook nodded. 'Did you get the call last month?'

'You mean the gay sex killer of Breadsall,' snorted Higginbottom, shaking his head. 'Don't get me started on Ford.'

'Was he really heading off in that direction?' asked Noble.

'In as much as DI Ford ever has a direction for his investigations.'

'You disagreed,' said Brook.

'As strongly as I dared, but he's not the type to listen to opinions that don't match his own. Stephen Frazer and Iain Nolan were two reputable middle-aged men living together who just happened to be gay,' continued Higginbottom. 'Ultra-respectable, successful businessmen and pillars of the community. Also one of the first gay couples to take advantage of the new legislation and get married.'

'You seem to know a lot about them,' said Brook.

'They were on the front of the *Derby Telegraph*, Inspector. You must have seen it – even made the odd national.'

'I don't read the papers.'

'Then take my word,' said Higginbottom. 'It was news.'

'That kind of exposure can infuriate all sorts of malcontents,' said Brook. 'Homophobes, religious extremists.'

'After their murder, the coverage in the local rag was bad,' said Noble. 'Brian Burton really did a number on the victims.'

'It wasn't bad, it was obscene, Sergeant,' said Higginbottom. 'That greasy little excuse for a journalist with all that sneering innuendo about sexual perversion just because they were tied up. Disgusting.'

'How did he get a detail like that?' demanded Brook, glancing at Noble.

'The word is Ford briefed him on his kinky sex killer theory, so Burton drenched the whole story in smut.'

'Why am I not surprised?' said Brook.

'Ford's a dinosaur and belongs in Jurassic Park,' continued Higginbottom. 'He figured it as a sex crime from minute one. Between them, he and Burton have set back gay rights in

Derby by thirty years. And I made a point of saying so to your superior.'

'You spoke to Charlton?' said Brook, fighting his own smile. 'What did he say?'

'Don't smirk, Brook,' chided Higginbottom. 'I realise he's no Terrence Higgins, but in spite of his religious views, he gave me a fair hearing and I got the impression that my thoughts on Ford's competence chimed with his own. Frank should've been pensioned off five years ago.'

'So *you're* responsible for getting me this plum job,' observed Brook.

Higginbottom smiled. 'You're welcome.'

'Just as well he's retiring next month,' said Noble.

'And not a moment too soon,' boomed Higginbottom. 'I don't envy him the professional embarrassment of being pulled off a case, but he'll get over it when he sobers up.'

'It's the poisoned well he leaves behind that bothers me,' said Brook. 'His sergeant was already giving me the Medusa treatment.'

'Caskey?' said Higginbottom. 'She's better off without him. And from what I hear, she's been carrying Ford for the last two years.'

'Was there *any* evidence in Breadsall to support Frank's theory?' asked Brook.

'Nothing to indicate a sexual motive of any kind.'

'As far as you were able to determine from your brief exam.'

Higginbottom conceded with a shrug. 'Fine, but it's been a month and the forensic reports will back me up. Talk to Frank if you think it's worth it, but take a large pinch of salt with you. As far as he was concerned, being gay was sufficient motive for their deaths.'

'Which would indicate a hate crime,' suggested Noble.

'Except there wasn't any hate on display at the scene,' replied Higginbottom. 'And the same applies here.'

'But if DS Caskey has been carrying Frank for so long, how come she signed off on his sex killer theory?' enquired Brook.

'I've no idea,' answered Higginbottom. 'I suppose she can only do so much.'

'Frank must have been a decent copper once,' retorted Brook.

Higginbottom shook his head. 'Why do you defend him? He doesn't have a good word to say about you.'

'Because one day I'll be a pathetic burnout too,' said Brook. 'And when I am, I hope someone will find something good to say about me.'

'People in the know rate you highly, Brook,' said Higginbottom. 'No one's ever said that about Ford.'

'People in the know have short memories,' snapped Brook. 'Now is there anything else on the Gibsons I can use?'

'It's the same killer as Breadsall,' said Higginbottom.

'In your opinion.'

Higginbottom counted out on his fingers. 'Both victims were killed by a single bullet to the heart. No sign of struggle. Death as close to instant as makes no difference.'

'But the Gibsons aren't gay,' observed Noble. Higginbottom acknowledged him with a shrug.

'No evidence of sexual activity,' pressed Brook.

'Without detailed examination it's impossible to be one hundred percent certain, but clothing is intact and seems unblemished by semen, so in my opinion, everything points away from a sexual motive, yes.'

'And presentation of the victims?'

'Very similar to Breadsall,' said Higginbottom. 'The Gibsons didn't or couldn't contest their fate, so no restraints. You know about the handcuffs?'

Brook nodded. 'Frazer and Nolan were younger and fitter . . .'

'. . . so the killer handcuffed them, then, after they were tied and gagged, removed the cuffs.'

'Presumably they resisted.'

'Wouldn't you?' The doctor threw his bag into the boot of the Mercedes, stifling a yawn. Brook didn't answer. 'And that's me done. I'll email the main points tomorrow.' He climbed into the car and drove away.

'I had no idea Higginbottom was such a passionate advocate of gay rights.'

'His son's gay,' said Noble. 'He's at Oxford now but there was some harassment at school a few years back.' Brook looked up. 'I have conversations with people. You find out about them that way.'

'Sounds exhausting,' said Brook, accepting the rebuke.

'And Higginbottom's right. Ford doesn't understand alternative lifestyles. Last month would've taken him out of his comfort zone. Some of the stuff he fed to Burton was way over the top. You should read it.'

'I've had enough of Burton's toxic world view to last me a lifetime, John.'

'The disc in the CD player?' repeated the scene-of-crime officer through his mask. He flicked through a row of evidence bags waiting to be carried out and held one up, allowing Brook to see it.

'*Classical Favourites*,' read Brook.

Noble returned to the crowded lounge now bathed in the powerful glare of arc lights. 'The Gibsons don't have any history with us and neighbours say they were good as gold.'

'What do we know about the son?'

Noble gestured at DS Morton.

'Gibson, Matthew,' said Morton, reaching for his notes. 'Retired accountant and professional landlord. Fifty-four years old.'

'Married?'

'He was cagey about that. Told me to mind my own business.' Brook raised an eyebrow. Morton shrugged. 'Given the circumstances, I didn't push it.'

'What time did he find the bodies?'

DS Morton flipped to the right page. 'This morning just before six.'

'So early?' said Noble.

'He says he came to collect the rent,' said Morton.

'Rent from his parents,' remarked Brook. 'What a prince!'

'Might explain the four hundred in cash,' said Noble.

'What about his house keys?' asked Brook.

'He had them with him,' confirmed Morton, rustling in a pocket and drawing out a plastic bag containing a pair of keys. 'He never needed them but always brought them just in case. Says he knocked a couple of times and when he didn't get a response he tried the door. It was unlocked and he walked in.'

A SOCO approached with the bagged unwashed champagne flutes. 'No obvious grains in the bottom of the glasses but we'll test for drugs obviously.' Brook nodded his thanks.

'Why would the killer drug them?' asked Morton. 'At their age, they'd be pretty docile.'

'A little something to make it easier on them, maybe,'

suggested Brook. 'From what I see, the killer didn't hate the victims. In fact the champagne makes it look less like an execution . . .'

'. . . and more of a fond farewell,' nodded Morton.

'A mercy killing,' suggested Noble. 'It's an angle.'

'Beats flying to Switzerland,' quipped Morton.

'On that note,' prompted Noble.

'Smee's collating all medications in the house and is chasing down their doctor to find out if one or both of them was terminal.'

'We're all terminal, Rob,' said Brook, absently. Morton and Noble exchanged a look. 'Did you ask Gibson about the champagne?'

'He says he didn't bring it,' said Morton. 'Claims his parents hardly drank apart from the occasional sherry, and even then it took them six months to get through a bottle.'

'And the champagne flutes?' said Brook.

Morton grimaced apologetically. 'You're right. They don't really belong, do they? Sorry.'

'Don't worry, Rob, we'll ask him at the station,' said Noble.

'You think Gibson's in the frame?' said Morton.

'If this were a one-off, yes,' said Brook. 'But if it's part of a series, then I don't see it. Any prints?'

'Plenty on the two dirty glasses, but they likely belong to the vics,' said Morton. 'Nothing obvious on the bottle, the washed glass or the CD.'

'What about the cash and envelope?'

'Gone off to the lab for tests,' said Morton. 'But if the doer didn't pocket the loot, he's unlikely to have fingered it.'

Brook shot him a glance. 'DNA?'

'Nothing visible to the naked eye on the vics, and the carpet looks clear,' replied Morton. 'Doesn't look like our guy pulled one off while they croaked, though you can never tell until SOCO get the spray out.' He winked slyly at the grinning Noble.

'Pulled one off?' repeated Brook with distaste. 'Fingered? Whoever bought *The Sweeney* box set, can they stop passing it around the squad, please?'

'Sir?' said Morton, trying to keep a straight face.

Brook glanced at his watch, determined not to rise to the bait. 'Never mind.'

'Do you need to be off?' asked Noble.

'Not without interviewing Gibson.'

'Sorry about your holiday.'

'Not sorry enough to let Ford and Caskey run the inquiry,' replied Brook. 'Why didn't DI Gadd get the poisoned chalice?'

'Jane's at the Policing and Partnerships Conference in London.'

'I didn't draw the short straw at least. Any more highlights from last month's murder book?'

'Until we get back to St Mary's, I'm working off what Read and Smee tell me,' said Noble. 'Neither of them remembers champagne or classical music. But we'll have a comparison on the bullets at least.'

'Ballistics could take a couple of days, until which time we won't know whether we're looking for a serial killer or not.'

'I'll ask Charlton to put the squeeze on,' said Noble.

'Get everything on the database from last month organised for briefing, and if you can, find any snippets Ford's people haven't had time to commit to the record.'

'Not sure Ford's people will be rushing to help, judging by Caskey's reaction.'

'Can't blame her,' retorted Brook. 'What's her background?'

'Worked her way up to sergeant in the Medway, where she was an AFO. Made the switch to CID and transferred to D Division two years ago.'

'She's an ex-firearms officer?' exclaimed Brook. 'Could be handy on a gun crime.'

'Thinking of getting her on board?' enquired Noble.

'She knows the ins and outs of Breadsall.'

'Doesn't mean she'll co-operate after what's happened to Frank.'

'She'll get over it if she's smart,' said Brook. 'And hopefully the Chief Super will be smoothing things over. As for Frank, let's hope he can be professional about it.'

'Good luck with that. Ford's been a liability for years. If this is a series, we're better off starting from scratch and drawing our own conclusions.'

'Has Gibson gone to the station?' Morton nodded. Brook checked his watch again and looked back at the property adjoining the Gibson house. 'You've not mentioned the neighbour.'

'We haven't spoken to her yet. Heather Sampson – Miss. She's in shock and went to hospital for a check-up. She's seventy-three years old, lives alone and, like most of her generation, is early to bed and early to rise.'

'Best part of the day,' declared Brook. He strolled to the grey plastic wheelie bin outside the Gibson house and lifted the lid with a latex-covered hand. 'And just in time to put out the bins.'

'I cancelled the collection for surrounding streets,' said Noble, unbidden. 'Uniform are lifting bin lids and grates in the unlikely event the killer dumped the weapon, or better yet, a bloodstained driving licence.'

'If only,' said Brook, managing a smile. 'And the Gibsons' bin?'

'SOCO are aware.'

'Are they aware who put it out for collection?' said Brook. Noble was puzzled. 'Well the Gibsons didn't, and I'd be amazed if their son did after finding their bodies.'

'See what you mean. He might have done it before he knocked.'

'Check with the neighbour and get a statement. She may have heard something to help us narrow our time frame.'

'Even if she heard the gunshots, she'd likely think they were fireworks this time of year.'

'Ask the question, at least.' Brook yawned. 'I've seen enough. Get a post-mortem slot, preferably for tomorrow morning so I can attend, though it's unlikely to tell us more than we already know. And send everything on file to my email so I can get up to speed tonight.'

Noble stared disconsolately over Brook's shoulder towards the crime-scene tape. 'Better yet, you could ask Frank in person.'

Brook turned to see a car pulling up. 'Great!' DI Ford, small and wiry with grey hair, leapt out and ducked under the tape before making a beeline for Brook and Noble. 'I wouldn't have to deal with him. That what you said, John?'

'Do you want me to . . . ?'

'Too late,' mumbled Brook through gritted teeth. 'Here to help, Frank?' he enquired loudly when Ford was in earshot.

'Help? What the fuck. I just heard from Caskey.' He waved his arms, his face puce with anger. 'Couldn't believe my fucking ears.'

'Control yourself, Frank.'

'This is my fucking inquiry, Brook.'

'Don't swear at me,' warned Brook. 'Didn't Charlton speak to you?'

'Oh, he spoke to me all right, but only after *I* rang *him*.'

'I'm sorry you had to hear like that. Truly.'

Noble nudged Brook, flicked his head towards the perimeter tape. Brian Burton from the *Derby Telegraph* was showing his credentials to the officer on duty, a photographer in tow, arguing that he should be allowed access to the site.

'The fuck you're sorry,' growled Ford.

'Go make sure Burton doesn't grease his way in, John,' muttered Brook, behind a hand. Noble stepped away, aiming an apologetic shrug at him behind Ford's back.

'Are you listening to me, Brook?' bellowed Ford.

'Unfortunately.'

'I wouldn't have believed a fellow officer would do the fucking dirty—'

'I'm following instructions from a senior officer, Frank. That's the job.'

'Don't tell me about the job.' Ford jabbed a finger towards him. 'I was nicking villains when you were in short pants.'

'I hear most of them got off on appeal.'

'Fuck you.'

'Keep it down,' said Brook. 'We're in the public gaze.'

'This is my case,' shouted Ford.

'I didn't ask for it, Frank.'

'The fuck you didn't.' Brook leaned away from breath laced with last night's alcohol. 'Where's the rest of my squad?'

'No idea,' replied Brook.

'They were stood down, sir,' said Banach, joining them. 'Chief Super's orders.'

'Chief Superintendent Charlton?' said Brook, beaming at Ford. 'That's our boss, isn't it?'

Ford glared. 'You're a real prick, you know that, Brook?'

'Better than anyone,' answered Brook, his manner softening. 'Look, Frank, we haven't always seen eye to eye, but you're retiring in a month.'

'So?'

'So why all the drama? Enjoy your lap of honour and leave the dirty work to us. An unsolved series is no way to bow out, believe me. That's how I left the Met.'

Ford's anger gave way to dismay and Brook saw defeat in his eyes. 'But this is *my* case. I'm a good copper. I closed that Black Oak Farm mess last year when you were on leave.'

Brook hesitated. 'I remember. Look, this isn't a slur on your record, Frank. The Chief Super wants continuity, and you can't provide that from your armchair.'

'But how will it look, me being yanked off my last case?'

'It'll look like what it is – a graceful handing-over of the reins, one good copper to another.'

Ford was taken aback at this and his features seemed to soften. 'You haven't always been so . . . respectful, Brook.'

'Neither of us has,' replied Brook, unwilling to let Ford have it too easy. 'But we no longer need to fight these battles.'

Ford lowered his head, quieter now. 'I thought you were on leave.'

'Back today,' Brook lied.

The rain started to pick up. 'Is it the same MO? If it's another pair of benders—'

'Go home, Frank,' said Brook. 'Make some lunch and have a glass of wine.'

'What's that supposed to mean?' snapped Ford, looking for offence.

'That's what retired people do, isn't it?'

'I'm not retired yet.'

Brook had run out of palliatives for soothing Ford's damaged ego. 'No.'

'You want my advice, Brook, you're looking for a pair of jilted arse bandits. There's your killers.'

Brook bit down on what Ford could do with his advice. He noticed Banach staring at him, willing him to use his rank to object to Ford's language. But as usual the demands of the case trumped all. 'What do you mean, a pair?'

Ford's yellow grin wasn't a pleasant sight. 'Didn't know that, did you?' he said smugly. 'We got the ballistics report back and it says the two benders in Breadsall were killed by different guns. You're looking for two killers.'

Brook saw Banach open her mouth to speak. 'Benders?' he repeated before she could say anything. 'You know we have standing protocols about using inappropriate language to disparage minority groups.'

'Fuck your protocols,' sneered Ford defiantly.

'For the last time, stop swearing at me,' said Brook, through gritted teeth.

'Or else?'

Brook took a deep breath, his fists balling, before saying quietly, 'Or else you're liable to get struck.'

Ford straightened as though he *had* been hit. He looked across at Banach. 'Did you hear that, Constable? DI Brook just threatened me. You heard him, didn't you?'

'I . . .' began Banach, her colour rising.

'Go home, Frank,' said Brook. 'Now.'

'You threatened me,' said Ford, agitated. He grinned maliciously. 'You can't do that. I'll have your job.'

'No, Frank, I'll have your pension when I tell the disciplinary panel that I'm gay and you provoked me. Now get off my crime scene before I have you escorted off.'

'You what?'

'You heard me.'

'You're gay?'

'Does it matter? I'm a middle-aged, divorced copper living on his own, so who's to say I'm not.' Brook smiled with that excessive bonhomie that drove his enemies to distraction, and Ford stood with his mouth open, too shocked to speak, unsure whether to be insulted or amazed. 'Now go home and make sure I get full access to your reports and anything that's not already on the database. You can start with the ballistics report. Is that clear?' Ford looked as though he were preparing an objection, so Brook sealed the deal. 'Then we can benefit from your fine groundwork.'

Ford hesitated, searching for sarcasm. Finally he nodded and his eyes found the floor. Resigned, he shuffled towards his car.

'Wow!' said Banach quietly, staring after him.

'I know,' said Brook. 'Two killers. Unexpected.' He watched Burton's photographer taking pictures of Ford as the reporter interviewed him on the other side of the perimeter. He wondered whether to wander across to make sure Ford stayed on message but decided against it. He had history with Burton, who'd made it his business to attack Brook and his work at every opportunity just because he wasn't a local man. Burton was the kind of journalist who always knew the right buttons to press, and Brook's shallow reserves of diplomacy were spent.

'You'd think with a month to go he'd be glad to be shot of it,' said Banach, following his gaze.

'You're too young to understand,' said Brook, eyes firmly on Ford. 'In a few weeks Frank stops being a somebody with power and purpose and starts being a nobody living on memories, sitting in a chair, waiting for death.'

Banach stared at Brook's blank features, waiting for a glimpse of levity that didn't arrive. 'Might be a good idea to give his retirement bash a miss,' she remarked.

Six

MATTHEW GIBSON SAT IN THE interview room in a white paper jump suit, face drawn, eyes glazed, clutching a polystyrene cup. His personal effects were in a plastic evidence bag on the table – watch, wallet, driving licence, loose change, handkerchief – having been removed from his civilian clothes, now gone for forensic exam.

Brook introduced himself, took a second to check the contents of Gibson's cup then glanced hopefully across at Noble, who stepped outside briefly to order more tea. When he returned, he started the interview tape and cautioned Gibson about his rights before naming those present.

'Firstly we're sorry for your loss, Mr Gibson,' said Brook.

'Thank you,' replied Gibson. 'Shouldn't I have my solicitor here?'

'You're entitled to be represented,' said Brook, a little surprised. 'However, that might delay the investigation. You're here as a witness at this time. I just have a few questions. If you agree to waive counsel but then don't wish to answer any or all of them, or feel the need to stop proceedings at any time, we'll postpone and you can leave. Fair enough?'

'Fine, but I don't know what else I can add.'

'We just need to get a few things clear.'

'To see if I contradict my earlier statement, you mean.' Noble and Brook exchanged a glance. 'When can I get my clothes back?'

'You entered a crime scene, Mr Gibson,' said Brook.

'There are certain tests,' explained Noble.

'You mean like gunshot residue?' Brook raised an inquisitive eyebrow. 'My hands were swabbed.'

'Your parents were shot,' said Brook. 'It's just procedure.'

'Then let me save you some time. I hold a valid firearms certificate and I'm a member of Swadlincote Shooting Club. I own several small-bore rifles, which I fire regularly at the club. From time to time I also fire other members' handguns, so gunshot residue is likely.'

'But you don't own a handgun.'

'I have a deactivated Glock 19.'

'We'll need to see that gun.'

'It's deactivated – it can't be fired.'

'Your parents were shot with a semi-automatic handgun, so we need to examine it,' said Noble.

Gibson's face soured. 'You don't dress it up, do you?'

'I'm sorry,' said Brook. 'But this is a murder inquiry and the immediate aftermath is the best time for gathering hard facts.'

'And deactivated weapons can be reactivated, I suppose,' nodded Gibson. 'I'll bring it in.'

Brook smiled indulgently. 'We'll send someone home with you to collect it. Presumably it's at your house.'

'In a drawer.'

'A locked drawer?'

'No, why would it be? It doesn't fire.' Sensing disapproval, Gibson added, 'It's little more than a toy.'

A constable entered with three mugs of hot tea and set them on the table, and Brook glimpsed Gibson's hand reaching for one, fingers still grimy from the fingerprint ink.

'What time did you arrive at your parents' house this morning?'

'As I told the other detective, a few minutes before six,' said Gibson.

'Define a few,' said Noble.

'About five.'

'Why so early?'

'Like a lot of old people, my parents are early risers.' He stopped cold. 'Were early risers. I like to get in and out before rush hour when I'm busy.'

'I thought you were retired.'

'From work, yes. But I own several properties around the city that I rent out. Today is rent day. Or should have been.'

'Rent day,' echoed Brook. 'So it wasn't a social visit.'

'No.'

'And when was the last time you saw your parents alive?'

Gibson hesitated. 'A month ago.'

'You sound very certain.'

'I am.' He took a sip of his tea.

'Would that be when you last collected their rent?'

Gibson caught Brook's eye, searching for a judgement. 'That's right. Every first of the month.'

'No visits apart from that?'

'Not this month, no. Like I said, I've been busy. I've got an ongoing building project.'

'When you arrived, what did you do?'

'I knocked on the door and waited.'

'Is that usual?'

'Yes.'

'And there was no answer.'

'No.'

'Then what?'

'I could hear music.'

'You heard it from outside?'

'Yes.'

'Did your parents routinely play music at that hour?' asked Noble.

'Yes, but not that loud,' said Gibson. 'I wouldn't normally hear it until I was in the house.'

'And you thought hearing music at the door was odd.'

'Unconsciously, I suppose.'

'What type of music?'

'Classical.'

'Go on.'

'I knocked again.'

'You didn't try to use your key to let yourself in?'

'No. My parents are . . . were tenants. And tenants have a right to privacy.'

'So formal with your own parents?'

'I'm a landlord,' said Gibson. 'It pays to treat everyone equally so they know where they stand.'

'Does that mean if they didn't pay their rent they could be evicted?' asked Noble.

Gibson's sigh carried a hint of resentment. 'My parents were comfortable, Inspector. They could have bought a house but didn't want the hassle of maintenance so they lived in one of my properties. I charged them a peppercorn rent to cover my costs, no more, and they always paid on time.'

'And in cash,' said Brook. Gibson hesitated. 'Most tenants

pay by direct debit, don't they?' Again Gibson declined to answer. 'The reason I ask is that there was four hundred pounds in an envelope in the bedroom. Was that the rent money, do you mind me asking?'

Gibson came to a decision. 'As a matter of fact, I do mind.'

Brook paused to let Gibson sweat before nodding. He made a note in his pad. 'No doubt we'll find out from their records. Old people do like to keep track of their bills, don't they?'

Gibson glared now. 'I'm not sure I like where this is going, Inspector. My parents have just been murdered.'

'And here you are worrying about undeclared income,' observed Noble.

Gibson pushed back his chair to stand. 'I'd like to leave now.'

'After the second knock went unanswered, what did you do?' Gibson glared at Brook. 'It's important, Mr Gibson.'

Gibson grudgingly dropped back on to his chair. 'I tried the handle. The door was unlocked. That was unusual.'

'Your parents always kept it locked.'

'Of course. They were old.'

'Where did they keep the key?'

'They always locked the door and left the key in the lock,' said Gibson. 'So it couldn't be misplaced, Dad said.'

'Which meant you couldn't unlock the door from the outside if there was an emergency.'

'Exactly. I told Dad not to do it because I might need to gain access, but . . . they were set in their ways.'

Brook nodded. 'Old people can be aggravating, can't they?'

'God, yes,' he said before he had time to think. 'That didn't mean I had any less affection for them,' he added, his eyes narrowing.

'Why take keys to your parents' house if you were routinely unable to use them?' asked Noble.

Gibson regarded him with derision. 'I'd look pretty silly if they finally paid attention and started removing the key and I couldn't get in because I'd left mine at home.'

'Old people and security,' sympathised Brook. 'It's a trade-off between locking the doors and being able to get out quickly if there's a fire.'

'Fat lot of good it did them, unlocking the door to a killer.'

'They may not have been careless,' said Noble. 'The murderer had a gun, after all.'

Gibson lowered his head. 'Of course. Will I get the keys back soon?'

'We're going to need them for a while, but as soon as it's practical, yes,' said Brook. 'Is it a problem?'

'I just need to know,' said Gibson.

'So you can re-let.'

'After this? No, it can go on the market as soon as you've finished your tests. I want nothing to do with the place.'

'Understandable. What happened after you entered the house?'

'The music was loud so I called out to let them know I was there. But even before I got to the lounge, I knew something was wrong. That terrible smell . . .' Gibson's eyes glazed over and he took a sip of tea to gather himself. 'Then . . .'

'You saw them.' Gibson nodded. 'Did you take a pulse?'

'I didn't need to.'

'So you didn't touch the bodies at all.' Gibson's mouth dropped open at the memory. 'Mr Gibson?' persisted Brook.

'No. They were clearly gone.'

'And the music?'

'I turned it off,' said Gibson, after a pause.

'Any particular track playing?'

'Pardon.'

'The track playing, you knew it, didn't you?'

Gibson looked up in surprise. 'Actually, yes – it was Barber's *Adagio*.'

'And that was their favourite.'

Gibson nodded. 'Yes, it was. It finished and then started again. It must have been on repeat. I shouldn't have turned it off, should I?'

'Not if you knew they were dead, no.'

'I'm sorry. I was in shock and struggling to think straight.'

'Understandable in the circumstances,' said Brook, resurrecting a more sympathetic tone. 'You told Sergeant Morton your parents weren't champagne drinkers?'

'No.'

'But you saw the champagne in the kitchen.'

'I saw it.'

'So you went in there.'

'My parents had been murdered,' said Gibson, narrowing his eyes. 'I thought someone must have broken in so I went to check if the back door had been forced. The intruder, the killer, might still have been in the house.'

'But the front door was unlocked,' said Brook.

'That doesn't mean the killer came in that way. He may just have left by the front door.'

'Pretty clear thinking,' said Noble.

'If I'd been thinking clearly, Sergeant, I would have realised the killer was long gone from the state of my parents' bodies.'

'Fair point,' conceded Brook. 'Did you search the rest of the house?'

'What do you mean?'

'If you thought the killer might still be on the premises, you might think it a good idea to search the house.'

Gibson nodded. 'You're right, I did.'

'You went into the bedroom.'

'Yes.'

'You saw the envelope with the cash in it.'

Gibson's gaze dropped. 'Yes.'

'Did you touch the money?' Gibson examined his hands. 'Mr Gibson?'

Barely audible, Gibson answered, 'Yes.'

'Louder for the tape, please,' said Brook.

Gibson looked up but was unable to meet their eyes. 'Yes. But . . . it was just there. I'm their eldest son, they were living in my property. I figured—'

'You figured with your parents dead the money was yours anyway,' nodded Brook.

'More mine than some light-fingered police officer's,' growled Gibson.

Brook took a leisurely sip of tea. 'You have a pretty low opinion of us, Mr Gibson. Any reason for that?' No answer.

'Touching the money compromised a crime scene,' said Noble.

'I'm sorry.'

'And we have to wonder why you did that.'

'It was a mistake. When I realised, I put it back.'

'After contaminating evidence,' continued Noble.

'I know. I was in shock, remember.'

'If it's any consolation, it's unlikely the killer would have touched the money without taking it,' said Brook. Gibson nodded, his features leavened by a measure of relief. 'Did you touch anything else?'

'No.' He looked up. 'Not that I'm aware of.'

'You mentioned you were the eldest son. Are there other surviving siblings?'

'My younger brother, Pete, and his wife Jeanie,' said Gibson finally. 'They went to Australia with the children.'

'Children?'

'Michael and Jessie.'

'Would those be the ones in the picture frames your parents had on their laps?' Gibson nodded. 'For the tape, please.'

'Yes.'

'When officers entered the scene, the photographs were face down,' said Noble.

'I didn't touch them, if that's what you're suggesting,' said Gibson.

'Then how did you know which photographs they were?'

'I recognised the frames. They were usually on the mantelpiece.'

'We didn't notice any pictures of you in the house, Mr Gibson,' said Noble.

Gibson hesitated. 'Pete . . . I never had children. Michael and Jessie were their only grandchildren.'

'And absence makes the heart grow fonder,' suggested Brook.

'Something like that.'

'Did you move the wheelie bin into the street?'

Gibson looked surprised at this change of tack. 'Er . . . no. There's an elderly neighbour. Heather Sampson. Whoever's up first puts out the bins. Dad sometimes forgot. Didn't you ask her?'

'Not yet,' said Noble. 'She's under sedation for shock.'

'Poor old girl. Yes, she's a bit frail. Going deaf, too. I doubt she'll be much help.'

'Did you notice the clothes your parents were wearing?' said Noble.

'What about them?'

'They were dressed quite smartly for a weekday morning.'

'They weren't students, Sergeant. My parents were always well turned out.'

'Your father routinely wore a tie?'

'Not around the house, but they were attentive to their appearance. They had old-fashioned standards.'

'Is it possible they might have been dressed for a special occasion over the weekend?'

'Is that when they were killed?' said Gibson.

Noble hesitated, glanced across at Brook, who shook his head. 'We haven't determined that yet.'

'Well they rarely went out,' said Gibson. 'And certainly not at night. There's nowhere to go in Boulton Moor. It's in the back of beyond. You need a car, but Dad didn't want one because his eyes were bad. I think Mum sometimes hankered to get out and about a bit more. But usually they just walked across the fields in the afternoon if it was fine. And in the evenings they had each other for company. They'd read and listen to music, then go to bed early. That's how they liked it. Normal for their age.'

'And alcohol?'

'The occasional glass of sherry, as I told the other officer, but never more than one.'

'What about the champagne flutes?'

'What about them?'

'Did they belong to your parents?'

'Yes. No.' Seeing Brook's confusion, he added quickly, '*I* like a glass of champagne if we have a celebration, so I bought them proper glasses so I wouldn't have to drink from a sherry glass whenever I went over with a bottle. They never used them, though.'

'But the bottle in the kitchen wasn't one of yours.'

'No. I never took them a bottle that I didn't drink myself.'

'Would they have joined you?'

'Mum was happy to have a glass. Dad would take one but only have a sip if there was a toast.'

'When was the last time you went round with champagne?'

'August the twenty-fifth.'

'For their wedding anniversary?'

'Correct,' said Gibson, impressed in spite of himself.

'Was there another significant anniversary over the weekend, something that might have caused them to celebrate?'

'Not that I'm aware of.'

'Maybe the date they met.'

'They met at school,' said Gibson. 'So I assume that would be sometime around the start of September. And they wouldn't have bought champagne to celebrate either way.'

'Did they have any regular visitors?' asked Noble. 'Social services, meals on wheels, that sort of thing.'

'No, they were still pretty independent. And proud of it. Though Dad was beginning to slip.'

Brook read down the list of medications recovered from the house. 'I notice your father was taking Angiomax. He had heart disease?'

'Angina, yes. But as far as I'm aware it was under control. Mum had high blood pressure. She took tablets for it and seemed fine. They were just old people with all the problems that can bring.'

'Would they have told you if one of them was terminally ill?'

'Are you implying this was some kind of suicide pact?'

'Not exactly,' said Brook. 'They were indisputably killed by a third party or parties but their valuables were left untouched, so we're looking for a viable motive. Your parents weren't subjected to any form of violence other than the bullets that killed them. We recovered a dozen bottles of medication from the house, so their deaths don't appear to be drug-related—'

'Drug-related?' exclaimed Gibson.

'Addicts don't discriminate,' said Noble. 'They're equal-opportunity thieves and, when the situation demands, killers. They don't check labels at the scene because they have a working knowledge of amateur chemistry. They'll bag any medication they can find and sort through it later to work up a cocktail that gets them where they want to be.'

'But wouldn't they have taken the cash?'

'Undoubtedly,' said Brook. 'So for the moment we're struggling on motive. But if we confirm champagne in your parents' bloodstream, we're forced to consider the possibility of some kind of mercy killing.' He stared unflinchingly at Gibson. 'You know, go at a time of their own choosing and all that. As a couple.'

'And perhaps people who have decided to die might consider vintage champagne a suitable celebration of their lives,' said Noble. 'Before someone puts them out of their misery.'

The colour drained from Gibson's face. 'And usually that someone is a person who knew and loved them,' he said softly.

'Usually,' confirmed Brook. 'Any other close relatives?'

'In the northern hemisphere, just me,' said Gibson.

'Then we need to know where you were on Saturday and Sunday,' said Brook.

'I was at home.'

'That would be at your address in Ticknall,' said Noble, checking a page of Morton's notes.

'That's right.'

'The whole weekend?' asked Brook.

'Yes.'

'You didn't venture into Derby at all?'

'No.'

'Or visit your parents.'

'I didn't drive anywhere at the weekend. I went for a walk both mornings. On Saturday I watched the rugby in the afternoon then made dinner. Same on Sunday.'

'Where did you walk?'

'There are plenty of footpaths and trails around Ticknall. It's very beautiful. I walk every morning if I can. Keeps me fit.'

'Except on rent day,' ventured Brook.

'Except on rent day.'

'Are you married?' said Noble.

Gibson didn't answer for a moment. 'What has that to do with anything?'

'Just background,' smiled Brook. 'And of course your wife would be able to help verify your movements.'

Gibson pondered for a moment. 'I prefer not to answer that at this time.'

Brook and Noble exchanged another glance. 'Mind telling us why?'

Gibson stared coldly at Brook. 'Yes.'

'You heard me say the bit about anything you fail to

mention but later rely on in court,' prompted Noble.

'I've not done anything wrong so I won't be going to court,' said Gibson. 'And I think I'd like to leave now.'

Noble was about to press the point but Brook shook his head minutely. He stopped the tape and ushered Gibson from the interview room, then turned back to Noble. 'Send someone with him to pick up the gun and get him to fill out a surrender form, then have it checked out. And ask Cooper to contact the gun people to check Gibson's certificates.'

'The gun people?' smiled Noble. 'You mean the National Firearms Licensing System?'

'Like I said. And while he's at it, tell him to check if Gibson has form.'

'He's a retired accountant,' said Noble.

'Whose first instinct was to ask for his solicitor,' retorted Brook.

'Think there's something he's not telling us?'

'Aside from his marital status? Definitely.' Brook drained his mug of tea. 'Do you love your parents, John?'

'As opposed to feeling affection for them?'

'You noticed.'

'That and Gibson housing his parents out of a sense of obligation. And he only calls round to see them on rent day. It doesn't mean he killed them, though.'

'No, it doesn't,' agreed Brook. 'I don't think he's our killer, so no need to push him into a corner just yet. We'll find out soon enough.'

Seven

BROOK PULLED UP OUTSIDE THE cottage just past noon. The rain was coming down hard and there'd be no walking today. In the kitchen, Terri was cocooned in the same blanket Brook had used for warmth earlier that morning. She cuddled a mug of hot coffee like it was a newborn baby, cigarette smoke drifting up into her vacant face from a saucer. Brook stubbed out the spent cigarette end and took the makeshift ashtray to the porch, opening a window for good measure.

'Sorry, I forgot,' she said, her voice husky with booze and tar, running a bloodshot eye over his worn jacket and trousers.

'Don't worry,' smiled Brook.

'I thought you were out walking.'

'Not without you, love.' He flicked on the kettle. 'How long have you been up?'

'Long enough,' she said, not looking at him. 'Where've you been then?'

Brook noticed that the empty wine bottles had vanished and two fresh bottles of red had been opened to breathe for the evening. 'I had to nip out and see John.'

'John Noble? I thought you were between cases.'

'I am,' said Brook. 'He wanted some advice, that's all.'

'You know I took a week off specially to come and see you.'

'I know.'

'I could've gone to Jersey for the week, or—'

'I'm glad you're here, Terri.'

'Not glad enough to leave work alone.'

'Sorry. But he rang early, and in three days you haven't been up before twelve.'

'I need the rest,' she protested.

'I wasn't criticising. I can imagine how hard teaching must be these days.'

'It is,' she mumbled.

'I just thought I had time to pop out and see him.'

Terri hesitated. 'Is it about this Black Oak Farm business?'

Brook turned from filling the teapot. 'What do you know about Black Oak Farm?'

'Are you joking, Dad? It was a big deal in all the papers.' She looked away under Brook's gaze. 'And I knew that poor girl, Reardon Thorogood, the one who was attacked and her parents murdered.'

'Really? How?'

'She was at Manchester in my last year.' She shrugged. 'And of course it was on your patch, so I followed it pretty closely, thinking you might be on the case . . .'

'I see.'

'Were you involved, Dad? You never mentioned it and I didn't see your name in the papers.'

Brook's gaze burned into her. 'Where is it?' Her face reddened, and from beneath the blanket she produced the letter Brook had received that morning. 'Terri, that's private correspondence.' He held out a hand and Terri reluctantly passed the sheets across the table.

'It was just lying around.'

'Lying around in my office,' corrected Brook.

'I was looking for matches.' Terri's expression betrayed injury. 'I'm sorry if I've invaded your space. If you tell me which parts of your home are out of bounds . . .'

'I didn't mean it like that.'

'Do you want me to leave? I can—'

'No, Terri, I'm sorry. It's my fault. You're right. I shouldn't have left it out. John rang and I got distracted.'

There was silence for a moment while Terri processed his apology. 'So was it your case?'

'No, I was on leave – camping around the Peaks. I invited you, remember?'

Terri nodded. 'I remember.'

'If I'd known the Thorogood girl was at university with you, I'd have said something.'

'So you know the background to the case.'

'Only bare details,' said Brook.

'Then why is this guy writing to you from prison?'

'Don't worry about it.' Brook plonked down a mug of a tea on the table. 'How much did you read?'

'All of it.'

Brook sat down opposite her. 'I'm sorry to hear that. The last thing you need – that anybody needs – is the ravings of a mass murderer bouncing around inside your head.'

'Mass murderer,' echoed Terri. She stared at the paper in his hand. 'Really? He sounds—'

'Of course he does,' cut in Brook. 'That's what organised serial killers try to sound like. They work hard to appear normal. They want you to think them intelligent and lucid. And in some ways they are. Their crimes are often methodically planned and carefully executed.'

'But they still get caught.'

'Of course. Their strengths are also their weaknesses. They obsess about what they do and it makes them vain and attention-seeking and completely lacking in empathy. And that breeds carelessness. But until we catch them, if you fit their victim profile they'll smile while they kill you then masturbate over the look on your face as you die.'

Terri was suitably shocked. 'Nice. So why is he writing to you?'

'He's not writing to me. I agreed to play postal chess in exchange for his confession.'

'You're kidding,' said Terri. 'You give too much of yourself, Dad. It damages you.'

'It's just chess. He sends me his moves, I send mine back.'

She pointed at the letter. 'That isn't just chess.'

'He's not done that before.'

'Dad—'

'The families needed closure. At the time it seemed a small price to pay.'

'And now?'

'It's irksome but I can cope.' He smiled to reassure.

'That's not what Mum said – she told me all about the Reaper all those years ago. She said that was how your problems started. Getting too close to these people.'

'That's all in the past.' Brook took a sip of tea and folded the letter into his jacket pocket. 'I'm better now, take things in my stride.'

'That letter was pretty familiar,' said Terri. 'Who is he?'

'Forget him, Terri.'

'But what if he's right about the case?'

'He isn't.'

'But what if he is? What are you going to do about it?'

'About Black Oak Farm? Not a thing. The case is closed.'

'But an innocent man might be languishing in jail.'

'If you've read the letter properly, you'll notice that not once does he say Coulson is innocent. That's part of the serial killer's sleight of hand. All it claims is that he didn't kill Mr and Mrs Thorogood.'

'But he's still gone down for their murder.'

'You've heard of joint enterprise, Terri. Luke Coulson was a co-conspirator. He was there with Jemson and possibly Reardon's missing brother. So even if he didn't actually kill anybody, which he did, he's still guilty of murder.'

'As I remember it, the only person Coulson's barrister said he'd killed was that guy Jemson, and that was to stop the attack on Reardon.'

Brook raised an eyebrow. 'As you remember it?'

Terri looked sheepish. 'I had a quick refresher on the internet.'

'In which case, you might also remember that Coulson never denied killing the parents.'

'He didn't admit it, either.'

'Coulson was there. He's guilty.'

'But he admitted to killing Jemson. Why would he do that and not admit to murdering the parents?'

'Because Jemson was a co-conspirator. He sexually assaulted Reardon. Having Coulson admit to the murder of Jemson is his brief's subtle way of casting his client as a protector of one of the victims.'

'But if he didn't kill the parents . . .'

'There were three of them, Terri. Jonathan Jemson, Coulson and the brother . . .' He cast around for the name.

'Ray.'

'Right. Coulson has a low IQ. He may not have been the instigator, but he went willingly to Black Oak Farm. There was security film of him brandishing the knife that killed Jemson and the Thorogoods, and a wealth of evidence to show that Ray Thorogood hated his parents and organised the attack. It was about money, pure and simple. As *I* remember it, Ray and Jemson knew Coulson was fixated on Reardon because all three had been at school together. And Jemson was an ex-boyfriend dumped by Reardon so he had his own grudge against her. Ray and Jemson planned the attack and Coulson was supposed to be the fall guy, only he deviated from the script when he stabbed Jemson. Coulson's conviction was cast iron.'

'Then why is this guy writing to you about it and why are you letting him get inside your head?'

'He's not getting inside my head, Terri, though he seems to be getting inside yours. He enjoys pushing people's buttons because he's got time on his hands. It's a game to him. He's insane, which you should know having read the letter in full.'

Terri's eyes dropped. 'Where he says he can see the ghosts of a killer's victims.'

'Exactly. And the only proof he offers that Coulson didn't kill the Thorogoods is that he can't see their ghosts standing next to him.'

'In which case a fruit loop like that shouldn't be your pen pal,' said Terri.

'We play chess,' retorted Brook. 'Nothing more.'

'What does he mean by "your own special companion"?' Brook stared at her, not knowing whether to answer or try to shut the conversation down. 'He mentions it in the letter.'

'I've read it.'

'Then who is he? Someone you knew?'

'Button-pushing, Terri. Remember.'

'Tell me.'

Brook didn't want to reopen this dark seam into his past but decided it was better to lance the boil before it became a sore point. 'He's talking about one of the Reaper's victims in 1991. Floyd Wrigley. In London.'

'When you had your . . . thing.'

'My breakdown,' corrected Brook. 'I found his body after the Reaper had paid a visit. A couple of years ago, when I went after Edward Mullen, he did some research into my past and concocted a story that I'd actually killed this Floyd. He assumed that having been a medium at one time, people might believe him. When I got too close, he hoped I'd back off if he threatened to expose me.' Brook shrugged. 'When I arrested him, he made the accusation.'

'And no one believed him?'

'Of course no one believed him, Terri. He's insane. Also he had a book about the Reaper case on his shelf with passages underlined – the passages mentioning Floyd Wrigley and his family.'

'Okay. If he's insane, why isn't he in a psychiatric hospital?'

'It's complicated.'

Terri pulled a face. 'Lucky I'm a graduate, then.'

Brook exhaled a long breath. 'Sometimes it's just easier to lock the door and throw away the key. And this man wasn't about to complain. He'd been in self-imposed solitary confinement for most of his life.'

'But while he's in prison, he's not getting the help he needs.'

'He's getting treatment,' said Brook. 'But you've got to understand, people like him are difficult to assess before they go to trial. They appear intelligent and articulate but their world view is that the rest of us are insane for not thinking as they do. It makes it difficult for them to contemplate that there might be something wrong with them and they invariably get their briefs to dispute the pre-trial diagnosis. In the end it's simpler just to lock them up and never let them out.'

'That's medieval.'

'It is what it is.'

'What if there was a chance of a cure?'

Brook smiled. 'If it's a choice between the misdiagnosis of an ambitious doctor armed with the latest psychobabble and locking people like Mullen away for ever, I know which option allows me to sleep at night.'

'But you don't sleep at night.'

'You know what I mean.'

Terri shook her head. 'I thought you were more progressive than that.'

'Being at the sharp end, seeing what I've seen, has a way of eroding whatever liberal instincts I once espoused,' answered Brook. He patted the letter in his pocket. 'This is a man who buried young boys alive in a makeshift coffin until he was ready to kill them and have their ghosts keep him company for eternity.'

'Shit. I had no idea.'

'There's no reason you should.'

'Why don't you tell me these things?'

'To protect you,' said Brook. 'These people, the crimes they commit . . . I can't share that kind of ugliness. I'm trained to soak it up and deal with it the best I can so you don't have to. It's my job.'

'But—'

'I know,' said Brook. 'Even with my training and experience, there was a time when I couldn't handle what I was seeing and my mind was nearly destroyed.'

'And now?'

'Now it's easier,' he said softly. 'But I'll never forget the sights I've seen. And it would be wrong if I did.' He touched a finger to his head. 'I have to carry those visions like scars. They're a memorial every bit as much as Auschwitz. And in a way, that's why people like Mullen and the Reaper do what they do. They want to make that mark on history. They want someone to remember them. People like me are the custodians of what they've done so ordinary people don't have to see, don't have to be exposed to the horror.'

Terri leaned over to him, the blanket falling from her shoulders. She put her arm round his neck and kissed his cheek.

Two hours later, Brook washed his hands and returned to the George's stone-flagged dining room, its open log fire beginning to die down though still radiating a soporific heat. As he passed the bar area, he waggled a hand towards the waitress who'd served their lunch. Returning to the table, he saw that Terri had ordered a second glass of wine.

'I thought we'd finished.'

'I fancied a *digestif.*'

Brook decided this was as good a time as any to broach the subject. 'Terri, you're drinking too much.'

'What?' She smiled pityingly at him. 'It's just a glass of wine, Dad.'

'No, it's a second large glass of wine at lunchtime, a couple of hours after you finished sleeping off the two and a half bottles you drank last night. And as far as I can tell, the only activity you've had this morning is making yourself a cup of coffee and opening two more bottles of wine for tonight.'

'You left out poking my nose into your private correspondence,' she added, her voice clipped, her eyes fierce.

'Don't change the subject.'

'Fine,' she said, reaching for the glass and downing a large gulp. 'You're right. I drink too much. It's because I'm from a broken home.'

The response Brook could never counter, only sidestep. 'So are thousands of others who don't have your gifts and advantages.'

'Advantages? You mean the guilt money you and Mum showered me with?'

'Guilt money? Is that what you think? Any guilt your mother and I carry about our relationship is between the two of us. We never let it affect how we behaved towards you after we separated. And because we had money, you wanted for nothing. What else should parents spend their money on, if not their kids?'

'So I should be grateful, then?'

'I didn't say that.'

'Because I didn't want money as a substitute for a stable childhood.'

'And that's why we didn't shower you with it, we gave it

with love when you needed it. We used it to put you through university not to assuage our guilt but because you're intelligent and wanted to go. We gave you all the love we could, even if mine was from afar. That was a constant that never waned despite the divorce. And in spite of our differences, neither of us once used you to attack the other.' He sighed and looked around the pub, glad they were the only diners left in the room. The waitress hurried over with the bill and, sensing the atmosphere, scuttled away just as quickly. 'At least I know I didn't. And your mother was the same until . . .'

The tears started down Terri's cheeks and her eyes narrowed to slits. When Brook declined to finish his sentence, she completed it for him. 'Until I stole her husband.'

Brook hung his head. 'God. We don't blame you for what that bastard did. Either of us. You were fifteen, Terri. Tony Harvey-Ellis was your stepfather and he abused you.' He sought the words least likely to inflict pain. 'Like all abusers he was cunning and self-absorbed. He betrayed your mother and made you a party to his deceit.' He waited for the inevitable rebuttal, but to his surprise it didn't arrive. Terri stared forlornly at the pine table. He moved his chair closer to take her hand. 'That's it, isn't it?'

'That's what?' she sobbed.

'Why you're drinking so much, why you're so unhappy. You're confused. There was a time you would have insisted you were in love with him. Thrown it back at me like a rock.' She peered up at him through the tears. 'But now you realise what he was and you don't love him any more. And you wonder why you ever did. That's why it hurts.'

'I know I hurt Mum. I ruined her life and she hates me.'

'Your stepfather ruined her life and he would've ruined

yours if he hadn't drowned. And your mother doesn't hate you. She hates herself for not seeing him for what he was. We both love you very much.'

She wept some more and burrowed her head into his chest while Brook rubbed her back. After a while, he got her to her feet. 'Come on. Let's take you home.'

Eight

Ds Noble's heart sank as he spied Chief Superintendent Charlton pushing open the door to the darkened incident room. By the encroaching light of the corridor he noticed a rolled-up newspaper under Charlton's arm like a cricket bat; the Chief Super looked like he'd been dismissed first ball. He seated himself at the back of the briefing and turned expectantly to listen to Noble.

'Pretend I'm not here, Sergeant,' he called from the restored gloom.

'Yes, sir,' acknowledged Noble. 'We're just finishing up.'

'Then you can let me have the bullet points. Where's Brook?'

'On leave, sir, remember?' Charlton's acknowledging grunt betrayed disappointment. 'He'll be coming in every morning to co-ordinate. That *was* the deal, wasn't it?'

'I suppose,' sighed Charlton.

Noble nodded at Banach, who turned on the lights. He gestured to the assembled detectives, who dispersed to desks and phones to hunt down lines of enquiry, and moved across to Charlton.

'So is it a series, Sergeant?'

'We're still getting to grips with the previous case, but the MOs look similar even if the victim profiles don't.'

'The first couple were gay.'

'And the Gibsons were an elderly couple, married for years, two grown-up sons. Neighbours say they were quiet, kept to themselves and seemed devoted. No enemies. No form.'

'But killed in similar fashion to the first victims.'

'Sat together and shot execution-style, yes.'

'Motive?'

'Unknown.'

'But Ford—'

'There was no indication of a sexual motive, sir. Not so far at least.'

'You're sure?'

'Not without a thorough forensic look-see, but we're pretty certain. And it seems unlikely to be a jilted lover in the Gibsons' case.'

'So Ford was barking up the wrong tree.'

Noble hesitated, not wanting to disparage a senior officer. 'I can't speak to that, sir, but any attack by someone with a psychosexual disorder would almost certainly manifest itself in more obvious signs of molestation.'

'And that's missing at Boulton Moor?'

'Completely. And, according to our information, at Breadsall too. No signs of disorganisation and disorder, which is the least we'd expect from the chaotic mindset of a jealous lover.'

'And the most?'

'Evidence of sexual violence on the victims, probably extensive.'

'But the two cases are still linked. Just not in the way Frank thought.'

'We're keeping an open mind until we get the ballistics report on the bullets, sir. That'll give us a definitive connection if there is one.'

'When will you be up to speed on Frazer and Nolan?'

'We're combing through the files and we've been watching the SOCO video. Looks similar, though Frazer and Nolan needed restraints. Handcuffs, then rope.'

Charlton nodded. 'Anything else I need to know before briefing the media?'

'There was one point that came up in DI Ford's inquiry, but for the moment it's better kept in-house.'

'Go on.'

'The ballistics report on the Frazer/Nolan killings showed the striations on the bullets were different. The bullets were from separate guns.'

'Two killers?' exclaimed Charlton.

'Unknown but strongly indicated, and that would definitely knock the sex killer theory into touch.'

'Why?'

Noble cast around for the simplest reason. 'Sex killers are almost always loners.'

Charlton nodded as though Noble's thinking chimed with his own. 'Was Ford aware of the ballistics report?'

'He mentioned it at the Gibson scene this morning, sir,' said Noble pointedly.

Charlton's facial muscles tightened. 'I'm sorry about that circus. I couldn't get hold of him in time.' He slapped the newspaper into Noble's chest. 'And tonight's *Telegraph* has all the gory details.'

Noble shook out the paper to read the headline. LOCAL HERO STOOD DOWN FROM INQUIRY. There were two photographs of the crime scene from beyond the tape, and quotes attributed to DI Ford bemoaning his fate at the hands of Brook.

'Sir, DI Brook—'

'Not his doing. I know, Sergeant. You'll be glad to hear Ford cleared his desk thirty minutes ago. He's on gardening leave until next month and I've threatened disciplinary action if he speaks out of turn again. And assuming it's of any use, he's to give you full co-operation on the first inquiry.'

'Just the paperwork, sir. We'll develop our own take on things from there.'

'Understood,' said Charlton. His expression soured. 'As for Brook, what's so important he can't forgo his leave and immerse himself in the case with his usual unhealthy intensity? In this weather I would have thought he'd be happy to postpone his walks for a few weeks.'

'It's not that,' said Noble. 'His daughter's paying him a visit.'

'Daughter?' queried Charlton.

'Terri, sir,' confirmed Noble. 'He doesn't see her very often.'

'I see,' said Charlton. 'Why not?'

Noble shrugged and held his tongue. He knew Brook wouldn't appreciate Charlton being privy to details of his troubled relationship with his only child. Noble wasn't supposed to know either, but he'd been able to read between the lines from past comments. Brook's daughter was damaged.

'Are you ready for the media, Sergeant?'

'Me?'

'Who else?' retorted Charlton. 'I'm briefing in half an hour, and if Brook's keeping his head down, then you're it.'

Brook said very little that evening and didn't comment on the two bottles of red wine that Terri gulped down during their meal. An air of unreality infected their occasional titbits of conversation. Chatting about the quality of the anchovies or the prospects for tomorrow's weather seemed surreal after the emotional outpouring of that afternoon, and it was a relief to Brook that at ten o'clock Terri staggered off to the sofa and closed the living room door on him.

Rather than follow his daughter into alcoholic stupor and brood about the crimes the late Tony Harvey-Ellis had inflicted on his ex-wife and daughter, Brook fired up the computer in the office. As always there was work to deflect him from the hard thoughts.

He eased out the misshapen drawer of his desk to check his passwords on the scrap of paper buried under a mesh of pens, pencils, paper clips and drawing pins. Once it was visible, he logged on to the CID system before concealing it under the same detritus. With some difficulty, he forced the crooked drawer home.

He started with his internal emails, clicking on the latest communication from Dr Higginbottom. He skimmed through the preliminary findings from that morning's crime scene, learning nothing he hadn't been told earlier.

Next he opened Noble's long update on the progress of enquiries. The canvass hadn't turned up any witnesses from the estate, nor could they find a single neighbour who had a bad word to say about the Gibsons. Certainly no one knew of any enemies they might have had, and all said the elderly couple kept to themselves and lived quietly. Neither victim had a criminal record, and Noble's suggestion that the Reaper had returned to Derby could be snuffed out in its infancy. The Reaper was a serial killer who only murdered dysfunctional families with petty criminal and antisocial tendencies – the Gibsons were the polar opposite of that victimology.

The next-door neighbour, Heather Sampson, had finally been interviewed in her hospital bed but could also shed no light on the death of the couple next door. She hadn't heard or seen anything suspicious and was unable to suggest a timeline for the killings.

Brook's iPhone vibrated and he opened a text from Noble.

Long day. 2 things. Gibson couldn't find his Glock, v. suspect. Plus Ford's ballistics report says a Glock used on Frazer and Nolan. Something about shape of the rifling on bullets. Also Ford canned and on gardening leave. See me on telly? If you didn't, don't bother. Charlton did most of the talking. Burton complaining about Ford's removal from case, then Charlton, bless him, gave him a kicking about the tone of his reporting re Frazer and Nolan.

'Welcome to the circus, John.'

Another text followed seconds later. *PS Don't read evening paper.*

'Thought we covered that,' mumbled Brook.

He texted back asking if Banach had identified the suspicious-looking man hanging around the crime scene that morning.

David Fry, ex-soldier and neighbour. Some previous for violence. Still looking.

After making tea, Brook printed out a large attachment to an email and began to read through DI Ford's files on last month's murder of two middle-aged white males in Breadsall, a well-to-do suburb on the north-eastern fringes of Derby.

Stephen Frazer was a retired businessman and Iain Nolan a librarian at the central library. Frazer was fifty-seven years old, Nolan ten years younger, and the pair had lived together, according to statements from friends and colleagues, for nearly twenty years, though only twelve of those in Derby after relocating from Carlisle. The men were 'self-confessed gays' according to Ford's sneering phrase.

'Confessions are for criminals, Frank,' muttered Brook, shaking his head.

The pair were killed around 29 September, a month before the Gibsons, and left bound together on a sofa in their home. Bruising on the wrists of both victims was consistent with handcuffing, but when discovered they were tied with rope. They were also close enough to hold hands as they died. Whether they had undone the ropes sufficiently to achieve a final caress or their killer had bound them specifically to enable it, Brook couldn't be certain.

In another departure, Frazer and Nolan had had large sticking plasters stretched across their mouths, presumably to prevent them from contesting their fate verbally.

After immobilisation, both men were shot through the heart. As Ford had implied that morning, the ballistics unit at East Midlands Special Operations Unit (EMSOU) had concluded the bullets were fired from different guns. Further, they had now identified the likely weapons as Austrian-made Glocks – the same make of handgun as Matthew Gibson's missing firearm.

In another parallel to the Gibson killings, the two men had lain undiscovered for days until found by the next-door neighbour, who had a key for emergencies. Not having seen them for a few days, she became suspicious at the drawn curtains and finally, after texts, phone calls and several knocks on the door had gone unanswered, let herself in to discover their bodies. Like the Gibson house, the door was unlocked. There was no mention of music or champagne in the report, so Brook made a note, then scrolled through the crime-scene photos.

Like the Gibsons, Frazer and Nolan's corpses were slumped together, heads touching, like a couple who'd fallen asleep in front of the TV. Again there was no suggestion of a robbery – expensive watches, mobile phones and cash had been left behind. Brook flicked through the photographs and watched the lengthy video attachment for any sign of a champagne bottle or drinking glasses. He lingered on an image of the kitchen sink in case the killer or killers had washed up and left glasses to drain. Nothing.

Next he leafed through the autopsy report to check stomach contents for Frazer and Nolan, noting with satisfaction that both victims had consumed a small amount of alcohol before their deaths, though it wasn't specified as champagne in the report. Presumably Ford and Caskey hadn't seen the relevance and had failed to press the point. Brook made another note.

One thing he wouldn't need to double check was the complete absence of rage or disorganisation pointing to a sexual crime, either of passion or violence. There was no sign of interference on the victims, visual or forensic – no semen on their intact clothing or skin, or anywhere in the room in which they died. The killer hadn't masturbated while his victims perished, and unless SOCO found something as yet undiscovered at the Gibson house, Brook felt the same conclusion could be drawn about that morning's crime scene.

Further, there were no fingerprints at the Breadsall scene that didn't belong to Frazer and Nolan, and it was a similar story with DNA. Ford's team hadn't developed a single forensic lead aside from the bullets recovered from the bodies, making it all the more strange that, in the absence of any supporting evidence, he had set them exclusively to pursue a killer driven by sexual motives.

Brook skimmed through reports detailing the search for Frazer and Nolan's former lovers, supposed by the strait-laced Ford to have become embittered and vengeful about a past snub. When that bore no fruit, the hunt began for a disgruntled gay sex worker from the local area, and Brook was dismayed at the manpower resources devoted to the futile search for both. He glanced again at the picture of the two dead men.

'No rage, no mutilation, no lust.'

No former lovers of Frazer and Nolan were identified in the Derbyshire area. The pair were found to be a devoted married couple. Tentative enquiries in Carlisle had also drawn a blank. Furthermore, it had been almost impossible to chase down gay sex workers in a solid working-class city like Derby. If they existed at all, they were extremely thin on the ground, and several sweeps around an area in Peartree known locally as the Mall had produced no leads.

Eventually DS Caskey had interviewed a young man called Derek Davenport, who had been arrested two years previously and subsequently convicted for public lewdness with an un-named tramp in Markeaton Park. Davenport denied knowing the victims or that he was a male prostitute or knew other male prostitutes plying their trade in Derby. It was all rather pathetic. Belatedly Ford's team had started to investigate the possibility of a religious component, given the hostility some churchgoers reserved for homosexuals. And that was the limit of the inquiry until the ballistics report had landed a few days before the Gibsons had died.

Given his limited knowledge of guns, Brook read the ballistics report twice then isolated the summary sheet. As Noble had suggested, identification hinged on the rifling marks on the two 9mm full metal jacket bullets recovered from the bodies in Breadsall. Both had similar distinctive features. Striations showed that both weapons were made by Glock, who were the only manufacturer of handguns to produce weapons with polygonal rifling, in this case hexagonal, in their gun barrels.

The rifling helped to propel the bullet from the gun, and any minor imperfections in the tooling left unique striations and scratches on the projectile as it moved at high velocity through the barrel. These impressions could then be studied under a microscope, where ballistic experts would match individual characteristics to a manufacturer and subsequently a particular model of weapon, if recovered.

Because the bullets removed from the victims were standard 9mm ones, it was only possible for EMSOU to narrow down the range of Glock models. Frazer and Nolan had been shot with either a Glock 17, 18, 19, 26 or 34, all of which chambered a 9mm slug.

With a manufacturer identified, Ford's team had stepped up their efforts to trace the weapons through local gun clubs, including Gibson's club at Swadlincote, but had turned up no missing weapons listed on the Firearms Licensing Database. After a cull of legally registered Glocks, ballistics tests were ongoing but had so far failed to turn up a weapon capable of firing the bullets recovered in Breadsall. It seemed likely that whoever shot Frazer and Nolan still had possession of the guns, which were almost certainly unregistered and illegal.

After another hour researching the UK availability of the Glock, Brook yawned and logged off, then took out his iPhone to text Noble, even though it was gone midnight. Like most reluctant mobile phone users, he assumed everyone switched off their device at night and any message would be read first thing in the morning.

Bad news, John. Glock, especially the 17, very popular in UK and US. Used by British armed forces and many police forces, including Met, PSNI and us.

As he stood to stretch, Noble replied.

Can't it wait for the morning!!!!!!!

Brook frowned at the row of exclamation marks and keyed in a reply. *It IS morning and I'm the one having my holiday ruined. While you're on, if I can't linger for the PM tomorrow, ask Dr Petty if she managed to identify alcohol in Frazer and Nolan's stomachs. Champagne?*

A few seconds later, a reply. *Whatevs!!!!!!!!*

Brook smiled and went to make more tea. With his brain working in overdrive, he wasn't yet ready to go to bed. He would only be mulling over the events of the day for hours on end. As he sipped his tea, he stared at the chess board in an effort to unwind. He'd already moved Mullen's rook as specified, and when he manoeuvred his white pawn to threaten, he jotted down a further series of countermoves before folding the paper into an envelope. Then he slipped the letter about the Black Oak Farm case into the same envelope and addressed it for posting to Wakefield Prison in the morning. No note to acknowledge the letter's receipt, or that it had even been read.

A message in itself. Brook did not want to play Mullen's mind games.

About to seal the envelope, he paused. He withdrew the letter, flicked on the printer and photocopied it before returning the original to the envelope and sticking the flap down firmly.

Nine

Wednesday 2 November

BROOK WOKE THREE HOURS LATER with his head lolling against the wing of an armchair. He crept through to the kitchen to douse his face and torso in cold water, changed his shirt, made a flask of tea, then set off in the dark for St Mary's Wharf, still barely awake.

Arriving at the station before six o'clock, he hurried to the office he shared with Noble, ignoring the baleful glance from Gordon Grey, the sergeant on duty at the desk. News of DI Ford's humiliation had travelled fast, and Grey, one of Ford's oldest friends in D Division, seemed on the point of verbalising a complaint before Brook scurried out of earshot. Safely ensconced in his office, he poured tea from his flask and logged back on to the database.

The door opened and Noble strode in carrying a vending machine coffee, stopping when he saw Brook. 'The early bird?' he said.

Brook's tired shrug was answer enough. His insomnia was a well-worn subject, and though others might applaud the virtue of his presence in the office, he knew it was a product of his emotional cowardice – work was a welcome distraction from his problematic relationship with Terri. 'What's your excuse?'

'I keep getting texts at ridiculous hours,' replied Noble, sipping the froth from his beaker.

'Try turning your phone off at night like a normal person,' said Brook.

'Old person, you mean.'

'Mature is a better fit,' quipped Brook. 'Exclamation mark, exclamation mark.'

'You're upbeat.'

'Light-headed more like.'

'You didn't see Burton's piece in yesterday's *Derby Telegraph*, then.'

'Do I ever?' He spotted the rolled-up newspaper under Noble's arm and held out his hand.

'Sure?' At Brook's nod Noble passed it to him. 'You made the front page.'

Unravelling it, Brook saw the headline and a picture of DI Ford standing disconsolately beside the tape of yesterday's crime scene. He decided to risk a few paragraphs.

Black Oak Farm hero Detective Inspector Frank Ford was dramatically ousted from a local murder inquiry by former London big shot Inspector Damen Brook this morning. Brook, whose spectacular failure to catch serial killer the Reaper in London in the late nineties resulted in a nervous breakdown and a hasty transfer to Derby CID, was not available for comment last night.

Local hero Ford was the latest victim of the force's baffling decision to accommodate a mentally unstable officer at the expense of local know-how, when he and his team were stood down from the inquiry into the deaths of Albert and Edith Gibson, an elderly retired couple in their seventies, reportedly shot to death at their home in Boulton Moor sometime over the weekend.

The murders are believed to show significant similarities to the recent slaying of gay lovers Stephen Frazer and Iain Nolan, who were murdered in their Breadsall home last month.

However, turning up to investigate this morning, DI Ford was forcibly denied access to the crime scene by members of DI Brook's squad.

Brook, originally from Barnsley, who has benefited from the support of successive Chief Superintendents despite a propensity for alienating fellow officers, became Senior Investigating Officer on the inquiry the morning the bodies were discovered and swiftly demanded DI Ford be placed on gardening leave after Ford objected to his removal from the case.

It was DI Ford, readers may remember, who was responsible for last year's arrest of Luke Coulson, leading to a conviction for his role in the murder of Monty and Patricia Thorogood and the vicious sex attack against their daughter Reardon at their farmhouse in Findern. Ray Thorogood, Coulson's co-conspirator in the attack, remains at large while a third conspirator, Jonathan Jemson, died at the scene.

'Gardening leave?' queried Brook.

'As soon as Charlton saw the paper, he told him to clear his desk.'

'Good for him.'

'And assuming we want it, Frank's been ordered to provide full co-operation or risk instant dismissal – which might affect his final pension.'

'I see.' Brook tossed the *Telegraph* on to the desk and sipped his tea.

'You're taking Burton's hatchet job well.'

Brook smiled. 'To be expected. Why else do you think Charlton wanted me as SIO?'

'What do you mean?'

'Don't tell me you fell for his "go-to guy" routine. Charlton wanted Ford off the investigation because he's past his sell-by date, but, since he's a popular officer, anyone stepping into Frank's shoes was going to get flak, so Charlton gives the poisoned chalice to someone who's accustomed to it. Me.'

'When you put it like that,' conceded Noble. 'Though I think you underestimate Charlton's respect for your abilities.'

'Do I? Either way, it's done, and at least it's been quick and brutal.'

'But Brian Burton—'

'Has done us a favour, John. We only started yesterday, so Charlton would know that Burton could only have picked up that garbage from Ford or one of his team. And you know how Charlton hates off-the-record briefings he can't control. At least now we have a clear run.'

'And if Frank's got any sense, he'll keep his head down until his retirement drink.'

'Don't hold your breath for the invitation. How's Caskey taking it?'

'I haven't seen her, but I'm guessing she's not happy.'

'If she's ambitious, she'll get over it. And when she gets

a chance to think about it, she'll realise Frank was on the slide.'

'Not soon enough to push him in the right direction,' argued Noble.

'Frank's stubborn and he's not a complete idiot. If Caskey made the running, Frank would be only too pleased to steer from the back seat.'

'That's what I hear,' said Noble. 'Black Oak Farm was all her work, apparently. Smee heard Ford was sleeping one off and Coulson was already in custody by the time he dragged himself to the scene. Still took all the credit.'

'Interesting that Caskey didn't mind.'

'Loyalty?'

'Who knows.' Brook shrugged. 'Any idea why she moved over from Armed Response?'

'Smee heard her partner was murdered in Kent and she transferred out soon after.'

'Go on.'

'That's all I know except that it was sudden and violent.'

'Really? I thought the station ran on gossip.' Brook took a sip of tea. 'Let me know if you hear anything else.'

'You mean find out.' Brook smiled his confirmation. 'Not like you to take an interest in people.' Brook didn't react, so Noble grinned and puckered his lips. 'Or do you have an ulterior motive?'

'No I do not.'

'Course, I forgot. Angie told me you came out of the closet yesterday.'

Brook frowned but didn't bite. 'Where are we on yesterday's legwork?'

'Nothing from door-to-door. No sightings of suspicious

callers, no one spotted any new faces on the estate, which, let's be honest, is on the road to nowhere.'

'And strangers would stand out a mile without the cover of darkness.'

'Agreed.'

'So, depending on the post-mortem, that gives us a window of between three and five hours on either Saturday or Sunday night,' said Brook.

'How do you work that out?'

'Because the Gibsons unlocked the door, John. It gets dark around five in late October, but even on Saturday and Sunday there'd still be people around, arriving home from weekend work or an afternoon's shopping.'

'Or the match,' nodded Noble. 'Derby were at home on Saturday.'

'On that basis I'd say we're looking at the killer's arrival time being later, when things have quietened down, say between seven o'clock and midnight latest.'

'No later?'

'Gibson said his parents were in bed early, after which I'd be amazed if they'd get up to answer the door, much less unlock it, especially for a stranger. Once in bed, it's a stretch for most people to do anything other than shout out of a window. That counts double for the elderly. Not to mention the sort of commotion you'd need to make, banging on the door, getting them to take notice.'

'And the Gibsons were still dressed.'

'Exactly. The killer arrived before they went to bed. If he'd broken in, that's another set of variables, but there's no evidence to support that. They opened the door for him, or them, and once inside, pacification was a simple matter. Though the actual shooting could've taken place a long time after ingress.'

Noble smiled faintly. 'And you think midnight might be too late for *ingress*?'

'If the Gibsons were anything like my parents, they'd be in bed before ten o'clock.'

'Which would narrow the window to three hours.'

'Something else to ask Matthew Gibson.'

'Speaking of Gibson,' said Noble. 'His parents would definitely open the door if he came knocking in the early hours.'

'That doesn't make him a more viable suspect, John. He'd still have to rouse them out of bed and get them dressed.'

'He had house keys, and we only have his word for it that his parents left their key in the lock. If he lied, he could have slipped in before they went to bed and shot them.'

Brook shrugged. 'Then why not leave it until later and shoot them asleep in bed. No fuss, no bother. He doesn't even have to see their faces. And why all the rigmarole with the music and champagne? Find me a motive and someone who saw him on the estate and we'll step into him. No hits on his car, I assume?'

'Cars,' corrected Noble. 'He's a wealthy man. He's got a BMW SUV and an Audi A3. But no hits on either. We're widening the search and trawling through traffic cameras, but it's a needle in a haystack.'

'Then concentrate on the three-hour window for Saturday and Sunday,' said Brook. 'Assuming the killer didn't park on the Gibsons' street, get DC Cooper on to appropriate CCTV and traffic film and expand the canvass to neighbouring streets.'

'He could've left his car anywhere within a mile radius and walked the rest,' said Noble. 'Maybe even further. It's not a major route, so we're struggling for serious film. We might get lucky with business premises, but there aren't too many and views will be limited, cameras lower quality.'

'Get it done and tick it off,' said Brook. 'Someone's prepared this carefully so I'm expecting a dead end, and we can assume Breadsall was the same. The choice of locations may be no accident.'

'Out of the way, quiet but with good access routes,' nodded Noble.

'Right. And canvass as far back as a month. If this is a series, the Gibsons would have been under the microscope soon after Breadsall.'

'On it,' said Noble.

'I assume there *was* a canvass in Breadsall.'

'Ford's not that far gone, but you're right – they turned up nothing. Posher area too, so residents that much more vigilant. I can get Cooper to have another look at the film, but it's semi-rural and cameras will be confined to the main road, if any.'

Brook made a ticking motion with his hand. 'Anything from bins and grates?'

Noble shook his head. 'The killers are hanging on to their Glocks for the next couple.'

'It's not a confirmed serial killer yet, John. Victimology isn't a perfect fit.'

'Two respectable married couples, quiet, devoted.'

'But age and sexuality set them apart,' insisted Brook. 'We need ballistics to give us a concrete link.'

'And two killers?'

Brook shook his head. 'That's very odd. A pair of armed men breaking into the homes of married couples, taking only their lives. What's the motive?'

'Maybe they stole something we don't know about.'

'From both crime scenes? No. There'd be evidence of a search at least, even assuming they didn't want the cash and other valuables. And I watched the Breadsall video last night. Frazer and Nolan were comfortable, no question, but they weren't fabulously wealthy, the Gibsons even less so.'

'We should ask Matthew Gibson for an inventory,' said Noble. 'Maybe he can shed some light.'

Brook stood and walked to the window to see the first fingers of dawn stretching above the horizon. 'If he knew his parents had something worth killing for, he would have told us already.'

'Not if he took it.'

'He's their son and heir, and with two high-performance cars and a number of tenanted houses, I'm guessing he's already well-off. With his parents elderly, whatever they owned would come to him soon enough. And what could they possibly have that he'd need to kill them for?'

'I don't know, but GSR showed he'd fired a weapon recently.'

'He told us that himself, John.'

'A clever way to divert suspicion.'

'Do you really think he'd kill his parents, send his mystery accomplice packing, then come back to discover the bodies a few days later and play the distraught son? Pretty cold. And again, why all the paraphernalia with the champagne and music?'

'To confuse us.'

'It's working,' answered Brook. 'And why handle the cash in the bedroom to implicate himself?'

'Another clever way to imply he's a bumbling idiot rather than an ice-cold killer.'

'It's not Gibson, doubly so if his parents are part of a series.'

'Unless he killed Frazer and Nolan to cover up his parents' murder. Make it *look* part of a series.'

'No,' said Brook emphatically. 'He would have chosen another elderly couple much closer to his parents' profile. Killing two middle-aged gay men, however devoted, doesn't fit the bill. And remember, they were difficult. They had to be tied and gagged.'

Noble shrugged, tiring of playing devil's advocate. 'Not so hard with guns and a partner to back you up.'

'But he might think he needs to kill again to make sure his parents' murder was well hidden.'

'Which he can hardly do now he's under scrutiny,' nodded Noble. 'Plus he wouldn't need help to kill his parents. Even unarmed, he's more than a match.'

'Agreed,' said Brook, pouring more tea from his flask and taking a comforting sip. 'Using a partner increases his exposure, makes him vulnerable. If Gibson had killed his parents he would've made it look like a simple robbery/murder. He would have shaken some pills on the floor and thrown the rest away, not complicated matters. The music and champagne personalise the crime and point the finger at him. Why would he do that?'

'He wouldn't,' conceded Noble, thoughtful. After a few seconds, he looked up at Brook. 'Son and heir.'

'What?'

He scrabbled for a piece of paper on his desk. 'He may be the son but he's not the heir.'

'What do you mean?'

'He doesn't inherit,' said Noble, locating the sheet. 'His younger brother in Australia does.'

'How much?'

'According to the solicitor's email, thirty-five thousand in various accounts and an insurance policy worth a hundred thousand.'

'People have killed for a lot less,' admitted Brook. 'What are Gibson's finances like?'

'Angie's sifting through them, but he owns two dozen properties – all but three outright.'

'Which would make him a millionaire on paper at least,' said Brook.

'Even millionaires have cash-flow problems.'

Brook checked his watch and lapsed into silence, staring out of the window at the pale sky. He shook his head. 'We're getting ahead of ourselves. Hold everything until we know this is a series. Anything else is just idle speculation. What about their health?'

'We pulled a pharmacy from the meds. The Gibsons were registered at the Raven Medical Centre in Alvaston. Smee and Read are chasing down their records.'

'Was the same done for Frazer and Nolan?'

'Neither was HIV positive, if that's what you mean.'

'It wasn't, but that still doesn't preclude other health problems.'

'If they did have problems and were desperate enough to ask a friend or relative to send them on their way, why would they need tying up?' asked Noble.

'It seems unlikely. More chance they were champagne drinkers, though.'

'Dr Petty might have something on their stomach contents this afternoon,' said Noble.

'What time?'

'Four,' said Noble. 'Sorry.'

'It's fine. You've got the experience, John. I'll work around you. And take Angie. It'll be good for her. Is Charlton okay with me taking the afternoons?'

'Fine,' replied Noble, avoiding Brook's gaze.

Brook eyed him doubtfully but didn't venture a comment. He glanced at his watch. 'We've got a couple of hours before briefing.' He drained his tea and headed for the door.

'Bacon sandwich?' enquired Noble hopefully.

'Where's the boundary tape?'

Noble looked around the dark garden. A frond of police tape lay twisted and inert on the drive. 'It's broken. It's been over a month.'

'Maybe Frazer and Nolan's relatives got a biohazard company in to clean.'

Noble fumbled with the keys, clumsy in his latex gloves, holding each one up to his face before trying to push it into the lock. He was beginning to get annoyed when he depressed the handle and turned to Brook in surprise. 'It's not locked.'

'Why am I not surprised?'

'Could be looters,' said Noble, his voice lowered. 'Or the killer coming back to jerk off.'

Brook flicked at a switch but the lights didn't work. 'Only one way to find out,' he said, pushing the door open. He stepped inside, puckering his nose. The ripe smell of decay had diminished since the house had been sealed, but the odour of death was still in the air. 'No bio-clean yet.' From Noble's hand, a thin beam of light illuminated the kitchen. 'You're well prepared.'

'My iPhone torch,' explained Noble.

'You're kidding.'

Noble sighed and held out a hand. Brook rummaged for his

new iPhone and handed it over. Noble shook his head and held down the start button. 'It's turned off.'

'Of course it's turned off. I don't phone people in the middle of the night.'

'No, you just text them. Do you pull out plugs before you go to bed as well?'

'The off switches do the job,' said Brook. He could feel amusement emanating from Noble in the darkness. 'What little sleep I get I don't want disturbed, John.'

'Disturbed? Last time I looked, you only had two numbers on speed dial and one of those is a daughter you see once a year.' Brook bridled but said nothing, sensing Noble's sudden regret. 'I didn't mean—'

'Forget it. You're right. I should leave it on.'

'What's the passcode?'

'Four ones.'

Noble exhaled disapproval. 'Don't you read the circulars about encryption?'

'What do you think?'

A second later, Noble flicked up the menu and tapped on the torch icon.

'Outstanding,' said Brook in wonder, wiggling his light around like a child with a bonfire night sparkler.

The pair moved into the house, their shoes clacking on the stone flags of a large kitchen complete with breakfast bar and stools, adorned by a marble-effect sink, drainer and work-tops. The large stainless-steel fridge, oven and hob gave the impression of expense and understated good taste. Noble opened the fridge and a bar of light illuminated him. It was empty.

'The sockets work at least,' he said, closing the heavy door again.

'Maybe a blown fuse.' Brook shone his torch on the wall above the breakfast bar. Wires hung down from a socket on to an empty bracket that might once have held a TV. 'Get Uniform to put a body on the house for the next week until we've had another look. I assume Ford took their computer to look for contacts.'

'There's a laptop on the inventory, though I've not had a chance to go through their emails. I've seen a screen dump of their Hotmail inbox, though.'

'And in English?'

'There was a printout of the inbox email addresses and subjects and hard copies of any useful content.'

'Such as?'

'Gossip with friends, Frazer and Nolan's plans, online shopping. That sort of stuff. Nothing caught the eye.'

Brook moved to a stack of magazines on the breakfast bar. He pulled the top one towards him and riffled through to a folded-down page. 'Any plans involving Thomson Holidays?'

'Come to think of it, there was something from them.'

Brook held up the magazine, and a sheet of A4 with handwritten calculations. 'Seems they were pricing up a skiing holiday to Japan.'

'Which they wouldn't do if one of them was seriously ill and they were planning an assisted suicide,' concluded Noble.

Brook placed the magazine back and wandered away into the large open-plan living space, picking up a framed photograph of Frazer and Nolan from a coffee table. Both wore brightly decorated Christmas cardigans and clutched a flute of champagne apiece. They were arm-in-arm and had streamers in their hair, and Nolan was blowing on a party horn. He replaced the frame and continued his search for a music centre. On an empty shelf he saw more disconnected wires hanging towards the floor. 'The CD player's gone,' he said.

'According to the SOCO photos it was an iPod dock,' Noble answered. Before Brook could work out what an iPod dock looked like, Noble approached illuminating a heavy green bottle in his gloved hand. It was empty.

'Champagne?'

'There's another four bottles in the rack. All vintage Laurent Perrier.'

'Unlikely the killer would bring a case,' ventured Brook.

'Then maybe Frazer and Nolan were drinking it when he arrived,' said Noble.

'And being the first of a series, he got the idea to use it in subsequent murders,' said Brook, nodding. 'Get it off to EMSOU.'

'But why didn't he leave the empty bottle and glasses on show?'

'Because it wasn't part of the plan until he saw them drinking it. The first kill he's careful so he sticks to the MO, but the second time he takes champagne himself because he wants us to see.'

'See what?'

Brook cast around for an answer. 'The element of celebration.'

Noble grunted, unconvinced. A noise from upstairs halted the pair. Noble extinguished his torch but Brook, unsure how to turn off the light, buried the phone in his pocket. He gestured Noble to the foot of the staircase and they crept towards a dark recess from which they could see the bottom step.

A torch beam from above provoked haste and both men

scuttled to hide. The light grew brighter and the stairs pronounced the descending chords of footsteps as a slim figure came down from the upper floor, panting under a burden.

Once on the ground floor, Brook scrabbled for his torch. 'Police,' he barked. There was a crash and a scream.

'Don't move,' ordered Noble, snapping on his torch to illuminate a middle-aged woman with her gloved hands held theatrically over her face. She had a duffle bag slung over her shoulder and a box lay spilled at her feet.

'Put the bag down,' commanded Brook.

She bent to oblige. 'This isn't what it looks like,' she said in a voice tight with tension.

Brook and Noble approached, fixing their lights on the woman's face.

'Who are you?' commanded Brook.

'Maureen McConnell,' said the woman. 'I live next door.'

'You found the bodies,' said Noble.

'I did.'

'And you have a key.'

She nodded. 'The lads . . . they had me water their plants whenever they were away. They were lovely lads. Lovely. They didn't deserve—'

'What are you doing here?' said Brook, forestalling a possible flood of tears.

'I'm doing what you lot should be doing,' she snapped, her trepidation forgotten. 'Safeguarding Stephen and Iain's property before the scumbags come for it.'

Next door in Maureen McConnell's warm kitchen, Brook read the handwritten note while she made tea and Noble emptied the duffle bag and the box of the iPod and dock, chunky watches, expensive sunglasses and items of jewellery and glassware.

Brook finished reading and handed the note to Noble.

To the police. Please apply next door to take possession of Stephen and Iain's belongings. Since you've abandoned the place, I've seen undesirables casing the joint so I've taken it upon myself to protect their property to pass on to loved ones.
Maureen McConnell (no. 23)

'Say we believe you really were going to leave that note,' said Brook.

'I don't care whether you believe me or not,' she said defiantly as she poured milk into cups. 'Since you taped off the house and left it to its own devices, I've seen all sorts of weirdoes sniffing around. Parasites.'

'They read the obituaries in the paper so they know when a house is empty.'

'Bloody ghouls.'

'So you decided to beat them to it.'

'That's right.'

'You took the TV?'

'It's in the spare room,' said McConnell. 'Look, I complained to your colleague but he was barely interested.'

'DI Ford?'

'That's him. Nasty little man with his insinuations. Bumboys, he called them. He didn't think I'd heard him, but I did. They were lovely lads, devoted, and that nasty man . . .' She broke off to stifle her emotions, took a sip of weak tea and gestured to the valuables unpacked on the kitchen table. 'Stephen and Iain had nice things. Very good taste. Expensive. Well, you know what the gays are like. Always well turned out.' She ran a swift eye over Brook's shapeless jacket and trousers, shiny with wear, and Noble had to look away. 'I couldn't let thieves help themselves. That glassware is Lalique. They collected it. They've got family up in Carlisle and they'll want keepsakes.'

'Then why the gloves?'

She shrugged. 'I didn't want to leave prints. In case you lot did more tests.'

'Any prints would have been found by now,' said Noble.

'How was I to know?' she complained. Her features softened and she rubbed away a tear. 'It's bad enough finding the boys like that...' She gazed off into the middle distance, an expression Brook had seen many times on the faces of stunned witnesses, their cosy worlds sullied by one brutal event. 'You haven't arrested anyone?'

'Not yet.'

'That's it then, isn't it? You're not going to catch them now, are you?'

'Them?'

She shrugged. 'Well, they were fit boys, Stephen and Iain. Always jogging or going for long walks. They took care of their bodies, you know, like the gays do. They were fit and strong, so whoever killed them . . . well.'

'Were they bodybuilders?' asked Noble.

'Not to that extent, but they exercised and ate right. They were toned and muscular. You could see that in summer when they were doing the garden.' She sighed. 'They loved that garden. Now what's to become of it?'

'You mentioned suspicious characters,' said Brook. 'Did you get a look?'

'Not really. They usually poked around at night. Young men mostly. I mean, they weren't all thieves. I expect a lot of them just wanted the thrill of seeing a murder house. I left a light on in their kitchen but there seems to be a blown fuse.'

'Any of them in cars?'

'Some.' Her face lit up. 'I jotted down a few number plates if that'll help.'

'Yes please,' said Brook with a glance at Noble.

'Did you give these numbers to DI Ford?'

'Oh yes,' said McConnell. 'Most of them.' When Brook raised an eyebrow, she continued, 'Well he didn't seem all that interested because it was after the . . .'

'After the fact,' suggested Brook.

'That's it,' said McConnell. 'Reckoned it was just looters.' She shrugged again. 'Well the killers are hardly likely to come back now, are they?'

'No,' said Noble, not wishing to alarm her with the propensity of some killers to fetishise a crime scene.

'Can I ask you a question about the day you discovered the bodies?' said Brook.

Ten

IN THE INCIDENT ROOM AN HOUR later, Brook gazed blearily at colleagues fiddling with papers or rushing around putting last-minute touches to their contributions. When activity dipped, he gave Noble the nod and the DS flicked a remote control and loaded the first crime-scene photograph on to the screen. It was the death shot of Mr and Mrs Gibson, slumped side by side in their separate chairs.

'Albert and Edith Gibson, shot to death in their home over the weekend. Exact time unknown and we're waiting on the PM for a guide.' Noble clicked on his mouse to load another image of death on to a split screen. 'Stephen Frazer and Iain Nolan shot to death last month in their Breadsall home. All four victims succumbed to a single gunshot and both couples were killed at home, seated beside their partner. Because of similarities in presentation and method, for the moment we work both cases together while we wait for ballistics to match the bullets. Or not. But for now, we have enough markers at both scenes to suggest a connection.' He enlarged the photo of the two dead men. 'There are, however, some differences.'

'Frazer and Nolan are tied,' said DC Cooper.

'We assume that's a control issue,' said Noble. 'Both men

were fit and active and would need to be pacified. Hence the gag, too. The Gibsons were elderly and both partners had health issues, which made them easier to manage. Cause of death and victim presentation are identical, even down to both couples holding hands as they died, and we think that too is no accident.'

'The killer wanted them like that?' said Banach.

'More likely he encouraged it as part of his vision,' put in Brook.

'His vision?'

'How he sees himself in the drama and what he wants to take from the act he's committing,' explained Brook. The less experienced members of his team took a moment to process his meaning, and he paused to let it sink in before nodding at Noble.

'Blood spatter and pooling from the Breadsall victims, combined with the angle of the gunshots, indicated that Frazer and Nolan were shot from close range by a standing gunman, or gunmen, and died where they sat. Reconstructions suggest their killer was between five-eight and six foot.'

'Narrows it down to about three million men,' said Morton to a short burst of laughter from assembled officers.

'And yesterday?'

'Initial blood analysis suggests the same MO, though we don't yet have a trajectory to confirm range or height of the killer.'

'Frazer and Nolan were gay,' said DC Smee. 'That's the biggest difference, surely.'

'Of course,' agreed Noble. 'However, they *were* married, like the Gibsons, and at this stage we're not fully convinced their sexuality was a factor. DI Ford's squad—'

'Ex-DI Ford,' interrupted Brook.

'Ex-DI Ford spent a lot of time and effort trying to flush out a jilted gay lover for the Breadsall killings, without success, and forensics also drew a blank on the usual indicators for a sexual motive. In fact, all four victims were unmolested and their bodies showed no signs of violence, apart from bruising on Frazer and Nolan's chests and wrists as a result of restraint.'

'So not a hate crime either,' suggested Banach.

'Given the lack of hate on display, I'd say no,' said Brook.

'Ruling out homophobia,' said Morton.

'And shooting is not the normal MO for a hate crime,' added Banach.

'It's limiting if you want to express rage,' agreed Brook. 'It's too cold, it lacks catharsis, and if a gun is ever a hate criminal's weapon of choice, you'd expect to see more bullets fired.'

'There would have been head shots as well,' said Banach. 'Hate crimes involve destruction of personality, and the face and head represent identity.' Impressed, Brook flattened his hands to mime *books* and Banach smiled, embarrassed.

Noble handed off the remote to DC Read, who loaded the next frame, showing a black handgun.

'Me and Smee were seconded to DI Ford's team for last month's killings,' said Read.

'Ex-DI Ford,' repeated Brook softly.

Read smiled apologetically. 'The weapons used on Frazer and Nolan were Glocks, one of the most popular handguns in the world because of its simplicity and versatility. It's used by the British Army as well as our own Armed Response Units in divisions up and down the country, including Derbyshire.' He loaded the next slide.

'The Glock 17 is the original design and still popular. It has a polymer frame, which makes it light and durable, and it fires a standard nine-millimetre bullet, two of which were recovered from the victims in Breadsall. It's hard to say which model was used because a lot of Glocks use the same ammunition, which is why it's such a popular handgun.

'But according to the ballistics boffins at EMSOU, the distinctive hexagonal filing in the barrel suggests both weapons were early-generation models. The original Glock 17 was first produced in 1982, but it could also be a Glock 18 or 19. Also, factory magazines will work in the 26 and the 34, and all generations of these handguns pack a nine-mill slug.' He paused for effect and loaded the next frame. 'Originally, DI . . . ex-DI Ford was thinking in terms of a lone gunman, but as you can see, the striations on the two bullets from Breadsall show they were fired from different guns.'

'Two handguns,' observed Morton. 'Two killers?'

'We're keeping an open mind,' said Brook. 'Nothing is certain until we confirm.'

'A single doer isn't going to take a separate gun for each vic,' insisted Morton. 'Has to be two gunmen.'

'It doesn't make sense, though,' answered Brook. 'Especially for victims as compliant as the Gibsons.'

'It's excessive,' agreed Banach.

'Very,' said Brook. 'But it's more than that. With multiple assailants there's invariably an element of escalation in the violence, and that's also missing from both scenes.'

'They egg each other on,' nodded Morton. 'Show off.'

Brook gestured at Read to continue.

'Last month we started tracking down all the nine-millimetre Glock firearms licensed to members of various gun clubs in the Derby area. All were legitimately held and securely stored. Nevertheless, DS Caskey had us collect them and send them for test-firing. So far EMSOU has found no match to the bullets removed from Frazer and Nolan.'

'How many guns are we talking about?'

'Fourteen,' said Read. 'We know that Matthew Gibson, Mr and Mrs Gibson's son, is a member of the Swadlincote club, but he wasn't spoken to because his weapon was decommissioned.'

'Any ex-army or police on the Boulton Moor estate, Dave?' asked Noble.

'Police?' exclaimed Morton.

'Frazer and Nolan were restrained with handcuffs before being tied and the cuffs were subsequently removed,' explained Smee.

'Anybody can get hold of handcuffs these days,' observed Cooper.

'But not anybody can get hold of a Glock,' said Brook. 'And that's what Authorised Firearms Officers in Derbyshire carry.'

'It's not like they can sign them out for a bit of freelance serial killing,' objected Morton. 'Security is tighter than a gnat's chuff.'

'Well someone talked their way into the Gibson house at the weekend, probably late at night and with a gun as backup, so it's possible they posed as a figure of authority.' There was a murmur at Brook's pronouncement.

'And there's no one with more authority than a police officer,' observed Banach.

'We're just throwing things out there at this stage, but with three pointers, we have to at least consider it,' said Noble. 'And for obvious reasons, this line of enquiry is not to be aired outside this room until we can discount it. Not even with family and friends, and especially not work colleagues. Understood?' There was an outbreak of nodding. 'Dave.'

'I've not managed to find any residents with links to guns in Breadsall,' replied Cooper. 'Although there are a number of retired police officers in the area, none of them were or are AFOs. Also no coppers living near the Boulton Moor crime scene. However, in the next street to the Gibsons there's an ex-soldier, David Fry.'

'Soldier?'

'Infantry, to be specific, so comfortable with weapons.' Cooper took a moment to load a mugshot of the man Brook had seen the day before taking a keen interest in the Gibson crime scene. In the photo, he had a black eye and looked the worse for wear.

'He was hanging off the boundary tape yesterday,' said Banach.

'He's local, so that may not be significant.'

Read nodded towards the mugshot. 'But he's clearly got form.'

'Fry returned to Derby from Afghanistan eighteen months ago, after leaving the army. Since being demobilised, he's amassed a jacket for drunkenness and affray but nothing with extreme violence and no suggestion that he has a weapon.'

'Veterans always have a weapon,' said Morton. 'Even if it's just a souvenir.'

'Service record?'

'Not got that far,' said Cooper.

'Employed?' said Brook.

'Officially unemployed.'

'Put him down for a follow-up, John,' said Brook.

'Bring him in?'

'No need. We know where he lives.'

Brook nodded at Read, who waved a hand at the display boards. 'Anyway, I put a list of the local Glock owners on the boards and in the record, for what it's worth, but it's looking like the guns used in Breadsall were either rogues or out-of-area. We're putting out feelers to other forces asking them to follow up question marks on the database about missing Glocks in Surrey, Hertfordshire and Scotland. Slim chance of a comeback, so a rogue is favourite. Somebody who's reactivated a weapon illegally or smuggled it into the country. There's quite a healthy trade in Northern Ireland because the army and the PSNI both carry Glocks, and when they get decommissioned it's not unknown for them to show up on the black market here.'

'In other words, any Glock used in a murder is likely to be illegal.'

'Afraid so,' confirmed Read.

'What about Gibson's gun?' said Noble.

'He's still not found it,' said Smee. 'Went round the whole house, but no sign.' He shrugged. 'Seemed genuinely put out.'

'Get a search warrant and have a proper look,' said Brook. 'What about his gun club?'

'First place we went after we checked his house,' said Smee. 'It wasn't in his locker or cabinet, but last night I spoke to the president of the club . . .' he consulted a note, 'a Mr Graham Warburton, and he confirmed he'd seen Gibson's gun at a social event at his Ticknall home and remembered the weapon was deactivated.'

'But presumably it can be reactivated,' said Brook.

'By someone who knows what they're doing, sure.'

'What about Gibson's financials?' asked Noble.

'He's a property millionaire twice over,' said Banach. 'He owns twenty-three houses around the city and county including his own, so no obvious financial motive.'

'Maybe he's overstretched,' suggested Morton.

Banach shook her head. 'Far from it. He acquired the bulk of his portfolio in his twenties and thirties, so debt repayments and mortgage liabilities are very low. His finances and cash flow are sound.'

'Another motive bites the dust,' remarked Noble.

'It doesn't mean he didn't kill his parents,' said Morton.

'Not without a motive I can believe in, Rob,' said Brook. 'One that explains the champagne and the music. If Gibson wanted his parents gone, the simplest thing to do would be to batter them over the head and ransack the place, make it look like teenage thrill killers or burglars. Instead we have an envelope full of cash with Gibson's prints on and two shots fired from a model of gun he owns . . .'

'. . . all of which implicates him,' said Noble.

'He's a retired accountant and property millionaire,' said Brook. 'I may be giving him too much credit, but if he had a motive, he'd plan it a lot better than that.'

A few heads nodded reluctantly.

'Speaking of champagne and music,' said Noble. 'This morning we re-interviewed the neighbour of the Breadsall house, the one who found Frazer and Nolan.' A few brows furrowed and Cooper glanced at his watch. 'Don't ask,' said Noble. 'She confirmed that both victims were partial to champagne, and we found several bottles in their wine rack, as well as an empty one. Forensics showed Frazer and Nolan had consumed alcohol before they died.'

'There were no empty bottles or champagne glasses in view,' said Smee.

'If Breadsall was the first kill, we could be dealing with an emerging MO,' said Brook. 'Frazer and Nolan could have been drinking when the killer arrived and he may have decided to make it a feature of future killings.'

'Where was the empty bottle?' said Morton.

'In the wine rack.'

'So the killer tidied it up?'

'Unless Frazer and Nolan had finished it before he got there,' said Brook. 'But fledgling serial killers are often chaotic in their thinking. Their first slaying is a basic model, which succeeding kills build on.'

'They keep going until they get it right,' nodded Cooper.

'So adding the champagne is a tweak,' asked Banach.

'It's possible.'

'What about the music?' said Smee.

'We think the killer may have been thwarted by technology,' said Noble. 'The neighbour, Maureen McConnell, said there was no music playing when she entered the house; however, she was certain the iPod was on.'

'So something might have been playing while they died,' said Banach.

'But why wasn't it continuous like at the Gibsons'?'

'Different technology,' murmured Banach. 'There was a CD player at the Gibsons'; maybe the killer tried to put music on repeat for Frazer and Nolan but didn't know how.'

'Meaning someone older,' said Cooper, nodding.

'Matthew Gibson's age,' offered Morton.

'It's not Gibson,' said Brook.

'You keep saying that, but he still hasn't given us a solid

alibi,' said Morton. 'Also he touched the CD player and the money and was positive for GSR.'

'He's a member of a gun club,' argued Brook.

'That doesn't alibi him just because he told us about it,' insisted Noble. 'He owns a missing Glock and he has a key to the second crime scene.'

'It doesn't give him motive for the first killing.'

'Both scenes are organised,' argued Read. 'Points to a mature perp.'

'It's *because* his parents' murder was organised that he didn't do it,' retorted Brook.

'Not if he organised it as assisted suicide,' suggested Banach. 'They both had health issues, after all. Maybe they decided their time was up. They want to go together so they ask their son to kill them. Gibson agrees and takes champagne to celebrate a happy life and plays them their favourite track as they die.'

'And being officially a murder and not a suicide, their life insurance is still valid so they can leave something to the grandchildren,' said Morton. 'Add in their savings and you're looking at over a hundred grand.'

'Works for me,' said Cooper.

'But not only does Gibson not need the money, he doesn't inherit,' said Brook.

'No, but his brother does, and if his parents are desperate to go, Gibson might see it as a good way to preserve the inheritance,' said Banach.

'So they have a little party and he kills them quickly,' nodded Morton, his enthusiasm rising. 'The insurance coughs up and everybody's happy. I like it.'

'Well I don't,' said Brook. 'Right now he's a person of

interest, no more. And in case you've forgotten, it was Gibson who told us the music was playing. Why tell us that if he put it on? In fact, why not remove the disc altogether when he turns off the CD player?'

There was silence as Brook's objections sank in.

'A hundred thousand pounds butters a lot of parsnips where I come from,' said Smee. 'Even if the whole bundle goes to the son in Australia, Gibson gets the house back and his parents avoid a miserable old age – everybody wins.'

'All arguments to revisit if the two murders are unconnected,' said Brook. 'Meanwhile we execute the search warrant on Gibson's house, and if it throws up something, all well and good. But if we get a match on the weapons from both crime scenes, then we're looking for a serial killer.'

'And he's out there looking for his next elderly couple to kill,' said Banach.

'Why elderly?' asked Read.

'Emerging MO,' said Brook. 'The Gibsons were a lot less trouble than Frazer and Nolan.'

'And they didn't have an iPod,' added Banach.

'What if we can connect Matthew Gibson to Frazer and Nolan in some way?' said Cooper.

Something in his voice made Brook sit up. 'Can we?'

Cooper flipped his terminal round. 'This just in. Matthew Gibson, fifty-four years old and a confirmed bachelor until this spring.'

'Confirmed bachelor,' said Brook, narrowing his eyes. 'Are you telling me he's gay?'

'He married a James Trimble in April, so I'd say yes. He's gay.'

'That's not much of a connection,' said Banach, first to speak after a moment's silence.

'It's more than we had before,' said Noble.

'There's more,' said Cooper. 'Gibson's got form. He's originally from Derby but left home at sixteen and moved to London the same year, 1978. A year later, he was cautioned for soliciting in Piccadilly Circus, and he has a string of related misdemeanours over the next eighteen months, including possession, affray and public indecency. That last offence was with a senior civil servant, who lost his job and subsequently killed himself.'

'Gibson was a rent boy?' said Smee.

'Reading between the lines.'

'Anything else?' asked Brook.

'Nothing,' replied Cooper, tapping his keyboard. 'He seems to have cleaned up his act after that. Went to college to study for his A levels and became an accountant. He bought property in London, then sold up and moved back to Derby to start building his portfolio here. Now has his own property company, and website. Nose clean ever since.'

Brook was deep in thought. 'Check Frazer and Nolan's laptop and phones again. Dig deeper into any social media they subscribed to. Matthew Gibson, too. And get moving on that warrant, Rob. Dave, I want more background on Gibson's misdemeanours. Also check on the family in Australia. Try to get a hint about relations between Matthew and his parents, and text John as soon as you have anything. It's time we filled in the blanks on Gibson's alibi.'

'I think we can guess, can't we?' said Noble, following Brook to the door.

'Since when did we start guessing?'

'Aren't you forgetting about Terri?'

Brook glanced at his watch. 'I've got time.' He hesitated,

then glanced surreptitiously back at Cooper. 'Meet you at the car, John.' Noble extracted a cigarette and headed for the stairs.

'Dave, I forgot to mention phone records.'

'John got me on to it last night,' smiled Cooper. 'Nobody rang the Gibsons over the weekend to arrange a visit, certainly not Matthew. Still waiting for the paperwork on his mobile, but if he did go to see his parents, he didn't ring ahead.' Brook nodded his thanks but didn't move off. 'Something else?'

'I was wondering if you could gather everything on file about Black Oak Farm and send it to my email,' said Brook quietly. 'Film, witness statements, forensics – the lot.' Cooper stared back at him as though he hadn't understood. 'You know the case I mean?'

'Of course,' said Cooper. 'Last year. DI Ford closed it.'

'Ex-DI Ford. And there's still an outstanding warrant attached.'

'Ray Thorogood,' nodded Cooper.

'Right.' There was an awkward pause.

'If I do a search, my ID will be on the record,' said Cooper. 'And?'

'And if somebody asks what I'm doing looking at another officer's closed case, what should I say?'

Brook paused. 'If somebody asks, tell them I wanted to see the material.'

'And if nobody asks?' Brook gave him a piercing stare and headed towards the door. 'Then keep it to yourself, Dave,' Cooper concluded.

Eleven

BROOK WAS SILENT ON THE drive out to Ticknall, unaware of the occasional glance from Noble.

'Everything okay?'

'Fine,' said Brook.

'Terri okay?'

'Fine,' repeated Brook, keeping his eyes on the road as they approached a brick bridge. 'Nice old bridge.'

Noble gave him a lingering stare, returning his gaze to the road. 'It's called the Arch. It was part of a horse-drawn tram system transporting stone and bricks to the canals.'

Brook looked across. 'I didn't know history was your thing.'

'My grandad had a canal boat near Ashby-de-la-Zouch. He used to take me out as a kid and told me all about it.' He smiled. 'Many times.'

At a pub called the Wheel Inn, Noble turned on to Banton's Lane and drove towards the five-bar gate that fed on to a track a hundred metres away. They passed several well-maintained brick and stone cottages on the way, the windows, gates and doors all painted in muted tones.

'We're in the heart of Farrow and Ball country here,' said

Noble. 'Posh paint,' he added when confusion clouded Brook's features.

They parked in front of Gibson's SUV on the drive of a brick garage belonging to the last property on the lane. Beyond was lush countryside, a pall of mist rising from the cold ground.

They walked through the gate towards the large two-storey house set back from the road. To the left stood a half-ruined stone barn with scaffolding on one side. The drone of a cement mixer filled the country air and two men – one middle-aged, one young – heaved large honey-coloured stones into position ready to add to the freshly laid course already fixed. At their approach, the older man laid a large stone on the ground and fixed Brook and Noble with a beady eye. He had short greying hair, arms covered in tattoos and wore a single gold earring, cut-off jeans and work boots. His bare legs were hairy and covered in cement dust, his knees soiled from kneeling on the wet ground. Through his chunky fleece jacket, steam rose from his torso into the cool air.

'Help you?' he called in a Scottish accent.

'We're looking for Matthew Gibson,' said Noble, holding up his warrant card.

'Police,' said the man, not bothering to look at Noble's ID.

Noble smiled his acknowledgement. 'Mr Gibson?'

'Up at the house.' Brook and Noble resumed their trudge along the path. 'Can you no' leave the man alone?' said the man, pacing after them. 'He just lost his parents.' The two detectives pressed on as though not hearing, aware of a string of muted expletives aimed in their direction. Brook glanced at Noble, who hung back to intercept while the DI walked on.

'Mr Trimble, is it?' asked Noble.

*

Brook reached the patio doors at the rear of the house just as Gibson emerged with a tray carrying three steaming mugs and a packet of chocolate biscuits. He wore similar garb to the agitated Scotsman and was equally grubby.

He stopped in his tracks when he saw Brook and put the tray down on a wrought-iron table. 'That didn't take long,' he said.

'The miracle of computers,' said Brook.

'I was just making tea,'

'Just milk for me. One sugar for my sergeant.'

Gibson stared at Brook before breaking into a lopsided smile. 'You're very sure of yourself, aren't you, Inspector?'

'I'm a DI,' replied Brook. 'People expect it. Inside I'm a quivering wreck.'

'No doubt.' Gibson picked up the tray. 'Just let me—'

'You don't have to speak to them, Matthew,' barked the Scotsman, marching towards them, Noble in close pursuit. 'You're in mourning, for feck's sake.'

'It's okay, Jim,' said Gibson. 'We knew there'd be more questions.' He removed his mug of tea and held out the laden tray towards his partner. 'I'll be down when we've finished.' Trimble hesitated, his cold blue eyes searching Gibson's face. 'It's fine, really.'

The Scotsman nodded faintly, then walked up to Gibson and gave him a long, lingering kiss on the mouth. After a defiant glare at Brook and Noble, he took the tray and turned in the direction of the barn.

Gibson ushered Brook and Noble into a spacious kitchen, a mixture of modern fittings and classical wooden units, cupboards painted in washed-out blue. Expensive chrome gadgets populated the surfaces, including a kettle, which

Gibson filled at a Belfast sink in an island in the middle of the room. The Mediterranean-red floor tiles were old and scuffed, and generous windows allowed bursts of low winter sun to flood the room with a warmth accentuated by the colour scheme, the ambience that of a comfortable Provençal home.

'Nice room,' said Brook.

'Yes, we gays are wizards at the old interior decor,' said Gibson tersely, flicking on the kettle and tossing tea bags into mugs. 'I assume my past is why you've come.'

'Amongst other things,' said Brook. 'You understand we have to ask.'

'It was nearly forty years ago.'

'There's no sell-by date on sex offences,' said Noble.

Gibson exhaled a little laugh. 'Offences, you say? Giving and receiving pleasure from other consenting adults is still offensive, is it?'

'Things have changed for the better on that score,' said Brook. 'But when it comes to sex, the law has always frowned on money changing hands.'

'Then the law's an ass,' snarled Gibson. 'Look around you, Inspector. This is Britain. Everything's for sale.'

'There's the added complication that you weren't an adult when you were picked up for soliciting,' added Noble.

'I was sixteen,' said Gibson angrily, plonking down two mugs of tea. 'An adult as far as heterosexual acts were concerned but a criminal when it came to exploring my own sexuality.'

'Society has moved on, Mr Gibson,' said Brook, taking a sip of tea. 'And the law has moved with it.'

'And yet my record is still on the books,' he said softly. 'If I'd been a sixteen-year-old girl turning tricks, I would have been treated like a victim instead of a criminal.'

'I wish we could go back and alter the past for you,' said Brook.

'I almost believe you,' answered Gibson. His manner softened and he managed a humourless laugh. 'Actually, don't bother. It's all water under the bridge. And between you and me, it was character-building. That period of my life was the making of me, and I look back fondly. Though I dare say I've forgotten most of the wailing and gnashing of teeth that happened with my parents.'

'They didn't approve?'

'That's putting it mildly.'

'Is that why they threw you out?'

'Nothing so dramatic, Inspector. My departure was mutually agreed and brought mutual relief. I was sixteen and gay. I didn't belong in seventies Derby, so I left as soon as I could scrape together the coach fare. My parents were glad to see the back of me.'

'Were they religious?'

'About average, I guess,' said Gibson. 'Church of England – not really a religion, is it?'

'No?' enquired Brook.

'No, it's more of a Conservative Party social club. You're a Catholic, I think.' Brook raised an eyebrow. 'I can always tell.' Gibson smiled maliciously. 'The look of pain and guilt in the eyes never goes away. My best customers back in the day.'

'We're here about *your* sins,' said Brook. 'Not mine.'

'Well my sins weren't the reason my parents were glad to see me go. It was just that my lifestyle, or the lifestyle I hankered after, was alien to them. They had no comprehension of how to communicate with me.'

'Nothing unusual there, straight or gay.'

'I suppose not,' said Gibson sadly. 'But parents want some kind of normality. A little common ground they can share with their kids. Without it family life becomes one long round of discomfort and embarrassment. No one wants that in their home, so when I was old enough, I left.'

'And arrived in London with little money and nowhere to live.'

'Something like that,' said Gibson.

'The money ran out and you were on the streets, hungry and cold,' said Noble.

'And forced into prostitution,' added Brook, sympathetically. 'Believe me, we hear the same story about runaways and missing persons every day.'

Gibson's stern features slowly broke into a grin. 'My God. You lot are so patronising, spewing out this identikit spiral-of-degradation crap for every missing teenager that crosses your desk. Do you ever stop to think that people are different, not just some damn statistic to be . . . interpreted?'

'That wasn't you?' said Brook.

'I was never forced to do anything I didn't want,' said Gibson. 'I was gay, and once I realised as much, I wanted to get fucked by men and fuck them in return.'

'Thanks for clearing that up,' said Brook, thin-lipped.

'My frankness upsets you,' sneered Gibson, pleased to have caused offence.

'More your inability to source appropriate verbs.'

'Very well. I wanted to have sex with men. Is that less offensive? And do you know something? I enjoyed it and I was good at it. And because I wasn't forced into it, I wasn't desperate enough to dose myself up with booze and drugs to get through. I never turned tricks for cigarettes and dime bags like some of the poor bastards on the meat rack – I earned top money. And since it was before the property boom, I managed to afford a little flat in Soho. I learned young that economic security was the key to happiness. Remove that security and you're at everybody's mercy, like the poor bastards who had to pimp themselves out for rough trade or give in to the limo-driving chauffeurs collecting jailbait for the House of Commons. I did whatever I wanted with whoever I wanted and got paid handsomely for the privilege.'

'But inevitably you were arrested.'

Gibson shrugged. 'Occupational hazard.'

'And did time.'

'A few months.' He grinned. 'The arresting officer said he'd let me off with a warning if I sucked his cock, but I wasn't going to pass up the chance to get locked up with hundreds of men, was I?'

Noble was stern, but Brook was briefly amused. 'What a heart-warming story,' he said. 'How did your parents react to your conviction?'

'I've no idea. I was in London, they were in Derby, living their dull little life, washing the Ford Anglia every Friday, roast beef on Sunday. As far as I'm aware, they didn't know anything about my life. I'd severed all ties.'

'But you were a minor,' said Noble. 'Surely the police contacted them.'

'If they found them. I certainly didn't volunteer information about my parents to the police. Said I was an orphan. Things were different then. It wasn't difficult to slip through the net. Child protection wasn't the big deal it is nowadays. The police didn't care and nor did social services. I was living my own life and wasn't bothered what anyone else thought, so even if Mum and Dad were told, I wouldn't have cared. They were miles away.'

'And when you moved back?'

'I never broached the subject with them – not out of shame, you understand, but because it would serve no purpose.'

'It never came up?'

'Never. And I was protecting *them*, not me. The older they got, the less relevant it became.'

'And before you left?' asked Brook.

'The only thing my parents ever said about my sexuality was that I was a disgusting little queer. Dad's phrase. When I came back to Derby, it was never mentioned. I wasn't sixteen any more and I guess they assumed I'd grown out of it.'

'How did they find out?'

'There was a boy at school. I misinterpreted some signals.'

'And was being a disgusting little queer why your parents disinherited you?' asked Noble.

Gibson smiled faintly. 'Probably, but I didn't care. They wanted grandchildren, and Pete and Jeanie were in a position to oblige. The irony is, having got their wish, the twins were whisked away to a better life in Australia, never to be seen again. Except in photographs. That hurt them, particularly Mum, and they wore it every day like a death in the family.'

'You weren't resentful?'

'About losing my birthright? No. I suppose I might have been had I not done so well for myself. I don't begrudge Pete. I never wanted a thing from my parents.'

'Except the rent,' observed Noble.

'They were my parents,' said Gibson, in an acid tone. 'They fed me and put a roof over my head for sixteen years. I had some kind of duty to house them, and the rent money was their idea, Sergeant. I didn't ask for it, but you know how proud old people are.'

'Neither a borrower nor a lender be,' said Brook.

'Words my dad lived by. Besides, the rent barely covered my expenses. I only took it for their sake.'

'Big of you,' said Noble.

'What can I say? I'm a giver,' Gibson snapped back, unwilling to be embarrassed.

'Your offences . . .' began Brook before correcting himself. 'Your criminal record spans a two-year period, but when you were eighteen, you enrolled at Golders Green College.'

'I'd had my fun and made good money doing it,' replied Gibson. 'But you only had to see some of the walking dead on the rack to know there was no long-term future in that game. And this was before we knew about AIDS, remember. Seventeen-year-olds who looked twice that, boys even younger doped up like zombies. I'd been lucky, but that life will claim you eventually. The wrong trick at the wrong time. Bent coppers. It was time to get serious. And respectable. I went to college. Ferdy helped.'

'Ferdy?'

'My late sponsor.'

'A sugar daddy?' observed Noble.

Gibson looked calmly at him. 'If it pleases you.' He laid down his cup and walked over to a drawer in the kitchen island. His hand disappeared and a second later he pulled out a gun, pointing it at Noble. Brook and Noble froze, mugs held halfway to their faces. 'Found it,' grinned Gibson, tossing the weapon in the air and catching it by its muzzle. 'Under the stairs.' He held the gun grip-first towards Noble. Both detectives stared at him.

'I'm starting to get the impression you don't care for the police, Mr Gibson,' said Brook, his voice soft and carrying a tremor of threat. He gestured at Noble, who drew out an evidence bag and held it open for Gibson to drop the gun.

'If you'd taken the shit I've had from your lot . . .' retorted Gibson. His grin tempered but its ghost remained. 'I'd like a receipt. Is there anything else?'

'Yes,' said Brook, gesturing at Noble, who extracted an envelope from his jacket and removed a pair of photographs before laying them in front of Gibson. 'Do you recognise these two men?'

Gibson stared at the photos, then looked sideways at Brook. 'These were the two men murdered last month. I read it in the papers.'

'Did you know them?'

'Why?' said Gibson angrily. 'Because I'm gay, you think I killed them in some kind of hissy fit?'

'We think the murder of your parents is connected to the murder of these two men,' said Brook patiently.

'The papers said they were shot,' said Gibson, his eyes narrowing. 'Same gun?'

'It's too early to know that,' said Noble.

'But the same method as my parents.'

'We can't go into details,' said Noble.

'You don't have to, I was there,' said Gibson. 'I saw how Mum and Dad died and I know you're looking for an experienced shooter, someone who knows their way around guns. Someone like me. Even from close range, hitting the heart with one shot is not as easy as you think. And to do it twice . . .'

'Four times,' said Brook. 'From three metres.' Noble glanced at his DI. It was unlike him to volunteer information.

'So I'll ask again.' He tapped a finger on the photographs. 'Do you know these men?'

Gibson looked into Brook's eyes, then away. 'We met them, Jim and me. On a march, and at a couple of parties. Stephen and Iain, right? They seemed nice enough, if a bit . . .'

'A bit what?'

'You wouldn't understand,' said Gibson sullenly.

'Give us some credit,' said Brook.

'They were a bit . . . gay,' said Gibson, his eyes challenging Brook to comprehend. 'Flaunting it, if that makes any sense. It was tedious.'

'You had little in common.'

'Apart from arse and interior design, not a thing. Look, I had nothing against them. It's just . . . this is going to sound bitter, but they came from nice middle-class homes with understanding parents and all the support that implies. And like it or not, that support softens you. Makes you think the whole world will let you cry on its shoulder.'

'Is that a problem?'

'Not for me,' replied Gibson.

'But it set you apart from them,' said Brook.

'Jim and I had it tough, and what we both went through growing up left its mark. So we don't slap people in the face with our sexuality. We don't flaunt it, because that shows a lack of confidence, a search for approval. We take people as we find them and expect others to do the same with us.'

'Happy in your skin,' quipped Brook.

'Confident would be a better word,' growled Gibson. 'But that doesn't mean we won't stand up and make a statement if we have to.'

'Not confident enough to make a statement about who you spent the weekend with,' observed Noble.

'My domestic arrangements are none of your business.'

'But your alibi is,' remarked Brook. Gibson was sulky. 'You were with your partner, I take it.'

Gibson nodded. 'And Sean. His son,' he added as qualification. 'We were working on the barn. You can ask them.'

'We will.'

'These parties,' said Brook. 'Were either of them at their house?'

'No.'

'You're sure?'

'The papers said they lived in Breadsall. I think I'd remember if we'd been to the house they were murdered in.'

'And were these parties . . . ?' began Brook.

Gibson's mouth curled into a malicious grin. 'Spit it out, as the bishop said to the rent boy.' Brook looked at Noble for help. 'Were they gay orgies? That what you mean, Inspector?'

'I wouldn't have put it quite like that,' said Brook, his face flushing.

Gibson smirked, taking pleasure in Brook's discomfort. 'How would you put it?'

Brook sighed. 'I've no idea. I'm out of my comfort zone, I admit it. So tell me. Is there an active gay community in Derby?'

Gibson laughed. 'You mean a *scene*, daddy-o? Sure. Vaguely. Like attracts like. But these weren't sex parties and we wouldn't go if they were. They were simply gatherings of friends, gay and straight. The sort normal people like even you could go to.'

'I don't go to parties,' said Brook.

'That's not a surprise.'

'We'd like the names of any partygoers you remember seeing there,' said Noble, extracting further pictures from the envelope and spreading them out on the kitchen surface. 'These were taken at parties in their home on Stephen and Iain's mobile phones. We've identified most people in the photographs except this man.'

Gibson followed Noble's finger to a man hidden behind a pillar. 'I wouldn't know him even if I could see his face properly. At their house, you say?'

'Yes.'

'I told you, I've never been there.'

'But you'd know some of the people in these shots.'

'Faces, maybe. Mutual friends of people with whom we attended a couple of parties – wedding receptions in fact. I can give you the names of the people getting hitched and you can get a guest list from them.'

'We're looking for a killer, Mr Gibson. Someone who may be responsible for the murder of your parents.'

'Nobody at the receptions we attended killed my parents,' replied Gibson coldly. 'Or Stephen and Iain.'

'If you're worried about getting your friends into trouble . . .'

'None of the friends I know by name are in these photographs,' insisted Gibson.

'Look . . .' began Noble before Brook placed a pacifying hand on his arm.

'No names then,' said Brook quietly. 'But answer a couple of questions and if the answer is no, we won't press you further.'

Gibson considered. 'I'm listening.'

'Did anyone at these gatherings have an argument with Stephen and Iain about anything when you were there?'

'No.'

'And did anybody at all – gay or straight – seem wrong to you?'

'Wrong?'

'Perhaps someone who gave off a vibe of hostility,' said Noble.

'Or even just seemed out of place,' added Brook.

Gibson mulled it over before shaking his head. 'Not that I noticed. They were weddings. Everyone was happy.'

'Were any of the guests at these parties acquainted with your parents?'

Gibson laughed. 'No.'

'As far as you know.'

'Knowing my parents, my answer stands. No.'

'What about anyone with shooting experience?' said Brook. 'Someone you knew from the gun club, perhaps.'

'That's more than two questions,' said Gibson.

'You don't want to answer questions to help find your parents' killer?' asked Noble.

Gibson sighed. 'I didn't see anyone I knew from the gun club, okay?'

'What time did your parents usually go to bed?'

'Seriously?'

'What do you think?' said Brook, stern now.

Gibson sighed. 'They were never up past ten.'

'Never?'

'Rarely. New Year's Eve, maybe, to hear the chimes, but that was it. They were early birds. Why?'

'Because they let the killer in, Mr Gibson,' said Brook. 'And we're fairly certain it had to be dark but that they were still up when the killer knocked on their door.'

'Assuming he didn't have a key,' said Noble, pointedly.

Gibson narrowed his eyes at him. 'So you think Mum and Dad knew their killer. Somebody from the neighbourhood?'

'Or maybe someone pretending to be officialdom of some kind,' said Brook. 'So if you know anyone who may have harboured a grudge . . .'

'God, no,' said Gibson with surprising venom. 'With all their faults they were the most obliging people you could wish to meet. Too obliging, if you ask me. Some travelling benefit bum conned them out of two hundred quid a couple of years ago after supposedly cleaning out their gutters. He can't have been up there more than ten minutes. I went ballistic at them.'

'Did you now?'

'You know what I mean. Old people are an easy target for scum like that.'

'Did you get a name?'

'No. He came back a month later looking for more work but they repeated the script I gave them and he never showed his face again.'

'What about someone called David Fry?' said Noble, consulting his notebook.

A brief hesitation from Gibson. 'Who's he?'

'Ex-soldier who lives round the corner from your parents,' said Brook.

Gibson shook his head. 'Don't know him. Should I?'

'No reason at all,' smiled Brook. 'We're just throwing names around, looking for an angle.'

'Names of people who know how to handle a gun, you mean.'

'Something like that. Did your parents ever mention him?'

Gibson shook his head. 'Anything else?'

'As we're here,' said Brook, 'what do you know about male prostitution in Derby?'

Gibson grinned. 'Are you serious?'

'As I'm completely out of the loop on *every* scene in Derby, and you being an expert in the field . . .'

Gibson's nostrils flared. 'I don't know a damn thing about male prostitution in Derby. There's no meat rack that I know of, but then I'm a happily married fifty-four year old so I'm not really the man to ask.'

'What do you think?' said Noble, when they were on the road back into Derby.

'What I've thought all along,' answered Brook. 'It's not him.'

'He was a bit shifty when we mentioned David Fry.'

'I noticed that. But that could be anything. And his partner confirmed his alibi for the whole of the weekend.'

Noble laughed. 'What else was he going to say?'

'It's not Gibson,' said Brook.

'You're taking that alibi seriously.'

'I'm taking it as evidence, until we have facts to the contrary.'

'What about the fact that the man's completely cold? He couldn't have cared less about his parents.'

'Coldness isn't a crime,' said Brook. 'And he made no attempt to disguise his relationship with them.'

'And Trimble?'

'What about him?'

'The tattoos. Prison ink, I shouldn't wonder.'

Brook considered. 'So he's been in prison. Plenty of people have.' Noble arched a stern eyebrow at him. 'But check him out, obviously.'

'You're sure you don't mind?' retorted Noble. 'I could nip back and interview him now. If he says he wasn't in prison, we could just take his word.' Brook rolled his eyes. 'Do we believe Gibson when he says he didn't know Frazer and Nolan well?'

'Their email account backs him up,' said Brook. 'And they didn't invite Gibson and partner to any of their parties.'

'But he recognised people in the photographs.'

'Some.'

'So why not give us names?'

'He doesn't trust us to be impartial, John, and with Gibson's past, do you blame him? Besides, we have most of the names.'

'Not all of them.'

'Then get the next-door neighbour to take another look. She was there.'

'She's hardly part of the scene. *Daddy-o.*'

'We don't have many options left.' Brook glanced at his watch. 'Can I leave you to chase that up?'

'As soon as I send Gibson's gun off to ballistics and get Cooper to check out this Trimble character so I can start punching holes in Gibson's alibi.'

Reardon Thorogood's eyes opened and she stared sightlessly into the dark, feeling the clammy hand of fear quicken her breathing. A noise downstairs had disturbed her light sleep and suddenly she was wide awake, senses heightened.

Sargent, a four-year-old Beauceron, dark and powerful with pointed black ears and an intelligent face, sniffed at her face with a wet nose before seeking out her hand to run a coarse tongue over her knuckles. 'You heard it too, boy.' She blinked herself awake in the darkness, but with thick curtains drawn tightly against the world, she was effectively blind. Her ears took up the slack and the noise came again. Downstairs, definitely. Maybe it was morning and the guys in the ground-floor offices were in.

Beginning to stir, she felt the pain in her back from sleeping on the too-soft couch. The stab of a headache behind her eyes followed. Another late night drinking herself to sleep. Another hangover. Another failure to reach her bed.

She sat up and Sargent put his paws up on to her lap. 'Hungry?' She glanced in the direction of the digital clock showing eleven in the morning, and her heartbeat began to slow. Office hours. She swung her feet to the floor, pausing to gather her wits.

Last night's full ashtray assaulted her nose, and she padded softly to the windows to haul back the curtains and welcome the dull grey light of a November morning into the flat, one of two on the top floor. The branches of large trees swayed gently in the wind beneath her, the thinning canopy of leaves partially shielding the park below from view, though from her vantage point, the rest of the city was laid out before her, the Trent flowing lazily in the distance.

Sargent set up a whine at the sight of greenery through the window. 'Walkies later, boy. Mummy can only go out when it's dark.'

The banging of the front door knocker made her heart leap, and she rushed to the security monitor to check who was at the door. She could see nobody on the screen.

She pressed the intercom button. 'Who is it?' No answer, and no one appeared in the camera's lens. 'I know there's someone there. Show yourself.'

Another fucking journalist looking for a human interest piece. Tragic Victim's Tears a Year On. What was that snake's name from the local Derby rag? Brian something.

'I know you're down there, Brian. The answer's no, so go away. And don't expect me to leave the flat any time soon, so you can tell your photographer to fuck off too.'

She headed for the kitchen, plucking the empty wine bottle from the floor as she went, but the banging resumed. Again the monitor showed no one there, so this time she opened the door of her apartment and tiptoed across the landing to the top of the staircase to look out of the casement window. Sargent tried to follow, but she pushed him back inside, guilt pulling on her gut. This was no life for an energetic young dog, cooped up indoors during daylight hours, rarely venturing out more than ten minutes a day and then often just on to the patio round the back of the house.

'One day soon we'll be normal again, boy. Promise.'

From the landing window, Reardon couldn't look directly down at the front of the house because of the flat roof of the bay, but it was her best view of the outside world. If there was a strange car in the street, she'd know it. And photographers were easy to spot, lugging all that gear around.

Today, however, she could only see people going about their normal business, walking by, on their way to work, taking dogs to the park, living life. Nothing out of place. She stood upright and caught her own reflection in the window – hair lank and lifeless, falling across her puffy pale face.

Another bang on the door. Maybe it was the postman. Feeling foolish, she took a few tentative steps down the stairs and unlocked the inner door, crouching to listen.

The next crash of the knocker made her jump out of her skin. She'd not heard it in such close proximity before. She tiptoed barefoot towards the peephole, leaned in to squint through the eyepiece at the front step, then, astonished, yanked open the door.

'What the fuck are you doing here?' she demanded. 'You frightened me half to death. Come in before someone sees you.'

Twelve

THE SUN CAME OUT OVER the Peaks on the drive out to Hartington. Normally Brook would've been heartened at the prospect of a walk with his daughter in the chilly afternoon sun, followed by a late lunch. But after the emotional scenes of the previous day, he had to admit he wasn't looking forward to it.

In addition, he was beset by guilt at leaving Noble to fend for himself. Not that Noble was incapable of running the inquiry. He was a fine detective, who knew all the moves, and should have been promoted to DI long ago. Indeed it pained Brook to take comfort that his friend was consistently overlooked, because a part of him knew that when Noble's promotion eventually happened, his own career would be over.

He was already past the age when most murder squad detectives opted for early retirement, and to continue without his friend and confidant at his side seemed unthinkable. After a sticky start, Noble had become indispensable, and together they had brought to book several dangerous killers in some of the most gruelling and intricate cases Brook had ever worked.

And this was at the core of his guilt now. Most of the inquiries he'd worked with Noble had become tests of endurance as much as brainpower, with eighteen-hour days commonplace. Brook drove himself harder than anyone in the search for justice and wouldn't let up until he had it, pushing himself and those around him to the limit. Thus far, Noble had stood with him, sharing his privations, his lack of sleep and his obsessive search for the truth. Now that exhausting legwork belonged solely to his DS, and Brook was troubled.

Approaching on the steep little back road out of Hartington, Brook noticed that Terri's lime-green Volkswagen wasn't standing on the small drive at the side of the cottage.

'Must be getting low on wine,' he mumbled unkindly, pulling the BMW to the front of the house to leave the drive free for his daughter. He ambled towards the front porch, pausing at the entrance to run a finger over the peeling white paint. 'Farrow and Ball, eh?'

Pushing open the unlocked glass door, he glanced at the full ashtray on the shelf, pleased that his daughter was remembering to smoke outside. As he slid his latch key into the front door, his eye fell on his muddy walking boots. Terri's boots, which should have nestled beside them, were gone.

Moving quickly into the kitchen, he headed straight for the note on the table.

Heard you go this morning. Sorry, Dad. Better if I don't stay. I've got a lot on my mind at the moment and I know all this drama makes you uncomfortable. And you're right as usual. I don't love Tony any more. Or even his memory. I realise now what he was and what he did to me and Mum and I hate him for it. Re your comments, I'm going to try and drink less but it's not easy. Love you. Will ring at Crimbo. x

Brook hung his head and screwed the note into a ball before flinging it through the open lounge door towards the unlit wood burner in Terri's makeshift bedroom, now shorn of her sleeping bag and rucksack. 'Well done, Damen. You've pushed her away. Again.'

After a few minutes' brooding, he made a cup of tea and slumped at the kitchen table, drawing out his iPhone. Nothing from Terri. He keyed in a brief message to her, denying his discomfort. It was a lie, but one he felt he had to tell. He followed up with *You know where I am if you need me*. A moment's thought and he deleted the second part of the message with its hectoring tone and replaced it with *Always here for you, darling*.

After sending the text, he roused himself and prepared to leave. With Terri gone, he had no excuse to stay away from the post-mortem, and the case could now have his undivided attention. Better than sitting at home for the rest of the afternoon brooding over his faults as a father.

After boiling the kettle again and renewing his flask, he hurried through the cottage to make sure Terri hadn't left a window open. Picking up a strong whiff of cigarette smoke, he paused at the office door. Instantly he noticed that the light on the printer was green. He felt certain he'd switched off both printer and computer after photocopying Mullen's letter. The absence of printer paper in the feed tray drew his eye. The night before, it had been full.

He flung off his coat and sat down, grimacing as the warped drawer of the desk bit into his hip. It had been pulled out, but hadn't been pushed fully home again. Forcing it out further, Brook stared down at the tangle of pens and pencils that had been swept aside, revealing his passwords.

'Terri, what have you done?'

He turned on the computer and keyed in his passwords to take him to the Police National Computer with its database of millions of British crimes old and new. With details of all serious crimes solved and unsolved, any obscure particulars could be entered to seek out a match with previous offences in any part of the country. It was a tremendous resource, first mooted in the early eighties after operational errors had allowed the Yorkshire Ripper to evade capture for so long.

Brook clicked on his search history to reveal details of the documents Terri had accessed earlier that day.

'Black Oak Farm,' he mumbled, closing his eyes briefly. He took out his iPhone and speed-dialled Terri's mobile, unsure what approach to take if she picked up. Her phone was switched off. He texted her to ring him, then tried the landline at her Manchester flat, to be greeted by a recorded message that announced the service had been disconnected.

'What? When?' He loaded his emails, pleased to see one from DC Cooper.

Sir, noticed you already accessed all material from Black Oak Farm. Do you still want me to send?

Brook typed his reply. *Hard copies of all printed material, please. I'll pick up tomorrow. Also, can you find out when this landline number was disconnected? Urgent response – please text news.* He added Terri's landline to the email and reluctantly typed in his own mobile number, dismayed that his store of contacts had expanded to five.

Given the circumstances, instead of driving into Derby to meet Noble and Banach at the Royal Derby Hospital, he sat down to read the reports and click through the scene-of-crime photographs of the Black Oak Farm murders that his daughter had printed off that morning.

He began with written reports. He knew the background to the case from internal bulletins and station gossip about Luke Coulson's trial, but the fine details had evaded him and made for grim reading.

Monty Thorogood, a local millionaire businessman, and his wife Patricia had been attacked and brutally stabbed to death in the kitchen of their farmhouse in Findern, a pretty village about six miles to the south-west of Derby. Their killing had been frenzied, with the perpetrator, Luke Coulson, striking over and over again at the two victims.

In addition to their murders, their daughter Reardon, in the house at the time, had been sexually assaulted by Jonathan Jemson, one of the attackers and a former boyfriend from their time at school together. Their relationship had ended years before, but Jemson had always harboured a grudge, and when the opportunity arose, he'd jumped at the chance to teach his former girlfriend a lesson.

According to Reardon's statements, Jemson's friend, Luke Coulson, also a former schoolmate, had entered her bedroom covered in blood and discovered the assault in progress. It seemed Coulson had also developed an unhealthy obsession with Reardon at school and was appalled to see her being attacked, so after failing to pull Jemson away, Coulson had stabbed him in the back and neck, severing an artery. He had then ransacked the property for valuables and changed into clothes belonging to Monty Thorogood.

Meanwhile Reardon, despite the trauma of the assault, had gone in search of her parents, discovering their mutilated bodies in a scene of bloodletting and carnage at which even Brook, with all his experience, blanched when he looked at the SOCO photographs.

Fortunately, Reardon had been able to flee the scene, partially clothed, despite a final confrontation with Coulson. She reached the village to raise the alarm while Coulson fled the farm in the family Range Rover with just over a thousand pounds in cash, items of jewellery he'd found in a safe in the master bedroom and a bag of his own bloodstained clothing for disposal. He'd made a desperate dash down the M1 in the high-powered car, heading for Dover and presumably escape to France on a ferry.

Unfortunately for Coulson, he'd become snarled up in the afternoon rush hour on the M25, and once details of the get-away car had been distributed, it was a simple matter to arrest him. He was detained at a service station without a struggle.

Brook's mobile vibrated with a message from DC Cooper. *Landline disconnected four months ago when property vacated.*

'Vacated?' exclaimed Brook, staring at the text. 'Terri, what's going on? And what's so important about Black Oak Farm?' He transferred the questions to his mobile, but once again his daughter failed to reply. Brook poured tea from his flask and switched on a couple of lamps to dispel the gathering darkness, then returned to read more reports.

The murders had occurred in early October last year, on a cool and cloudy Monday afternoon between twelve and one p.m. That morning, Jemson and Coulson had finished their preparations for the raid before taking the bus to Findern village. They had approached the farm on foot, both dressed in hiking gear and boots and carrying a small rucksack, which was later recovered from the scene. In it police found a detailed map of the area around Findern, with suitable escape routes highlighted in red, as well as damning evidence of an inside job – a plan of the farmhouse.

Handwriting and fingerprint comparisons showed beyond a doubt that Reardon's missing brother Ray had drawn the plan. On it he'd identified the location of the safe, the security control room and Reardon's bedroom. Clipped to the map was a photocopied printout of all the valuables – jewellery, expensive watches and gold coins – likely to be found in the safe. The photocopy was from an insurance policy document taken out by the Thorogoods only three weeks before the murders – at Ray's instigation, according to his sister's statement. In a corner of the photocopy, the safe's combination had been written in biro in Ray's own handwriting.

Also in the rucksack investigating officers found an empty plastic bag containing remnants of the drugged meat the pair had fed to the family dog, Sargent, to prevent it attacking the intruders or alerting the Thorogoods to their presence.

The farm itself should have been well protected by its sophisticated alarm and security camera system, installed the previous year again at Ray's insistence. However, according to its internal clock, and unknown to the victims, the system had been disabled the night before, allowing Jemson and Coulson to approach the house unseen and break in without setting off an alarm. The telephone landline had also been disabled.

In addition, footage of all film prior to the attack had been expertly erased from the hard drive, presumably to remove the record of Ray Thorogood approaching the control room to turn off the system on the eve of the murders. A Post-it note attached to the police report referred to Jemson having previous employment as an installer at a security company in Derby, and it was subsequently discovered that he had exchanged a series of text messages with Ray Thorogood giving detailed instructions on disabling and erasing material from a security system.

Without this footage, the exact sequence of events inside the farmhouse before and during the attack was difficult to pin down. It was believed that Coulson had entered through the front door and murdered Mr and Mrs Thorogood while Jemson proceeded to Reardon's bedroom, where she was lying on her bed listening to music on her headphones, oblivious to the fact that her parents were being attacked a few rooms away.

The fact that Coulson was right-handed – Jemson was left-handed – confirmed to police and prosecutors that he had struck the fatal blows that had killed the Thorogoods. Significantly, Coulson declined to defend himself, claiming he had no memory of events, neither denying nor admitting his role in the attack. In fact from the moment of his arrest he uttered barely a word to police interrogators and didn't submit to cross-examination at his trial.

This wasn't unusual for Coulson. Defence lawyers produced paperwork confirming that he had learning difficulties and had left school with no academic qualifications. He also suffered from a speech defect and never spoke in lessons – a good reason for Coulson and his brief to sidestep the ordeal of cross-examination, although that didn't explain his reluctance to make a pre-trial statement about his role in the murders.

Not that a full confession would have mitigated his crime. Coulson's life sentence was a formality once he'd been examined by experts and declared criminally responsible and fit to stand trial. He might have been educationally subnormal, with a couple of de rigueur personality disorders thrown in, but Luke Coulson was deemed capable of understanding the gravity of his crime and was duly punished.

Brook drained his tea and sat back to check his phone again – still nothing from Terri.

Resuming his reading, he clicked through forensic and crime-scene reports, all of which damned Coulson further. After the attacks, he had rifled through Monty Thorogood's wardrobe for fresh clothes in which to make his escape, but stupidly had stuffed his own bloodstained clothes into a carrier bag and thrown them into the boot of the Range Rover – presumably for disposal at sea. Blood from all three bodies had been discovered on his clothes and shoes and subsequently under his fingernails and on his hair.

Brook clicked on another link, surprised to see that CCTV film was available. He soon learned why. After being attacked by Jemson, Reardon had made her escape, but not before rebooting the security cameras in the control room near her bedroom in order to locate Coulson and other possible intruders. The grisly sight of her blood-soaked parents on the control room monitor subsequently drew her to the kitchen to check in vain for signs of life.

Being unable to call the police on her dead mother's inert mobile phone or the disconnected landline, she headed for the front door, only to run straight into a knife-wielding Luke Coulson. Security footage showed the encounter, but Brook paused it so he could skim through Reardon's transcript of what she could recall of their conversation before restarting the film.

It was bleak, fascinating stuff and Brook watched their dance of death intently. Both Reardon and Coulson were eerily calm after the bloodbath. Such a reaction was not uncommon.

People often responded to extreme traumatic events with unnatural composure, at least in the initial stages of an ordeal. Shock could make people block out harrowing events like the death of loved ones and, worse, make them oblivious to imminent danger.

The possibility of sudden death, even one's own, was such an extreme and unique situation that the mind was often incapable of processing the information, suppressing unpalatable outcomes. The consequences could be fatal if individuals were unable to sense the need to run from, or fight against, danger – the fight-or-flight instinct required to force those at risk to act in their own interest.

But whatever her state of mind, Brook watched rapt as Reardon made all the right moves, maintaining eye contact and keeping her opponent talking, at the same time treating him with a respect he'd probably craved, and been denied, for most of his short life. The fact that Coulson had just rescued her from a violent ex-boyfriend must have given her sufficient confidence that she could dissuade him from doing her harm, and gradually she was able to talk him down until Coulson dropped the knife.

After discarding it, he moved towards Reardon for a hug, holding on to her tenderly and pressing his head into her neck. According to Reardon's statement, at this moment Coulson had whispered something in her ear. Her response was brief before she disengaged and moved warily to the front door. Once outside, a CCTV camera showed her sprinting to safety along the grass fringes of the gravel drive in the direction of the village.

Brook looked at the transcript to see what had been said.

Coulson: If I let you go, will you forgive me?
Reardon: Of course I will.

He clicked off the film and loaded further reports on to his monitor. DS Rachel Caskey's name was prominent, and Brook was pleased to see she knew her stuff. After the attack, while SOCO did their grisly work, the first port of call had been Jonathan Jemson's flat, which had thrown up an unregistered prepaid mobile phone hidden in a drawer.

The phone contained dozens of text messages exchanged between Jemson and Ray Thorogood, revealing the extensive planning leading up to the attack on Black Oak Farm. The texts also made known the full scope of Ray's venom towards his parents, hinting at unpaid debts and speaking of his determination to free himself from their purse strings.

Brook skimmed through more transcripts as the two men put their plan together. The content of the messages painted a picture of Ray Thorogood as the brains behind the operation. Under instruction from Jemson, Ray would disable the security system and landline the night before and delete any film of his actions. Jemson meanwhile was charged with recruiting Coulson, whom both Jemson and Ray knew from school. Texts referred to his low IQ and it became clear that Jemson and Ray were lining him up to take the rap for the murders of Monty and Patricia Thorogood as well as Ray's sister Reardon.

Brook read through some of the relevant transcripts.

Do Mummy and Daddy first, and then try to get Luke to fuck or at least jizz over my bitch of a sister. He always had a thing for her. Should be simple. Then do them both with the same knife and make it look like they croaked each other in the struggle so we can hang everything round Luke's neck. Ray.

Can't wait to see the look on her face when I walk in on her. LOL.

Almost wish I could be there. Ray.

Brook sat back to contemplate the exchange. *Almost wish I could be there. Ray.* He narrowed his eyes. 'And why weren't you there, Ray?'

With Coulson's body at the scene and his DNA inside Reardon, it wouldn't be hard for investigating officers to construct a version of events placing Coulson at the heart of the crime. The obsessed loner seeking out a former schoolmate for whom he'd developed an unhealthy obsession, killing her parents before taking his revenge on her. She fights back, inflicting fatal injuries on her attacker before succumbing to her own wounds.

The perfect crime.

The beauty of the plan was that Ray would be on hand to fill in the gaps, to confirm Coulson's sleazy fascination with his sister, and with the rest of the Thorogoods dead, he would be free to inherit the family fortune. After a suitable but unspecified period, he would reward Jemson for services rendered. When things had died down, Brook had no doubt that Jemson's death would be the next item on Ray's agenda.

Of course, the plan had fallen down on Coulson's reluctance to be a party to the assault on Reardon. His crush was apparently more about unrequited love and less about straight-forward lust, as Ray and Jemson had presumed. For that reason, it was speculated that Jemson had initiated the attack on Reardon to stimulate Coulson's interest. Or maybe he really had wanted to teach his former girlfriend a lesson and had got carried away, though he should have been intelligent enough to know that a rape on his part would leave unmistakable evidence of his presence at the farm. For someone with a criminal record, that meant a certain DNA match against his stored profile, and arrest within days.

Whatever the trigger, the sexual assault had spawned further violence, Jemson striking Reardon several times about the face – the likely trigger for Coulson's deadly intervention.

Unfortunately for Ray Thorogood, this turn of events effectively left him in limbo, and instead of being able to bury his family and claim his inheritance, he'd been forced to run. With Reardon alive and able to testify that he'd been at the farm the night before the murders, his part in the attack became clear, despite the failure of security cameras to confirm his presence, or that of his car, a silver Porsche.

Brook leaned back in his chair to think. He was impressed by the fact that Ray had disappeared so completely. This hinted at preparation, at contingency plans, as well as betraying Ray's lack of faith in his co-conspirators. He clicked through more reports, looking for information on Ray's whereabouts at the time of the attack. He couldn't find any. However, a few days after the murders, Ray's car was discovered at the East Midlands Airport long-stay car park.

Brook scrolled down for further information but couldn't find what he was looking for, so he scribbled a reminder in a fresh page of his notebook before reading through reports of subsequent checks carried out on airline passenger manifests, including available film of passengers boarding flights at East Midlands on the day of the Black Oak Farm massacre.

As soon as Ray's car was found, airport police began checking all departing passengers for weeks after the events in Findern. But if Ray had taken a flight from East Midlands, security checks were unable to discover it and CCTV couldn't definitively identify any viable suspects leaving the country, even though all male passengers in their mid-twenties, especially those matching Ray's description, had been thoroughly checked.

In fact, all British males passing through the airport were traced and eliminated from enquiries, although three men travelling under foreign passports had never been found – two Frenchmen and one Pole. However, not one of them matched the description of Ray Thorogood closely, and because of that, the search had been expanded to include ports and other airports as well as the British motorway network.

But in spite of all these measures, Ray Thorogood had never been found. Either he had escaped disguised as a foreign national, complete with forged passport, or he had laid down a false trail and made a run for it across country – destination unknown.

Brook loaded Google Maps to remind himself of the extensive motorway system around the airport site. The M1 and the M42 link road were under a mile away, so if Ray hadn't taken a flight out of the country, he could feasibly have dumped his Porsche at the airport and driven another vehicle north, south or west – there was no nearby motorway east of the airport. But without knowing if there *was* a second vehicle, checks on motorway film were pointless. If he was still in Britain, Ray Thorogood could effectively be anywhere.

Brook read on, loading more files documenting the search for Thorogood, both forensic and physical. A SOCO team had descended on Ray's small cottage in Repton to build the case against him and Jemson. Forensically the search was routine. Evidence of Thorogood's presence was abundant, but it confirmed little more than his occupancy, as well as providing plentiful DNA and fingerprint samples. Not that samples would be of much use in the murder inquiry, as his DNA and fingerprints were also to be expected at Black Oak Farm, the parental home.

On the other hand, officers had found plenty of other evidence at the cottage. Trawling through his financial papers, they had been able to substantiate the rumours of Ray's mounting debts. Significantly, he didn't own the Repton house – his mother did. He was a tenant, albeit one allowed to live rent-free in a valuable property in a desirable area, yet still unable to sell the house to pay his debts.

Original copies of the work order for the farm's security systems were also found, as was a copy of the insurance policy Ray had insisted his father take out to cover the farm contents and his parents' lives.

Ford's team also found a couple of items of jewellery that the insurance document suggested should be in the safe at Black Oak Farm. After the attack, Coulson had emptied the safe of one thousand pounds, half a dozen gold coins and a pair of cheap watches. The rest – rare coins, another thirty-nine thousand pounds and easily portable items of expensive jewellery such as rings and earrings – had not been found on Coulson or Jemson and were missing, assumed to be in Ray Thorogood's possession after he was forced to flee.

As his passport was also missing, it wasn't a stretch to speculate that, before absconding, Ray had removed most of the cash and valuables from his parents' safe *before* the murders to fund his escape in case Jemson was tempted to keep the best items for himself.

Brook flicked quickly through the rest of the reports. There were no mentions of finding the prepaid phone that Ray had used to exchange messages with Jemson. He considered this and made a note, then searched for copies of documents about Ray's other mobile phone, the official one, a Samsung, under contract. It too was not to be found at the cottage in Repton.

'Both of Ray's mobile phones missing,' he muttered. It didn't matter. Finding the pre-paid phone at Jemson's flat meant they could study the shared history of Ray and Jemson's text messaging.

Interestingly, no actual calls were made – the two conspirators communicated exclusively by text message on untraceable phones, presumably purchased for the sole purpose of planning the attack. Obviously both phones would have been destroyed afterwards if the plan hadn't gone so badly awry, allowing Jemson's to be recovered from his flat.

Brook checked the records for Ray's Samsung. Use of his official mobile had become sporadic in the month leading up to the attack and had ceased entirely a week before. There was no record of any contact on the actual day between Jemson and Ray on either phone in their possession. Brook poured more tea and pondered this.

'So how did you know things were unravelling at the farm? Are you sure you weren't there, Ray?' A moment later, he shook his head. 'No. Of course you weren't. How could you be?'

He reloaded the transcripts of texts between Jemson and Ray. The final one from Ray, sent a couple of days before the attack, caught his eye. It was brutal stuff.

When they're all dead, JJ, torch the fucking place. Hideous building. More money than taste, my parents. Hacienda doors FFS. Make it look like an accident so start it in R's en suite. She always has a dozen tea lights going when she takes a bath. Pretentious cunt. Make it look like they got knocked over in the struggle. Farm insured to the hilt so an extra 10K in it for you. Plus it gets rid of your DNA and stuff. Ray.

Brook checked his own mobile again – still no reply from Terri.

'Is this your first?' asked Noble, as he and Banach approached the brightly lit post-mortem suite.

'My first PM,' answered Banach. 'Not my first stiff, obviously.' Noble nodded, thin-lipped. She peered closely at him. 'Don't worry about me.'

'I'm not,' panted Noble. 'I'm worried about me.'

'You? You must have seen dozens.'

'I have,' said Noble. 'But never as the lead. Normally I switch off and stare at the wall, and when things get a bit hairy, the boss sends me out to fetch tea. He's good like that.'

'After all you've seen?'

'Oh, I'm fine at a crime scene,' said Noble. 'It's all the digging around in cavities and skulls that I'm not so keen on.'

'Does it affect the boss?'

'Not so you'd notice,' answered Noble. 'And honestly, after the things he's seen, post-mortems are a walk in the park.'

'You really rate him, don't you? As a detective, I mean.'

Noble pressed the buzzer on the wall. 'You've had a few months with him. What do you think?'

'He's clever, no doubt,' said Banach. 'And considerate without appearing to be.'

Noble looked quizzically at her. 'I sense a *but* coming.' Banach hesitated. 'You can speak freely to me *and* the boss. He's insult-proof.' He grinned. 'Providing you use appropriate vocabulary.'

Banach smiled, but it was clear Noble wouldn't be deflected. 'There's something about him, something closed off that's eating at him.' When Noble didn't ask her to expand, she nodded. 'You've seen it too. A darkness that he can't share.'

'The Reaper,' said Noble softly. 'Before I knew him.'

'The serial killer who killed families in London?'

'Derby too.'

'He was never caught.'

'That's the official version.'

'You know different?'

'No,' said Noble cautiously. 'But sometimes he slips and I get the impression he knows something I don't.'

'Like?'

'Like the Reaper is really dead, even though there's no way he can know that. It's just an impression.' His expression became wary. 'This stays between us.'

'Of course,' she said quietly, not wishing to deflect him.

Noble took a breath. 'When he moved from the Met to Derby CID, he was a broken man. I mean, in pieces. It was quite a sight. Divorced. Estranged from his daughter, with a nervous breakdown on his sheet. I drew the short straw because I'd only just made DS. Nobody liked him. He didn't join in banter, didn't learn the ropes or stand a round at the pub after a big win. Even now, if you asked him to name three quarters of the people at St Mary's, he couldn't do it. It's like he's using all his mental energy, all his resources, to hold himself together. And making the effort to learn even minor social skills would upset the delicate balance he tries to maintain. He's like a high-wire artist. He can only concentrate on the case. Any distractions and he'd fall to his death. That's why he works so hard.'

'Like a shark, always moving forward.'

'Right. He has to keep busy because he doesn't have the skills to relax and switch off. It would give him too much time to think.'

'He's on leave now, though.'

Noble smiled. 'Oh, he's miles better than he was. But it's still there, whatever it is. He carries it always. And when a case becomes too much, you can see him starting to come apart.'

'What happened to cause all that?'

Noble hesitated. 'Besides me, you're the only member of the squad who's noticed it. What do you think?' Now it was Banach's turn to hesitate, so Noble pressed on. 'You saw something up at Animal Farm, didn't you? Before we got there. He did something. Or said something. I could tell.'

'I know he risked his life to save me from a bunch of nutters who were preparing to cut me open,' said Banach defiantly.

'You know what I mean.'

Banach hung her head, not wanting to dredge up memories of her first CID investigation, a case that was nearly her last after she'd fallen into the hands of a violent group of fanatics. 'I might be wrong. I was in a bit of a state.'

Noble smiled encouragement. 'We're just talking, Angie.'

'Something he said.' She gazed into Noble's eyes and took a breath. 'I think a long time ago he might have killed someone.'

Noble opened his mouth to speak, but at that moment, the

double doors to the mortuary suite swung open and Dr Ann Petty, a handsome blonde woman in her early forties, stood before them.

'Sorry to keep you waiting,' she said.

'You were right,' said Petty. 'The alcohol from both Frazer and Nolan's bloodstreams contained traces of Chardonnay and Pinot Noir; both grape varietals used in champagne production.'

'Quick work.'

'Not really,' said Petty. 'I did the analysis two weeks ago. Didn't DI Ford mention it? I emailed him.'

'Perhaps he told DI Brook,' said Noble diplomatically. 'Two grape varieties. So it was a blended champagne.'

'All champagnes are blended, Sergeant,' replied Petty. Noble raised an eyebrow. 'I spent three months in France as a student, harvesting grapes.'

'And you got a taste for it,' said Noble. 'Champagne, I mean.'

'Who wouldn't?'

'Anything else?'

'It was vintage champagne, if that makes any difference.'

'How do you know?' asked Banach.

'Because most non-vintage is made from only one variety of grape blended from different years. Vintage is a blend of two varieties, occasionally with Pinot Meunier in the mix, though that tends to be left out these days because it doesn't age well.'

'I'm impressed,' said Noble.

'I'm sure you're just as big an expert on gassy lagers,' replied Petty, grinning.

Noble's expression didn't change. 'And the Gibsons?'

'They had champagne in their systems as well, though they hadn't drunk as much as Frazer and Nolan.'

'How much?'

'Frazer and Nolan put away a bottle between them according to their blood tests. But the Gibsons' levels were much lower – no more than a glass, I'd say. I'll need more time to be certain.'

'No need,' said Noble. 'The killer left half the bottle.'

'Thoughtful.'

'Anything unusual about their deaths?'

'Only the fact that they were shot,' said Petty. 'Two old codgers like that. Hardly seems necessary.'

'So everyone says. When?'

'From all indicators, I'd say between eight o'clock in the evening and midnight on Saturday. Sorry I can't narrow it down further. Lividity confirms the victims died in their chairs, same as Frazer and Nolan. You should be able to get an approximate height from ballistics. Death instantaneous or near as damn it.'

Noble nodded. 'Bullets?'

'Gone off to EMSOU by courier. They were the same calibre as last time, I think – nine millimetres. And presumably an experienced shooter.'

'How so?' asked Banach.

'Assuming you're tying the four gun deaths together, your killers have fired a total of four rounds, each delivering a single bullet into the hearts of four separate victims,' said Petty. 'Shows some level of expertise, I think.'

'What about their health otherwise?'

Petty considered. 'They had the usual ailments for their

age. Some arterial weakness around the heart on Mr Gibson commensurate with his underlying problems, but nothing to suggest imminent decline. I assume their GP said the same. Were you thinking this might be a suicide pact of some kind?'

'It was an angle,' said Noble.

'Well, I'd rule it out on health grounds,' said Petty. 'But that doesn't mean people at their age don't decide they've outgrown their usefulness and choose to go before things get ugly. Maybe they had depression?' She looked at Noble expectantly.

'Not so their GP noticed,' he answered.

Petty nodded. 'I can't help you on mental outlook, I'm afraid. But it was the same picture with Frazer and Nolan. And they were as fit as the proverbial. A real shame. Such a devoted couple.' Noble narrowed his eyes at her. 'I remembered them from the personals in the *Derby Telegraph* not so long ago. *Together for ever. Stephen and Iain.* Touching.'

'Personals?'

'Personal ads. Weddings and anniversaries. Lonely hearts.' She laughed, holding up her hands in self-defence. 'I'm a singleton, Sergeant. I'm allowed to look at the personal columns. You'll get there.'

'Never happen,' sniffed Noble.

'And speaking of singletons,' grinned Petty. 'Where's Derby's most ineligible bachelor?'

'DI Brook is on leave.' Noble eyed her reaction. He'd got the impression from previous visits that Dr Petty carried something of a torch for Brook.

'Well deserved, I'm sure,' replied Petty, giving nothing away. 'And I'm not complaining. Gives me a chance to meet DC Banach and thank her for her efforts last year.' Banach reddened. 'The sisterhood owes you a vote of thanks for stopping those butchers up at Animal Farm.'

'Just doing my job,' said Banach, with an embarrassed glance at Noble.

'And doing it damn well, which is why we need to thank you.'

Thirteen

AVING READ ALL THE WRITTEN reports, Brook loaded the SOCO photographs of the bloody events at Black Oak Farm and examined each slowly and methodically, occasionally making a note before clicking on to the next one. He stared impassively at shots of the Spanish-style kitchen disfigured by arterial sprays of blood on the walls and the terracotta tiles on the floor; at the vast lakes of deep scarlet under the bodies of Monty and Patricia Thorogood, beginning to dry on the scuffed tiles; at the body of Jonathan Jemson, his jeans pulled below his knees, head and neck deeply scored and dotted by gouts of blood. At the foot of the bed, a large red pool had eaten across the bedroom carpet, and the covers were splashed dramatically with the first jets of blood surging under pressure from Jemson's neck.

Brook would've preferred hard copies that he could place in order as he walked himself mentally through the unfolding drama, but he didn't have any printer paper left, thanks to Terri.

When he'd scrolled through all the uploaded pictures twice, he reloaded the security camera footage taken after Reardon

Thorogood had rebooted the system and watched it through again, starting with the opening frame of her poking her bruised and battered head out of the security control room.

He watched her hesitate at the front door before moving to the kitchen to check on her parents. He watched her kneel over the bodies of Monty and Patricia Thorogood, looking for signs of life, standing in their blood, paying no heed to the possible presence of a killer in the house. He watched her leaning against the wall in despair when she discovered the disabled landline before rummaging in her mother's bag for a mobile that was equally useless.

When she ran into Luke Coulson by the front door, Brook paused the film again for a closer read-through of the transcript of their conversation put together from Reardon Thorogood's testimony and the expert opinion of a lip reader. Coulson, of course, had failed to contribute a statement at any point after his arrest and had offered no defence at his trial, so the transcript relied heavily on Reardon's recollections.

Brook restarted the film and tried to follow the dialogue exchanged between Coulson and Reardon. Confirming his previous impression, what transpired was a delicate game of cat and mouse between a knife-wielding murderer and a desperate but quick-thinking victim. Coulson was calm for the most part, though revelation about his long-held feelings for Reardon betrayed him at his most agitated. Imagined slights from over a decade ago revealed his paranoia and preceded his sole outburst of aggression towards Reardon.

She, on the other hand, displayed incredible coolness under pressure to counter Coulson's ravings. Her responses were textbook examples of how to verbally pacify an unstable and potentially violent suspect. When she finally broke away from

Coulson's clutches, she made sure to get off the road at the earliest opportunity, knowing that he might be following close behind in the Range Rover and liable to change his mind about leaving a living eyewitness.

Moving the film on, Brook sat back as Coulson climbed into the Range Rover after throwing his plastic bag of bloodied clothes into the boot. A few moments for him to understand the controls and the vehicle roared out of sight. With a fresh tea in his hand, Brook scrolled back to the final clinch as Reardon pulled her head away from Coulson to reply to his whispered entreaty.

'Of course I will,' said Brook, as her mouth moved.

Noble took a sip of his coffee in Maureen McConnell's warm and welcoming kitchen. 'Any more prowlers?'

'Not since your forensic team moved back in. Did the number plates help?'

'Afraid not,' replied Noble.

McConnell nodded. 'Thanks again for being so understanding about the other night, by the way. I can only imagine what it must have looked like, me sneaking around gathering up all the boys' valuables.'

'It looked like you were looting,' said Noble.

'Well thank God you could tell I wasn't.'

'Looters don't tidy up,' explained Noble.

Banach placed a large brown envelope on the table. 'As Sergeant Noble mentioned on the phone, we could use your help identifying someone you may have met.'

'I'll try.'

'These photographs were downloaded from Stephen and Iain's mobile phones,' said Banach.

'You may have been asked to identify him before, but we'd like you to take another look,' continued Noble.

'These would be of the parties at their house.'

'Yes.'

'I suppose I'm in a few of them, but I wasn't at every party they threw.'

'We know,' said Noble.

'Were you the only woman there?' asked Banach.

'At the ones next door, yes,' said McConnell. 'A big barbecue every summer and a do at Christmas, as well as their engagement party. Such lovely food and drink, too, though the music was a bit raunchy for me.' Her features darkened. 'You're not going to ask me if there was sex going off during these parties, are you? That's what that other detective wanted to know, like it was some kind of orgy. Then some grotty journalist turned up, sneering and insinuating about drugs and sex. The boys just weren't like that.'

'Mrs McConnell . . .'

'Lovely to me, they were. Couldn't do enough for me after my divorce.' She laughed. 'I think sometimes they tried a bit too hard. Always matching me up with some waif or stray they'd run into or some misfit they'd invited to their party with a sob story of his own.'

Banach and Noble exchanged a glance. 'Misfit?'

'You mean straight men?' said Banach.

'Oh yes. Not all the guests were gays. But the last thing I needed after kicking out that bastard' – she mimed spitting on the floor – 'was to dive into another relationship with a man coming off the back of his own problems. Stephen and Iain never stopped trying, though. If a man was single and the right age, they'd invite him along to the house and introduce me. It was embarrassing, and the poor blokes were as uncomfortable as I was.'

'Remember any names?' McConnell shook her head. 'Please try. It could be important.'

McConnell sighed. 'Well, there was one that stood out, the last one they introduced me to. Alex? Ollie? Something like that. A very shy man.'

'He stood out from the others.'

'Oh yes. Terrible state he was in. I felt really sorry for him. His wife had died the year before and he hadn't been out since. Socially, that is.'

'Then how did he come to be at Stephen and Iain's party?' ventured Banach.

'The boys had met him somewhere – shopping, I think – sobbing his little heart out doing the things he'd done with his dead wife. And Stephen and Iain, being so soft, befriended him and invited him to their party to cheer him up.'

'Did it work?' asked Banach.

McConnell shook her head. 'He tried to have a good time, but the poor man was inconsolable.'

'Did he know Stephen and Iain were gay?'

'I wondered about that,' said McConnell. 'The boys liked to act a bit more butch when they were out and about. You know, to discourage bigots and such.'

'But at the party it was clear.'

'Oh yes. Iain in particular was very, you know, camp. Especially around his friends.'

'So maybe this Alex or Ollie got a shock when he found out,' suggested Noble. 'Maybe he said something.'

'Not to me,' said McConnell.

'He didn't seem disgusted or appalled?' offered Banach.

McConnell shook her head. 'He seemed fine about it. Really. In fact, now I think about it, he said there wasn't enough love in the world and we shouldn't hate people for expressing it differently. I remember thinking that was nice.'

Noble's interest waned. 'Was that the only time you saw him?'

She laughed guiltily. 'Yes, thank God.'

Banach indicated the photographs. 'Is he in any of these?'

McConnell moved the photos around, grouping them in batches, staring at them with a mixture of pleasure and sadness. 'These were Christmas. These were summer. Their engagement party. That was a lovely day.'

'We're interested in this man ringed in red pen,' said Noble. 'The rest have been identified and eliminated.'

'It's not very clear,' said McConnell, picking up a couple of pictures, her eyes narrowing in concentration. 'Did you try Stephen and Iain's computer?'

'We did,' said Noble. He picked up another photograph to show her the image of a man in a cable-knit V-neck sweater leaning behind a pillar. He was mostly obscured but he appeared to be shaven-headed. 'This isn't much better, but that's you there and you look like you might have been talking to him.'

'That's Alex,' said McConnell with a laugh. 'But he wasn't called Alex. Something slightly less common. Ollie? Willie? God, my memory. Anyway, he was very shy and intense. Didn't have a clue about small talk, to be honest, though he wasn't bad looking. But there was no spark.'

'How old?'

'Forty. No more. Younger than me. Is that the only shot of him?'

'Unfortunately. Do you remember anything else about him? Where he lived, perhaps.'

'He didn't live in Breadsall because he drove to the house and I remember he told me about his journey. Roadworks and all that. I mean, who cares, right?'

'Do you remember any details?'

McConnell considered before shaking her head. 'Sorry.'

'Did he mention work?'

She shook her head again. 'Not a word. He didn't like talking about himself, and when he did, he was *very* boring. No social life, you see.'

'Did anything at all strike you about him?'

'I remember he was extremely fit – muscular. Now you mention it, he did talk about going to a gym to lift weights.'

'Did he say which one?'

'Afraid not.'

'And have you ever seen *this* man at one of Iain and Stephen's functions, or in any other context?' said Banach, laying down a photograph of Matthew Gibson, taken from his application for a National Firearms Licence.

'Never seen him before,' said McConnell after a few seconds of contemplation.

'Or this man.' Banach laid down another photograph, this time the mugshot of David Fry.

McConnell shrank back. 'He looks like he's been in the wars.'

'Do you know him?' McConnell shook her head. 'Okay. You've been a big help.'

Brook had dozed off in the office chair when the vibrations of his mobile woke him. He snatched it up from the desk. 'Terri?'

'It's me,' said Noble.

'John,' said Brook, rubbing his eyes and trying to work his dry mouth. 'What time is it?'

'Nearly eleven,' replied Noble. 'You thought I was Terri?'

Brook stood to massage his back, scouring his brain for a believable lie. 'She went to the Duke for cigarettes half an hour ago. She must be having a quick drink.'

There was a pause at the other end of the line. 'Everything all right between you two?'

'Course. What's up?'

'Frazer and Nolan. Petty confirmed they were drinking champagne before they died.'

'Another connection to the Gibsons.'

'And I spoke to Maureen McConnell again. She didn't know Gibson or David Fry.'

'Fry?'

'We had a mugshot, and as he was a similar build to one of the unidentified partygoers, I thought it was worth a punt.'

'No joy?'

'None. Though interestingly, McConnell did say the guy we still can't trace is straight. And according to her, he was grieving for his wife.'

'How did he end up at Frazer and Nolan's house?'

'She reckons he was a stray they picked up and tried to matchmake, but they didn't hit it off, and anyway he was too cut up about his wife to be back on the market.'

'Homophobe?'

'The opposite.'

'Doesn't rule him out,' said Brook. 'Maybe he saw the blissful couple and resented their happiness. Did you get a name?'

'Alex, Ollie or Willie.'

'And this was the guy hiding behind the pillar.'

'Right. That was the only party he attended. He was only on a couple of pictures and he managed to avoid getting his face clocked on both.'

'Check Frazer and Nolan's social media again.'

'I have. He's not there.'

'Don't their friends have camera phones of their own?'

'Sure, but do you go to parties and spend your time taking pictures of everyone?'

'I don't go to parties. Is it worth putting McConnell in with an artist?'

'Might as well. We're getting nowhere. Oh, Matthew Gibson's partner, Trimble, also has ancient form, though not quite as long ago as Gibson's.'

'Soliciting?'

'No, he was married with a baby when he was seventeen. Most of his jacket is connected to booze. D and D, assault, ABH. And he did eight years for armed robbery. Released in ninety-nine.'

'Armed as in with a gun?'

'The same. But he's been clean since, apart from an affray charge on a Stonewall march in London ten years ago.'

'Interesting. What time are you briefing tomorrow?'

'Eight,' said Noble. 'Too early?'

'Mid-morning to me,' mumbled Brook, feeling the stab of guilt again. He sensed Noble about to ring off. 'Ask Caskey to attend, see what she can contribute on Frazer and Nolan.'

'Are you sure?' said Noble eventually. 'She may have baggage.'

'We all have baggage. Do it anyway.'

*

Brook woke at four after fitful sleep. He padded downstairs to make tea, then returned to his office to check for messages on his iPhone. Still nothing from Terri.

He opened the desk drawer and rummaged around for his ex-wife's phone number, pocketing the scrap of paper before taking his mug out to the porch to drink his tea in the cold, sharp air of late autumn. Winter was in the air and the thought depressed him. Getting out on to the hills to spring-clean his mind was a lifeline he missed during the dark months. Even if he wasn't entangled in a case, too many of his favourite walks were too boggy to attempt. For the first time in an age, he hankered after a cigarette.

Instead, resolved on his course, he drained his tea and left the cottage.

Thirty minutes later, Brook approached the end of the A52, the road damp from rain and the traffic sparse. A flask of tea and a bulky torch sat in the passenger seat next to him. At Markeaton roundabout, instead of heading into Derby and then on to St Mary's Wharf, he swung right on to the A38 and powered down the trunk road heading towards Birmingham. Ten minutes later, he pulled off the A38 on to the old Burton Road and headed for the village of Findern.

Skirting the village to the east, Brook turned on to Longlands Lane and drove through an attractive housing estate before taking a single-track lane heading back out into countryside, following it until it began to peter out.

About a mile from the village the track widened out towards an open five-bar gate, a FOR SALE sign bolted to the gatepost. Beyond, the gravel drive opened into a circular turnaround. As

Brook drove nearer, Black Oak Farm reared up out of the darkness like a ghost ship. From what he could see, the farmhouse was a large and imposing modern bungalow built in an L-shape of pale stone, dotted with darker stone and wood trim for a Spanish ranch effect.

He parked and turned off the engine and headlights, plunging himself back into virtual darkness. Apart from the glow of the occasional lorry tearing by in the distance, the only other artificial illumination came from hazard lights blinking faintly on the abandoned cooling towers of Willington Power Station a couple of miles away.

Stepping out of the car, he flicked on the powerful torch and trudged towards the squat building, sweeping the beam around him as he walked. He arrived at the front door, a sturdy gnarled wood and mottled glass affair, recognising it from the scene-of-crime film. He turned the handle, expecting it to be locked. It was.

He stepped back to look out into the blackness before setting off to walk full circle around the empty property. Even in the eerie gloom he became quickly convinced that there was no ground high enough to afford a clear view of the farmhouse. If Ray Thorogood had wanted to monitor the progress of Jemson and Coulson on that fateful day, it would have been hard to find a vantage point on surrounding land. Unless, of course, he was in the house the whole time, hiding from cameras.

Brook shook his head. 'No. You weren't here, were you, Ray? You couldn't have been. Someone either tipped you off that things were going badly, or ...' He left the thought hanging while he mulled it over, then walked around the property a second time. At the rear of the house he came to the French windows. Inside was the kitchen where Mr and Mrs Thorogood had perished.

He leaned on the handle to point his torch through the glass, and to his surprise it gave way in his gloved hand and the door opened inwards. After a superfluous look round, he stepped quickly into the murder room, closing the French window behind him, and stood for a moment to get his bearings, his pulse quickening.

When he walked, his footsteps echoed in that way unique to an empty house, where sound is no longer absorbed by carpets and furniture. The faint smell of disinfectant and new paint reached his nostrils.

Sweeping his torch around the room, he realised that the entire kitchen had been refurbished. It was now a completely different space. The blood-stained wallpaper on the walls had been replaced with washable white paper, the ruddy terracotta tiles had been pulled up and in their place were wooden floor panels painted with white non-slip paint. Everything he remembered as having colour of any kind had either been removed or painted white. Not his favourite colour scheme, but then the house had been the scene of a violent triple homicide. Not surprising that the seller, presumably Reardon Thorogood or her representatives, would want neutral colours throughout, especially in the room where two people had been so horribly butchered. For some crimes, even the chemicals of a professional trauma cleaning service couldn't expunge the horror.

The pine table and chairs had gone and the garish hacienda-style doors had been replaced with modern double doors, also white. The kitchen surfaces, which had been pine, were now blocks of marble, light grey with darker flecks for contrast.

The security camera was still in place, though, high on its bracket in the corner of the room. It was dormant, much to Brook's relief.

After a thorough examination by torchlight, he made his way across to the brand-new white telephone. From its cradle on the wall, he lifted the handset to his ear. It worked.

He gently returned the receiver to the cradle, which nestled next to a thermostat, then made his way towards the interior of the house. At the double doors, he flicked idly at a wall switch, flooding the kitchen with dazzling light from new recessed ceiling fittings.

He blinked at the harshness and flicked off the lights immediately, plunging himself back into torchlight. In the redecorated white hall he briefly flicked on more lights to get his bearings before heading for Reardon's bedroom. On the way, he recognised the door of the security cupboard that had provided the dramatic opening frame from that day after Reardon had rebooted the system. He tried the handle, but the suite was locked, then swung the torch towards the ceiling to find the camera that had recorded that opening scene. It was in the same position but, like the one in the kitchen, appeared to be off.

Brook's smile was bleak. It wasn't as if he'd broken in, he reasoned, failing to alleviate his own disquiet.

With a deep breath he pushed at the white door of Reardon's bedroom. More white was inside. White walls, white blinds, white woodwork. The bed and the rest of the furniture were gone. The carpet too. The boards were bare, awaiting the flooring of choice of the new owner, if one could be found after such an infamous act.

Brook stepped noisily on to the boards, staring down at the

grain in case Jonathan Jemson's blood had soaked through to the wood. If it had, there was no longer a visible stain.

He moved into the en suite bathroom, again retiled in white. The original had been pale yellow, he remembered. There were no tea lights around the bath, and he made a mental note to recheck SOCO photographs and film to see how far, if at all, Jonathan Jemson had prepared the conflagration, a final act of destruction against the Thorogood family, before unexpectedly meeting his own fate.

Returning to the kitchen, he headed for the French windows and left the house the way he'd come in, closing the door firmly behind him.

Back at his car, he heard a noise from the lane and a small but lively dog panted its way over, jumping eagerly at him for attention, its big wet nose pushing at his hands.

Brook ruffled its friendly head, felt the collar and looked down the lane for an owner. An elderly man was leaning his hands and chin on a long hiking pole. The first fingers of dawn stretching above the horizon framed the man's head sufficiently to show him squinting suspiciously at Brook.

'Morning.' Brook tried to sound nonchalant. He opened the passenger door and dropped the torch on to the seat.

'Morning,' said the old man doubtfully. 'Here, boy.' The dog abandoned Brook and ran excitedly back to its owner.

Brook gestured over his shoulder at the farm. 'Nice spot.'

'Used to be,' drawled the man, showing no sign of moving off, despite the dog's zeal.

'Any idea what it's selling for?'

The old man thumbed at the estate agent's board. 'Reckon they could tell you.'

Brook smiled. 'Course. Just wondered if you knew.' He made an ostentatious note of the estate agent's number and climbed into the car, setting off back towards the village under the slowly rotating gaze of the old man.

Fourteen

BROOK SAT QUIETLY AT THE back of the darkened incident room, staring at the photograph of the elderly couple slouched in their chairs, as Noble began.

'First things first.' Noble glanced at Cooper and heads turned to him.

'An hour ago EMSOU confirmed a match on the bullets that killed Mr and Mrs Gibson with those taken from the bodies of Stephen Frazer and Iain Nolan.' A murmur of excitement and trepidation travelled around the darkened room.

'It's a series,' confirmed Noble.

'Great,' mumbled Charlton, sitting next to Brook.

'The other new information is that, according to the post-mortem, Mr and Mrs Gibson died between eight o'clock and midnight on the night of Saturday October the twenty-ninth,' said Noble. 'And based on evidence at the scene and the victims' habits, we estimate that the killer gained entry to the house sometime between eight and ten o'clock.'

'Habits?' enquired Charlton.

'They were dressed,' explained Noble. 'Their son says they went to bed no later than ten o'clock every night, so if they opened the door to their killer, which we think they did, it must have been before ten. After that, getting their attention might involve a lot of noise.'

'Do we know why they let him in?' said Charlton.

'They may not have let him in,' said Noble. 'But they were trusting enough to open the door.'

'And with a gun, if he couldn't smooth-talk his way in, he'd simply enter by force,' said Smee.

Charlton nodded, deep in thought. 'Okay. But if the killer was in the house by ten, why think they could've died as late as midnight?'

'Because he brought champagne,' said Noble. 'And all three took the time to have a glass before the fatal shots were fired.'

'It wouldn't take more than half an hour to drink a glass of champagne,' said Charlton.

'But getting to know the victims would take longer,' said Brook softly.

'You're discounting the possibility the Gibsons knew their killer?'

'For now we are,' said Brook. 'Which means he needed to make their acquaintance.' He moved reluctantly towards the light. 'Give them time to prepare.'

'Prepare for what?' demanded Charlton.

'Their send-off. In my opinion this was a farewell party. A short celebration of their lives. Champagne, music, photographs of loved ones on their laps. Bang. You're dead.'

'That's why they were holding hands?'

'I think so.'

'But what makes you think he got to know them?' demanded Charlton.

'Because he took the trouble to ask them their favourite

classical track, which was playing as they died,' replied Brook.

'Maybe he already knew it,' suggested Charlton. 'Their son would.'

'No,' said Brook. 'Mr and Mrs Gibson were strangers. We'll do the legwork to be sure, but I think the profile is solid. If the killer knew anyone, it would be Frazer and Nolan.'

Noble nodded. 'First principles – Frazer and Nolan were the first kill.'

'So when our shooter was ready, he started the series with someone he knew,' ventured Banach.

'Why?' asked Charlton.

'Every serial and spree killer needs a trigger, and that invariably involves a victim or victims that he knows or has seen, even if only from a distance.'

'So Frazer and Nolan may not have actually met their killer,' said Charlton.

'Also possible,' said Brook. 'But being one of the first gay couples to get married in Derby, they were in the public eye and he may have got to know them that way.'

'We seem to be assuming the killer is a man,' said Banach, with a glance at the mute DS Caskey sitting nearby. 'Isn't that rather patronising?'

'It's just shorthand based on the statistics,' said Brook. 'Women nurture. Men kill.'

'Not exclusively,' argued Banach.

'No, of course not,' agreed Brook. 'We keep an open mind – always – but the figures for organised serial killers are even more skewed towards a man.'

'Female serial killers are like hen's teeth,' added Noble.

Banach shrugged her acknowledgement before glancing again at DS Caskey for support that didn't arrive. In fact the newcomer was gazing into space and Banach couldn't even be sure she was paying attention. 'I suppose.'

'However Frazer and Nolan came to the killer's attention, they fitted the pathology and he – *or she* – started to make plans,' said Brook.

'How exactly?' said Charlton.

'They were a happy couple,' replied Brook. 'Like the Gibsons.'

Chief Superintendent Charlton nodded slowly as though he understood. 'And after that first kill, like all organised serial killers, he needs more.'

'Especially if things have gone well and he deems their deaths to have been worthwhile,' added Brook.

'So what's his purpose?' said Charlton.

'To feed his urges, his mania, his desire to set the world straight as he sees it.'

'How?' demanded Charlton.

'No idea. But if this man feels he has to kill happily married couples, to find him we'll need to work out why.'

'It's not sexual?' said Charlton.

Brook shook his head. 'Forensics says not.'

'No semen at either scene,' said Morton.

'What about prints and DNA?' demanded Charlton.

'Nothing,' said Brook. 'The victims weren't touched. The only sign of violence was the bullets.'

'Then what did he want?'

'When we know better, we'll have him,' said Brook.

'So how do we catch him?' demanded Charlton.

'We do the legwork, get to know him, his methods and how he thinks.'

'What's the legwork telling you?'

'That he's very careful,' answered Brook. 'We have no witnesses to either incident. No one saw or heard anything despite the killer being on the scene for some time. We think he may be an experienced individual, strong and forceful and maybe with a position of some authority in his public life.'

'How do you conclude that?' interrupted Charlton.

'Because he was able to control four people with little struggle or commotion,' said Noble. 'Even knowing they were about to die didn't help Frazer and Nolan. He had the strength of character and physical presence to pacify them.'

'He had a gun,' pointed out Charlton.

'Which helped, no doubt,' said Brook. 'But Frazer and Nolan were fit enough. If they thought they were about to die, it would make sense to take him on. Maybe they'd both still be dead, maybe not, but they ought to have tried. Instead they followed his instructions until both were bound and gagged, and by then it was too late.'

'You keep referring to a single assailant. EMSOU said different guns were used,' said Charlton. 'That tells us there were two killers.'

'Actually it only tells us there were two guns,' said Brook. 'I'll believe there were two killers when I have evidence to that effect. Everything else points to a single individual.'

Caskey's features showed her conjuring an objection. 'So if the killer *or killers* knew Frazer and Nolan, why wasn't there music and champagne at their crime scene?'

'We think there was,' said Noble.

'But the killer didn't get the idea until he got there and found them drinking it,' said Brook.

'An emerging MO,' said Caskey, deep in thought.

'And in light of the bottle at the Gibson house, we asked

Pathology to take another look at stomach contents. Frazer and Nolan *had* drunk a bottle of their own champagne.'

'Then why was there no mention in reports?' said Charlton, turning to stare at Caskey.

'We suspect the bottle was empty so the killer removed it and washed the glasses,' said Brook. 'Only later did it occur to him that he should make it a feature because it fits the pathology of the crime.'

'With its suggestion of a celebration,' added Caskey.

'Quite.'

'But why wash the glasses?' demanded Smee.

'The killer sees them as a distraction from what he's trying to present to us. For his first kill he only wanted us to see what he'd done to the victims. Thinking about it later, he decided to incorporate the champagne into his next tableau, but even then he removed the bottle and glasses to the Gibsons' kitchen so they didn't get in the way.'

'But there was no music in Breadsall,' said Caskey, warily.

'The next-door neighbour thinks the iPod was on when she discovered the bodies, that there had been music,' said Brook.

'But whoever put it on didn't know how to put it on repeat,' added Noble.

'Which suggests someone more mature,' said Charlton. 'Not au fait with the technology.' Brook smiled his agreement. 'So where are we?'

'Where we always are at the beginning, sir,' replied Brook. 'Feeling our way. A bit like our killer.'

'What do you mean?'

'He's new at this but getting better. The planning is methodical and he's becoming more confident, refining his

MO. Things went smoothly in Boulton Moor. He gains entry without difficulty and doesn't need restraints. After the preliminaries, he shoots Mr and Mrs Gibson . . .'

'. . . with two separate guns,' added Caskey.

'With two separate guns,' conceded Brook. 'Then he exits the house, leaving no trace, walks back to his car and drives away.'

'Where's he parked?'

'Walking distance obviously,' said Noble. 'But he wouldn't risk being too close in case he annoys residents, draws attention to his parked car. We've widened the canvass to a mile radius, asking for information about anyone seen carrying a bottle or carrier bag in the vicinity of Boulton Moor on Saturday evening. It's a long shot.'

'Dark nights,' said Charlton, nodding. 'Any idea where he went afterwards?'

Noble moved over to a map of the city. 'Good escape routes from both locations.' He tapped the map with a ruler. 'From the Gibson house on the southern extremities of Derby, you're two minutes from the A50. The ring road is even closer, so he can take his pick. He knows his way around.'

'So he's local to Derby.'

'Undoubtedly,' said Noble. 'Breadsall is also on the fringes of the city, only this time north-east. He knows where to strike.'

'We're not suggesting victims are selected on the basis of nearby trunk roads, are we?'

'Not especially, sir,' said Noble, smiling. 'But we're noting the location and the absence of heavy foot traffic. Makes movement easier from vehicle to crime scene.'

'Nothing on film?' asked Caskey.

'We're trawling through traffic cameras, but we have a big window and only a limited view of the main highways,' said Cooper. 'If the shooter knows the area or has scouted out the kill zone, he'd have little trouble parking in a nearby residential street and walking the rest.'

'Same problem as Breadsall,' nodded Caskey. 'Though obviously we ended up canvassing on the two-killer theory.'

Brook didn't react, aware that the subtle dynamic of his squad was altered by Caskey's assertiveness. She was rightly protective of the assumptions Ford's team had reached regarding Frazer and Nolan, but her certainty was at odds with the prevailing ethos of his squad: nothing is certain until it's *absolutely* proven.

'No vehicles on film common to both scenes?' asked Charlton.

'None,' replied Cooper.

'Should married couples in west Derby be worried?' ventured Charlton, to a ripple of amusement. 'If the killer is striking at different points on the compass . . .'

Noble's smile was cryptic. 'It's not a factor we've considered, sir.'

'The victims are connected by cause of death,' said Brook. 'Using a gun implies a need for speed and precision. The killer wants the victims dead but takes no pleasure in the kill. He lingers on the celebration but not the murders.'

Noble clicked his mouse until all four victims were together on a split screen. 'Four bullets, four victims.'

'Two guns,' repeated Caskey.

'Two guns,' agreed Brook. 'Again we keep an open mind, but all science on this type of crime suggests a lone gunman. And the champagne at the Gibson house would tend to support that,' he added quickly, as Caskey began to form an objection.

'How so?' said Charlton.

'There were only three glasses,' said Banach. 'Both victims had champagne in their stomachs, so . . .'

'That leaves one washed glass for the killer,' concluded Morton.

'Maybe the second gunman didn't drink,' offered Charlton.

Brook shrugged. 'Like I said – open mind.'

'So being a series, Matthew Gibson is now out of the picture,' remarked Caskey.

Brook and Noble exchanged a look. 'Almost,' said Noble. Charlton raised an eyebrow.

'Gibson's a gun owner and shoots regularly. He owns a deactivated Glock 19 . . .'

'Being tested,' said Caskey.

'Yes,' said Brook. 'But we don't see him as a viable suspect because he has an alibi and no real motive.'

'Ballistics on Frazer and Nolan suggested early-model Glocks,' said Caskey.

'We saw the report,' said Brook. 'But Glocks are plentiful in Britain.'

'I don't doubt it,' she replied. 'It's a great gun and there are always rogues in circulation.'

'For those who aren't aware, Sergeant Caskey is an Author-ised Firearms Officer,' explained Charlton.

'A long time ago,' said Caskey, smiling hesitantly.

'Do you still shoot?' asked Smee.

'Most weeks. I live near the Ripley range and I use a Glock too. It's the best handgun in the world, and Inspector Brook is right. It's not hard *or* expensive to pick one up if you know where to go.'

'Maybe we shouldn't dismiss this Gibson so quickly,' said Charlton.

'But the Champagne Killer is now a series,' pointed out Caskey. 'We'd need to link him to Frazer and Nolan.'

Charlton was crestfallen. 'Right.'

'Champagne Killer,' remarked Read, smiling.

The sudden disdain on Charlton's face was withering. 'I do not want to hear that sobriquet outside this room, DC Read. And I don't expect to see it in the newspapers.' Read lowered his head, frowning.

'Sir,' said Cooper, with an apologetic glance at Brook. 'We did kind of connect him to Frazer and Nolan.'

'How?'

'Matthew Gibson is gay and was acquainted with the first two victims. Also we contacted his brother in Australia, who confirmed that Matthew's sexuality caused difficulties with their parents.'

'That was over thirty years ago,' argued Brook.

'According to Gibson,' pointed out Noble.

'Gibson *knew* Frazer and Nolan,' exclaimed Charlton. 'Then why—'

'They were acquainted, no more,' interrupted Brook, glancing at Caskey to see if she was preparing to resurrect DI Ford's sex killer theory.

'Could be significant,' said Caskey, looking carefully back at him.

'Motive and alibi,' repeated Brook. 'He spent the entire weekend with his partner.' He held up a hand to forestall the objections. 'I know, I know. But he has no motive and the method makes no sense.'

'Easy access to the house,' shrugged Caskey. 'Gun owner.

Does he drink champagne?' Brook remained silent.

'We'll take that as a yes,' said Charlton.

'Gibson's a wealthy man,' said Brook. 'And highly intelligent.'

'You mean the sort who plans carefully,' said Caskey, with a hint of flippancy in her voice.

'Exactly that sort,' said Brook. 'And if he was going to kill his parents, he wouldn't have done it like that.'

'He might if they asked him,' said Caskey. 'A final celebration before he sent them on their way. And it would explain why they weren't tied.'

'Suicide pact,' pondered Charlton. 'Did they have health problems?'

'Nothing life-threatening,' said Noble. 'And no reports of depression, though you can never tell, obviously.'

'If Gibson killed his parents, why would he need a second shooter to help?' ventured Banach.

'Exactly,' agreed Brook.

'So *now* it's two shooters,' smiled Caskey.

'And why show up three days later and pretend to discover the bodies?' demanded Morton.

'It *was* rent day,' said Noble, with an apologetic glance at Brook. 'If their bodies hadn't been discovered, he'd have to turn up to collect or it would look suspicious.'

'So he kills them and returns to the scene to play the bereaved son,' said Caskey, encouraged. To Charlton she added, 'Think we're being a bit hasty putting a line through his name, sir. The man I saw on Tuesday looked pretty calm for someone who'd just found his parents executed.'

'But he has no motive for Frazer and Nolan, and their deaths were nothing to do with mercy killing,' said Brook.

'Both were in good health, even planning a ski trip to Japan. And the fact that they were tied shows they resisted.'

'Then maybe he had a different reason for killing them,' retorted Caskey.

'A gay hissy fit?' mocked Brook, using Gibson's own phrase. 'Organised serial killers don't have different reasons for killing, Sergeant. They only have one and every kill is a variation on a theme.'

'Then maybe Gibson's not a serial killer, just someone eliminating those who have pissed him off,' said Caskey. 'Parents, ex-lovers – they top the list of most domestics.'

'Frazer and Nolan were not Gibson's ex-lovers,' insisted Brook.

'So they snubbed him and he takes it badly,' suggested Caskey.

'There's no social media or any emails to prove a relationship between Gibson and Frazer and Nolan,' argued Brook. 'And may I remind you that ex-DI Ford's team worked to that theory extensively and found nothing.' Caskey's colour began to rise.

'If Gibson knew them, it's a connection,' insisted Charlton. 'We can't rule him out. You were the one saying do the legwork, Brook. Start with his alibi for *both* killings. Did we check out his partner?'

'James Trimble,' said Cooper, with a hesitant glance at Brook. 'Born in Glasgow. Divorced with one son, Sean. The son has minor violence on his sheet, but Trimble Senior served eight years for armed robbery. Out in ninety-nine.'

'Armed as in *with a gun?*' asked Caskey, raising an eyebrow at Brook.

No contradiction from Cooper. Silence for a few seconds.

'Open mind, Brook?' enquired Charlton. Brook nodded faintly in response. 'So what now?'

'With no forensic leads from either scene, we're looking harder at the Frazer and Nolan murder,' said Noble.

'First principles,' nodded Charlton, sounding pleased with himself.

'It's our baseline,' replied Brook. 'Changes he made for the Gibson killing show his development. We'll know more when we've finished playing catch-up on DI Ford's inquiry.'

'There's not a lot to catch up,' said Caskey. 'We eliminated most of their friends and contacts.'

'Most,' said Noble, flicking at a remote. The photograph of Maureen McConnell and the partially visible shaven-headed man appeared on the whiteboard. 'We couldn't put a name to this man, though the neighbour thought he might have been called Alex or Ollie.'

'That was the only decent picture of him, and we drew a blank on ID,' said Caskey. 'But the neighbour told us he was harmless.'

'Her assessment of harmless would be about as helpful as her memory for names,' said Brook. Caskey acknowledged with a faint dip of the eyes.

'Any concrete reason to think this man's a suspect?' enquired Charlton.

'Only that he wasn't a friend. Frazer and Nolan had just met him and invited him to their party because they felt sorry for him,' said Banach. 'He'd recently lost his wife.'

'Looks a bit like that ex-squaddie I was doing background on,' said Cooper, fumbling with his keyboard. 'David Fry.'

'It's not him,' said Noble. 'McConnell didn't ID his mugshot.'

'Who's David Fry?' enquired Charlton.

'A neighbour with form,' said Noble. 'Ex-army.'

'So he knows about guns.'

'I wondered when we'd get to him,' said Caskey. 'I arrested him a couple of times for various drunken scuffles and I noticed he was taking an unnatural amount of interest in Tuesday's crime scene when I was *briefly* there.'

'What do we have on him?' said Charlton.

Cooper clicked his mouse to load a photograph of the shaven-headed ex-soldier. 'Returned from a tour of Afghanistan eighteen months ago and has had a few problems reintegrating. As DS Caskey said, he's been tugged for drunkenness and affray.'

'I was reading that the army's had more casualties from post-battlefield suicides than were killed by Afghan insurgents,' said Banach. 'Doesn't make him a murderer.'

'Any hint of serious violence?' asked Charlton.

'Isn't being a soldier a hint?' said Caskey.

'Check out his service record,' ordered Charlton.

'In the works, sir,' replied Cooper.

'Did Fry's name come up in the canvass?' asked Caskey.

'I was coming to that,' said Morton. 'The next-door neighbour, Heather Sampson, remembered him pounding on the Gibsons' front door last year. She couldn't say why, just that he was angry and shouting to be let in.'

'This is the first I'm hearing of it,' exclaimed Brook.

'Sorry, but the poor old girl's been in hospital with shock,' said Morton. 'It was a while ago and she only just remembered and mentioned it to one of the SOCOs after she got home.'

'When?'

'Yesterday afternoon.'

Brook's expression betrayed impatience. 'No, when was Fry banging on the Gibsons' door?'

Morton checked his notebook. 'Just before Christmas.'

'Nearly a year ago,' said Brook. 'What happened?'

'Unknown,' said Morton. 'Apparently the Gibsons were out. He was there for a few minutes, hammering and shouting, then he went away and that was it.'

'Any other neighbours corroborate?' asked Noble. Morton shook his head.

'An unresolved conflict with an ex-soldier,' said Charlton. 'Does he have weapons?'

'He doesn't have a licence,' said Cooper.

'He's ex-army,' said Morton. 'My brother's in the Royal Marines and reckons squaddies always leave a posting with guns they've picked up locally. They smuggle them back in their kit for souvenirs.'

'Married?' asked Banach.

'Ten years, no children,' said Cooper.

'Well he's got more of a connection to the Gibsons than the rest of the estate,' said Charlton. 'That's three viable suspects already, Brook.'

'Three?'

'Gibson, Fry and this man at Frazer and Nolan's party.'

'At least two shooters right there,' observed Caskey mischievously.

'And if the unidentified partygoer had lost his wife, we can assume he was heterosexual,' added Charlton.

'We assume nothing,' said Brook quietly. 'He may have had a dead wife, but plenty of gay men feel the need to hide their sexuality behind a conventional marriage.'

'Yes, yes, but if he *was* straight and went to a gay party—'

'It wasn't a gay party, sir,' said Banach softly. 'It was a party.'

'But the point is it's possible he felt uncomfortable when he realised the sexuality of other guests,' insisted Charlton. 'Threatened, even.'

Caskey grunted doubtfully. 'If he did feel homophobic rage, it would have manifested at the party, sir. And even assuming he could control his anger, to return months later and kill Frazer and Nolan means he nurtured the kind of hate that would produce a savagery which was sorely missing from the victims' corpses. The victims I saw, at least.'

'Agreed,' said Brook. 'These are definitely not hate crimes. The opposite, if anything.'

'Then what about Gibson?' said Charlton, a little chastened to have his detecting abilities undermined. 'His parents lived in his property, so that's *his* door David Fry was banging on. Do they know each other?'

'Gibson says not,' said Brook.

'Dig deeper, Brook,' said Charlton, standing. 'And keep me informed. I'm briefing the press and TV this evening and I want you sitting beside me, so make sure you have something of substance to announce.'

'Can't do it, sir,' replied Brook, his features hardening. 'I'm officially on leave.' Charlton glared at him, preparing his riposte.

'Happy to sit in with you, sir,' said Caskey before the Chief Superintendent could verbalise a complaint.

Charlton stared at Brook, then nodded at Caskey. 'Very well. Might look good after all the nonsense about your former DI. Make sure you're up to speed on the Gibson inquiry.'

'Shouldn't take long,' quipped Caskey.

*

'Result,' mumbled Noble to Brook, when the briefing had ended.

'You think so?' Brook's eyes were on Caskey, chatting earnestly with Cooper.

'Don't tell me you enjoy holding Charlton's hand with the media.'

Brook turned to Noble. 'No, I don't. But DI Ford has retired, John.'

'So?'

'So if the budget allows, a deserving DS is going to get promoted.'

Noble also fixed his eyes on Caskey. 'See what you mean.' He shrugged. 'Well she's certainly impressive.'

'Apart from one thing,' said Brook.

'What's that?'

'She wants it too much.'

'How do you know?'

'Because when she found out that Gibson is gay, she had the perfect opportunity to defend Ford's sex killer theory.'

'So why didn't she?'

'Because Ford is history and now she's playing the game with different contestants.'

Noble nodded. 'And playing it well.'

While Noble nipped out to the car park for a crafty cigarette before their drive over to Boulton Moor, Brook sidled across to DC Cooper, busily tapping away at his keyboard. 'Dave,' he said, part greeting, part enquiry.

Without reply, Cooper looked around the room before handing over a thick folder.

Brook nodded his thanks and left the incident room,

marching briskly to his car. Once there, he dropped the file on the passenger seat and took a quick inventory of its contents. Everything was there. Forensic reports, witness statements, photographs of the crime scene as well as Ray Thorogood's cottage, transcripts of text messages and a disc of CCTV footage taken at Black Oak Farm. Brook only needed one more piece of information that wasn't in the file. He texted his query to Cooper.

A minute later, his phone vibrated. It was a text from Terri.
Don't contact me, Dad. I'm okay. Just need some time.

He frantically tapped at the screen to phone his daughter, but by the time he'd hit the speed dial, her mobile had been turned off again.

'Damn it, Terri,' he cursed.

Before he could compose a message to her, a text arrived from Cooper, and Brook noted down the address he needed for the afternoon.

A tap on the window made him jump.

Noble stood at the passenger window. 'Ready?'

Without wishing to, Brook glanced down guiltily at the bulging folder on the passenger seat. Noble followed his gaze, so Brook leapt from the BMW, leaving the manila folder on the seat.

'We'll take your car, John.'

Fifteen

NOBLE PARKED THE CAR OUTSIDE the Gibson crime scene, next to two scientific support vehicles. Activity had dwindled and the knot of watching spectators had followed suit now that the bodies of the victims had been removed and the TV cameras departed. Scene-of-crime officers were still doing tests, steadily trudging back and forth to the house, but they too would soon be finished and the property would be sealed.

Noble locked the car and the pair walked away from the crime scene. 'Are you going to tell me what's going on?'

'Going on?'

'The file in your car. The furtive conversations with Cooper. The problems you're having with Terri.'

'You'd make a good detective, John,' quipped Brook, trying to put Noble off the scent.

'I should mind my own business, is that it?'

Brook hesitated, then nodded at their destination. 'Number thirty-two.' Noble frowned. 'It's nothing to worry about.'

'So it is to do with Terri.'

Brook opened the wooden gate and headed towards the

front door. Long grass covered the garden. 'We're having . . . problems. Let's leave it at that.'

'Is this to do with the abuse?'

Brook found Noble's eyes. 'What?'

'Don't worry. It's not station gossip. She let slip something a couple of years ago, that time you spent a night in hospital. I read between the lines.'

'And you said nothing for two years.'

Noble shrugged. 'I respect your privacy.'

'So what changed?'

'You tell me.'

Brook rapped firmly with the door knocker. 'Like I said. It's nothing.'

The door was opened by a full-figured woman in jeans and baggy jumper, perhaps thirty-five though she looked older around the eyes. Cigarette smoke floated sinuously from hand up to face. 'You lot again,' she said with a resigned sigh.

Noble smiled. 'Mrs Fry?'

'What is it this time?'

'Is your husband in?'

'Pubs aren't open for half an hour. Where else would he be? Who's he smacked around this time?'

'It's nothing like that,' said Brook. 'We're talking to everyone about the Gibson murder.'

'We already said our piece yesterday. We didn't see nothing, we don't know nothing.'

'We just have a few more questions.'

After a beat, she stepped back from the door, taking a long drag on her cigarette and turning to holler over her shoulder. 'Davey. Police.'

Brook and Noble followed her down the hall as she padded

back into the dark interior and pushed open a door. Without breaking stride, she gestured to the room on her right before wandering off in apparent indifference to the kitchen at the back of the house.

In the living room, the burly, shaven-headed ex-soldier Brook had seen a couple of days ago lay sprawled across a white leather sofa, the console of an Xbox in his huge hands. He was playing a muted game involving racing cars though Brook could hear faint noise leaking from a pair of headphones on the floor. Fry had a cigarette jammed between his lips and an open can of beer at his feet and wore the same tatty, paint-stained fatigues, with a sleeveless T-shirt in camouflage green.

Seeing Brook and Noble, he sat up, swinging his bare feet to the carpet, but remained resolutely seated and examined the brandished warrant cards thoroughly before pausing his game. 'Help you?' he asked, his voice hoarse with tar.

'We'd like to ask you a few questions.'

Fry removed his cigarette and extinguished it between his fingers. 'If this is about the Gibson murders, I spoke to one of your lot yesterday. Terrible shame but I don't know what else I can tell you.'

Brook looked around the bare room – at the TV with various black boxes stacked in a pile underneath, wires heading off in all directions towards sockets; at the sofa and a lone armchair; at a pair of fully laden dumb-bells nestling in a corner. He could make out little else in the room, though it was hard to see with the venetian blinds closed. He saun-tered over to the window and pulled the blind up sharply, allowing the low sun to flood the room and pick out the blue-brown toxins of cigarette smoke. For good measure he opened a small casement to freshen the brewery air, then nodded at

Noble, who closed the door to the hall.

Fry held a hand to his eyes, smiling faintly. 'If you're thinking of beating me to a standstill, matey, you're going to need help.'

'We can open the door if it makes you feel safer,' smiled Brook.

Fry took a swig of beer and restarted his game. 'Leave it open on your way out.'

Brook considered for a moment, then looked around at the mass of cables and bent to pluck one from its socket. The room was flooded with the explosive roar of the cars racing around a virtual circuit. Fry threw his hands to his ears in terror, then banged, panic-stricken, on the console to pause the game and return the room to silence. He jumped up and advanced aggressively on Brook.

'Do you know how many ways I could kill you right now?' he seethed, a foot from Brook's face, his shoulders flexing like a cat before a fight.

Noble bristled and took a step towards the pair, but Brook halted him with a gesture, finding his grin. 'Let me see. Is it more than one?'

Fry narrowed his red-rimmed eyes and after a few seconds his breathing seemed to slow and he nodded at the middle-aged detective, a curious expression on his face. 'You'd like me to, wouldn't you? Fuck me, you would.' He stepped back, his breathing returning to normal, and moved back to the sofa, turning off the game. 'We could have used a few more like you at Camp Bastion.'

'Flat feet,' replied Brook.

Fry laughed bitterly. 'At least you've got feet. Ask your questions and keep it down. I don't react well to loud noises.'

'You can get treatment for PTSD, you know,' said Brook.

'Ask your questions or go,' insisted Fry, swigging from his can.

'Why were you banging on the door of the Gibson house before Christmas last year?' asked Noble.

'I wasn't.'

'You made quite a racket,' said Noble.

Fry gazed malevolently at him. 'Wasn't me.' He grinned at a joke as yet untold. 'And they're not around to contradict me.'

'You've misunderstood,' said Brook. 'We're not asking if you were there; we already know you were. And you also spent a long time hanging on the perimeter tape after the bodies of your neighbours were discovered.'

Fry smiled. 'So DS Caskey told you.'

'I saw you myself.'

He shrugged. 'Not much excitement around here. Course I'm going to see what all the fuss is about.'

'You haven't answered our question,' said Noble.

'Which one was that?'

'A witness saw you banging on Mr and Mrs Gibson's door,' said Noble.

'That's not a question,' he replied, staring at the two men in turn. He glanced at his watch and drained his can before standing. 'I don't have time for this. I have an appointment.'

'The pub can wait,' said Noble. 'Unless you'd prefer to answer questions at the station.'

'You and Miss Marple here taking me in, son?'

'You forget we have half a dozen officers around the corner, Sergeant,' said Brook, smiling.

'It's Mr Fry. I left the army, remember.'

Brook nodded. 'Mr Fry, you weren't stupid enough to hit

me just now and I seriously doubt you murdered the Gibsons. So let's dispense with all this posturing. Tell us about the dispute and we'll go away. I assume it was a problem with the decorating.'

Fry's expression tightened and aggression resurfaced in his eyes. He sank back on to the white leather, which squeaked at his arrival. 'What decorating?'

Brook flicked a glance towards the paint stains on his combats. 'I'm a trained detective, Mr Fry. And the Gibsons' living room was pleasantly refurbished.'

Fry examined the paint as if only just seeing it. 'I can give you my card if you'd like.'

'Just answer the question.' Fry didn't respond. 'We're not interested in untaxed income,' said Noble, attempting to seal the deal. 'This is a murder inquiry.'

Fry took a deep breath, coming to a decision. 'About twelve months ago I printed off a few flyers and posted 'em locally. I'm pretty handy, thought I might earn a crust working as a jobbing painter and decorator. It was a rough time. I'd been out of the army for about six months. Money was tight. And it was Christmas.'

'You couldn't find work.'

'Not a chance. Still can't. Not official. Not unless I want to stack shelves in the pound shop for a bag of peanuts. Help for heroes!' Fry shook his head. 'This fucking country.'

'So you put yourself out there to do a little decorating?'

'Right.'

'And the Gibsons offered it?'

Fry hesitated. 'No. Their son rang me.'

'Matthew?' Brook glanced at Noble, remembering Gibson's earlier denial.

Fry nodded. 'His parents were away for a week and he wanted a couple of rooms freshened up. He'd picked up my flyer so he asked me to do it.'

'Which rooms?'

'The bedroom and lounge.'

'And?'

Fry hesitated, choosing his words with care. 'I did the work but Matthew Gibson . . . refused to pay me. Said some cash had gone missing or something.'

'Did you steal it?' asked Noble.

'No,' growled Fry.

'And you felt aggrieved,' said Brook.

'I was owed and I'm not a thief.'

'So you stormed round there to get your money.'

'I don't know about stormed,' said Fry. 'Their son lived out in the country somewhere so he wasn't around. So I went to ask the old couple.'

'But you were angry.'

'It was Christmas and I needed the money, so when Mr and Mrs Gibson got back, I decided to go round and mention it. That nosy old trout next door,' he said, shooting a glance at Noble for a rebuttal. 'She must've got the wrong impression. I was banging loud 'cos they were old and a bit deaf. Anyway, turns out they weren't home till the next day, so I went back then and told them I was owed money and that their son had refused to pay.'

'Did you tell them why?'

'You bet I did,' said Fry. 'Turns out they'd taken the cash with them to Cornwall. They were embarrassed, so they paid me.' He smiled. 'Said their son was the landlord and they'd claim it back off him. Problem solved.'

'And no hard feelings.'

'None.'

'Not even against Matthew Gibson.'

'I'm not gonna shake his hand if I see him in the street, but I got my money, so . . .'

'When did you last see the Gibsons alive?'

Fry shook his head. 'A few weeks ago, maybe. In the street.'

'And Matthew?'

'Not seen him since. I got the impression he doesn't get on too well with his parents. They said they only saw him on rent day.' He laughed without humour. 'I mean, rent from your parents. Tight-fisted cunt – with all his money.'

'All his money?' Brook repeated.

Fry continued without a beat. 'You've seen his motor. And he owns his mum and dad's house. Must be loaded.'

'Must be,' agreed Brook. 'The odd thing is, when we mentioned your name to Mr Gibson, he denied knowing you.'

'Probably embarrassed because he stiffed me.'

'His parents were shot to death and he was embarrassed,' said Brook. 'Sound reasonable to you?'

'You'll have to ask him.'

'Oh, we will,' said Brook. He glanced at Noble.

'Do you know someone called Stephen Frazer?' asked Noble.

'Should I?'

'Just answer the question.'

Fry appeared to give it genuine thought. 'No.'

'He lived in Breadsall.'

'That's the other side of Derby and I don't have a car,' said Fry.

'What about Iain Nolan? Same postcode.'

'Same answer. I don't know anyone in Breadsall. Why?'

Noble's mobile began to croak and he nipped outside to answer it.

'Matthew Gibson knew them,' said Brook.

Fry narrowed his eyes. 'Knew them? Are they dead?'

'Do you own a gun?' said Brook, ignoring the question.

Fry's expression hardened. 'I didn't kill Matthew Gibson's parents. They were a nice old couple. I liked them.'

'I asked if you owned a gun.'

'No,' said Fry, thin-lipped. 'I'm finished with guns.'

'Not even a sneaky souvenir from your tour in Afghanistan?'

'Why would I want a souvenir of that shithole?'

'I've no idea,' said Brook. 'But if you have, tell us now and we won't take any further action if the gun is clean. You'll lose the weapon, obviously.'

'I *don't* have a gun,' insisted Fry, resurrecting a little aggression.

'But you used a handgun in the army.'

'No, we controlled the camel-fuckers with sarcasm,' sneered Fry. 'Course I had a fucking gun, I was infantry.'

'What type?' said Brook. 'Gun, I mean.'

'A standard-issue Glock 19.'

Brook glanced at the beer can. 'Ever drink champagne?'

'Do I look like I do?' Brook waited him out. 'No, I don't drink champagne.'

'So none in the house.'

'The wife likes a glass of Chardonnay, but I'm strictly a beer man. Maybe spirits if a horse comes in. Is that it?'

'Notice any bottles of champagne at the Gibson house when you were working there?'

'No, but then I'm not the type to go rooting around other people's cupboards, am I?'

'How much did the Gibsons pay you?' asked Brook. Fry hesitated. 'Out of interest.'

'Three hundred quid.'

'Cheap.'

'Yeah, well I don't exactly have a glowing CV, do I?'

'No government help?'

Fry smiled pityingly. 'You're kidding, right? This is Britain, Inspector. You help yourself or you don't eat.'

Noble returned. 'That was Cooper.' He glanced at Fry and gestured Brook outside.

'Coop says they found a fingerprint match from the Gibson house,' said Noble, once they were outside on the pavement. 'It's David Fry's.'

Brook turned back to gaze at the house. Fry was staring malevolently at them from the window. 'Where?'

'On a light switch in the bedroom.' Noble waited for a reaction.

Brook's expression didn't encourage. 'He just told us he was decorating there, John. Besides, the killer wore gloves. That's why we've got no prints where we know he had his hands. Champagne bottle, CD player, glasses. It's not Fry.'

'It doesn't matter,' countered Noble. 'Fry has a history of violence and a working knowledge of guns; he had access to the house and had had an argument with the owner.' He waited. Brook sighed, not wanting to concede the point. 'Charlton's not going to be impressed if we don't bring him in for a GSR test.'

'You saw his short fuse,' said Brook. 'No way he killed the Gibsons. Any conceivable motive he might have would involve impulsive and messy violence. And don't forget there was an envelope full of cash, untouched.'

'We have enough for a warrant,' insisted Noble. 'We have to do the legwork. We've got his DNA and prints on record but we need to take him in for a GSR test to see if he's fired a weapon.'

Brook sighed, turning reluctantly back to the house. 'I suppose you're right.'

'I'll call for backup,' said Noble. 'He could be a difficult takedown.'

'He didn't do it, John.'

'Doesn't mean he'll come quietly. And he's not an idiot. He's going to know that his criminal record as well as the circumstantial evidence stacks up against him. He'll hit the bricks if he thinks we can pin it on him.'

Fry turned from the window and sprinted upstairs to gather up a rucksack that sat ready packed in the spare room. He threw in his night-sight binoculars and hurtled down the stairs to the kitchen.

His wife saw the rucksack. 'Where are you going?'

Fry ignored her and pulled open the fridge, hauling out a packet of cheese and a carton of ham before stuffing them into the empty top pocket of the rucksack. He picked out a loaf from the bread bin and flattened that into the same pocket.

'Where are you going?' she shouted.

'Pub.'

'Bollocks. You're taking food and your go bag.' Fry didn't answer. 'Shit, Davey, what have you done?'

He turned to her briefly but couldn't maintain eye contact. 'Nothing.'

'You're lying,' she said, shaking her head. 'It's another woman, isn't it?'

Fry closed his eyes in despair. 'How many times . . . ?'

'Then what is it? You can tell me, I'll understand.'

'I have told you,' he said, rounding on her angrily. 'It's nothing, I swear. Now leave me alone.'

Fear flitted across her eyes and she shrank away from him. 'You're scaring me, Davey. Something's wrong. Something's been eating you up ever since you got back from Bastion.' He didn't answer, instead pulling on his boots. 'Why don't you—'

'Shut up,' he seethed, fastening the rucksack and slinging on his army camouflage jacket before heading back to the lounge to peer out at the front of the house. The two detectives were sitting in their car and DS Noble was talking into a radio handset.

Fry raced back to the kitchen and opened the back door before turning to his wife, his face containing an apology of sorts. 'I'm sorry, love, but you have to trust me. I'm fine. I just have a few things to take care of at the lock-up. I'll be away for a couple of days, that's all. When the cops come back in, don't tell them anything and don't mention the lock-up. You don't know anything, okay?'

'That wouldn't be a lie, would it?' she snapped back, tears filling her eyes. She stared back at him and he moved in to give her a kiss, but she shrank back and turned her head away, raising a hand to push at him. 'Just go.'

With barely a pause he marched smartly to the back fence, lifted his rucksack into next door's garden and vaulted over to the other side.

His wife lit a cigarette with a shaking hand and slammed the back door.

Sixteen

NINETY MINUTES LATER, BROOK WAS alone in the BMW, dividing his attention between his map book and looking for the turn-off. He spotted Canning Circus police station, his cue to swing off the main Nottingham road towards Park Terrace. As he drove, he admired the handsome houses, properties from another era, a time when the wealthy merchants of Nottingham lived on the heights to the west of the city, overlooking the sweep down to the famous castle and beyond to the River Trent, the artery around which the city had flourished for fifteen hundred years.

The houses were solid and imposing, some in traditional red brick but others updated with cream or grey stucco. All were large, and sadly only a few were still residential, but one such property was his destination.

Finding the address he sought, Brook manoeuvred the BMW on to the pavement on the opposite side of the street and placed his police logbook on the dashboard to avoid a ticket. Then he climbed out for a lingering examination of the house. It consisted of two floors, with a third elevation created by a partial extension on one side of the roof. The walls were grey stucco, which picked out the white trim of the rectangular

Georgian windows. Two imposing wooden doors provided admittance to the building; one of them opened into a protruding flat-roofed lobby on the left and served offices on the ground floor. At the side of the property a patio wound around to the back of the house, bordered by wide public steps heading down the hill towards a small park.

Brook's mobile vibrated in his pocket.

'Fry's well and truly in the wind.'

'Did his wife say anything?'

'She's not speaking,' replied Noble. 'Should I take her in?'

'No. Check their financials and his mobile records. Find out where he might go.'

'He's ex-army. He could go anywhere, maybe even live off the land.'

'Maybe. But he didn't kill the Gibsons. I don't care how much circumstantial evidence there is.'

'That doesn't make him any less dangerous if the wrong person gets in his way.'

Brook sighed heavily. 'Make sure his mugshot is out there.'

'Charlton wants us to do a media appeal.'

'That's unnecessary. Just put someone on his house and wait until he tries to slip back home, take him there. If we escalate, he's only going to feel more desperate and act accordingly.'

'But Charlton . . .'

'. . . doesn't realise that we know best, John. I suggest you remind him. No media appeal.' Brook ended the call before Noble could reply and examined the left-hand door, a brass plaque declaring it the entrance to a computer software company. The buzzer and microphone grille were supplemented by a large brass knocker. He peered through the ground-floor window, noticing the security shutters bunched up at either side of the bay. Several very young-looking people were working at computer terminals and the whole space was bright and airy.

The right-hand door was identical to the left, but there was no brass plaque beside the buzzer and intercom, though there was a functioning security camera. Brook pressed the buzzer. Several minutes passed, but no one answered, so he stepped away just in time to glimpse a heavy curtain twitch on the upper floor. He buzzed again and barked his name and rank at the grille of the intercom.

After waiting a further five minutes, he strolled around the house via the patio at the side of the property. At the rear, he had a magnificent view of treetops and a glimpse of the well-tended park below. As he turned the corner at the back of the property, his progress was halted by a forbidding wrought-iron gate complete with protruding spikes on one side. Behind the bars, a weathered wooden table and chairs sat on stone flags. Looking up at the first floor, Brook spotted an elaborate wrought-iron fire escape with retractable ladder for added security. The fire escape protruded from an incongruous door set high in the house and firmly shut.

Retracing his steps, he noticed that every window on the ground floor was fitted with security grilles, to be fastened at night to protect all the computer hardware, no doubt.

A young man on the patio blocked his return to the front of the house. 'Help you?' he demanded.

'Perhaps,' Brook replied, flashing his warrant card to take the wind out of his sails. The young man's manner softened immediately. 'I'm looking for Reardon Thorogood.'

'I can't help you.'

'Can't or won't?' replied Brook. 'According to my information, this is her address.'

The man hesitated. 'I've never heard of her.'

'But there is somebody living in the upstairs apartments,'
said Brook, raising his eyes to the house. 'And this is her
address.'

'Sorry,' repeated the man, then he turned without another
word and scuttled round the corner, the front door slamming a
second later.

'I must be slipping,' muttered Brook, trudging back to the
front of the house. He buzzed the right-hand door again,
stepping back to crane his neck to the first floor. He saw the
curtain fall again so pressed his mouth to the intercom and
held his warrant card to the camera. 'I know you're in there,
Miss Thorogood.'

Finally he was answered by a scratchy voice through the
grille. 'What do you want, Inspector?'

'To talk to you about your parents' murder. Shall we have
the conversation through the intercom?'

There was silence and Brook tried to think of an alternative
strategy, but the buzz of an electronic entry mechanism
followed by the click of the latch invited him to push through
into the entrance hall, where he was greeted by another locked
door. Another electronic latch unfastened and he pulled open
the door on to a staircase and jogged up to a spacious landing
illuminated by a high skylight in the roof. Here he was faced by
two solid-looking doors. A second later the left-hand one
opened.

Assuming an invitation, he stepped into a spacious
L-shaped room drenched in soft winter sunlight. At the far
end, the room was bookended by two doors, one of which was

the entrance to a bright modern kitchen, visible through a hatch – the other was presumably a bedroom. Another door was set into an exterior wall and was doubtless the one that opened on to the fire escape he'd seen from below.

Walking to the centre of the room, Brook's feet were loud on the stripped wooden floor, painted in a washed-out industrial white similar to the new flooring at Black Oak Farm. Looking around, he saw plush suede furnishings, including an ample sofa angled towards a huge flat-screen TV hung on brackets across one corner of the room. A glass-topped coffee table serviced the needs of the sofa-dwellers, but that was it as far as furniture was concerned.

Moving across a large cream rug that extinguished his footfall for a few seconds, he was drawn to the stunning view over Nottingham Castle from the outsized window. He stared out across the park for a few seconds, then, remembering his purpose, turned to face Reardon Thorogood, who was peering at him from behind the door through straggly uncombed hair.

'Inspector Brook, you said.' She locked the door behind him and drew across two well-oiled, sturdy bolts. Her voice was squeaky, hesitant, almost breathless with anxiety. 'What happened to DI Ford and Sergeant Caskey?'

'DI Ford retired,' said Brook, trying not to stare at the transformation from the young woman he'd seen on the security camera footage to this pale, shapeless imitation that stood before him, one socked foot perched nervously on the other, like a bird in a cage.

What he could see of her face was dull-skinned and sallow, her eyes red, her cheeks pinched and lacking colour. She fidgeted with reddened, sore-looking fingers and Brook observed her bare nails bitten to the quick. She wore baggy

jogging bottoms and a shapeless woollen sweater that swallowed whatever figure she may have possessed.

Even though serious trauma rarely improved a victim's
appearance, Brook was shocked.

'And DS Caskey?'

'Busy on another case.'

'Is he?'

Brook turned his head quizzically, puzzled for a second.
She was testing him. 'She.'

Reardon nodded, satisfied, and the tension in her frame
seemed to ease a notch. She licked her lips each time she
spoke. 'What did they say downstairs?'

'Not a thing,' replied Brook. 'You've got them well trained.'

She smiled nervously. 'I own the building. They're a software
start-up and I gave them a favourable lease as long as they don't
answer questions about me.'

Brook glanced at the monitor by the door. It had a four-
way split screen showing the ground-floor entrance, the roof,
the fire escape he'd seen from the rear and the patio on the
ground floor.

'And you chose a software company because they'd be
equally enthusiastic about their own security, thus enhancing
your own.'

Reardon's smile was lips only, which she licked again before
speaking. 'That's perceptive of you.'

'Well there's no need to evict them after the way they
stonewalled me,' said Brook. 'Pretty tight security just to keep
out journalists.'

'I'm not afraid of journalists,' said Reardon. 'I'm afraid of
people pretending to be journalists. Or police.'

'Do you need to see my warrant card again?' She shook her

head. 'Anyone in particular you think might come round masquerading as a policeman?'

Reardon padded across to the fire escape door and pushed out on to the wrought-iron platform. She turned towards Brook and leaned back on the rail, producing a pack of cigarettes from beneath her baggy layers. There wasn't room for two on the small metallic walkway – brightened, Brook noticed, by a couple of pot plants – so he stood in the doorway, facing the city below. Reardon lit up with an urgency he would once have recognised and offered him a cigarette, which he refused with more regret than he was comfortable with.

'My loving brother Ray is still out there, isn't he?'

Brook was surprised. 'Wherever he is, your brother is a fugitive.' She didn't answer, inhaling deeply from her cigarette. 'Ray can no longer benefit from your death. He has nothing to gain by trying to find you.'

She smiled faintly. 'You're probably right.'

'I am right,' said Brook. 'You've had a traumatic experience, but trust me, things will get better and you *will* get over it.'

'I won't get over it if he kills me,' she replied, taking another huge drag.

Brook raided his memory. 'The last sighting put him in Spain.'

'He's not in Spain.'

'Why so sure?'

'Too foreign. Ray hates the sun. And greasy food.' She laughed without mirth. 'Not like Mum and Dad. They loved all things Latin. You'd know if you'd been to the farm before . . . before . . .'

'I've seen the crime-scene photographs,' said Brook, quickly, not wanting to mention his unsanctioned visit.

'Of course.' Another huge pull on her cigarette. 'Then you saw.' Her smile disappeared. 'Sorry, I'm talking a lot. It's nerves. Plus I don't get out much for conversation.'

'Don't worry,' said Brook. 'I'd like to hear more about your parents.'

'Really?' She seemed pleased. 'They loved Spain and decorated the farm like a hacienda – doors, tiles, cartwheels, the colours of the Mediterranean.' She laughed. 'It was pretty garish, to be honest. With all their money they could have had . . . I don't know, something better than a tasteless bungalow in the middle of a few bare acres. But they were happy. Dad had made his money and retired, and they did pretty much what they wanted.'

'They liked to travel?'

'Travel is overstating it. A few months in Tenerife every winter to escape the weather suited them down to the ground.' She smiled at a memory. 'When we were young, we went for two weeks in the summer. I loved those holidays, but Ray refused to go as soon as he was old enough. When I stopped going too, they'd jet off for a lot longer and come back with ridiculous tans and cheap knick-knacks for the pair of us. That annoyed Ray even more than the holidays, seeing them waste their money on shit he didn't want. Just give me the cash, he used to say.' Her eyes glazed over, her smile dying. 'But they never did. And now they're dead.'

'It must be hard.'

'The hardest thing is that the signs were all there and Mum and Dad missed them. Ray was nine when he first started asking for cash instead of presents at Christmas. Nine! And every year Mum and Dad would laugh and hand him some cheesy gift from Spain or Mexico, a bullfighter's cape or a three-cornered hat or something. Then he'd have one of his tantrums.' She stared off into the distance. 'He seethed over what he couldn't have – a motorbike when he was sixteen, a car when he was eighteen. If only they'd seen what he was like.'

'It's easy with hindsight,' said Brook. 'How did Ray treat you?'

'Normal. Like a brother treats a sister,' she said. 'But then I didn't control the money.'

'And yet he tried to have you killed.'

'It wasn't personal. I was an obstacle, nothing more.'

'How much money are we talking about?' asked Brook.

At first she bridled at his bluntness, but a moment later saw no reason to withhold an answer. 'I'm not sure exactly. Even now.' She flicked away the ash of her cigarette with a shaky hand and watched it fall through the air to the patio below. 'The funny thing is, Ray was completely hopeless with money. He could never keep it, didn't know how to handle it. When we were kids, his pocket money was gone the same day, I don't know what on, then he'd ask for more. Every Friday he'd turn on the waterworks because he'd spent his allowance on God knows what.

'After he left home, the problem became more acute because he couldn't or wouldn't get a job and had crazy dreams of being a successful entrepreneur. Of course he wasn't, so he was always on the phone, hitting Dad up to support this or that dodgy scheme. Guess he thought after all the crappy holidays and crappy presents, he was owed.'

'Did he get support?'

'Not as often as he wanted.' She shrugged. 'My parents believed in tough love. They were right. You can't succeed in life with Ray's mindset. Everything he did turned to shit, and when his business ventures went down the toilet, it was just too easy to ask for a handout.'

Brook nodded. 'So if he's not in Spain, where do you think he is?'

She looked him in the eye now. 'He's here in Nottingham.'

Brook was taken aback. 'What makes you say that?'

She hesitated. 'I think I'm being watched.'

'Think?'

Reardon seemed about to confide in Brook but instead shook her head. 'You think I'm paranoid.'

'I don't know, but why would anyone be watching you?'

'Not anyone. Ray.'

'Same question.'

'Because I survived, and his life and all his plans are screwed. He wants payback for that.' Her lips sealed tight against an imagined fate, until she licked them again with a lizard dart of her tongue.

'That makes no sense. Even assuming he knows where you are, he can't inherit.'

'Maybe that's not why he wants to kill me,' said Reardon.

'What other reason could there be?'

'Ray's a fuck-up, Inspector. He could never finish anything. Maybe, just once in his life, he wants to do something properly.'

'If he wanted to do something properly, he should never have put your fate in the hands of Jonathan Jemson and Luke Coulson.'

Reardon flinched at the sound of their names. 'Ray won't see it like that. Nothing's ever his fault.'

'So he's come back just to kill you.'

'If he ever left,' replied Reardon. 'Rachel – DS Caskey, that is – said they had no record of him leaving the country.'

'They found his car at the airport.'

'But if he got on a plane, why was there no sign of him?' she demanded, stubbing out the cigarette in the soil of a nearby herb planter that already contained dozens of spent butts.

Brook could only shrug. He'd had the same misgivings. 'So you shut yourself away in this gilded fortress.' He took a moment to admire the view.

Reardon lit another cigarette and followed Brook's gaze. 'It's not like I'm a prisoner.'

'Really?' Brook ran a gimlet eye over her shapeless clothing while her focus was on the distant horizon. 'How often do you go out?'

'This is out,' she said, gesturing at the horizon.

'I mean out of the front door and into the city, for a drink or to see a film.'

Reardon hesitated. 'I climb down to the patio when it's dark sometimes but I don't stay long. I feel safer at night, hiding in the shadows. No chance of being snapped by journalists and paraded on the front page of some local rag – Tragic Survivor of the Findern Massacre.' She laughed without mirth.

'Then effectively you're a prisoner.'

'Maybe. I have the internet to wander around in. And Netflix.'

'Are you sure that's a life worth protecting?'

'I beg your pardon.'

'I'm sorry, I shouldn't have said that,' said Brook. 'But if past traumas stop you living your life properly, then you might as well be dead. Locking yourself away like this, chain-smoking, seeing nobody. Surviving isn't the same as living, and I speak from experience.'

'Do you?' she said. She stared at him, her face a mixture of anger and astonishment. 'I must say, you're very free with your opinions.'

'I admit I am,' conceded Brook. 'But then I've seen too many victims of violent crime. It comes with the job. Doesn't your friend try to coax you out?'

Reardon narrowed her eyes. 'My friend?'

'I'm not your first visitor today,' said Brook.

She stared. 'Have you been watching the house?'

Brook gestured at the makeshift ashtray, rows of crushed cigarettes mocking their once-pristine appearance in the pack. 'Some of those butts have lipstick on. And you're not wearing any.'

She stared down at the herb planter then thoughtfully back at Brook. 'I could've been wearing lippy last night.'

Brook splashed his shoe in a small puddle of rainwater on the platform's metal floor. 'It rained last night. Most of these cigarette ends are soggy apart from a dozen fresh butts that are dry. And I can see at least three with lipstick on. That suggests a lengthy conversation.'

After a moment's silence, Reardon broke into a bashful smile. 'You're good.' Brook waited for his answer. 'My dog walker. She takes Sargent out every day.'

'Sargent?' said Brook, surprised. 'Your dog.'

'That's right.'

'You've still got him.'

'Of course I have. He's the only good thing left from my previous life. What? You think I should give him away so he doesn't remind me of that day?'

'A lot of people would.'

'Getting rid of a dog I love isn't going to make me forget

what happened, Inspector. Sargent was a victim too. And victims stick together. The bastards drugged him before they came into the house. He could've died. Thankfully . . .' She paused, bit her lip, her eyes moistening. 'Sorry, that sounds terrible when my parents . . .'

'You endured a horrific experience.' He studied her, recalling Terri's ongoing struggles. 'Have you thought about therapy?'

'I've thought about everything,' said Reardon. She turned her head towards the view. 'Even throwing myself down there.'

Brook shook his head. 'No, you haven't.'

'Excuse me?'

'The girl I saw facing down a knife-wielding killer wouldn't throw her life away so easily. I've watched the film, Reardon. You were at the front door, free and clear. With Jemson dead and Coulson roaming the house, you could've run. Instead you risked everything to find your parents.'

Her lip wobbled. 'I had to know . . .'

'Of course you did,' said Brook. 'But there was still a cold-blooded killer in the house. Don't underestimate the courage it took to do that.'

Reardon smiled at him. 'Thank you. That's a nice thing to say. And you're right, I didn't come through all that just to throw myself off the fire escape.' She grinned. 'It might hurt.' Her mirth subsided quickly. 'I shouldn't joke about suicide, but that doesn't mean I don't feel terrible guilt about surviving when my parents died.'

'A natural response.'

She cocked her head at him. 'For a policeman, you haven't asked many questions. About that day, I mean. I've talked more about it than you've asked.'

'I didn't come here to make you relive it,' said Brook. 'I've seen the photos and the film, read the reports.'

Reardon licked her lips. 'Then why are you here?'

'One question is bothering me.'

Her brow furrowed. 'Go on.'

'Ray wasn't at the farm that afternoon, right?'

'I honestly don't know,' said Reardon. 'I only know I didn't see him.'

'He was there the night before, though.'

'Yes, he came over late that evening and stayed the night.'

'But his car was gone in the morning.'

'I assumed he took off early.'

'I see.'

'What is it?'

'If Ray wasn't there, how did he know things weren't going to plan and that he should make a run for it?'

'DS Caskey wondered the same thing,' frowned Reardon.

'And what did she conclude?'

'She thought maybe he *was* there, watching. Either that or Luke phoned him somehow. Told him the deal was off.'

'What do you think?'

'I don't know.'

Brook could see the rising panic in her eyes. He was tempted to ask her what else Caskey had concluded, but decided against it. He didn't want to upset her or tip his weak hand. 'From all I've seen and read, I don't think there was a deal between Luke and Ray. Jemson and Ray I can accept. But Coulson was lined up as the fall guy. He wasn't supposed to survive the attack. And if Luke didn't phone Ray, and Jemson was already dead, how did Ray know things were turning sour?'

'I don't know,' she said quietly. 'To be honest, I've tried not to think about it. After Mum and Dad died, I kind of shut myself down until the trial. When it finally came to court, Luke didn't even testify. He just sat there day after day with a strange smile on his face, staring at me. Truthfully, I'm still not sure what happened that day. Maybe I'll never know. The fall guy, you say.'

'Made to measure,' said Brook. 'The lone weirdo, low intelligence and obsessed by an unattainable beauty.'

She blushed. 'He'd be cured if he could see me now.'

'You'll get better,' offered Brook, with no great certainty. She smiled hesitantly. 'If this is too painful . . .'

'Ask your questions.'

'Well, according to phone records, around the time of the attack there were no texts or calls logged on any of the mobile phones carried by any persons at the farm that day,' said Brook. 'And the landline was down.'

'What of it?'

'Ray's official phone, a Samsung, was never found. We know the number of a second, pre-paid phone because of texts sent from a phone belonging to Jemson, hidden in his flat. Jemson didn't have it at the farm and it hadn't been used that day. His regular phone was in his jeans, but that also hadn't been used since that morning, when he'd arranged to meet up with Coulson and travel to the farm.'

'I remember,' nodded Reardon. 'If I'd known JJ had it on him, I could've called the police on it.'

'So my question stands. How did Ray know to run?'

Reardon pondered this. 'Couldn't JJ have warned him some other way?'

'I don't see how. They communicated exclusively by text, and that day there was no record of any activity on either of their mobiles. Besides, things were going to plan up to the moment Jemson was attacked.'

'I see what you mean,' she replied, blanching slightly at the memory.

'The only other mobiles were yours and your mother's.'

'Mine was smashed . . .'

'. . . and your mother's couldn't be used because the battery was flat.'

'Right,' said Reardon, shaking her head. 'Mum's phone was ancient and she always forgot to charge it. What about Luke?'

'He had his mobile on him when he was arrested on the M25, but apart from the texts exchanged with Jemson that morning, it hadn't been used. Also, his history showed no contact with Ray and no mention of the attack in his texts from Jemson.'

'So how did Luke know what was going to happen that day?'

'It's entirely possible that he didn't. Jemson had been texting Luke for over a month before the attack but never mentioned you or the farm in any message. I suspect if he wanted to plant the seed about his plans, he would've done it verbally. He and Ray wouldn't want any record of links to Luke apart from a few innocent messages from Jemson suggesting a drink with an old friend.'

'Strange.'

'Not really. They were using him. They had to make it appear that Luke was the creepy loner, following through on his long-held obsession with you. The one he told you about before you escaped.'

'And I thought that was just a teenage crush.'

'Oh, it was much more than that, as Jemson would have known. Ray too. And if you and Coulson had died at the scene, it would have been a simple narrative to construct, especially with Jemson a witness to Luke's infatuation with you.'

'He could have said anything,' agreed Reardon.

'And would have.'

'And Ray's official phone?' said Reardon. 'The Samsung. Even if he destroyed it . . .'

'We checked,' said Brook. 'He stopped using it a week before the attack and presumably dumped it when he ran.'

Reardon shivered in a sudden breeze that whipped up over the treetops. If it were possible, her colour seemed to drain further. 'It's hard to believe your own brother and an ex-boyfriend could cook up something so cold and painstaking.'

'Not painstaking enough,' said Brook. Reardon's lip began to wobble again and she put a hand up to dry a tear. 'Are you okay?'

'There was a time when JJ . . . we . . .' She waved a hand across her face, seeking control.

'Was it serious?'

'We thought it was,' she said, composing herself with a large expulsion of air. 'We were just kids, of course, but we felt our love was like no other, that it would last for ever.' She shook her head. 'Thinking of him now makes me want to throw up. Ray too. I remember a few things they said from the trial. So brutal.' She blew out her cheeks again, her face red, but this time there was no stopping the tears and she started to sob.

Brook stepped in to squeeze her arm. He wasn't good at this sort of thing. He had more questions but they would have to wait.

The piercing mid-morning sun had disappeared and a chilly breeze was stirring.

'You're freezing,' said Brook. 'Come inside.' He pulled Reardon back into the warm apartment and guided her towards the kitchen. 'Let's get you a hot drink,' he said, flicking on the kettle. After rummaging around, he made her a cup of Earl Grey with two spoonfuls of sugar and manoeuvred it between her icy hands.

From behind a tree in the park below the house, a pair of eyes watched through binoculars as Reardon Thorogood levered herself up from the fire escape rail to follow Brook into the apartment. As the pair retreated from view, the fire escape door closed and the binoculars were lowered.

On the first-floor landing on his way out, Brook glanced at the adjoining door and turned to Reardon. 'You have a neighbour?'

'It's empty,' said Reardon, gripping the door frame, desperate to return to her sarcophagus.

'You say you own the whole building?' She nodded. 'The lawyers sorted out the estate then.'

'Yes and no,' answered Reardon. 'I have access to funds but a lot of Mum and Dad's money could be tied up for years.'

'Because Ray is missing and not dead.'

'Right. It's complicated. The lawyer has to apply for some kind of order so he can distribute funds in Ray's absence.'

'A Benjamin Order?'

'A Benjamin Order,' she repeated. 'I don't understand the ins and outs.'

'It indemnifies your legal people, allowing them to divide the estate between surviving family, even if one of the heirs is not officially dead.'

She shrugged and Brook could see she was wishing him gone.

'Changing the subject, apparently you were at Manchester University with my daughter,' said Brook, watching her face for a reaction. 'Terri.'

Reardon narrowed her eyes to concentrate. 'Terri Brook?' she said, shaking her head.

'She'd be using Harvey-Ellis as her surname.'

Reardon's face lit up in recognition. 'Yes. I know Terri. American literature, right? How is she?'

Despite the simplicity of the question, Brook was always unprepared for it and had to think for a second. 'She's fine,' he lied, eschewing the response that first entered his head. *As damaged as you.*

'Give her my best,' smiled Reardon. Brook nodded and turned to the stairwell. 'Inspector!' He turned. 'I'll think about what you said. About living my life. Really I will.'

He smiled back and set off down the stairs.

Out in the rapidly cooling afternoon, Brook unlocked the car and glanced up at the first-floor window. Reardon Thorogood peered down at him like a ghost in a haunted house – statuesque, other-worldly. Her pale, expressionless features reminded him of Terri four or five years ago, when the memory of her abuser was at its keenest. Dealing with the traumas she'd suffered had left Terri confused, her emotions in tatters, and the only course for a while had been to withdraw behind the drawbridge of a blank face. That was Reardon's face now.

Seventeen

THREE HOURS LATER, BROOK WAS ushered into an office that appeared to have been modelled on the set of *Dial M for Murder* – plush leather seats, a solid oak desk in front of large sash windows. Floor-to-ceiling bookshelves along one wall contained multiple volumes on criminology. The spaciousness and decor were at odds with the functional prison building through which Brook had just been escorted by a monosyllabic prison officer.

Dr Trevor Marshall, a middle-aged man with a monk's tonsure, sat behind the desk, radiating a vague air of academia. His bald dome was freckled and shiny, his ear-high fringe grey and cut tight to the skull, yet his dark suit was dotted with specks of dandruff across the padded shoulders.

Marshall stood, his hand extended across the desk, and Brook returned a firm handshake, knowing how much significance some attributed to such things.

'Welcome to Monster Mansion,' said Marshall with a dry smirk. Brook raised an eyebrow. 'Oh, we're under no illusions about what we do here at Wakefield Prison, Inspector Brook. It's a supermax facility for a reason, and we house the baddest of the bad so that people can sleep soundly in their beds.'

He narrowed his eyes as though reminding himself of some ephemera he'd once known well. 'Brook,' he muttered cryptically. He gestured to a chair and sat down behind his desk, flicking open a manila folder and checking its contents against a flat monitor blinking at him. 'This is rather short notice, Inspector.'

'I'm sorry about that,' replied Brook, sitting. 'A recent development.'

Marshall nodded, waiting in vain for Brook to elaborate. 'You're the chap who sends vintage port to one of our guests every Christmas.'

'Edward Mullen,' confirmed Brook, reaching out with his left hand to place a half-bottle of port on the desk and steeling himself for the derision to come. 'Thought I'd save myself the postage this year.'

Marshall's grin was laced with a hint of scorn. 'My catering people *love* the problems that causes, not to mention the precedent.'

'Somehow I don't see Mullen getting drunk and giving the game away.'

Marshall conceded with a lift of his eyes. 'Tell me, how on earth does a child killer get a deal like that?'

'It was the coldest case on our books,' replied Brook. 'The victim's families wanted closure, I made concessions to get it.'

'But jumping through a hoop like that . . .'

'We didn't think a few sips of Christmas port from a plastic cup too high a price to put away an active serial killer.'

Marshall's smile was icy. 'It amazes me how everyone's an expert on what prisons can and can't handle when managing dangerous criminals.'

'Try managing them without a locked door between you,'

retorted Brook. Marshall's eyes glazed and Brook reproached himself. Ruffling the feathers of a prison governor was not going to get him in to see Coulson. His face creased into a smile. 'But you're right, Doctor. Even in my job, it's impossible to appreciate the unique problems you must face in a facility like Wakefield – until you actually visit one, that is.' He looked around theatrically. 'I'm impressed.'

Marshall returned his gaze to the monitor, apparently mollified. 'Thank you. Usually nobody pays us any mind until we screw up, and then the public and politicians are all over us like a rash. What do they expect?'

'Miracles on a shoestring budget,' nodded Brook sympathetically.

'Exactly!' said Marshall, warming to his theme. 'Though there's only so much we can achieve on the resources they provide.'

'Whatever you do, I'm sure it's never good enough for the Home Office,' continued Brook, shaking his head, trying not to overdo the smarm.

'No.' Marshall clicked at his mouse. 'Luke Coulson, Luke Coulson.' His eyes flicked from side to side. 'By all accounts not one of our scariest monsters – or the brightest spark.' He read from the screen, ' "Subject is quiet, well-behaved, respectful to staff but easily led by other inmates. Responds negatively to aggression and becomes tearful when verbally bullied. Clearly vulnerable. Recommend restricted circulation." Not one of life's alpha males,' he concluded, with a grin to imply his own membership. 'And in here that puts him at risk from those happy to manipulate and intimidate. Of whom we have an abundance.'

'Anyone in particular getting into his head?'

'We have our suspicions,' said Marshall.

'Mullen?'

'No,' said Marshall emphatically. 'Not his style, for one thing. They're both on the isolation block and we don't allow Mullen near other inmates. This may be where monsters live, but there are still those who think they're superior to the child killers.'

'But Coulson's not a child killer. Has something happened?'

'He got badly cut on the face when he first arrived but wouldn't say who did it. As he had no privileges earned, I had nothing with which to threaten him, so we isolated him for a while.'

'Doesn't a reluctance to point the finger earn respect from other inmates?'

'Not as often as you'd hope,' replied Marshall. 'Certainly not in Coulson's case, and certainly not here. Frankly, Coulson's a bit dim and hasn't adapted. He has no idea how to behave or carry himself, which makes him a sitting duck, and we moved him out of general pop for his own safety. Inmates here have their own cells anyway, so it wasn't a huge upheaval.'

Again Brook glanced at the criminology texts in the bookcase. He spotted *The Criminal Mind*, by Dr Trevor Marshall, prominently displayed. It was well-thumbed. Nearby, to his surprise, he noticed Brian Burton's book *In Search of the Reaper* – a badly written, badly researched hatchet job of Brook's efforts to catch the serial killer operating in London in the early nineties, and many years later in Derby, after Brook's move north. 'Then maybe he did know how to carry himself.'

Marshall gazed at Brook as though trying to figure him out. 'That's an intelligent observation, Inspector.'

Brook smiled. 'Should I be writing a book?'

Marshall couldn't prevent an appreciative laugh. He returned his gaze to the screen, then back to Brook. 'Black Oak Farm. Triple homicide. Correct me if I'm wrong, but wasn't that Frank Ford's case?'

Brook's heart sank. 'You know Frank?'

'We go back a way. I did a ten stretch at Sudbury.' Marshall's lips twitched with satisfaction at his pun. 'How is the old devil?'

'Frank's fine,' smiled Brook, his eyes unable to join in.

'Any reason why *he's* not here to reinterview?'

'He retired last week.'

'I had no idea,' said Marshall, surprised. 'He's in good health?'

'Fit as a fiddle. Just had enough of red tape and unsocial hours.'

'Copy that,' nodded Marshall, depressing an intercom button. 'I must ring and wish him well.' Brook maintained his beaming smile, but it was beginning to hurt. 'Coulson hasn't said anything but yes-sir-no-sir since he arrived. What makes you think he'll talk to you?'

'He likely won't, but with a new lead, I have to try.'

The same prison officer who'd escorted Brook to the governor's office entered with a carrier bag. He handed a note to Marshall, then showed him the contents of the bag.

'Makes a change from cigarettes,' observed Marshall, nodding at the prison officer.

Coulson shuffled over to the table, eyes cast down, baggy sweatshirt billowing, low-slung jeans hindering his movements. Brook noticed a recent vivid scar running the length of his left cheek.

The prison officer stepped ahead of him and pulled out a plastic bucket chair. After a brief glance at Brook, Coulson slumped down opposite him and resumed his examination of the floor.

Brook introduced himself and asked permission to record their conversation – *help me with my notes* – but received no reaction. Not even a meeting of eyes.

'I'd like to ask you some questions about Black Oak Farm and the deaths of Mr and Mrs Thorogood.' Deliberately refusing to apportion responsibility, he paused to see if Coulson reacted. Nothing. 'And your friend Jonathan Jemson.' No movement, no eye contact. 'Jonathan *was* your friend, wasn't he?' Still nothing. Brook wasn't discouraged. He knew how to play this game, how to keep chipping away until he hit the mother lode of self-justification buried deep inside every criminal. Patience was the key.

'Ray Thorogood was your friend too. The three of you were at school together.'

Coulson dug his hands further into his jeans pockets and glared sulkily down at the tabletop.

Brook decided it was time to play a high-value card. 'Four, if you include Reardon.' He noticed a brief flicker of eyelash and followed up. 'I saw her this morning.'

Coulson's head lifted momentarily, but a second later he resumed his stare. Too late – Brook had seen the ripple of emotion coursing across his features. The affectation of nonchalance was a facade. Brook had found his pressure point.

'It's fine, Luke,' he continued. 'You don't need to tell me how much you like Reardon. You're the man that saved her from JJ and her brother. They were going to kill her. She appreciates that and she's grateful for what you did.'

This time a glare from Coulson, his face hot and bothered. Now it was Brook's turn to let Coulson stew for a few minutes, part of the push and pull of working his man, keeping him off balance.

'She told me as much . . .' he checked his watch, 'four hours ago.'

Coulson resumed his sulky stare but threw in a couple of malevolent glances.

'I've been reading your school reports, Luke. Do you know what I discovered?' he asked, not expecting an answer. 'I discovered that other pupils thought it was funny to bully you. They bullied you at primary school, they bullied you at secondary school. I don't like bullies, Luke. I never have. It happened to me when I was at school. I was an only child, like you, and it used to bother me until I worked out that all they wanted was a reaction. After that, I stopped reacting even when they badmouthed my parents. I never talked to them, never sought their friendship. Nothing. I wouldn't give them the satisfaction. They loved to see me get angry and aggressive, but I soon realised that when that happened they laughed and taunted me all the more. That's what they enjoyed. That's when they won. So I ignored them until they got bored and moved on to someone else.'

He sat back, eyed Coulson. 'We have that in common, Luke. That's how you handle bullies too, isn't it? Never react. Treat them like they don't exist, pretend you can't hear the hurtful things they're saying. Make them feel that talking to you is a waste of their time. And, most importantly, don't ever tell on them, because if you do, they'll know they've hurt you.

'But you didn't tell, Luke. Even when someone cut you recently. I admire that. At school, people said hurtful things to you. About your mum. About the way you speak.' Brook moved his hands in a dismissive gesture. 'No reaction. Even when someone spat in your face, you ignored it. You could've hit out. You could've told. But you didn't. You wouldn't let them win.'

Luke's thousand-yard stare became less of a defence mechanism and more of a conduit back to the past. His expression was no longer blank as his mind's eye replayed real events, and Brook could see the consequences manifested on his face. Events that had damaged him, pushed him deeper inside himself so no one could see the hurt. Brook watched him for several minutes until he was convinced his past had finished cascading through his consciousness and he'd returned to the present.

'Did DI Ford bully you, Luke?' he said. 'Did he threaten you when you wouldn't speak? If he did, I'm sorry. If it helps, you won't be seeing DI Ford again. Ever. I've taken over the case.'

'Is he dead?' said Coulson softly, his voice hoarse and rasping with a slight inability to fully sound out the consonants. A mixture of surprise and respect invaded the watching prison officer's face. Brook barely registered it as he considered his response, not wanting to rush Coulson, not wanting to say the wrong thing. 'Retired.'

Coulson nodded, though his expression betrayed a search for meaning. 'He was old.'

Brook gestured to the prison officer standing, hands behind his back, at the wall. He marched forward revealing the carrier bag and deposited it on the table. Brook extracted a soft drink and placed it in front of Coulson. Then he tipped out the rest of the contents – three packs of fun-size Mars bars. Coulson's eyes gorged on the sugary treats.

Brook pushed a bag of chocolate towards him. 'Go ahead.' Coulson hesitated, but after a few seconds he opened the can and took a deep swig of the sugary drink, then tore into the pack of chocolate bars. He ripped the wrapper from one Mars bar after another, gobbling down five with barely a pause for breath.

Panting, he took another swallow from the can before sitting back, satisfied. A loud belch followed and he smiled guiltily before considering Brook. 'I like Mars bars.'

'I know,' smiled Brook. 'You had Dr Pepper and Mars bars on the passenger seat when they arrested you.'

Coulson stared at him. 'Clever.'

'Not really.'

'And now you think I'm gonna start telling you stuff just 'cos you brung me chocolate.' He peered at Brook. 'Stuff about what me and JJ done.'

Brook shrugged. 'That's up to you.'

'Wasting your time. I'm a killer. I'm where I belong.' He folded his arms – a classic mental and physical barrier. Defensive. Protective. 'Why'd you even bother?'

Brook considered the answer to a question he'd thought about on the drive up to Yorkshire, preparing the response he'd need when Chief Superintendent Charlton eventually found out about his visit and posed it himself.

'Ray Thorogood is still at large,' he said. 'For Reardon's sake, we'd like to find him.'

'What's Ray got to do with it?'

'The attack was Ray's idea,' said Brook. 'His and JJ's.'

Coulson glared at Brook. 'I was at the trial. I ain't deaf.'

'Then you know they planned to use you, Luke.'

He shrugged. 'Seems like it. Don't change what I done.'

'And you don't mind if Ray gets away with it?'

'Looks like he already has.'

'Reardon will be disappointed,' said Brook. 'She's scared stiff. She's hoping we can find Ray so she can start living her life again.'

Coulson was brooding now, his voice clipped. 'You won't find him.'

'What makes you say that?'

Coulson thought about his next answer, then seemed pleased with his choice. 'Because he's too smart for you.'

'Not that smart,' answered Brook. 'His plan failed. Reardon was supposed to die, Luke. And if things had gone to plan, so were you. Jemson was preparing to kill you and make it look like Reardon did it in self-defence. He was just waiting until your DNA was all over Reardon.' He paused for effect. 'Or better yet, inside her.'

Coulson stood in a rage, shooting his chair behind him. 'Don't be disgusting.'

'Sit down,' ordered the prison officer, at Coulson's shoulder with the chair in a trice, his hands lightly pressing him down on to it. Coulson stood for a second longer, his eyes burning malevolently into Brook's, before he finally sat down, his face glowering.

'You're dirty, you,' he said, panting, the worst of his sudden rush of anger subsiding. 'I wouldn't never do that with Reardon 'less she wanted me to and we was married. You're just dirty.'

'Not me,' said Brook, holding up his hands. 'Ray and JJ. *Their* plan. And with you and Reardon dead, Ray inherits his parents' estate and Jemson gets paid handsomely for his troubles. If that had happened, we'd be none the wiser and the case would've been closed. To the police it would look like victims *and* killer were dead – end of story. But that didn't happen, Luke. The plan failed because of you.' No reaction. Brook pressed on. 'Ray and JJ underestimated your feelings for Reardon. That's why he wasn't smart.'

'Well if he's so dumb, how come you ain't found him?' leered Coulson.

'I didn't say he was dumb,' said Brook. 'Just that he under-estimated you. You spoiled everything, Luke. You saved Reardon's life.'

Coulson couldn't completely suppress his grin at such praise. 'I did, didn't I?' He paused, hesitant, framing a question. 'How . . . how is she?'

'Scared.'

'She weren't scared at the farm.'

'Oh, she was scared all right, but she managed to hide it. People can do that in a life-or-death situation.'

'She was very brave,' Coulson agreed, nodding. 'Considering.'

'If we can find Ray, she can stop being scared. Do you know where he is?'

'Have you tried his house?' said Coulson, with a little smirk.

Brook smiled, studying him, before shaking his head theatrically. 'No, I didn't think you'd know. JJ's not likely to have confided in you, and Ray certainly didn't.'

'There you are then,' said Coulson, sulky again.

'Pity. Reardon was depending on you.'

'Is that what she said?'

Brook nodded. 'She needs your help, Luke. You don't have to, but if you answer my questions, it might help her.'

'I don't like questions. Teachers made me answer them and people laughed.'

'Then listen instead.' Brook waited for an objection that didn't arrive. 'Your mobile phone records show texts and conversations with JJ leading up to that day, but there's no mention of the attack.' Coulson shrugged. 'What about Ray? Did you see or speak to him in person before you went to the farm?'

Coulson said nothing for several minutes and Brook had almost given up on an answer.

'No,' he replied eventually.

'What about on the day?' asked Brook softly. 'Did you see him at the farm?' Coulson shook his head. 'When *was* the last time you saw Ray?'

'The day we left school. I ain't seen him or spoken to him since that day.'

'That was seven years ago.'

'If you say so.'

'And you never spoke on the phone?'

'Nope.'

'So all the planning that went into that day at the farm, you had no part in it?'

'Nope.'

'Did JJ mention Ray to you at all?'

Coulson considered for longer than seemed necessary, then nodded and helped himself to another Mars bar. 'At the farm, JJ told me Ray was in charge. But I never spoke to Ray and I never saw him.'

'When did JJ mention Ray?'

'I asked where he got the map of the house. He said Ray give him it.'

'But you didn't see Ray?' Another head shake. 'Why do you think that was?'

'Guess he din't want to get his hands dirty.'

'And Reardon?'

Coulson's expression darkened. 'What about her?'

'When was the last time you saw her before that day at the farm?'

'Same as Ray.' Coulson broke off eye contact, and when Brook moved his head to re-establish it, Coulson shifted his position. *He's lying.* 'So you hadn't seen Reardon since the day you left school?' Coulson shook his head, eyes lowered. 'That's a long time, Luke. No wonder Ray underestimated your feelings for her.'

'Feelings?'

'You've got feelings for her, Luke. Anyone can see that. You let her live and that cost you your freedom. You had a better chance of escape with her dead.' Coulson said nothing. 'But you couldn't harm her because you liked her.' Coulson nodded. 'You've liked her since the day you first saw her.' He went bright red. 'That's a long time, Luke. Were you friends at school?'

'Nope.'

'So not like with Ray and JJ.'

'They were boys,' said Coulson softly.

'So boys spoke to you, girls didn't.'

'Girls din't like me.'

'I see,' said Brook. 'How often did you see JJ after you left school?'

'On and off.'

'And how long since you'd seen him to the time he texted you a month before the attack?'

Coulson stared at the ceiling, trying to make the calculation. 'Couple of years. Maybe three.'

'So out of all three of them, you've only seen JJ since you left school.'

'Yep.'

'You're lying,' said Brook, trying to stir things up. Coulson met his eyes briefly. 'Not about JJ and Ray. Course you've seen JJ. He was like you – had trouble holding down a job, no qualifications, from a poor family. You moved in the same circles. But Ray and Reardon's family were rich. They moved in *different* circles. I'd be surprised if either of them even knew you existed once you left school. Especially Reardon.'

'You're wrong,' protested Coulson, a note of petulance in his voice. 'She remembered me. She said.'

'What else was she going to say?' demanded Brook. 'She wanted to live. She barely knew who you were. She had to act like she remembered you but that was all it was – an act.'

'She knew my name,' snarled Coulson.

'JJ must've said it just before you killed him.'

'No, she . . .' Coulson was panic-stricken for a second, trying to remember, before finding a malicious grin. 'You just said I was lying,' he said triumphantly. 'How am I lying then if you say she din't know me?'

'I didn't say Reardon had seen *you*,' said Brook, his eyes boring into Coulson. 'But you've seen her. You've watched her, admired her from a distance and for a number of years, I'd guess.' Coulson went white. 'We had a lip reader look at your conversation with Reardon in the hall. I have the transcript here.' He picked up a sheet of paper and read, '"But your dad shouldn't have shouted. He shouldn't have chased me." That's nothing to do with the day of the attack, is it?' No answer, no eye contact. 'Reardon's father saw you watching her one time, didn't he?' No answer. 'He chased you, shouted at you. Where were you? Hiding in a field, or behind a tree? Were you watching her undress?' Coulson's eyes darted from side to side.

'No, it wasn't like that, was it? You weren't interested in her body. You loved her for who she was and what she represented. She was distant and beautiful and you watched her from afar. You wouldn't dare start a conversation with a girl like Reardon. You'd be too scared of rejection.' Brook chuckled. 'And Reardon wouldn't be seen dead talking to someone like you, and would probably have told you so to your face.'

'JJ was like me,' said Coulson, defiantly. 'She went out with *him*, din't she?'

'JJ was handsome and popular. But even he didn't last and he resented it. What sort of resentment did you carry all those years before you visited the farm, Luke?' Coulson drained the Dr Pepper so he wouldn't have to answer. 'Was she mean to you at school?'

'Not so much.'

'So she was.'

'Not as much as other girls.'

'No,' considered Brook. 'Because she'd be dismissive, looking at you like you didn't even exist.'

Coulson shook his head. 'I got it wrong. We sorted it out at the farm.'

'So you're friends now?'

Coulson smiled. 'We sorted it out.'

Brook allowed himself a little chuckle. 'I saw the film, Luke. You sorted out nothing. Reardon was scared of you.'

Coulson breathed heavily through his nose and blinked a couple of times – a nervous tic. 'At first maybe. 'Cos I had a knife. But we sorted it out, I'm telling you.'

'So you forgave her for being mean.'

'I forgave her for being mean,' said Coulson haughtily, as though the phrase was his.

'And that's why you let her live.'

'What else was I going to do?' pleaded Coulson. 'I couldn't kill her. I love her. She's beautiful. Every time I seen her . . .' He stopped dead, his face a mass of suppressed emotion.

'I understand,' said Brook. 'Watching her all this time, maybe even close up, when you wouldn't need the binoculars.' Coulson's head shot up, his eyes widened. 'They were found in your bedroom after you were arrested.' Brook sat back to let things settle. 'No photographs?'

'Couldn't never afford one of them posh cameras,' he said sullenly. 'Didn't need one, mind.' He tapped his forehead and smiled. 'It's all up here. Including when we kissed at the farm.'

Brook didn't point out the element of coercion in Coulson's only embrace with Reardon. 'So when JJ mentioned going to the farm, you were pleased.' A nod. 'And loving her as you do meant you couldn't rape and kill her?'

'Not married,' he mumbled. The prison officer grinned behind Coulson's back, but Brook admonished him with a glare.

'None of that prevented you from tying her up. You could've done that. Then you might have reached Dover and caught the ferry.'

'I couldn't hurt her no more after what JJ done. Did you see what he did to her face? That weren't right.' Coulson lowered his head. 'I should never have listened to him. That's what got me in here. My fault for listening.'

'Why did you go?'

'JJ said he just wanted to talk to her and did I want to come.

I never seen her since school. Not real close up. He knew I liked her. I told him so. That's why he asked me.'

'And when did you realise something was wrong?'

'When he gave that meat to Sargent . . .'

'Sargent?'

'Reardon's dog.'

'I know it's her dog. How did you know its name?'

'I heard her calling it one time.'

'One time when you were watching her.' Coulson nodded. 'Did Reardon ever see you watching?'

'No. I was real careful.'

'But her father saw you.'

'Just that one time.'

'Reardon didn't mention anything in her statement about stalking.'

Coulson shrugged. 'Her father didn't want to worry her maybe.'

Brook nodded. 'Did you ask JJ what he was doing when he drugged the dog?'

'Course. He said we was just gonna take a few quid and some rings and stuff and the dog might bark.'

'Did you believe him?' Coulson shook his head. 'But you were only in the grounds. It wasn't too late to turn back.'

Coulson hesitated. 'I wanted to see Reardon.'

'To protect her from JJ.'

'No, I didn't know JJ was gonna be dirty,' said Coulson, his face reddening again.

'You must have had some idea when he sent you away to look around the house. You must have suspected.'

'I never.'

'You must.'

'I din't know, I tell you,' said Coulson, his breath shortening. 'Not until I walked in on him.'

'You mean when JJ had his trousers round his ankles and Reardon was naked, her face bloody and bruised.' Coulson nodded. 'What did you do?'

'I told him to stop, but he never. He just laughed and told me it was my go.'

'But you refused.'

'Yes.'

'And?'

'JJ started laughing, taking the piss, and then he started hurting Reardon some more and I din't like that.'

'The knife was in your hand.'

'Yes.'

'And you stabbed him.'

'I din't wanna. But he wouldn't stop, so I cut him.' Coulson gulped on the memory. A tear made its way down his ruddy cheek. 'He was hurting her so I cut him and he stopped. And then he was dead.' He looked down at his clothes as though he was Lady Macbeth. 'I was covered in blood and I knew I'd been bad. Then I went to a bedroom to look for clothes.'

'You didn't stay to help Reardon.'

'She was crying,' said Coulson, blowing out a huge breath. 'And she was . . .' He hesitated, panic-stricken, his eyes wild.

'Naked?' Coulson's head dipped to acknowledge his embarrassment. 'What about Mr and Mrs Thorogood?'

'What about 'em?'

'Did JJ tell you to kill them?'

He took a breath and set his jaw. 'I knew what I had to do.'

'You killed them.'

'Like I said.'

'But that's just it, Luke – you didn't say. Not a word. You never said *I killed them*. I read the custody interviews, the trial transcript. Not once did you say it.'

''Cos it was obvious.' He shrugged.

'Then why not say so?'

Coulson sighed. 'My brief reckoned I better not testify, so I never. He reckoned they might think I was a hero or something for saving Reardon.'

'*They*, meaning the jury.'

'S'right.'

'Well the jury's not here now and neither is your brief. So tell me.'

'Tell you what?'

'Tell me you killed them. Say the words.'

'They're dead. What does it matter?'

'It matters to me.'

Coulson stared back. 'I killed them. Happy now?'

'Delirious,' fired back Brook. 'Who did you kill first – Mr Thorogood or his wife?'

'I don't remember.'

'Really? Mr Thorogood was attacked first. You attacked him from behind. How did you manage to surprise him?'

'I rushed him. He never knew what hit him.'

'I thought you said you don't remember.'

'I remember that.'

'Enough to convince DI Ford, maybe,' said Brook. 'But I'm not so easily persuaded. Are you sure it wasn't Ray who killed them?'

'Nope. I killed them. I done Mr Thorogood first . . .'

'No you didn't.'

'What?'

'Thorogood was *attacked* first but his wife died before him. He had a disabling wound but her injuries were more severe. After neutralising her husband, the killer could attack Mrs Thorogood without interruption. And as she lay dying, he managed to crawl across the floor for a final embrace before bleeding to death himself.'

'That's right,' said Coulson, smiling. 'He put his arm round her.'

'You remember now.'

'Like it was yesterday.' Coulson tore the wrapper from another Mars bar and popped it whole into his mouth, chewing enthusiastically before swallowing.

'And how do you feel about what you did?'

'I done a bad thing and they didn't deserve it, but at least they're in heaven.'

'So, no remorse.'

'No use crying over spilt milk,' said Coulson, shrugging.

Brook narrowed his eyes. 'But you do cry, don't you?'

Coulson stared back at Brook, then at the floor, as though the Thorogoods lay at his feet. 'I never killed no one before, so yeah, I see them, the two of them lying there. At night. Blood all over the floor, sticky and hot, on my clothes, my hands.' He gazed saucer-eyed at his palms. 'I had to wash my hands.'

'What else do you remember?'

'Eh?'

'Did they say anything when you killed them? Did they beg for their lives or cry out as they died? Did the knives make a noise as they cut? What could you smell? If I killed someone, I'd remember every tiny detail.' Coulson didn't answer. He simply stared as though in a trance, seeing the bodies by his feet in a farmhouse kitchen. 'So tell me.'

Coulson blinked and took a breath. 'They didn't make a sound and that's a fact. But I remember the smell. The blood was sweet and sickly.' His expression became coy. 'And I think they done a number two in their pants.' He giggled in spite of himself, and Brook noticed the prison officer also crack a grin. 'They were nice people.'

Brook narrowed his eyes. 'How would you know that?'

"Cos they went to heaven,' said Coulson proudly. 'I felt them go.'

'What do you mean, you felt them go?'

'When I leaned over, I felt their souls leave their bodies. It's like they went right through me to go up to Jesus.'

Brook glanced across at the prison officer, whose expression he interpreted as *What do you expect?*

'What makes you say that?'

Coulson's eyes widened at the memory. 'Because when I leaned over them, there was this massive heat pouring off 'em. They was well dead but they were hot. That's when I knew. It was their souls going up to heaven.' He pointed a finger at the ceiling, then at the floor. 'If you've been bad, you go down to the devil.'

Brook took a moment before his next utterance. 'Is that where you're going, Luke?'

He lowered his head as though about to cry. 'Prob'ly.'

'What did you say to Reardon when you kissed her?'

He looked at the ceiling to remember. 'I asked her to forgive me.'

After a long pause, Brook clicked off the recorder and pushed back his chair. 'Enjoy the rest of the chocolate, Luke.'

'Did you really see Reardon this morning?' asked Coulson before Brook could step away.

'Yes.'

'Is she still beautiful?'

Brook paused, sensing a final opportunity. 'Fear has changed her. Fear of her brother returning to finish the job.'

'Never happen,' said Coulson, shaking his head. 'He ain't coming back. When you see her, tell her not to be scared. Tell her she's safe.'

Brook waited on the spacious landing of the isolation block while the prison officer locked Coulson in his cell. Looking around, he lifted his eyes towards the furthest metal door. The observation flap was open and two cold black eyes stared back at him.

'So you did read my letter,' shouted Mullen balefully from beyond the door. His voice had deepened since Brook had last been in his presence. Now it seemed sonorous, booming. Perhaps the acoustics were responsible. 'And yet you try to avoid seeing us, and after we've waited so long.' He turned back to his cell. 'Haven't we, children?' The prison officer returned and Brook was glad to see his key already out. 'Don't you want to introduce your dead companions to mine?' called Mullen, chuckling. 'What a story they'll have to tell. One day we'll be neighbours.' His voice reverberated around the whitewashed walls.

When the block's exit door was finally unlocked, Brook pushed past the prison officer into the cool corridor beyond, dimly lit by weak light bulbs. He marched hurriedly towards the exit a hundred yards away, his blood pressure slowing as the isolation block receded.

'I'll escort you to the barrier.' He turned to see Dr Marshall appear at his side. 'By the way, how did you do that?'

'What?'

'My officer says Coulson was singing like a bird.'

'He didn't really tell me anything I didn't know,' said Brook.

'But he was talking at least. And it couldn't just be the Mars bars. You realise my staff don't have the time or the resources to dig so deep into all my inmates' psyches.'

Brook smiled to placate. 'I had the advantage, Doctor. I know it.'

'You did. Nevertheless, I gather you handled Coulson impeccably. I look forward to hearing the interview.' Brook looked quizzically at him. 'We record everything too. For clinical reasons, you understand.'

'And you don't mention it in case it's inhibiting.'

'You have a good grounding in psychology, Inspector. You didn't judge Coulson and you didn't patronise him.'

'It's the only way to invite the monster inside to come out and talk.'

'Mullen, on the other hand, needed no second invitation, I noticed,' said Marshall.

'We have a special relationship,' retorted Brook.

'The port tells me that much,' replied Marshall. 'Of course, you know what he's got to say about you? That many years ago you killed a man named Floyd Wrigley. A man who'd raped and murdered a young woman, according to Mullen.'

Brook's blood was running cold and he barely heard himself speak. 'Floyd Wrigley and his family died at the hands of the Reaper. It's all in the record.'

Marshall smiled. 'Forgive me. Of course murderers cry foul against their captors all the time.'

'That's what comes of being insane.'

'And yet Mullen was sufficiently lucid to be able to function in society for years while he harvested his victims.'

'The only times he managed to venture out of the house,' said Brook. 'And he had considerable help when it came to evading capture, don't forget.'

'Nevertheless, a very intriguing case, this Reaper. A disinterested serial killer is so rare.'

'Disinterested?'

'The victims were strangers to him. They died quickly and the Reaper appeared to take little pleasure or profit from their deaths, sexual or otherwise. Very unusual.'

'You sound like you've done some research.'

'A little background, perhaps.'

'Brian Burton's book?'

Marshall allowed himself a little laugh. 'I've skimmed through it, but I prefer hard facts to the kind of sensationalism employed by that seedy hack with his petty grudges – particularly against you, Inspector.'

'We share an opinion then, Doctor.'

'I'd like to share more than that, Brook. I've been studying what I can find on the Reaper killings and I'm thinking of writing a paper on the case.'

'Are you now?'

'And since you were the lead detective in London and the SIO in Derby, I'd love to pick your brains about it.'

Brook hesitated. 'I can't discuss an open case.'

'You don't really believe it's still open, do you, Inspector?'

Brook was taken aback. 'Why wouldn't I? It's unsolved.'

'But my sources in the Met tell me your prime suspect, a Scandinavian industrialist, died some years ago.'

Brook tried to hold the governor's penetrating stare.

'You're well-informed, Doctor.' Marshall accepted the acknowledgement with a dip of the head. 'And he was *my* prime suspect, nobody else's. But you're forgetting the Reaper murdered a family in Derby after that particular suspect's death.'

Marshall smiled. 'Ah, yes. Careless of me.'

Fry shivered over the small camp stove, cupping his hands above the blue flame that was helping to drive the cold and damp from the lock-up. When his hands were warmer, he busied himself repacking his belongings. His lightweight camouflage tent and sleeping bag were already in the body of the rucksack, so he filled the side pockets, starting with the rolled-up plastic wallet housing his array of hand-made German hunting knives. Finally he loaded cans of Irish stew from a cash-and-carry pallet into every remaining space that he could manage.

Finishing his cup of black tea, he changed the canister on his mini-stove and, after stowing it securely in the top flap, bound the rucksack to the back of his old Norton motorbike, then knelt to examine the small black stain underneath the engine. 'You'll have to do, Graham.'

He unlocked the padlock on the double doors and pulled the chain through, peeking out into the cold night air before turning back and glancing across at the jumble of stained decorating sheets piled high on a filthy old armchair. After a pause, he knelt to retrieve a small box from under the sheets and opened it.

For a moment he stared at the Glock, then he picked it up, unloaded the magazine and, seeing that it was full, rammed it home again, making sure the safety was back on.

Slipping the gun into a pocket of his combat jacket, he pushed the front wheel of the Norton against the door, forcing it open, then rolled the bike into the night. He retrieved the chain, threading it through both handles before fixing the padlock.

The street was cold and dark in this post-industrial slice of the city. If the street lights worked at all, they were pale and not fit for purpose, and even the desultory sex workers were elsewhere on such a forbidding winter's night.

Fry swung his leg over the bike, jumped down hard to kick-start the engine and roared off into the darkness.

After a full day, Brook tried to switch off on the long drive back to Hartington. It helped that the rush-hour traffic had receded and progress was swift along the M1. But as soon as he turned off towards Chesterfield and home, he was forced to abandon his ruminations and focus on the dark and twisting country roads, slick with winter rains. Shortly after pulling out of the village of Rowsley, his mobile began to vibrate, and in case it was Terri, he pulled into a convenient lay-by to answer.

'Where are you?' said Noble.

'In the car.'

'Terri with you?'

Brook hesitated. 'Yes, we're just setting out to eat.'

'Great. Let me say hi.'

'She just nipped back into the cottage for cigarettes.'

There was a pause at the other end. 'Okay, give her my best.'

'I will. Something urgent?'

'Not if you're on your way out.'

'Any sign of Fry?'

'None.'

'I'll be in early tomorrow to pick things up.'

'See you then.'

Noble threw his mobile on the passenger seat then stepped out of his car. He walked up the flagged path of Brook's cottage, a bottle of red wine in hand, and opened the porch door of the darkened building. He placed the bottle of wine on a shelf and propped the card for Terri against it before heading thoughtfully back to his vehicle.

Eighteen

Friday 4 November

AT SIX THE NEXT MORNING, BROOK pushed through into the entrance foyer of St Mary's Wharf to be met by a malicious grin from Sergeant Hendrickson, yet another of ex-DI Ford's oldest friends in the division, standing behind the polished wood counter.

'Inspector,' said Hendrickson with a sneer.

'Sergeant,' replied Brook through barely opened mouth, surprised to be the target of the man's malevolent attentions after a run-in a couple of years before had culminated in Hendrickson being severely reprimanded. He'd sworn at Brook in front of the Chief Superintendent, and whatever Charlton's other faults, his unbending confidence in the chain of command meant that Hendrickson's act of insubordination was dealt with rigorously. In fact he'd only avoided dismissal by the skin of his teeth, and from that day on had handled his encounters with Brook using kid gloves. But today something had clearly changed.

When Brook had rounded the corner, Hendrickson picked up the phone and pressed a button. 'He's here.'

*

Opening the door to his office, Brook laid laptop and flask on the desk. Noble didn't look up from the report he was reading, so Brook poured himself tea while he worked out what to say.

'Thank you for the wine, John.'

Noble didn't look up. 'No problem.'

'And the card.'

'Did she like it?'

Brook waited for Noble to crack. He didn't. 'Terri left a couple of days ago, but I expect you worked that out.'

Noble looked up. 'I knew you were unlikely to go for a meal in two cars. Two days, you say?'

'I should've told you.'

'You don't have to tell me anything,' said Noble. 'You were on a week's leave until three days ago, and thanks to Charlton, you got dragged into Ford's investigation against your will. And I went along with it just so I wouldn't have to work with Frank, so I take my share of the blame.'

'John . . .'

'In fact you're *still* on leave, so go home if you want. You and Terri are obviously having problems, and if you need to sort them out, I'll cover for you until Monday.'

'I wish it were that simple, John.'

'What do you mean?'

'The less I tell you, the less you'll have to lie when the proverbial hits the fan.'

'What are you talking about? Where is she?'

'I don't know. We haven't spoken.' Brook hesitated. 'She broke the law.'

'Terri broke the law? How?'

'I can't tell you. Suffice to say, it's my fault.'

'I don't doubt it,' snorted Noble. 'The amount of law-bending you get up to, it's in the poor girl's DNA.'

'It's not a laughing matter, John.'

'I'm not joking.'

'John . . .'

'What did she do?' asked Noble.

'Don't worry, no one got hurt.'

'Then tell me.'

Brook sat down heavily and took a swig of tea. 'Black Oak Farm.'

Noble's brow furrowed. 'Last year's triple in Findern. Ford's case,' he added after Brook's confirmation. 'What about it?'

'That's what I'm trying to find out. Three days ago, I got a letter from Mullen.'

'Edward Mullen, serial killer?' Brook's dip of the eyes confirmed it. 'What about him?'

'You know how we play chess.'

Noble frowned. 'Still? I've told you. Cut him loose. You owe him nothing.'

'I gave my word, John.'

'Just tell me,' said Noble with a sigh.

'Three days ago, he sent his usual envelope with his moves in. But this time there was a letter about Luke Coulson as well.'

'Luke Coulson?'

'He's serving life for the Black Oak Farm murders.'

'I know. What of it?'

'In the letter, Mullen claimed Coulson was innocent.'

Noble stared for a moment. 'You didn't actually take it seriously, did you?'

'Give me some credit.'

'How does Mullen know anything about Coulson?'

'They're in the same block at Wakefield Prison.'

'Monster Mansion?' Noble thought it through. 'Three days ago. That's the day I dragged you to the Gibson murder.'

'I left the letter on my desk, and when I got home, Terri had read it and started quizzing me about it.'

'What did it say?'

'Just that Luke Coulson was innocent of two of the Black Oak Farm killings.'

'Based on what?' said Noble. When Brook didn't answer, Noble reached his own conclusion and shook his head. 'Based on Mullen's lunatic notion that he can see the dead. What did you tell Terri?'

'That he was insane and to forget it.'

'But she didn't.'

'Apparently not. That night between us was strained. The next morning when I snuck out to the station, she cleared out her things. What I didn't realise until later was that she'd logged on to the PNC and photocopied everything on file about Black Oak Farm.'

'How did she manage that?' Brook looked away and Noble folded his arms in disapproval. 'Don't tell me. You write all your passwords down and leave them where they can be found.'

'Something like that.'

'Scribbled Post-it notes stuck to the monitor?'

'Close enough,' said Brook quietly. 'This stays between us, John. If there's any flak, I'll take it. It's my footprint on the file after all.'

'That still doesn't explain her interest in Black Oak Farm.'

'No,' agreed Brook. 'But there is a possible connection. The girl who was attacked – Reardon Thorogood . . .'

Noble racked his brain. 'The daughter?'

'She was at Manchester University with Terri.'

'And you think she asked Terri to have a butcher's and see where we're at?'

'I don't rule it out.'

'You say you haven't spoken to Terri.'

'Her mobile is switched off,' said Brook.

'You can't ring her at home?'

'That's the other thing. She moved out of her flat in Manchester. Months ago. Lock, stock and barrel. Without so much as a word.'

Noble was hesitant. 'Have you spoken to her mother?'

'I've not had a chance.'

'Why not?' Brook didn't answer. 'Why not?' persisted Noble. 'You've had your afternoons free at least.'

Brook's reply was barely audible. 'Actually, I haven't. I've been reinvestigating the Black Oak Farm case.'

'Oh God.' Noble stared at him before casting around for justification. 'I suppose, if you looked at a few files . . .'

'I spoke to Reardon Thorogood yesterday afternoon.'

Noble's expression was weary. 'Great. That it?'

'Afterwards I drove up to Wakefield to interview Coulson.'

Noble was incredulous. 'You drove up to Monster Mansion? I don't believe it.'

'I was coming home last night when you rang.'

'Learn anything?' demanded Noble sarcastically.

'Enough to know there are unanswered questions.'

'Of course there are,' scoffed Noble. 'Coulson didn't make a statement or offer up a defence, as I remember. That doesn't mean he isn't guilty as sin.' Brook was silent. 'How's it going to look, you reinvestigating a closed case on the say-so of a deranged serial killer?'

'Bad,' conceded Brook. 'But there is something wrong, something missing.'

'You mean the brother.'

'Amongst other things.'

'And you think Coulson is innocent.'

'No, that's just it,' retorted Brook. 'He's a killer and belongs in prison, no question. But something's nagging at me.'

'And when Charlton finds out?'

'I suspect he already has. Hendrickson just gave me the high hat at the front desk. He hasn't done that in a while.'

'You think Hendrickson knows.'

'I'd say so. He looked very pleased to see me.'

'You're paranoid. Charlton's not going to keep that old fossil in the loop, and anyway, how could the Chief find out so quickly?'

'The Wakefield governor is an old friend of Frank's,' said Brook. 'He promised to ring to wish him a happy retirement.'

'That would do it. You think you're for the high jump?'

'I'm not worried about Charlton. He's going to look pretty incompetent suspending the man who took over from the other DI he suspended.'

'It doesn't mean he won't throw the book at you down the line.'

The phone rang. Glancing at his watch, Noble picked up. He listened before raising his eyes.

'Yes, he's here, sir,' he said, staring at Brook. 'We'll be right there.' He put the phone down. 'He wants us.' He stood, pulling on his jacket.

'There is no *us* here, John,' said Brook. 'He wants me, not you.'

'Don't even bother,' replied Noble, holding the door open.

*

Outside Chief Superintendent Charlton's office, Brook put his arm across Noble. 'John, I can handle this.'

'Forget it,' flashed back Noble. 'It's my fault you're not at home with your feet up.'

Brook managed a smile. 'Is that really how you picture me on leave?'

'Well . . .'

The door opened and DC Cooper emerged. He glanced apologetically at Brook and hurried away in the direction of the incident room.

'Come in,' said Charlton. His voice was quiet, modulated, revelling in the full majesty of his rank. Brook entered, followed by Noble. 'You don't need to be here, Sergeant.'

'With respect, sir, I think I do.'

Charlton hesitated. 'Very well. Sit.'

Brook and Noble both paused when they spotted DS Caskey in a chair next to Charlton's desk. Facing their chairs. She avoided eye contact.

'I expect you know why I asked you in, Brook,' said Charlton.

'New initiative, sir?' replied Brook. 'That scrap-metal crackdown was a masterstroke.'

Charlton eyed him spitefully, resisting the temptation to rebuke. 'It's come to my attention that you've been spending your time reinvestigating one of DI Ford and DS Caskey's old cases. A case that was closed over a year ago and went to trial six months later.'

'You mean Black Oak Farm,' answered Brook. Caskey's head shot up at the admission and she glanced across at Charlton before resuming the inspection of her knees.

'Thank you for your candour, at least,' said Charlton.

Brook flicked a glance at Caskey. 'What brought my enquiries to your attention, sir?'

'We received reports of a prowler at the farm,' explained Charlton. 'And being a well-to-do area, a man walking his dog jotted down your number plate and phoned it in.'

'A prowler?' said Brook. 'I was visiting a crime scene.'

'In the middle of the night?' queried Caskey, cautious but insistent, adroitly steering clear of the full-frontal aggression to which Ford would have resorted.

Brook smiled. 'Time pressures, Sergeant. With my squad snowed under, I went there early, yes, but it is late autumn so naturally it was dark.'

'You admit it, then,' said Caskey.

'Would there be any point in denying it?' said Brook.

'None. We did some checking of our own,' continued Charlton. 'And we noticed, with the assistance of DC Cooper, that you've been accessing reports and files about Black Oak Farm on the database.'

'That's correct,' beamed Brook with as much swagger as he could muster. 'DC Cooper was acting under direct orders from me.'

'As you say,' said Charlton.

Brook's grin widened. 'Anything else, sir, or did you have questions?'

Caskey's mouth tightened but she remained silent, turning to Charlton for his response.

'Let's start with what the hell do you think you're playing at,' said Charlton softly. 'Leaving aside the severe breach of etiquette you've committed, haven't you enough on your plate without gallivanting around the countryside looking into ancient history? Other officers' ancient history, I might add.'

Brook's expression aped confusion. 'Ancient history? I'm sorry, sir. But I thought, with DI Ford's retirement, that you wanted me on the case.'

'I didn't sanction you looking at Black Oak Farm,' snapped Charlton. 'That investigation is closed. A conviction was secured.'

'I'm aware of that, sir. But I was only taking a peek because of similarities with Breadsall and Boulton Moor.'

Charlton and Caskey were stunned into silence. Out of the corner of his eye, Brook registered Noble's puzzled expression.

'What similarities?' said Caskey, finding her voice.

'The fact that a married couple were murdered in their own home and died in each other's arms.'

'But the Thorogoods were stabbed repeatedly, not tied up and shot,' said Caskey.

'I didn't say there weren't differences,' said Brook.

'DI Ford and DS Caskey caught the killer ...' countered Charlton, waving a hand at Caskey.

'Luke Coulson,' she obliged.

'Coulson,' confirmed Charlton. 'It went to trial and he's serving a life sentence.'

'I'm aware of that,' said Brook.

'Then what the devil are you playing at?' roared Charlton.

'Correct me if I'm wrong, but isn't there an open warrant on Ray Thorogood?'

Caskey was incredulous. 'You think Ray Thorogood might be responsible for Breadsall and Boulton Moor?'

'I've no idea,' said Brook, arms outstretched. 'I've only just taken over DI Ford's caseload.'

Charlton and Caskey were silent for a moment before Charlton found his voice. 'Why didn't you think to clear this with DI Ford or DS Caskey? Or better yet, me?'

'This may be my fault, sir,' interrupted Noble. Heads turned, including Brook's.

'I'm listening,' barked Charlton.

'Well, when I spoke to you about DI Brook taking over the Gibson inquiry, I did suggest that we would need a free hand to develop our own theories on the crime.'

'A free hand,' repeated Charlton softly, beginning to see the pay-off marching over the horizon.

'That's right. Sir.' Noble paused to let his words sink in. 'And if memory serves, you agreed.'

Tight-lipped, Charlton glanced at the po-faced Caskey, then at Brook and Noble for a few seconds. Eventually his head began to nod. 'Yes. Yes, I did.'

'So when DI Brook and I noticed the similarities between Black Oak Farm and the latest killings, I relayed your instructions about a free hand immediately. Sir.'

'Of course you did,' agreed Charlton softly. He took a second to digest the result, fully aware of the defeat beckoning, then turned to Caskey, who appeared to be composing another question. 'Answer your concerns, Sergeant?'

Caskey was speechless, but with the spotlight on her, she summoned the wherewithal to nod her head.

Brook got to his feet. 'Well if there's nothing else, sir, I have an inquiry to run.'

Brook, Noble and Caskey trooped out of Charlton's office together, though the latter ducked towards the toilets as soon as convenient.

'Could be awkward,' said Noble, gesturing at Caskey's retreating frame.

'You go on, John.'

Noble's eyes narrowed. 'What are you going to do?'

'I'm going to apply the smooth balm of man-management.'

'Christ,' said Noble. 'Should I fetch the Federation rep?'

'Your vote of confidence is noted,' retorted Brook, frowning.

Noble made to leave, then paused, looking around to see if they could be overheard. 'You didn't actually believe any of that garbage about Black Oak Farm, did you?'

Caskey emerged from the toilets rubbing hand cream into her palms. She stopped momentarily, registering Brook's presence, before resuming her progress as though he was invisible. Brook fell in with her.

'I assume you've come to tell me you want me off the Gibson inquiry,' she said, eyes straight ahead.

'Quite the opposite. I wanted to commend you on your loyalty to Frank. You fought his corner well.'

'It's my corner too.'

'But the clever thing was you didn't paint yourself into it,' said Brook. 'I hate to mix metaphors, but Frank would've burned *all* his boats in that situation. One of his weaknesses.'

'Weaknesses?' exclaimed Caskey. 'And I suppose you don't have any.'

'You can ask John for a list if you like. It's quite a read.'

Caskey stopped and faced Brook, fighting for control of her anger. 'You know, you're very self-assured for someone . . .'

Brook raised an eyebrow when she stopped in mid-sentence. 'Someone who suffered a nervous breakdown?'

Her eyes found the floor. 'I . . . I didn't say that.'

'But you were going to,' replied Brook. Caskey didn't deny it. 'Believe me, I'm a long way from self-assured, though a toe-to-toe with the boss generally brings out the best in me.'

'One of your strengths?'

'You'll pick them up as you go along.'

'I've already heard the station gossip, Inspector.'

'Nothing good, I hope.'

'I'll make up my own mind.'

'I'm sure Frank had you believe I was irredeemable, but I hope I'm not.'

'Not as bad as the worst opinion and not as good as the best?' she ventured.

'Something like that.' Brook smiled. 'Dangerous thing, station gossip. If I hear anything about you, I'll be sure to check my facts directly.'

She glared at him. 'I try to avoid being a topic.'

'You've succeeded,' said Brook. 'You're a blank canvas.'

'That's because my past is *my* business.' Her lips tightened aggressively around the words and Brook saw pain in the quiver of her cheek.

'Will you tell Frank I've been climbing all over his case?' said Brook.

She threw her head back. 'No. But for his sake rather than yours.'

'That's the better reason,' said Brook. 'But if he *should* find out from another source, you can tell him from me that Coulson is a murderer, you got that spot on.'

Caskey's eyes narrowed. 'I'm sure he'll be very grateful, but I sense a *but* coming.' Brook didn't contradict her. 'You found mistakes in the casework?'

Brook sought the diplomatic route. 'Omissions is a better word.'

'Omissions?' she repeated, thin-lipped. 'We arrested a killer whose co-conspirators were either dead or in the wind. There wasn't a lot more we could do.'

'But there were questions not fully explored. If they were asked at all.'

Caskey folded her arms. 'For instance?'

'For instance, where was Ray Thorogood when his parents were being murdered?'

'You think we didn't ask that question?'

'You may have asked,' said Brook. 'But did you attempt an answer?'

'As far as we could ascertain, Ray Thorogood was not at the farm that afternoon. According to Reardon, he stayed over the night before and was gone the next morning.'

'Didn't you consider that he may have been there without Reardon knowing, especially if he didn't want to be seen?' said Brook.

'Of course we did,' snapped Caskey. 'We rejected it.'

'On what basis?'

'Circumstantial evidence. Namely the rather obvious point that if Ray had been present, he would have intervened the moment his plans for Reardon began to go wrong. Her survival ruins everything for him. If his sister lives, she can place him at the farm at the same time as the security system and the landline were being disabled. So if he had been there, he would have stepped in and killed her. As that didn't happen, it stands to reason he couldn't have been there.'

'Then how did he know things were going wrong and he should make a run for it?'

Caskey paused. 'We're not sure. Nobody contacted him that day, at least not on any phone we know about.'

'I know,' said Brook. 'Jemson didn't get the chance because everything was going well up to the point when he got it in the neck in Reardon's bedroom. Coulson didn't contact him for the simple reason he was a patsy not a co-conspirator, as the text messages between JJ and Ray prove.'

'That wasn't conclusive. Coulson could have been involved . . .'

'Coulson didn't have the first clue about the plan. He claims, convincingly, that he hadn't seen or heard from Ray in years.' Caskey's expression registered an objection. 'That's right, Sergeant,' continued Brook, before she could speak. 'I asked him.'

'You went to Wakefield Prison?'

'Last night.'

'Why?'

'I thought I made it clear in Charlton's office,' said Brook. 'If I'm taking over Ford's caseload, I look at what I please.'

'And you managed to get Coulson to speak to you.'

'Another of my strengths.'

'Coulson's a convicted killer,' sneered Caskey. 'They tend to lie.'

'Everybody lies,' said Brook. 'But that doesn't alter the fact that there's no record of a call or message from Luke to either of Ray's known mobile phones.'

'Ray may have had a third phone, unknown to us.'

'Then there'd be a record from one of the phones at the scene, yet there were no outgoing calls or texts on *any* devices belonging to *any* person at Black Oak Farm that day – certainly not once the attack was under way. Not Jemson's, not

Coulson's, not Patricia Thorogood's, not her husband's. And the landline was disabled *before* the attack. The only mobile phone I don't know about for sure is Reardon Thorogood's.'

'It was smashed in her bedroom during the attack,' said Caskey.

'And?' said Brook, prompting her with an eyebrow.

'We checked the history, obviously,' said Caskey, indignant. 'No calls were made, no messages were sent once the attack was under way. Her last communication was a text to a girlfriend in Derby, half an hour before Jemson and Coulson arrived. After that, it was unusable.'

'And no rogue phones at the farm,' said Brook.

'No, and we searched the place from top to bottom. No emails or messages of any kind were sent either, before you ask. As for Coulson not being in on the plan, the jury's out as far as I'm concerned. If Coulson had a prepaid phone, he could've warned Ray then discarded it at any point on the M1.'

'So Ray had a third phone solely for communicating with Coulson,' concluded Brook. 'I don't think so.'

'Seeing as how you're so chummy with Coulson, why didn't you ask him?'

'I did. Coulson claimed he knew nothing about the planned attack until he got to the farm and Jemson drugged the dog. He hadn't seen Ray since secondary school and didn't know he was involved until Jemson told him where he got the plan of the farmhouse.'

'Like I said, murderers lie,' said Caskey.

'If so, he's lying way above his IQ.'

'I wouldn't know, I've never heard him speak.'

'Lucky I taped the interview, then.'

'I do know he was smart enough to turn off his *official* phone to immobilise the GPS locator when he made the dash to Dover.'

'And then forgot to dump his bag of bloodstained clothes,' said Brook. 'I don't consider that smart. But you're right. He did lie to me. He was hiding something. Something very personal.'

'What?'

'Coulson had stalked Reardon for years.'

'He was a peeper?' said Caskey.

'He had binoculars he used to watch her.'

'At the farm?'

'I think so.'

Caskey was thoughtful. 'Reardon never mentioned it in her statement.'

'She may not have known,' said Brook. 'Though her father did. He chased Luke off one time. Luke says that's why he killed him.' He took a breath. 'So my question about Ray's whereabouts during the attack stands.'

'He wasn't there or he'd have finished the job when Reardon ran,' insisted Caskey.

Brook smiled. 'Then I have another question, one that you won't be able to answer, but if you can work out why I've asked it, you can choose whether to stay on my team or not.'

'And if I don't?'

'Then *I* get to choose.'

She considered for a moment. 'Ask your question.'

'If Ray wasn't at the farm, why wasn't he somewhere else?'

Nineteen

'HOW DID HE REACT?'

'Gibson? About average,' said Morton. 'Not happy when we took his champagne away, but overall okay.'

'His partner, Trimble, was angrier,' said Read. 'You'd think with his previous he'd know the routine, but he was seething, insisted on watching us search every room.'

'But nothing of interest,' said Brook. Read shook his head.

'Dave?'

At the back of the darkened incident room, Cooper loaded the obscured image of the shaven-headed mystery man at Frazer and Nolan's party on to the whiteboard screen.

'It's going to be a long haul tracing this man,' he said. 'All we know about him is that his wife died.'

'And that he might be called Alex or Ollie,' offered Noble.

'That's not much help,' said Cooper. 'I don't know if the suspect is from Derbyshire, Nottinghamshire, Staffordshire or Leicestershire. Checking for widowers could throw up hundreds of suspects.'

'It's a start,' said Brook. 'Artist's impression?'

'McConnell's not coming in until this afternoon, so we're still flying blind.'

'Make some assumptions,' said Brook. 'Confine it to Derbyshire and don't go back more than two years.'

'Then narrow it down to males aged thirty-five to fifty, and start comparing,' said Noble.

Cooper seemed on the verge of verbalising further difficulties but decided against it. 'I'll do my best.'

'Do we even know this is our guy, or have a viable motive for him?' said Banach. 'I mean, what's his angle? My wife's dead so I'm going to kill happy couples to make me feel better?'

The door to the darkened room opened and Brook turned, expecting to see Charlton putting in an appearance. Instead, the slim figure of Rachel Caskey scuttled towards a chair at the back. A few heads turned to her, not all friendly after news of her complaint to Charlton had spread.

'The music and champagne speak to a different agenda,' said Brook. 'The killer is attentive and caring. If he harboured resentment against his victims, we'd have seen it on the bodies.'

'And he certainly wouldn't be letting them hold hands,' said Banach.

'We're sure that's deliberate?' said Smee. 'Maybe he just tied the knot wrong.'

'Twice?' said Banach.

'Angie's right,' said Brook. 'Everything is deliberate, particularly when it comes to presentation. The first view we have of the victims is what the killer wants us to see – it's a direct line into his head.'

'And it would be the easiest thing in the world to rearrange the bodies once they're dead,' said Noble. 'Depend on it, the hand-holding is a feature.'

'But why is he so caring if he doesn't know them?' said Morton.

'He does know them,' said Caskey softly, gaze fixed on the floor, still aware of the ill-feeling generated towards her. Heads turned to listen. DS Morton's expression suggested an imminent gibe.

'How?' asked Brook, to head him off.

'I think it's all tied up with his wife's death,' answered Caskey. 'And he doesn't care about the victims exactly. It's more than that.' She sought the right words. 'He envies them. His victims are part of a loving relationship, something he once took for granted. Part of what he's doing wants to celebrate that.'

'What kind of celebration is killing them?' said Smee.

Caskey took a deep breath. 'It's his gift to them. He's offering something he never experienced and wishes he had.'

'What's that?'

'A journey into eternity with the love of his life.'

The room was quiet as everyone stared at Caskey, then at each other. Caskey didn't look up.

'So how is he selecting them?' asked Brook.

Caskey blinked. 'The victimology is weird. Serials normally select from the same social group because that's where your psychopathy is formed and honed.'

'So where do you encounter both well-heeled gay professionals and elderly retired heterosexuals on a low income?' enquired Banach.

'Nowhere socially . . .' began Morton.

'Personals,' said Noble suddenly.

'Sorry.'

Noble's expression betrayed excitement. 'Something Dr

Petty said at the post-mortem. She reads the personal columns in the *Derby Telegraph*.'

'That's right,' said Banach. 'Births and deaths obviously, but also marriages, engagements, messages from lonely hearts – a smorgasbord of personal relationships all in one place.'

'Frazer and Nolan announced their wedding in the *Telegraph*,' declared Noble. 'Petty remembered it because it wasn't long afterwards that she was performing their autopsies.'

'*Together for ever. Stephen and Iain*,' Banach uttered solemnly.

'Together for ever,' repeated Caskey. 'That's it. Maybe the Gibsons took out a similar announcement.'

'That could throw up hundreds of potential vics every month,' suggested Smee, aghast.

'Get the press office on to the *Telegraph*, John,' said Brook. 'Find out when Frazer and Nolan were in the paper. Then ask if the Gibsons made a similar proclamation.'

'August,' nodded Noble, making a note. 'Their wedding anniversary.'

'Good,' said Brook. 'And if they had, they would've kept a copy of the newspaper at home.'

'I'll check with the exhibits officer,' said Noble.

'And get the press office to ask the *Telegraph* management to suspend all personal columns, especially those dealing with relationships – marriages, anniversaries, engagements. You know the drill.'

'They might have a problem with that,' said Noble. 'It'll cost them.'

'My heart bleeds,' retorted Brook, pausing in embarrassment when a few wry smiles broke out. 'Poor choice of words, but it's been six days since the Gibsons were murdered, and if the killer hasn't selected his next victims already, he'll be doing it soon.'

'What if they don't comply?' said Caskey, finally able to look at him.

'Charlton wants something meaty for his briefing. If the *Telegraph* doesn't suspend, we announce how we think the killer is selecting his victims, let the public apply the pressure.'

'They're going to love you for that,' said Noble.

'And after all that good press I've been getting,' quipped Brook.

'So maybe this guy at the party was incidental,' said Banach, nodding at the mystery man on the screen. 'Maybe our killer hasn't physically encountered the victims.'

'We still need to eliminate him,' said Brook.

'Couple of emails,' said Cooper, clicking on his mouse. 'A ballistics tech wants to see you about a reconstruction at EMSOU.'

'Who?' demanded Brook.

'Donald Crump.'

'Crumpet,' said Noble, smiling. 'Not seen him since he moved out to the Badlands. What about a reconstruction?'

'That's all it says. He wants you and DI Brook over to EMSOU,' said Cooper.

'Schlep all the way to Nottinghamshire?' groaned Noble. 'Better be important.'

'That's wild country,' said Morton, winking at Noble. 'Need an armed escort?'

'You said two emails,' said Brook, frowning.

'David Fry's service record,' said Cooper. 'Do we still want it?'

'He was in the Gibson house, and he's missing,' said Brook.

'Left the army with a dishonourable discharge,' said Cooper, scanning his monitor. 'He assaulted a soldier under his command, put the guy in hospital for a week.'

'Any reason why he's at liberty in Derby instead of in the Colchester Glasshouse?' asked Noble.

'That's all they gave me,' said Cooper.

'Interesting,' said Brook.

'So he's quick with his fists,' argued Banach. 'Trouble is, none of our victims were beaten.'

'Champagne and shooting is not his style,' agreed Brook, thoughtful. 'Nevertheless, he's a person of interest, so maybe it's time to put something out there.' He looked at Noble. 'Make it clear we want him as a witness rather than a suspect at this stage, though.'

'I'm not traipsing out to Hucknall?' ventured Noble.

'Too dangerous,' quipped Brook, glancing at Caskey. 'Sergeant. With me.'

On the M1, Caskey was first to break the awkward silence after their last exchange. 'I'm sorry about my attitude before.' Her voice was hesitant, unused to apology.

'Forget it.'

'Your question about Ray Thorogood. It hadn't occurred to me. If Ray *wasn't* at the farm, he should have taken the opportunity to get himself an alibi, make sure he was seen somewhere else.'

'Seen and remembered,' said Brook. 'With his entire family about to be slaughtered and Ray set to inherit, he needs a cast-iron alibi to put to bed a lot of the suspicion. You'd expect to find his dibs and dabs in the family home, but we'd have been all over him if Reardon had died.'

'And an alibi prevents all that,' nodded Caskey.

'You found no traces of him on or around the victims?'

Caskey looked across at him. 'Nothing anywhere near the major trauma sites. Some hairs and prints in his old room and common areas like the kitchen. But nothing in blood or on the bodies. The security suite had his prints all over it, but that doesn't prove he shut down the system. It was the texts he exchanged with Jemson that put him in the frame.'

'I saw them,' said Brook. 'Grim reading.'

'You wouldn't think someone could be so cold about killing his own sister.'

'Never underestimate the depravity of the human race, Sergeant. And Jemson was just as callous, prepared to rape and murder a girl he once professed to love.'

'She's lucky she's alive to tell the tale,' said Caskey. A slight edge in her voice made Brook look across at her. 'Without her statement, we'd have no way of placing Ray at the scene the night before.' Large rain droplets began to distort the view through the windscreen and Caskey flicked on the wipers.

'How hard did you look for Ray?'

'Trust me, his picture was everywhere that same evening. And I do mean everywhere. National TV and newspapers. All the agencies. The case was very high-profile.'

'But no response.'

'Not a sniff. Nothing that panned out, at least. No one saw him on the day of the murders, including Reardon. And no one saw him scarper. He disappeared without trace until that sighting in Spain and even that's never been confirmed.'

'Financials?' ventured Brook, even though he knew the answer. 'Electronic witnesses are a lot more reliable than people.'

'First port of call,' answered Caskey. 'Same story – no spending on his plastic for the week before his parents were butchered.'

'I read that in the file,' said Brook. 'I thought it odd.'

'So did I until I found out his cards were maxed out the week before,' said Caskey.

'Maxed out?'

'He withdrew cash from ATMs up to his credit limit on all plastic the week preceding the murders. A contingency plan in case things went awry, we thought.'

'And not worried how suspicious it would look if things went to plan,' answered Brook. 'ATM film?'

'Scarf across the face and a hoodie,' replied Caskey.

'Strange,' said Brook.

'What?'

'The mix of detailed preparations and rank incompetence.'

'Incompetence?'

'Recruiting people like Jemson and Coulson to carry out his plans.'

'Jemson was no Einstein, but he had a reasonable IQ,' replied Caskey.

'And he held a grudge against Reardon.'

'Not to mention the know-how Ray needed to shut down the security system and wipe the cameras,' said Caskey.

'You've left out the most important reason Jemson was recruited,' said Brook. 'Not only did he know about Luke's secret obsession with Reardon, he also knew he had a viable grudge against Mr Thorogood. Both made him the ideal patsy.'

'A patsy who managed to turn the tables.'

'I wouldn't call life in prison turning the tables,' said Brook.

'He's alive,' replied Caskey. 'That's more than you can say for Jemson.'

Brook glanced across at her, his eye drawn by a pendant, the letter G on a silver chain, peeping through her shirt. She caught him looking. 'Sorry,' he said.

She touched the letter lightly as though caressing it, then pushed it back through the gap in her shirt. Her smile couldn't hide the pain. 'My late partner.' Brook kept quiet out of respect, but evidently she took his silence for a prompt. 'George.'

'And he had a matching pendant?'

She looked at Brook, then away. 'Something like that.'

'He must have been young. When he died, I mean.'

Caskey maintained her attention on the traffic. 'Same as me.' Again she mistook his silence for a question. 'Twenty-nine.'

'Dare I ask what happened?'

'Home invasion while I was at work.'

'And you found the body.' She nodded imperceptibly. 'I'm sorry.'

Her eyes were fixed on the dark lanes of the A38. 'I'm over it,' she said, her voice hoarse, affirming the opposite. Brook accepted the lie as a conversation closer. No one was *ever* over the death of a loved one, especially if it was sudden and violent.

He indicated the next turn-off and Caskey manoeuvred into the inside lane on to the roundabout. 'So what do you want to do?'

'Do?' asked Caskey.

'You worked out why I asked the question. You get to choose.'

She took a moment to consider. 'I thought it was obvious. I'd like to stay on the inquiry, please.'

'You won the wager, you don't have to say please.'

'And if I hadn't won?'

'But you did,' insisted Brook.

'I'd like to know.'

He considered for a moment. 'After your insights in the briefing, I need you on the team. You got inside the killer's head. Where the monsters live. That's the job. That's where we need to be if we're going to catch him.'

She looked searchingly at him, a hint of mockery playing around her lips. 'Where the monsters live?'

'A little trip I make from time to time.' Caskey was silent, but he could see the questions forming about his past. 'You can ask.'

'I know most of the details from DI Ford.'

'I'm sure he was very sympathetic,' grinned Brook.

Caskey smiled briefly. 'He wasn't your biggest fan. But I'm not so naive that I'd accept a single opinion. And from what I've seen Sergeant Noble is fiercely loyal.'

Brook smiled. 'To a fault sometimes. He's helped me a lot. When I first came to Derby . . .'

'You don't need to tell me,' said Caskey. 'I know about keeping personal stuff where it belongs.'

'I know you do,' said Brook. 'But you need to know what happened.'

'Why?'

'Because I'm your senior officer, and at some point in the future I may need to order you to put yourself in danger.'

'And?'

'And that won't work unless you have complete confidence in me.'

Caskey shrugged. 'I'm listening.'

'It was a long time ago. I was young and I made a mistake, got too involved with a case. A case that took my marriage and nearly my sanity.'

'The Reaper killings,' said Caskey. Brook let his silence act as confirmation. 'Was he your first monster?'

'That's something I'm still trying to work out,' smiled Brook. 'But he was the cleverest prey I ever hunted and he beat me fair and square. I was outthought and outmanoeuvred.'

'Sounds tough.'

'There were consolations,' said Brook. 'I learned a lot about evil and even more about myself.'

'Like what?'

'That it's important to know where the monsters are, Sergeant.' Brook turned to look at her. 'But you wouldn't want to live there.'

A couple of minutes' silence followed, Brook concentrating on directing Caskey through more roundabouts.

'Can I ask something?' she said.

'I can see you need inducting into the squad.'

She smiled. 'I've heard that you're impossible to offend.'

'I don't know about that, but you can speak freely as long as you use decent English, avoid swearing in my presence and, most important, don't ever call me guv.'

'Because it brings back your time in the Met?'

'Something like that. We're here.'

Caskey pulled her Saab into a small car park, guiding it into a space next to the drab building that housed the East Midlands Special Operations Unit. For a site housing departments that oversaw every aspect of forensic services for the entire East Midlands, stretching across five counties, the building didn't give off any hints about the breadth and strategic importance of the work that went on beneath its dog-eared flat roof.

The archaic design and shabby construction screamed post-war prefab, and Brook found it so depressing that he routinely avoided as many EMSOU seminars and training courses as he could get away with.

'What's your question?'

Caskey thought through her wording before settling on simplicity. 'You didn't really believe all that rubbish about a link between Black Oak Farm and the Champagne Killer, did you?'

Brook studied her. 'You didn't really believe all that rubbish about a gay sex killer, did you?'

'Touché!'

'What are we looking at, Don?'

Donald Crump turned to Brook with red-rimmed eyes, housed in a sweaty face, heavy on the jowls.

'How are things with you, Don?' he began. 'I'm good, Inspector. Nice to see you. How was your move out to this shitty building in the middle of nowhere, Don? Like walking off the edge of the earth, Inspector.'

Brook had forgotten Crump's bluff manner and heightened sense of self-importance. He glanced at Caskey, who raised an amused eyebrow. 'How was the move out to Hucknall, Don?' he said in a voice guaranteed to communicate lack of interest.

'Don't ask,' replied Crump, shaking his head. 'It's like the Wild West out here. Hard to believe this country has gun laws with all the drug-related shoot-'em-ups in the Nottingham 'burbs.'

Brook nodded and paused for a beat before indicating the four crash-test dummies arranged on separate chairs. Wires protruded from rods inserted into the dummies and were attached to two posts about three metres away. 'So what are we looking at?'

'A reconstruction of the two shootings,' said Crump, indicating first the dummies on the left and then on the right. 'This is Breadsall, and this is Boulton Moor.'

'And this is the position of the shooter,' said Brook, pointing to the two posts.

'Right. As you see, from the position of the bodies recorded by SOCO at the crime scenes, we were roughly able to extrapolate the angle of each bullet's journey from the weapon. And with the use of lasers, we can also plot the bullet back to its source and get a fairly accurate indication of the shooter's height. The killer is between five-eight and six feet as you know.'

'Killer?' said Caskey, glancing at Brook. 'So we're talking about a lone gunman.'

'Sorry if that queers your profile, but I thought you'd need to know,' said Crump. 'Two different guns were used, but there was only one shooter.'

'How can you be sure?' said Caskey. 'Couldn't two shooters be a similar height?'

'Maybe if they were Siamese twins,' said Crump. He moved to the two wires emanating from the dummies on the right. 'When we traced the path of the bullets back to source, it was clear, from the second incident in particular, that the guns were held no more than six inches apart.' He raised his hands to the wires to prove how close the shooter's hands would have been. 'See? We didn't notice it quite so obviously in the Breadsall shootings because one of the victims must have turned his body slightly when the fatal shot was fired. Even so, that put the two weapons no more than twelve inches apart. Boulton Moor is more clear-cut. Neither victim tried to turn away and the bullets entered at the angle you can see, fired from the position plotted. There's no mistake. Your shooter was alone and fired with a gun in each hand.'

'One killer,' said Caskey, her brow creased in bewilderment. 'Two shots fired but from two different guns. What am I missing?'

'He wanted both victims to die at the same time?' exclaimed Noble.

'The exact same time,' said Brook, taking a welcome sip of tea. 'That's why he used two guns, so he could fire simultaneously.'

Noble held up his hands. 'Why?'

'Because he's lost his own life partner,' said Caskey. 'His soulmate. He feels cheated, alone.'

'More than that,' added Brook. 'He's obsessed with the idea that he should have died with her so they could continue their journey together.'

'Hand in hand?' ventured Noble.

'Exactly.'

'Why not just kill himself if he's that depressed?' asked Banach.

'Because death is no release if he has to make the journey alone,' said Caskey. 'Live or die, he can't face either alone.'

Noble nodded, thinking it through. 'So as a public service, he decides to start offing happy couples to spare them the pain of their partner croaking before them.'

'A service,' agreed Brook. 'A gift. That's how he sees it.'

'It's almost poignant,' observed Banach.

'And the trigger?' asked Morton. 'I mean, assuming our guy didn't off Frazer and Nolan the day after his wife died.'

'It could be anything,' said Brook. 'Something he's seen, something he's heard. Something that brought it all back, convinced him that killing happy couples would spare one of them a lifetime of solitary anguish.'

'And our mystery man at the party is our prime suspect again,' said Morton.

'Insofar as we know, he's grieving, so he fits the profile,' said Brook. 'Also he's strong, and around the right height, according to Maureen McConnell's description. And he knew the first victims.'

'Matthew Gibson is a six-footer,' said Noble hopefully.

'It's not Gibson,' said Brook. 'He's gained a partner, not lost one.'

Noble conceded with a lift of the eyebrows. 'And I suppose we can disregard Trimble for the same reason.'

'Yes.'

'And David Fry?'

'We can't rule him out officially,' said Brook.

'But his wife's alive.'

'You're assuming Fry's wife is his true love,' said Banach. 'Perhaps he has another object for his grief, a secret girlfriend.'

'Or boyfriend,' said Banach.

'You think Fry could be gay?' said Noble.

'Why not?' answered Banach. 'It happens. Even in the army.'

There was silence for a second while people absorbed the implication.

'This beating that got Fry discharged,' pondered Brook. 'I had a case years ago in the Met. A soldier on leave stabbed another squaddie and we held on to him until the Red Caps arrived. I found out later that he got the same discharge as Fry.'

'Instead of a custodial sentence?' enquired Morton. 'Sounds iffy.'

'That's just it. A month down the line, we heard there were mitigating circumstances. Apparently the wounded soldier had made a sexual advance.'

'And so it was okay to stab him?' enquired Banach. 'I don't call his sexuality a mitigating circumstance.'

'Nor did we, but attitudes in the army were different, and we're talking twenty years ago,' said Brook. 'The army back then took it into account. The interesting thing was, a couple of years later, the soldier who committed the stabbing got pulled for grooming a teenage boy.'

'He was gay all along?'

'So it would seem,' said Brook.

'It's sad that there are still people so conflicted about their sexuality that they'll resort to violence to avoid uncomfortable truths,' said Banach.

'Could you dig a little deeper, Dave?'

'I'll try,' said Cooper. 'But the army aren't being overly co-operative.'

'At the very least flag up any incident that might have Fry involved in a significant death or severe trauma.'

'Fry would know plenty of soldiers killed in Afghanistan,' said Noble. 'Civilians, too.'

'So what are my search parameters for our mystery man now?' asked Cooper, with a heavy sigh.

'Go with the stats, Dave,' said Brook. 'Assume a male killer with a dead wife for now. Cross-reference with likely weapons experience, age and height, and draw up a list of possibles.'

'And expand the search as we clear each category,' concluded Cooper softly.

'I still say the killer could just as easily be a grieving woman,' suggested Banach.

'We have to start somewhere,' said Noble.

'I don't buy it being a woman,' said Smee.

'Is that so?' sneered Banach, with a sly wink at Caskey. 'You don't think women are capable of cold-blooded murder?'

'Of course they are, but even with a gun, Frazer and Nolan would have taken a lot of handling.'

'And only men have the required strength of character?' continued Banach, turning to Caskey for support. Caskey's return smile was weak.

'Well, no . . .' began Smee.

'Would you like to see how easily a woman can handle a couple of men?' demanded Banach.

'I'll get you a shovel, mate,' said DC Read to Smee. 'You can dig yourself a deeper hole.'

'Let's just say the statistics tell us it's a man,' declared Brook, nodding at the photo array. 'To that end, I want every person at Frazer and Nolan's party reinterviewed. Find out who spoke to our mystery man. What sort of things were talked about? Where did he meet his hosts? What was his accent? Did he bring anything to the party? Did his mood change? When did he arrive and leave and did anyone see his car? Note down any scraps of information, however insignificant they appear.'

'We asked all these questions at the time,' said Caskey. 'Memories are unlikely to improve.'

Brook acknowledged with a shrug. 'What happened with the *Telegraph*?'

'Both dead couples put a notice in the paper,' said Morton. 'Frazer and Nolan in mid-July, just before their wedding, and the Gibsons at the end of August for their anniversary.'

'*Together for ever?*' said Noble.

'Something along those lines.'

'Prophetic, at least,' said Noble.

'Maybe it's more than that,' suggested Brook.

'You mean the killer's looking for that phrase?'

'Maybe not that exact phrase, but something that echoes the sentiment that's driving him.'

'The Gibson ad was paid for by their son, Matthew,' said Cooper. 'Don't know if that's significant.'

'It's a conversation-starter,' said Brook.

'Do the *Telegraph* do obituaries as well?' said Banach softly. Everyone looked at her. 'I mean, if the killer is picking victims from the personal columns . . .'

'Then maybe he used the paper to announce his wife's death.'

'Or husband's,' pointed out Banach.

'It's a thought,' said Brook. 'Dave.'

'How far back?' sighed Cooper, starting to look put-upon.

'This wound is still raw, so for now don't go back more than two years.'

'Try annual anniversary notices for the death as well,' said Noble. '*Still much missed*. That sort of thing.'

'And prioritise anything that feels incredibly heartfelt, maybe even to the point of sickly-sweet,' said Brook. 'Our killer really means it, so he won't write anything perfunctory.'

Noble raised an eyebrow at Cooper. 'Nothing perfunctory, Dave. Got that?'

'I will when I've looked it up.'

'So if the killer's using the personal ads to select his victims,' said Morton slowly, 'how does he get from the text of the ad to a name and address? I mean, it's one thing to pick a victim from the paper, quite another to find out who and where they are. I can't imagine the *Telegraph* gives out that sort of information.'

'Easy enough with a wedding party,' said Smee. 'Check with the church and cross-reference with the time of the service and dig from there.'

'And don't forget our suspect may already have known Frazer and Nolan,' said Banach.

'But if we're right about the profile, he wouldn't have known the Gibsons,' remarked Morton. 'So how did he get their address without asking the paper?'

Twenty

'ＩＴ'Ｓ ＭＥ. Ｉ ＮＥＥＤ ＭＯＮＥＹ.' A pause, Fry's breath steaming in the cold air. 'That's not enough. The police have been on to me. The next-door neighbour saw me at the house . . . Never mind that now, what about the money? . . . Five hundred? Don't take the piss. I know where you live now, so don't make me come out there . . . A grand? It'll have to do . . . No, of course I won't ask for any more. When and where?' He checked his watch. 'I'll be there.'

He rang off, then took the brand-new mobile apart and shoved the parts into the same pocket as his dormant iPhone. Sitting on the tarpaulin, he glared up at the stars winking at him from the cotton-wool sky. There was no light pollution out in the sticks, and the lights above reminded him of the amazing starscape visible from the deserts of Helmand. Melancholy invaded his features, hardening his face.

He drained his hot drink, wiped the mug round with a leaf and broke camp. The mini-stove had cooled sufficiently to be packed, so he shook the moisture from the tarp and rolled it into a side pocket of the rucksack, the stove wrapped inside. Finally, slinging the rucksack over his shoulders, he straddled his Norton and plotted his way through the gloom back to the road. The dark patch beneath the engine caught his eye and he knelt with some urgency to run a couple of fingers over the stain. The leak was getting worse.

A second later the Norton coughed into life with a pungent belch. Without turning on his lights, Fry chugged along the path next to the river until he picked up the rudimentary lane that would take him back to the main road.

Despite the late hour, the incident room was still a hive of activity, so Brook slipped away and headed for the office he shared with Noble, pleased to find it dark and deserted. He turned on his iPhone and dialled a number from a small address book in his desk, hesitating before he flicked at the green call icon.

'Hello?'

Brook heard laughter in his ex-wife's voice. 'Amy? It's me.' There was silence at the other end of the line, though he could hear muffled conversation and conviviality in the background. 'I'm sorry. I'm interrupting something.'

'It's okay,' she said. 'What do you want?'

'It's Terri.'

Panic invaded Amy's voice. 'Is she all right?'

'As far as I know. That's why I'm ringing you. She came to stay for a few days, but since then when I've tried to get in touch she won't return calls.'

'What happened? What did you say to her?'

'Nothing. But when she visited, she was . . . she seemed very unhappy, drinking herself to sleep every night.'

'And you picked her up on it, I suppose.'

'It's not healthy, Amy. We're talking about three bottles of wine a day.'

'Ever thought that might be just when she sees you?' Brook bit down on his instinctive reply. 'Sorry. Out of order. I had noticed last time she was down.'

'So what do we do?'

'Nothing. She's having a tough time but she'll work through it. You'll see.'

'You sound very sure.'

'Terri's an intelligent girl.'

'That's part of the problem,' said Brook. 'She thinks too much.'

'Wonder where she gets that from.'

'Did you also know she'd moved out of her flat?'

A pause. 'In Manchester. Yes, I did. She gave up her job, too.'

'She told you?' exclaimed Brook.

'I'm her mother.'

Brook bit his lip. 'Did she say why?'

'Bored, I expect. You always said she was overqualified for teaching.'

'I'm not worrying about a career change, Amy. I'm just wondering where she's living and why she can't confide in me.'

'Don't take it personally, she doesn't confide in me much either,' said Amy.

'At least you know where she's staying.'

'Actually, I don't.'

'I don't believe you.'

'Believe what you like.'

'Then where is she, and what's she doing for money?'

'She's fine for money, Damen, just leave her to it. Terri's smart. She'll work things out.'

'What things?'

'Relationships.'

'With us?' No answer. 'Who, then?'

'I don't know. I told you, she doesn't confide in me.'

'But you think there's another man in the picture.'

'She's in her twenties, Damen. There's always someone in the picture, or have you completely forgotten the search for love and acceptance?'

Brook sighed into the phone. 'I suppose I have.'

'I've got to go.'

Brook heard a guffaw in the background. 'Sounds like you're having a good time.'

'What does that mean?'

'It doesn't mean anything.'

'I can't do this, Damen. Goodnight.'

'Take care, Amy.'

'You mean don't fall in love with another manipulative abuser.'

'That's not what —'

The line went dead. On an impulse Brook tried Terri's mobile again but it was still turned off, so he left the office, hurried past the busy incident room to the car park and drove out of St Mary's Wharf into the dark night.

Banach sidled over to Caskey at the kettle. 'They're quite lovable when you get to know them, Sarge.'

'Who?'

'Smee and the other DCs.'

'Are they?' said Caskey.

'How are you settling in?'

'It's only temporary,' said Caskey.

'Well if you want promotion, this is the squad to be in,'

replied Banach. 'DI Brook is great to work for, although he can be a bit brusque if you don't give your best.'

'You don't say.'

Banach laughed. 'The upside is you get all the credit for your work and sometimes some of his. It's a bit of a boys' club at times, but there's no backbiting and we're all on an equal footing.' Her grin found little response.

'Heart-warming,' said Caskey, unmoved.

'Sarge?'

'It may be all lovey-dovey in DI Brook's squad, but don't ever forget, Constable, that we're living in a man's world.'

'You're wrong . . .'

'Your superiors are men, aren't they? I'm pleased you've made friendships that have made you forget that harsh reality, but when the chips are down, men will stick together.'

'You're my superior and you're a woman,' said Banach, fixing Caskey in her gaze. 'And with you on board, we can whip them into shape.'

'Isn't that DI Brook's job?'

'Ultimately,' said Banach. 'But we're all adults here and the Inspector treats us as such.'

Caskey considered a moment. 'I'm used to fighting for elbow room.'

'Well you made a good start.' Caskey cocked her head. 'The profile. I've been with him less than a year, but I could see he was impressed.' Caskey nodded. 'Must have been tough.'

Caskey raised an eyebrow, a challenge in her expression. 'What must?'

Banach reddened. 'What can I say? Station gossip. No escaping it, I'm afraid.'

'Go on.' Banach hesitated, so Caskey softened her tone. 'I mean it, Angie. I'd like to hear what's being said.'

'It's all a bit vague.'

'Good.' Caskey's laugh was short. 'That was the intention.'

'Mystery woman, eh?' grinned Banach.

'Not any more, obviously. What have you heard?'

'Just bits and pieces.'

'Tell me.'

Banach could feel the force of Caskey's probing and picked her words carefully. 'They say your . . . partner was killed in a home invasion – burglary gone wrong or something – while you were at work.'

'Is that what they say?' said Caskey, refusing to confirm or deny.

'I'm sorry. It must have been terrible.'

Caskey's eyes glazed over. 'Yes.'

'It's still raw, I can tell,' said Banach. 'Those things you said in the briefing about feeling cheated when a loved one dies . . .'

'It never goes away.' Caskey smiled faintly and rubbed Banach gently on the arm to forestall any further sympathy. 'Let's hope you never have to find out.'

At the end of her shift, Caskey drove home to her compact terraced house in the small town of Ripley, half an hour's drive to the north of Derby. The bare boards of the entrance hall were leavened only by a large carpet sample of indeterminate shape, and the door slammed behind her with the kind of echo reserved for an empty property.

Running up the bare steps to her bedroom, she changed hurriedly into jeans and a sweater from the pile of unironed clothes on a chair, aware of hunger pulling on her insides – another day without a proper meal.

Opening the fridge in her stark kitchen, she found no fresh food, and despite rummaging amongst the jars of preserves and pesto, she couldn't rustle up any decent leftovers. A glance at the dirty Tupperware in the sink confirmed she'd eaten every scrap of cold pasta, dry pizza crust and hollowed-out baked potato in the house, and the pile of unwashed plates, dehydrated substances adhering to the glaze, spoke of a life lived on takeaways and frozen meals.

Apart from tins of baked beans, the cupboards and shelves were bare. She grabbed the last bruised apple from a bowl, took a few bites, then threw the rotting fruit in the bin.

'It's no good, Georgie,' she said with a sigh. 'I need to see you.'

She pulled a pair of cowboy boots from a cupboard and slipped them on, then left the house to drive the short distance to Butterley Hall, the headquarters of the Derbyshire Constabulary, the presence of a firing range at the complex the deciding factor in her move to the town.

Ten minutes later, she trotted down the steps to the range, calling a greeting to the portly uniformed sergeant behind the Perspex screen of the booth.

'Back again, Rachel?'

'Evening, Freddie.'

'A bit later than that, my love.' Sergeant Freddie Preston glanced at a clock behind him. 'I've just turned off the fans and was on my way.'

'I only need twenty minutes,' she smiled, trying to keep the desperation out of her voice. 'Can't afford to get rusty.'

'I'm on my own,' said Preston. 'No RCO.'

'Lucky it's just me to control then,' she said, trying to seal the deal.

Preston frowned. 'What are you after?'

'Just targets.'

Preston studied her before gathering his armoury keys. 'Twenty minutes and not a minute more,' he said. 'Some of us have got a life, you know.'

'I love you, Freddie.'

'I'll bet,' he chuckled. 'And you're not rusty, you're the best marksman on the books. You should stop poncing about in CID and get back to the ARU.'

'I will when I've caught all the bad guys.'

'Oooh! What are you working on, love? Something juicy?'

'I could tell you, Freddie, but then I'd have to kill you.'

'Teach me to ask,' he sighed, handing her the logbook to sign, then adding his own name. He filled in the time and date, then his hand disappeared beneath the desk to buzz her in and she trotted after him towards the armoury. 'You should bring a sleeping bag, save on petrol.'

She contorted her face into yet another grin, paying the price of admission gladly. 'Not a bad idea at that.'

'Fancy a quick brew while you get set up?'

'Love one.'

Preston studied her. 'You all right, Rachel? You look tired.'

'New diet,' she beamed back.

Preston sucked in a deep breath, pulling in his stomach. 'The dreaded word,' he sighed, exhaling heavily. He unlocked the metal munitions door to reveal the array of ordnance, kept separate from the weapons. 'How many?' he asked.

'Twenty okay?' From a shelf Preston pulled down a small

box and slapped it into her hand. 'I was hoping for live rounds,' she said, encouraging him with a helpless smile.

'You trying to get me canned?' he replied in mock censure. 'Those things cost money. Twenty nine-mills, no more,' he said, scrabbling in a different box and handing her twenty rounds. He filled in a form attached to a clipboard and gave her the pen to sign.

While Preston locked the ammunition store and turned away to make tea, Caskey headed into the locker room to open her cubicle, extracting a pair of clear goggles and a set of ear defenders. Opening the door wider, she stared lovingly at the picture of the smiling young woman with short blonde hair and flawless skin gazing out across the metropolitan expanse of Paris from a platform of the Eiffel Tower. Her perfect mouth was wide with laughter, sparkling eyes slanting off-camera, aware of the picture being taken.

Caskey smiled as though Georgia was standing beside her, held for a moment by the sheer exhilaration and joy on her lover's face.

'We'll always have Paris,' she croaked, the emotion catching in her throat. She kissed the tips of her fingers and held them against Georgie's disembodied face before closing the locker and returning to the range.

Two minutes later, Preston came in with two steaming mugs, dribbling hot tea on to the rubber matting. He placed them on the loading bench and unlocked the adjoining armoury door.

'The usual?' he enquired, passing her a Glock from the rack, followed by another form to sign.

Caskey took a large swig of tea in lieu of food, wishing she'd asked for sugar to provide a little energy. She fed ten bullets into a speed loader and moved across to the fourth and last lane, putting the clear protective glasses over her eyes and pulling the ear defenders around her neck. She rammed the clip into her weapon. 'Ten going in,' she called.

Preston had moved across to the target lever and was busy slipping on the same eye and ear protection in addition to a high-vis slipover. 'Make ready,' he shouted above the noise of the fans circulating fresh air to prevent the inhalation of weapon discharge toxins.

Approaching the firing lane, Caskey manoeuvred the ear defenders into place, stepped up to the hazard tape and spread her feet, raising the gun in both hands.

'Watch and react,' called Preston, pulling on the lever.

Caskey rapid-fired her ammunition at the targets, emptying her clip quickly. 'Clear,' she shouted after the tenth round. 'Reloading.'

'Reloading,' echoed Preston.

She fed the remaining ten bullets into her speed loader and pushed the clip into place, then went through the same rapid-firing sequence.

'Shoot complete,' shouted Preston when she stood at ease. 'Unload and prove.' Caskey unloaded the weapon and held out the breech for inspection. 'You're clear,' he confirmed, removing his gear. 'Ease the springs, love. Line is clear.'

Caskey stepped forward to inspect her target. 'Think I lost one there, Freddie.'

'Too eager,' he replied. 'That's your weakness. Take it slower and feel the shot as though the bullet is fired from your brain and down your arm.'

'I'll try,' she smiled, stooping to sweep up her spent cartridges and dropping them into a bin, then returning the gun to Preston.

As she stowed her kit in her locker, she gazed once more at Georgia's beautiful smile, toying with the idea of taking her home but realising she'd likely spend the whole night just staring at her face. 'I love you,' she told her, and with a deep breath locked the door. A moment later, she logged out and bade Preston a cheery farewell.

Brook drew to a halt opposite Reardon Thorogood's building in Nottingham. It was cloaked in darkness, the ground-floor bays securely shuttered and barred for the night. Mist seeped from the cold ground of the park and hung in the damp air like smoke from a bonfire, illuminated by the ethereal glow of the street lamps. A desultory firework exploded in the distance, purple and green fronds flowering briefly before dying in the sky.

He emptied his flask of lukewarm tea and gazed at the up-stairs windows, curtains drawn, no signs of life or light. After draining his drink, he emerged into the sharp November air and stood at the front door, still uncertain whether he should be disturbing Reardon's fragile peace of mind again.

Instead of pressing the buzzer, he made for the patio at the back of the house, rounding the corner in darkness and coming to a halt at the wrought-iron fence barring his way. Looking up to the first-floor platform of the fire escape, he was pleased to see a light on. A second later, the door swung open.

Instinctively he stepped back behind the corner of the building to avoid detection, his eyes trained on the metal platform. A slight figure dressed in shapeless clothing emerged into the cold night air. As on his previous visit, she lit a cigarette and rested what weight she had on the damp rail, looking out across the shadowy park below. A muffled voice from within the apartment spun her around.

'I'm having a cigarette,' she called. The muffled voice said something by way of reply. 'Then let him shoot me,' retorted Reardon defiantly. 'What do I care? Call this a life? Get it over with, I say.' The muffled voice spoke again, but Brook couldn't make out what was said. Reardon took a huge belt of smoke and flicked the lit cigarette from the platform. It landed near Brook's feet with a spray of orange. 'Okay, okay,' she complained. 'I'm coming in. Happy now?'

When the door slammed closed, Brook trod on the lit cigarette and returned to the front of the building. He'd barely got round the corner when he heard another door slam somewhere on the street. He held his ground.

A large dog appeared, straining at a leash. Brook wasn't sure of the breed, but it bore a strong resemblance to the one he'd seen in photographs in the Black Oak Farm files. He was looking at Reardon's dog, Sargent, a four-year-old Beauceron.

He dipped back behind the corner of the house as a figure followed holding on to the leash, tilting backwards to restrain the eager animal, which pulled powerfully towards the park. The dog walker was taller than Reardon, wearing jeans, boots and a waterproof, hood up against the elements.

Half walking, half jogging, the pair reached the top of the steps and descended in the direction of the park below. A minute later, Brook followed.

At the bottom of the steps, a circular gravel path around the grassy interior hived off left and right. Adjusting his eyes to the gloom, Brook spotted the figure ambling along in the shadow of the trees lining the path, while the dog, off the leash, pelted giddily around on the moonlit turf, relishing its twice-a-day freedom. It seemed unperturbed by the odd explosion of gunpowder as revellers rehearsed for the following night.

To allay suspicion, he took the path in the opposite direction, looking across every now and again to monitor the progress of the hooded figure. As they approached each other at the far end of the circuit, he darted furtive glances at the dog walker's face. It was impossible to discern features under the pitch-black cloak of night, but when he was five yards from his prey, a rocket exploded overhead and the darkened figure was briefly illuminated.

'Oh my God,' exclaimed a familiar voice.

'Terri,' said Brook, sounding almost annoyed.

'Dad!' she shrieked. 'What are you doing here?'

'What am I doing? I'm following you.'

'Following me? Why?'

'I'm a detective, Terri. This is what I do. And don't tell me it's a shock. Reardon must've told you about my visit.'

Terri hesitated. The light from the rocket had gone, but Brook saw the hood nod. 'She told me.'

'Is this where've you been the last few days?'

'Of course. Helping Reardon, walking the dog, supporting her.'

'I did wonder why someone claiming to be terrified of her missing brother would drag me out to the fire escape and put herself in full view like that. You were down here in the park and she wanted to let you know I was in the flat.'

'It's a signal,' said Terri. 'You don't seem surprised to see me.'

'You heard me mention I was a detective,' replied Brook. 'I've emptied enough ashtrays to know your shade of lipstick.

Not to mention the paper trail you left to Black Oak Farm.'

'I'm sorry about that,' said Terri, sombre now. 'But Reardon was really upset when I phoned her about the letter from that killer in Wakefield Prison. I knew you'd look into it, Dad. I told her all about you, about what a great detective you are and that with you on the case, Ray is as good as behind bars.'

'You flatter me,' said Brook, though a part of him was secretly pleased. 'Now if the dog's finished its walk, I'd like to get back to the light so I can see your face.'

'You missed me then.'

'Of course I missed you,' said Brook. 'Running off like that. It wasn't right. I've been worried sick. Especially finding out you'd packed in your job and left your flat. Why didn't you tell me?'

'I'm sorry,' sighed Terri. 'But I knew you'd worry and I didn't want that.' She called the dog, which bounded towards her and sniffed excitedly at her hands. She fixed the lead on to its collar and they mounted the steps. 'I had to come, Dad. Reardon's in danger. She needs me.'

'From what I just heard, it sounds like she's coming to terms with her situation and wants to move on.'

'You heard our conversation?'

'Some of it.'

'Being a detective gives you permission to eavesdrop on people, does it?'

'Pretty much,' nodded Brook, unabashed.

Terri pursed her lips in disapproval, then softened. 'I suppose you've every right after what I did. At least you're not angry.'

'Just because I'm not shouting and shaking my fist doesn't mean I'm not angry. Terri, you broke the law.'

'I had to,' she insisted. 'We needed to know how close you are to catching Ray.'

'Well now you know. He's missing and presumed to be in mainland Europe.'

'Spain.'

'That was the last sighting, though it was unconfirmed.'

'So you can't be certain?'

At the top of the steps, the street lamps threw their pale radiance across their faces.

'Nothing is certain.' Brook threw out his arms and the dog bounded up to sniff for doggy treats. 'Anything else I can help you with?'

'You *are* angry,' said Terri.

'I think I've a right. You hack into confidential files using my password, then leave without a word, knowing full well I wouldn't rest until I'd found you. All to get me to help your friend, I assume.'

Terri lowered her head. 'Dad, I had to do something. When I saw that letter . . .'

'That letter was from a borderline lunatic and serial killer. I should've thrown it away.'

'But you didn't, and now you're interested, aren't you?' Brook didn't deny it. 'If you could solve the case and find her brother . . . Reardon's been beside herself. She's had no information about what happened to him, nothing since the trial.'

'What information does she need? Her brother conspired to kill her and her parents for money. She was lucky to escape with her life.'

'She doesn't feel lucky,' replied Terri. 'Not when she doesn't know where Ray is. That other detective . . .'

'DI Ford.'

'Right. He never once briefed her about the search or what was going on.'

'There should be a Family Liaison Officer involved at least.'

'Well she never hears from them.'

'What about DS Caskey?'

'Not a word,' said Terri.

'They probably had no information to give her. Ray did a thorough job of disappearing, you know.'

'Which is why I had to do what I did. I'm sorry, but Reardon needed me.'

'Did she put you up to it?'

'Quite the opposite,' said Terri defiantly. 'It was all my idea. Reardon just wants to forget it ever happened.'

'Then why don't you respect her wishes?'

'Because she just says that to stop me worrying. She's scared stiff and too proud to ask for help.'

'Or maybe she genuinely wants to try and live a normal life instead of hiding herself away.'

'She said you'd tried to talk her round.'

'And I meant every word. Shutting yourself away from the world is no life. I've tried it.'

'But she's in danger.'

'You don't know that,' insisted Brook. 'Ray could be on the other side of the world by now – or dead for all you know.'

'Or he could be here, watching and waiting for his chance.'

'She can't live the rest of her life on that premise.'

'Then find out, Dad, so we can be sure.'

'There's no evidence he's even in this country, Terri.'

'Is that so? Well, something happened six months ago, when I was still in Manchester.'

'Six months ago?'

Terri hesitated. 'She phoned me. From the hospital.'

'What happened?'

'Reardon was trying to come to terms with things – like you said she should. So one afternoon, she plucked up the courage to go out in the car.'

'Reardon has a car?'

'Not any more.'

'What happened?'

'The brakes failed and she crashed into a wall, damaged her hip. She was lucky she wasn't killed.'

'The brakes can fail if the car hasn't been used for a while.'

'She's not an idiot, Dad. She'd had it serviced the week before. It was tampered with.'

'Cars are machines, Terri. Machines fail – especially when people don't use them properly.'

'I knew you wouldn't believe me.'

Brook sighed. 'Where's the car now?'

'She had it fixed and sold it.'

'Police involved?'

'She said she got a reference for the insurance. Will you check it out?'

Brook hesitated. 'If I get time. What did she say about it?'

'She claimed it was an accident, but she only said that so I wouldn't worry. Deep down she thinks Ray tampered with it.'

Brook sighed. 'Terri, you must realise, Ray can no longer profit from killing his sister.'

'What if it's not about the money?'

'Haven't you read the files you stole?' replied Brook sternly. 'The whole case is about the money. And now Ray Thorogood is a fugitive, wanted for murder. Reardon could drop dead this minute and he still wouldn't inherit. All he's got left is his liberty, and trying to kill Reardon puts that at risk.'

'So you think he's out of the country?'

'All the evidence suggests it. Not one sighting puts him in Britain.'

'Which proves precisely nothing.'

'His car was found at the airport,' pointed out Brook. 'You have to stop worrying, let Reardon move on.' He sighed before adding softly, 'And so should you.'

'I have moved on, Dad, I'm looking out for my friend.'

'Then concentrate on helping her get well.'

'Get well?' repeated Terri, incredulous.

'Reardon is damaged, Terri,' said Brook, becoming impatient. 'Traumatised.' And before he could stop himself, 'And she's not the only one.'

A look of shock transformed Terri's face before her countenance set hard against her father and she stomped away, yanking at the dog's leash.

Brook closed his eyes in self-recrimination and set off after her. 'I didn't mean it to sound like that. I know you've had a bad time . . .'

She turned at the door, her face awash with tears. 'A bad time?' she screamed. 'My fucking stepfather abused me.'

Brook flinched at her rage but saw his chance. 'Yes, he did, and you're scarred, Terri. I wish it hadn't happened. But it did, and I can't change that. And the abuse was all the worse because of the lie he nurtured that you'd given consent where none could be given. You were a minor and he was a criminal.' Now the shame came, and he looked down, panting with emotion. 'If I'd been there, I would have killed the bastard with my bare hands. But I wasn't, and I can't change that either. I can only give you the advice that I was given when I had my breakdown. Get help before it's too late, because until you sit down with a professional and talk it all through, you're not going to get better, that I guarantee.'

'Reardon's helping me,' she sobbed.

'No she isn't,' growled Brook. 'I know she's your friend, but she's got her own demons. You must see that you are her crutch, Terri, and limping along together isn't getting help, it's just company on the way down. Talk to a professional, I'm begging you. And get Reardon to do the same.'

The front door opened, Brook and Terri turning at the noise. Reardon stood there barefoot, in her shapeless jogging bottoms and baggy sweatshirt.

'I heard shouting.'

'You remember my daughter Terri,' said Brook sarcastically. 'Manchester University? American literature?'

Reardon flushed and Terri turned coldly back to Brook. 'Thank you for your analysis, Dad. I'm sure it's sound. Only you got one thing wrong. Reardon isn't my friend, she's my lover, and has been for a while.' She grabbed Reardon roughly by the neck and pulled her mouth to hers, planting a long and passionate kiss on her shocked lips. A few seconds later, Reardon's surprised expression gave way to reciprocal passion, and the pair absorbed themselves in their embrace while the dog jumped excitedly up at them.

When they finally broke free, Terri threw a final malevolent glance in Brook's direction and disappeared into the house, stomping up the stairs.

Reardon grinned sheepishly. 'Well this is awkward.'

'I'm used to it.'

'I'm sorry you had to find out like that. She did want to tell you.'

Brook took a deep breath. 'That she's a lesbian? I'm not sure she knows what she is.'

'She's sure,' said Reardon.

'You've both been horrifically betrayed by men,' said Brook. 'But I'm not sure that's enough to make either of you certain of anything.'

'Well it'll have to do for now,' said Reardon. 'But if our relationships upsets you . . .'

'It doesn't upset me,' said Brook, shaking his head. 'Not in the least. If Terri's happy, I'm happy, that's all any parent wants for their child. But does she look happy to you?'

'We'll get there.' Reardon prepared to close the door but hesitated. 'Is this about the letter Terri showed me?'

'Partly.'

'Inspector, could that man be right? Is it possible Luke Coulson didn't kill Mum and Dad?'

'Edward Mullen is insane,' said Brook, suddenly feeling very tired. 'Terri should never have read that letter, and she certainly shouldn't have shown it to you.'

'I wish she hadn't.' She waited a beat. 'So you think he's wrong about Luke? Because Ray may be a cold-hearted bastard, but the way Mum and Dad—'

'Anything Mullen says should be treated with extreme caution,' said Brook. 'Men like him – lifers – like to play games. It's the only fun they get.' Reardon nodded, satisfied. Brook looked round at his car. 'I should go.'

'You mustn't blame Terri for stealing the files,' said Reardon. 'She thought she was helping me. Will she get into trouble?'

'She used my name.' Brook smiled faintly. 'So no.'

'But you will?'

'My boss might think I've lost my marbles again, but that's nothing new.' Brook flashed a look at her to see if she understood the implication of what he'd said. It seemed she did. '*You* could get in trouble, though, just by having the files. You should destroy them.'

Reardon licked her lips. 'Wait here.' She disappeared up the stairs and returned a moment later, handing Brook a plastic bag full of A4 papers. 'Here. I don't want the bloody things. They . . . remind me.' Brook looked inside the bag. 'It's all there – reports, photographs, the lot.'

He took the bag, but hesitated. 'Terri mentioned a car crash six months ago.'

'She shouldn't have.'

'What happened?'

'The brakes failed and I crashed into a wall,' replied Reardon. 'Why?'

'She thought . . .'

Reardon nodded. 'So did I. But you're right. Ray can't come back to Britain. It makes no sense.' Brook turned away, but was drawn back by Reardon's voice. 'She's quite a girl, your daughter.'

Brook managed a smile. 'No thanks to me.'

'Don't be fooled,' said Reardon. 'She's very proud of you, talked about you all the time at uni. All the cases you worked on, all the killers you caught. She loves you very much.'

Twenty-One

BROOK OPENED HIS COTTAGE DOOR just before midnight and dumped his flask and laptop on the table with the plastic bag full of photocopied files. He went to make tea but found he'd run out of milk so poured himself a small malt whisky topped up with a large splash of water instead. Taking a sip, he slumped at the table and drew out his iPhone to tap out a message.

Every time we're together we argue, Terri. I know it's my fault but it's because I love you, because I want what's best for you and I hate to see you unhappy. When you're ready to give me another chance, I'll be here. x

With a heavy heart, he sent the text into the ether, took another sip of whisky and composed a message to Cooper.

Dave, can you find details of a car crash involving Reardon Thorogood about six months ago? Also find out if Ford requested East Mids car park film for Black Oak Farm dates. Either side if possible. Email immediately please.

Cooper acknowledged almost instantly, then Brook turned his attention to the bag of Black Oak Farm papers Terri had copied. He emptied them on to the table and split them into two neat piles – photographs and reports, including the forensic team's findings. As he'd seen the photographs before, he drew the larger stack of statements towards him and began to divide them up. After a few minutes he had three piles of documents in rough chronological order – statements from Reardon Thorogood and attending officers, post-mortem findings and forensic reports.

He'd only read the PM reports once before, and then only fleetingly, as cause of death for all three victims was not in dispute. He read methodically but didn't learn anything new. Core body temperature indicated that Mr and Mrs Thorogood had died between twelve and one o'clock on the afternoon in question. Both died from a combination of blood loss and organ failure. Arterial damage in the neck and heart for both victims was extensive.

The sheet for Jonathan Jemson told a similar story. His fatal injury was the neck wound inflicted by Coulson, and Dr Petty had noted the frenzy in the attack. When Jemson assaulted Reardon in front of Coulson, he triggered an unexpected savagery in his former schoolmate that cost him his life. Jemson's throat was cut from behind, his windpipe and carotid artery severed. Reardon Thorogood had been drenched in arterial spray as Jemson collapsed on top of her in his death throes.

Moving down the page, Brook tried to compare descriptions of the wounds against the photographs, but Terri's black-and-white printouts, taken from his cheap home printer, were inadequate, so he padded through to the office to retrieve the folder of identical full-colour crime-scene photographs given him by Cooper. He checked them against the black-and-white photographs to make sure they were all there, then proceeded to examine them against the written reports.

He thumbed down to the colour pictures of Jemson, his trousers around his knees, slumped forward and lifeless. He'd struggled briefly against Coulson's fatal attack but had been hampered by his state of undress and had died where he was attacked, bleeding out comprehensively as his brief, useless life had shuddered to a close, the shock on his face surviving his departure from the corporeal world.

In the same set of colour photographs, Brook retraced Coulson's steps to the murder of the Thorogoods and gazed briefly at the blood-drenched couple. Moving past the Jemson shots, he paused over a mundane-looking pair of photographs he hadn't really registered before when riffling through the black-and-white copies. Perhaps the absence of vivid blood-staining had caused him to overlook them amongst the surrounding gore. Both shots were of barely visible blood smears on the cream carpet of Reardon's bedroom.

One of the shots was a close-up next to a numbered yellow evidence marker, the other a longer shot to establish location within the room. The smears were about three feet from the bedroom window, some way from the bed and the rigid, blanched corpse of Jonathan Jemson.

Brook put the pile of colour photographs to one side and picked up Terri's black-and-white printouts, thumbing through them to make sure the same two images were there. He found them sandwiched between the images of Mr and Mrs Thorogood's lifeless bodies and shots of Jemson's bloodless remains. In black and white the two photographs hadn't been especially striking, particularly as blood spatter in most of the other images was spectacular, to say the least.

He placed the two photographs back into the pile and counted them. There were the same number of black-and-white shots as colour – all were accounted for. He did the same with the written reports. As promised, Reardon had given back everything Terri had stolen from the PNC database. His daughter was now beyond the reach of criminal charges.

Relieved, he flicked through the papers to find the reports detailing with forensic examination of Reardon's bedroom. He scanned down the page for the relevant number on the evidence marker. Don Crump had analysed the blood smear: *The sample (Evidence Marker 7) was found to be the blood of Mrs P. Thorogood. Likely transference from kitchen via perpetrator's (LC) footwear.*

Brook checked the close-up shot again. It didn't look like a footprint. Then again, Coulson's shoes had left clear footprints on the hall carpet on the way from the kitchen to the bedroom, so perhaps a less generous trace after such abundant transference was only to be expected. The real question thrown up was why, after attacking and killing Jemson, had Luke Coulson walked round his dying friend towards the window? Signalling to Ray?

He put the pictures aside for a minute and thought about it before shaking his head. The same objections he'd raised before still applied. If Ray was there, he would've acted when things began to go wrong.

Cross-checking Reardon's lengthy statement about events in the bedroom, Brook could find no mention of Coulson being anywhere but the route from the bedroom door to Jemson, at the bottom of the bed, and back again. She made no reference to him crossing the room to go towards the window. He made a reluctant note to ask her about it if the opportunity presented itself, aware that vast experience had shown that looking for logical behaviour from someone who had just killed another human being was often the worst way to approach a puzzle.

Next, he re-examined the PM findings on the Thorogoods, this time comparing them against the pictures of the devoted couple lying dead in their garish red kitchen, framed by a vast pool of drying blood.

Dr Petty's notes showed that Mrs Thorogood had been stabbed in the heart and neck – both major traumas that would have proved fatal on their own. She also had slash marks on her hands from where she had grabbed at the knife in self-defence. All the injuries were on the front of her body. She'd known she was under attack.

Mr Thorogood had fewer wounds, only one of which would have proved fatal – a deep cut across his windpipe. Being the stronger, and the main threat to Coulson, it was only natural that he'd been attacked first, though he'd died after his wife. Coulson had been content to incapacitate Thorogood before turning his attention to a more prolonged attack on Mrs Thorogood.

Then, with his wife dead or dying, and despite massive blood loss and physical trauma, Thorogood had summoned enough will and strength to crawl across the floor, through the expanding pool of blood, to die in his wife's arms. Brook stared at the couple's final resting place.

'Together for ever,' he said. 'Just like the Gibsons. Just like Frazer and Nolan.' He stared at the image of the two victims. 'Different time frame, different weapon, different MO.' He took another sip of whisky. 'Different killer.'

He thumbed through the rest of the kitchen photographs, comparing them against any forensic findings relevant to a particular shot. Most needed no explanation, such as the photograph of the dead landline dangling from its cradle, or Mrs Thorogood's drained mobile lying inert on the floor.

Brook pushed aside the papers and drank the final swig of watered-down whisky. He swilled it around his mouth before swallowing, revelling in the unfamiliar heat. For a few seconds he considered turning in, but memories of his spat with Terri came flooding back and he knew he wouldn't be able to sleep. He glanced at the whisky bottle, then, turning his head against oblivion, dragged himself out to the car and set off back to St Mary's.

Twenty-Two

CASKEY TURNED THE KEY IN the lock and stepped softly into the dark kitchen. Given the lateness of the hour, she eased the door back to stop it creaking and lifted it on to the latch before securing the mortise.

She flicked a hand to the light switch and fluorescent tubes blinked into life, flooding the kitchen with piercing light. After filling a glass of water at the sink, Caskey picked a crisp apple from the fruit bowl and devoured it. Work had got in the way of food again but it was far too late to eat anything substantial or she knew she'd never sleep.

She drank the water, turned off the kitchen light and slid off her jacket and shoes while her eyes adjusted to the dark. She'd finally become accustomed to the house and was able to pad to the stairs without turning on more lights. Once there, she hung her jacket on the circular wooden newel cap, removed her phone and warrant card from a pocket and placed them on the bottom step. She unfastened her trousers, let them drop to the floor and stepped out of the moist warmth of the garment before picking them up and flinging them across a chair against the wall.

She smiled, imagining Georgia's oft-repeated complaints

about the trail of discarded clothing throughout the house. Creeping upstairs, she unbuttoned her blouse, winding it into a ball to stuff into the laundry basket on the landing, then pushed through into the warmth of the bedroom. The bedside clock ticked over to one o'clock.

She unhooked her bra, dropping it silently to the floor, and slid the cool T-shirt out from under her pillow to pull over her head and torso. She lifted the necklace over her head and laid it on the bedside table, adjusting the heavy G-shaped pendant on the chain so the letter was standing the right way up.

She smiled at this. 'OCD,' she whispered, aping Georgia's amused warning. Georgia's own R-shaped pendant would invariably be dropped on the carpet by the bed, forgotten until the morning.

Caskey slid between the soft sheets, pleasantly cold to the touch, and wriggled closer to the sleeping form on the other side of the bed.

'It's cold,' she whispered suggestively, running a hand across her bedmate's smooth waist. She stopped at her belly button. Her partner was icy to the touch. 'Georgie?' Sitting up, Caskey withdrew her hand and felt stickiness on her fingers and now along her own bare thigh.

Leaping to the light switch by the door, she fumbled to turn it on and sprang back to the bed to yank the duvet away from Georgia's unresponsive body. She recoiled in horror at the snapshot of blood and brains adhering to the congealing muss of blonde hair, now streaked with red. Georgia's shattered teeth were barely discernible, distributed around the gore of the pulped crater where her lovely face had once been.

Time seemed to stand still for Caskey as the image seared into her eyeballs. She couldn't hear anything above the sound of her own blood pumping in her eardrums. She tried desperately to make sense of what she was seeing. And then suddenly she did. Her hearing returned and she began to hyperventilate, her mouth instantly arid, her pulse rate through the roof. Her beloved Georgia was dead.

'Oh God. Oh God,' she panted, scrambling to her feet, filling her lungs to scream, but nothing came out.

'Happy now, you sick bitch?' snarled a voice behind her, drooling lovingly over the last word.

Caskey pivoted as the wardrobe door swung open and a man appeared, a face she recognised, angry and tearful, yet filled with hate, dotted with flecks of blood.

'Why . . . ?' began Caskey, but the words wouldn't come.

'Why?' he seethed. 'This is my fucking home.' He nodded at the disfigured mass on the mattress. 'Georgia's my wife and you took her from me, you perverted *cunt*.'

'Georgia,' gulped Caskey, trying to think, to remember her training, but her head was swimming in a whirlpool that had already sucked her future into the void. She tried to get her bearings. A house that had begun to seem familiar was now alien to her.

'You're divorced,' she managed to wrench out.

'You think that was my idea, bitch?' He moved slowly round the bed towards her and Caskey saw the baseball bat held tight to his leg. He noticed her looking and pointed the bloodied end at her. A shard of brain matter flapped as the bat hung in front of her eyes. 'You turned my beautiful girl into a fucking dyke.' Tears welled in his pale eyes as he looked at the bloodied corpse on the bed. 'I loved her,' he croaked, his face disfiguring with sudden anguish. A second later, his features hardened again and he took another step. 'You turned her against me.'

Caskey broke eye contact and made a dart for the door, but he kicked it closed and swung the bat at her head. She ducked and tried to retreat, but there was nowhere to go, the bedside table digging into the back of her thighs. Feeling behind her, she knocked over the lamp in a frantic search for some kind of weapon. The metal of her pendant was touching her right hand and she tightened her fingers around it.

'Don't look so worried,' he leered. 'You got a little time yet, bitch. After I knock you senseless, I'm gonna put one in you.' He blew her a kiss and, to make his meaning clear, leered at her sharp nipples through the T-shirt. 'Figure you owe me that much. And when I've shot my wad, if you can say, "Thank you, Barry. That was great, Barry," and make me believe you, I might just let you live.'

Caskey looked for an escape route. There wasn't one. She screwed up her courage. 'You really think I'd want to live after you've had your dick inside me?' she panted, trying her best to add a breathless laugh.

The grin on Barry's face evaporated and he swung the bat wildly at her head. With nowhere to go, she was forced to block the blow with her arm, taking a hit on the elbow and yelping in pain. She caught hold of the slim handle, though, and tried to wrench the weapon from his grip. But he was too strong, pulling the bat up to his chest, dragging her towards him and following up with a head butt to her forehead.

Caskey groaned and fell back on to the bed, in danger of blacking out. In a trice, a rough hand seized the back of her neck, jerking her up off the bed before flipping her round and pushing her face down on to the mattress. She heard the bat clatter to the floor, then a knee pressed down on the small of her back as her flimsy knickers were ripped away.

'No,' she moaned into the duvet. She tried to wriggle free, but it was impossible with his full weight on her, arms pinned under her body. For good measure he slapped the back of her head to quieten her.

A second later, the weight eased as he stood to grapple with his zipper, and Caskey managed to lift her head. Georgia's bludgeoned body filled her vision. Beautiful, tender, loving Georgia, caked in blood and viscera.

With a howl of rage, she pushed herself up to free an arm and slashed blindly behind her with the heavy pendant. Instinctively, Barry stepped back, more cautious with an erect penis to protect. She kicked out with her heel, then got to her feet, scratching at him like a cornered wildcat. With his trousers around his ankles, she was able to knock him off balance and he fell back against the wall.

He fumbled to pull up his trousers, but there was no time as Caskey launched another barefoot kick at his head, landing a glancing blow, enough to put him back against the wall, where he slid to his haunches. She made a leap for the door and yanked it open, but he knocked her ankle as she passed and she stumbled clumsily on to the landing. Using the balustrade to pull herself up, she turned back to see him tearing towards her, baseball bat cocked in readiness.

'You bitch,' he screamed, swinging the bat at her head.

Ducking low, Caskey sidestepped his powerful frame and he crashed into the stair rail. As he hit the flimsy structure, she heaved herself on to his upper body to unbalance him further, and his feet lifted from the floor. Wriggling like an upturned turtle, he tried to right himself, but Caskey grabbed one of his flailing feet and heaved it towards the ceiling. With an anticipatory wail, he did a forward roll into the darkness, landing with an audible crack and moan on the solid flooring below.

Caskey put hands to knees to get her breath back, then collapsed sobbing on the top step. A minute later, reality rushed in. *Beautiful Georgia. Dead. For ever.*

She was brought round by the sound of pained movement below. Flicking on the hall light, she saw Barry trying to haul himself along on his belly like a slug, grunting with the effort of every centimetre.

'Bitch,' he managed to wrench out when he realised she was watching. 'You broke my back.'

In response, Caskey descended the stairs, slow and deliberate, and disappeared into the kitchen, re-emerging a few seconds later with a large carving knife. Calmly she approached the struggling Barry and straddled him, but face down, he couldn't see her raise the knife. Couldn't see the glint of the blade and death following behind. Couldn't beg for mercy.

Roughly she yanked him up by the belt and flipped him unceremoniously on to his back, registered his accompanying scream with grim satisfaction. She moved over him, waiting until he opened his eyes before brandishing the knife. His neck was at a strange angle, she noticed, and he couldn't lift his head. His smile was a grimace of effort, his teeth smeared with blood. 'Go on then, bitch. Do it.' Tears appeared in his eyes. 'I can't live without my Georgie.'

Caskey gripped the weapon harder, but realised her hand was shaking. It wasn't from doubt. She wanted this man dead, but even more than that, she realised, she wanted him to suffer, to know he'd been bested by a woman, to know that his Georgie could never take him back.

At that moment, Caskey didn't care about her career, didn't

care if she lived or died. Georgia was gone. The love of her life had been taken from her, and she had no reason to exist other than to see her killer live a long life in agony. The animal who had so brutally taken Georgia away from her was pleading for a quick and painless death. To that she could not accede.

'Get used to crapping into a bag, *bitch*,' she mumbled, lowering the knife. She picked up her phone from the bottom step and calmly made the call. Her voice seemed surreal in the banality of Georgia's Medway home, like she was listening to someone else report the attack to the operator.

When the call ended, she dropped the phone and trudged to the top of the stairs, knife in hand. Exhausted and disbelieving she sat and let the tears come – and come they did, dripping down her juddering face, dropping on to the weapon held loosely in her palm.

Barry's pained laughter brought her back. 'Wanna know something?' he mumbled, panting with the effort.

Don't listen. Don't listen. Don't . . .

'When I fucked my Georgie, she cried just like you are now, 'cos she thought you'd be home to save her . . .'

With a howl from the depth of her being, Caskey leapt to her feet, planted both hands on the banister and heaved herself into the abyss, dropping feet-first towards Barry's chest. He saw her falling towards him and opened his mouth to scream, but she landed with a shattering of ribs before he could form a note, the last sound to leave his mouth the gurgle of escaping blood surging up his throat from ruptured lungs.

A lifetime later, she heard the enforcer ram dismantle the kitchen door, colleagues shouting her name. She lifted Georgia's alabaster hand to her lips to brush a farewell kiss on to her long blood-flecked fingers. Then reluctantly she let go and withdrew the blade from her own wrist, letting the knife fall to the floor.

'We'll be together again, my love. And next time it'll be for ever.'

As she straightened, she noticed Georgia's chain with its R-shaped pendant on the carpet by the bed and picked it up, placing it over her own head with great solemnity.

'Up here!' she screamed at the bedroom door.

Caskey woke drenched in sweat, entwined with the pillow, her only reliable lover since that awful night two years before. She unclenched herself from its unresponsive embrace and sat on the edge of the bed, elbows on knees, hands covering her damp face. The clock ticked over to half past three, but despite the hour, she trudged to the shower, dragging her soaking sheet to the floor as she went.

Thirty minutes later, she was out in the cold Derbyshire night.

Twenty-Three

BROOK COULDN'T HIDE HIS SURPRISE at seeing Caskey push through the door at 4.30. She was equally taken aback to see him.

'Trouble sleeping?' queried Brook, pausing the film on his monitor.

'Almost always,' she said, doing her best to crack a smile. 'Especially on a case.' She filled the kettle, then flicked a glance at Brook's monitor. 'What's that?'

'This,' said Brook, waving a hand at the paused film, 'is several days' worth of CCTV footage from East Midlands Airport Long-Stay Car Park One. You requested it, remember.'

'The sequel's better,' she quipped.

'You should watch it,' replied Brook. 'Help you sleep.'

Caskey's smile faded. 'I've already seen it.'

'Have you?'

'Some of it,' replied Caskey, hesitant. 'I could have told you there was nothing to see.'

'I would've looked anyway,' said Brook. 'I'm not the best delegator. Another of my weaknesses.'

'Mine too,' said Caskey, sitting down at a spare desk. 'Did I miss anything?'

'Not a single thing,' remarked Brook. 'From midday on the day of the killings to the exact time Ray's Porsche was discovered, you missed nothing.' He paused for effect. 'Doesn't that strike you as odd?'

'Odd?'

'That there's no sign of his Porsche approaching the airport on any access road and no image at the number plate recognition camera at the ticket barrier. And yet the car is there.'

Slowly Caskey stirred hot water into her mug. 'We figured some kind of malfunction. It's the only explanation.'

'We?'

'DI Ford and myself.'

'So you actually checked the ticket barrier camera?'

'DI Ford did.'

'And he didn't find an explanation for why there's no sign of Ray's car on the barrier film.'

'Like I said.' Caskey struggled to keep her tone businesslike. 'Some kind of malfunction.'

Brook nodded. 'I suppose you were entitled to expect your SIO to do his job.'

Caskey took a sip of hot black coffee, remembering DI Ford's exact words. *It's not important, Rach. We've got Coulson. Move on.* 'Did you find anything?'

'Yes and no.'

'What does that mean?'

'I found no evidence of a malfunction.'

'How can you tell?'

'Because if the cameras weren't working properly, there'd be breaks on the digital clock,' said Brook softly. 'There aren't any.'

'No?'

'No.' He took his time to let the implication sink in. 'The film I've seen proves that Ray's Porsche did *not* drive under the car park barrier from noon on the day of the killings to the moment we found his car. Yet there it was.'

Caskey was confused. 'There's only one entrance and one exit, right?'

'The ticket barrier going in and out.'

'Then I don't quite know what your point is. The fact that the Porsche was in the car park proves it must have been driven under the barrier.' The first doubt infected her voice. 'Meaning there's something wrong with the film.'

'You know what they say about cameras,' smiled Brook.

'They lie if they're faulty,' snapped back Caskey, her sangfroid beginning to slip.

'In which case there'd be time gaps in the clock.'

'You've watched the film in real time?'

'Course not,' conceded Brook. 'That would take days.'

'Then you must have missed it.'

'I don't think so,' said Brook.

'How can you be sure?'

'Easy. You see, Ray didn't pre-book the car park . . .'

'Of course he didn't pre-book,' scoffed Caskey. 'He wouldn't want a card payment against his name when he's trying to disappear.'

'Clearly. In which case, to get in he'd have to take an on-the-day ticket.' Brook raised an eyebrow, challenging her to understand.

She stared hard at him and then into space before closing her eyes when she understood. 'And every ticket is time- and date-stamped.'

'To the minute. Which means . . .'

'You can fast-forward to every on-the-day ticket issued to check the number plate and make of vehicle.' Caskey was sombre now, and Brook saw no reason not to let her stew. 'But if the car was in the car park after the murders, it *must* have been driven in.'

Brook took a sip of tea. 'Wrong on both counts.' Caskey narrowed her eyes. 'It didn't drive in through the barrier, at least not under its own power.' He scrabbled for a sheet of A4 paper. It was a plan of the long-stay car park. He pointed to a mark on a particular bay. 'This is where you found the Porsche, right up against the fence, yes?'

'Correct,' said Caskey. 'Ray was cute. He parked at the furthest point from the barrier as possible.'

'And as far away from the fixed CCTV cameras as possible,' continued Brook.

'Maybe so, but the car was there,' said Caskey. 'He couldn't hide that from us.'

'No, he couldn't,' smiled Brook. 'But then he didn't want to.'

'I don't understand.'

'It's simple, really. The car suggests he got a flight out of the country, yes?'

'Yes,' she said slowly.

'So not only did he not want to hide the car from us, he actively wanted us to find it.'

'Why?'

'So we'd think he got on a plane when in fact he didn't.'

Caskey took a sip of coffee to give herself some thinking time. 'You think he's still here in Britain.'

'I've no idea. All I know from this film is that he didn't take a flight from East Midlands after the murders. Leaving the car there was a misdirection to make us think he'd fled the country after his parents were killed.'

'Okay, he misdirected us,' replied Caskey defensively. 'Does it matter whether he left the country by plane, train or automobile?'

'In this case, yes,' said Brook. 'You see, the Porsche was dumped at East Midlands *before* the attack at Black Oak Farm began.'

'Before? I don't understand.'

'Don't you? Ray wasn't trying to hide the car, he was only trying to hide *when* it was parked. That's why you and Frank couldn't find it on the film.'

'He couldn't possibly have dumped the car before the attack.'

'That's what we're meant to think,' said Brook. 'And believing it to be impossible, we're more likely to conjure up a camera malfunction if we're convinced the car was driven to the airport after the attack.' He shrugged. 'It helped that you already had a built-to-order culprit under lock and key and that you'd developed a clear narrative of the crime.'

Caskey took a sip of coffee. 'So when *was* the Porsche left at the airport?'

Brook clicked on the monitor to load a different file and pressed play to start a piece of film. 'It's dark and difficult to make out much more than shapes, but you'll get the gist.'

On the monitor, a large van drove up to the ticket barrier. Caskey could make out two indistinct figures inside, both dressed in dark clothing, baseball caps pulled low over their faces. The vehicle came to a halt at the barrier and a man's arm reached across to take a ticket.

Brook froze the film. 'Judging by the height and general bulk, I'd say Jemson is driving.'

'So you think Ray is the passenger.'

'Possible. But we don't get a good enough look.'

'Which makes this a hell of a leap,' said Caskey. 'You can't even see their faces.'

'I think that's the idea.' Brook clicked on another file. It was a higher view of the car park from a fixed CCTV camera. In one corner of the screen he pointed to a white van, barely visible in the distance. 'Same van five minutes later, near the bay where you found the Porsche.'

Caskey looked at him, beginning to understand. 'Wait a minute. You think they brought the car in inside a van and unloaded it?'

'It's the only credible explanation.'

Caskey shook her head. 'I don't believe it.'

'Watch.' A minute later, the van drove away from the parked cars towards bays nearer the departure building. Brook pointed at the screen to a distant car. 'You see. There's the Porsche.'

'How can you be sure?'

'It's Ray's car,' insisted Brook.

'Is that the only view?'

'I'm afraid so.' He moved the film backwards and forwards. Although indistinct, it was clear that the parking bay was empty before the van arrived and occupied after it pulled away, although it wasn't easy to identify the car.

'That's far from conclusive,' said Caskey.

'There's more,' answered Brook. He clicked on a new piece of film showing the rear of the van much closer to the fixed CCTV camera. This time the driver hopped out of the cab and marched purposefully towards the airport hangars.

'You say that's Jemson,' muttered Caskey.

'Right height, right build.'

'What's he doing?'

'He's gone to pay for the ticket,' smiled Brook. 'With cash, obviously.' He clicked off the film and sat back. 'In five minutes he comes back and the van drives away. Not sure where yet, but fingers crossed Cooper can find us a route. And the plates were fake, before you ask.'

Caskey's eye wandered to the digital display and her mouth fell open. 'Three days before the murders.'

'Yes.'

'We never saw this film.'

'Because Frank never thought to look at it.'

Caskey was stunned. 'Three days *before* the murders. I don't understand.'

'I'm not sure I do either,' said Brook. 'It all seems a bit elaborate. But the net result of obscuring *when* the car was parked was that ex-DI Ford and you were more likely to accept that he'd driven from Black Oak Farm on the morning of the murders to catch a plane.'

'Why was there no mention of this in Ray and Jemson's texts?'

Brook smiled. 'Good question.' Caskey waited expectantly. 'I don't know the answer to that either. Yet.'

'So if the Porsche was at East Midlands three days before the killings, Reardon must've lied about Ray being at the farm.'

'Not necessarily,' replied Brook. 'I checked her statement. She said Ray got to the farm late and was gone in the morning. She never saw the car, only her brother.' He poured more tea from his flask. 'He may have had a lift.'

'In the van?'

'Who knows?' Brook emitted a one-note laugh. 'But he didn't book a taxi.'

Caskey was thin-lipped, her face drained of colour. 'So where is he now?'

'My guess is that he never left the country.'

Caskey managed a strained smile. 'Guess?'

'It wasn't my case,' said Brook. 'So I have to guess until I can develop my own take. But Reardon Thorogood thinks he's here. She's holed up in a top-floor fortress in Nottingham, in fear for her life.'

Caskey's shock was tinged with anger. 'You've spoken to Reardon?'

'Thursday afternoon, before I drove up to Wakefield to interview Coulson,' said Brook. 'Is that a problem?'

'Would you care if it were?'

Brook was taken aback by her direct, almost rude manner – he liked it. 'Not really. I have the Chief's backing. Ford's cases are my cases.'

'But DI . . . we closed it.'

'To a point.'

Caskey drained her coffee, unable to contradict Brook. 'How was she?' she asked quietly.

'Reardon? A shadow of the girl I watched talking Coulson down at the farm. She seems diminished, damaged.'

'I've no doubt she'll get over it.'

'Given time,' said Brook. 'And professional help.'

Caskey shook her head. 'No way will Ray come back to kill her when he can't inherit. I told her as much.'

'You kept her informed, then?'

'To a point,' said Caskey. 'There were precious few developments.'

'There was mention of a car crash six months ago.'

Caskey nodded. 'She thought her brakes had been tampered with.'

'You knew about it?'

Caskey hesitated. 'Reardon rang me from hospital to report it.'

'I didn't see anything in the file.'

'I looked into it. The mechanic said the brakes were fine. It was driver error. Wet day, wet shoes. Her foot slipped off the brake and she went into a wall.'

'No witnesses?'

'None.' She stood to flick the kettle on again. 'I didn't put a report in the file because it was an accident. It had no relevance to events at Black Oak Farm.'

'Fair enough.' Brook rustled through papers on the desk. 'Speaking of the farm, what was your take on these blood smears?'

Caskey pulled the offered photographs towards her and examined them. 'That's Reardon's bedroom carpet . . .'

'About three feet from the window,' added Brook.

'I remember. It's Mrs Thorogood's blood. Transference from Coulson's shoes, we assumed.'

'Assumed?'

'That was EMSOU's analysis.'

'It's not an analysis,' said Brook sharply. 'You're the detective. Forensics can tell you what the clues are, it's your job to interpret them . . .'

Noble walked into the room and halted in surprise, flicking an instinctive glance at the clock. 'Morning,' he said curtly, dropping his laptop on a desk.

The monosyllabic grunts he received gave him pause. 'Any

news on Fry?' Brook shook his head. Caskey examined the floor, appearing not to hear him. After an awkward few seconds, Noble backed out of the door again. 'Think I'll just nip downstairs for a Kit Kat. Anyone want anything?'

Brook and Caskey shook their heads without looking up and Noble took a lingering gaze at the two combatants then beat a hasty retreat.

Caskey turned to Brook. 'Is there something you want to get off your chest, sir?'

Brook hesitated. Handling people with strong egos wasn't his strong suit. 'I'm trying to ask the questions DI Ford should've asked.'

'Sir, DI Ford—'

'Should have retired five years ago,' interrupted Brook. 'Two years ago he would have been pushed if you hadn't joined his squad and started improving his clear-up. The whole division knows you were running the show for him.'

'DI Ford was a good copper . . .'

'Rubbish. If he'd been a doctor, he'd have killed someone by now. Ford hasn't been a decent copper for years and you know it. I've had to clean up several of his past catastrophes, cases he could have cleared himself with a little due diligence. You papered over the cracks for a while, but you can't be expected to smooth things over for ever.'

'I was just—'

'Don't bore me with declarations of loyalty. They're no justification for ignoring bad practice.'

'So you don't value loyalty, then?' demanded Caskey, waspish now.

'Not if it's based on my rank,' argued Brook. 'Detectives in my squad are under no illusions that loyalty is all well and good, but the result is everything, and for that I want them to speak freely if colleagues aren't doing their job, even if noses are put out of joint.'

'And if that involves criticising you?'

'If I'm slipping, I want people to tell me so I can pull my socks up or step aside. I've seen too much indifferent policing over the years to want anything less.'

Caskey's face was like thunder and Brook blew out his cheeks with the effort of it all.

'Look, Rachel.' She flinched at her first name as though she'd been slapped. 'A DI's job is to be strategic. I ask the questions and direct the inquiry where it needs to go until every facet of the investigation makes sense, not simply nod through a speculative report from EMSOU. *I'm* in charge and *I* carry the can. Remember that when you get promoted.'

'Fat chance of that,' she replied. 'People talk about inclusion and *my door's always open*, but that's just management speak, and when push comes to shove, management is all about protecting its own position.'

'Believe me when I say I know exactly what you mean.'

'More management double-speak,' she seethed. 'Please stop *handling* me.'

Brook smiled. 'Fine. But trust me, I'm a lot further away from management than you are.'

'It's amazing they managed to accommodate you at all then,' she retorted, with a sarcastic lift of the eyebrows. Doubt seeded her expression a second later and she looked away guiltily.

Brook stroked his chin. 'Right again. Political correctness makes it harder than it should be to dump mentally unstable officers.'

'That's not what I meant,' she mumbled.

'Yes it is.' His expression softened into a smile. 'But I'm virtually impossible to offend, remember.'

'Part of the healing process?' she mocked. Brook's smile widened. 'So it's just poor policing that gets up your nose, then?'

'Especially my own.' There was silence for a moment as Caskey worked through the implications of all the insults she'd hurled at a senior officer. 'You'll make a good DI, Rachel.' Brook met her eyes. 'But you have to avoid the distractions.'

'Distractions?'

'The ones afflicting you since Black Oak Farm.'

Her expression became defensive. 'What are you talking about?'

'I've been looking at what you've achieved since you arrived in Derby. Before Black Oak Farm your record was flawless and Ford was the beneficiary. But since then it's like a switch was flicked and you haven't been the same copper.' Caskey stared at a point behind Brook's head. 'The whole investigation was a shambles. Okay, you got a partial result, but only because Coulson fell into your lap. Then five weeks ago, you stood by while Ford spouted all that nonsense about a gay sex killer, and even Charlton began to realise all was not well. Something changed in you at Black Oak Farm. What was it?'

Her expression assumed a haunted quality and she made an instinctive grab for the pendant under her shirt. 'Nothing.'

'This is about losing your partner, isn't it?'

She glared at him. 'That's none of your business.'

Brook smiled sympathetically. 'Yes it is. This is a police station, Rachel. Lives are at stake. If we can't function, criminals escape and people die.' He gestured at the pendant.

'Tell me about the murder. What happened to George?'

Her face flushed. 'I can't.'

'You have to,' said Brook.

'Is that right?' she snorted.

'If not me, then someone who can help.'

'Help how?'

'George was killed over two years ago,' said Brook. 'Then you arrived at Derby CID and hit the ground running, throwing yourself into your work.'

Caskey was tight-lipped, her answers clipped. 'A new job. New colleagues to impress.'

'Of course. But then something happened at Black Oak Farm that took you out of your comfort zone and back to that night. Something reminded you of George's death, didn't it?'

She stared at him, finally nodding as though her head didn't work properly. 'The victims . . .'

'Mr and Mrs Thorogood.'

'They were . . .'

Brook located the photograph he'd stared at the night before – the one of Mr Thorogood enfolding his dead wife in his arms. He held it up and Caskey glanced at it briefly then looked away.

'They were together at the end,' said Brook. 'Is that what you wanted?'

The tears began to roll down Caskey's face. 'The night I came home and found George's body, I remember I held . . .' she blinked away a tear, 'I held . . . his . . . hand. It was cold. Like marble.'

'And you wanted to die with her so you could be together.' Caskey's head shot up and their eyes met. 'Did you think we wouldn't understand, Rachel?'

'That I'm a lesbian,' she croaked. 'I just didn't want . . .'

'We have inclusion policies . . .'

'Fuck the inclusion policies,' she spat back. 'I'm not ashamed of my sexuality.'

'Good,' said Brook, for once content that a swear word was appropriate. 'Then what *are* you ashamed of? Weakness?'

More tears rolled down her cheeks. 'I should have died with my soulmate so we could never be parted. I even had the knife over my wrist. Instead . . .' She lowered her head in shame.

'Here, blow your nose.' Brook handed her a tissue. 'How I could have used your strength twenty years ago.' She looked up at him. 'You're headed where I've been, Rachel, if you don't get counselling.'

'Where the monsters live?' She dried her eyes. 'I don't think so. I'm just being pathetic.'

'No, you're not. You've experienced something that not many of us will have to go through. And that's how you were all over the Champagne Killer's profile the other day. The loss, the rawness of it.'

'I dream about it every night, wake up drenched in sweat, panting like a schoolgirl.'

'Been there,' said Brook quietly. A smile began to distort his mouth. 'Maybe not the schoolgirl bit.'

Caskey let out an explosion of short-lived mirth that cut the atmosphere, then stared into the past as though it were a book in front of her. 'Doesn't it get to you? The awfulness of what you've seen.'

'Of course.'

'But you got past it.'

'After a fashion,' said Brook. 'You see, I realised our dreams exist to house our demons. We may not like it, but as long as we wake up in the morning, we're fine. Yet even knowing that, I had to get help.'

'But you always seem to be in complete control.'

'Control is what they pay me for,' replied Brook. 'My team have to have faith in me. Without it, they become rudderless and can't function. Like DI Ford's lot until you turned up.'

Caskey loosed a groan then sat up with a deep breath. 'Don't worry, I'm finished crying.'

'Thank God for that,' quipped Brook. He fumbled in a pocket and handed her a ten-pound note. 'You look half-starved, Rachel. There's a chuck wagon on the corner about to open. Get bacon sandwiches for the three of us, and when you've eaten, call the estate agent for Black Oak Farm, then organise a forensics tech from EMSOU to swab for blood samples.'

'Blood samples? The whole house has been gutted and refurbished, and that was after the clean-up.'

'I know, but if I'm guessing right, there's one particular place that might still yield a result.'

Caskey moved to the door, then turned. 'How did you know I was a lesbian?'

Brook shrugged modestly. 'I'm a trained detective.'

'Seriously.'

'Station gossip.'

Caskey was confused. 'But there isn't any.'

'Exactly.'

Twenty-Four

'YOU AND CASKEY SEEMED TO be going at it,' said Noble, wiping the bacon fat from his hands.

'Just discussing anomalies in the case,' said Brook, putting down the report he was reading. 'Do you know any more about her story?'

'Caskey? No. Only that she worked in the Medway and her boyfriend was murdered.'

'George,' said Brook, declining to elaborate.

'Sounds like you know more than I do.'

'Do you know about the night he died?'

'Smee reckons Caskey discovered the body after a late shift, face bashed in, and the killer was still there.'

'Still there?' exclaimed Brook. 'What happened?'

'She took him down. Apparently the guy tried to rape her, she fought him off. He died from his injuries.'

'Clean kill?'

'The board cleared it,' said Noble.

'Do you know *how* she took him down?'

'What do you mean?'

Brook frowned, turning up his palms. 'Gun? Knife? Flamethrower? Poisoned mushrooms? Atomic device?'

Noble smiled. 'No idea.'

'Find out, will you?'

'Seriously?' Brook took the trouble to raise an eyebrow. 'When are you not serious?' muttered Noble, answering his own question. 'Where is she?'

'Arranging for a tech to go to Black Oak Farm,' said Brook, pouring more tea from his flask.

'Black Oak Farm!' said Noble. 'Would those be the anomalies you were discussing?' No answer from Brook. 'And there was I thinking you added Caskey to the team because she was second lead on Frazer and Nolan.' Still no reply. 'You wanted her on the team so you could dig around on Black Oak Farm, didn't you?'

'Maybe.'

'Definitely. Haven't we got enough to do?'

'I'm here, doing it, John,' said Brook, nodding at the papers on his desk.

'Then why do you need a tech to go to the farm?'

'To look for blood samples and a fingerprint.'

'It's over a year. Surely the place was bleached and steam-cleaned months ago.'

'Nevertheless.'

'This is because of Terri, isn't it?'

'No.'

'Mullen, then – Black Oak Farm was closed.'

'It shouldn't have been,' said Brook. 'Gathering up Coulson and finding Ray Thorogood's car at the airport gave Ford a nice neat bow to tie things up.'

'It doesn't mean there was anything else to find.' Noble waited for a reply. 'There are unanswered questions in every inquiry.'

'Unanswered questions are one thing, John, legitimate lines of inquiry ignored quite another.'

'Such as.'

'I checked the airport film. Two people used a van to transport Ray Thorogood's car to East Midlands Airport three days before the murders. Now why would they do that?'

Noble took a moment to ponder. 'To make us think Ray had hopped on a plane.'

'The car already does that, so why didn't Ray just drive it there himself?'

'Maybe he couldn't.'

'Why?'

'He was busy?' ventured Noble, taking little interest.

'It was the middle of the night, John.'

'Then perhaps he was already out of the country when his parents were being murdered and he didn't want us to know he'd done a runner.'

'Why not?' replied Brook. 'Isn't being in a different country about the best alibi you can get? If things hadn't gone pear-shaped at the farm, Ray's parents *and* his sister would be dead and there'd be no one to point the finger. Being abroad puts him above suspicion for life, John. So if he left *before* the attack, he should've flagged that up.'

'How sure are you that he didn't take a plane?'

'As sure as I can be.'

'Fake passport? Disguise?'

'No one matching Ray Thorogood's general description left on any flight three days either side of the murders,' said Brook. 'He didn't take a plane and he wasn't trying to create an alibi for himself. All of which suggests a different agenda.'

'What?'

'I don't know.'

Cooper wandered over from his terminal with a wad of papers. 'Reardon Thorogood's car crash.'

Brook ignored the offered sheaf and raised a bloodshot eye. 'Just give me the summary, Dave.'

'Long story short, there was nothing suspicious about it. The garage tested the brakes and they worked perfectly. No worn discs, no loss of fluid in the chamber, no sabotage.'

'So Caskey was right,' muttered Brook.

'Caskey?'

'She looked into it six months ago. Unofficially.'

'Then I'm sorry for wasting your time,' said Cooper, feigning annoyance.

'You've done fine work today, Dave,' soothed Brook.

'It didn't earn me a bacon sandwich, though, did it?' mumbled Cooper.

'You wouldn't have enjoyed it,' said Noble, pulling a face. 'Far too greasy.'

'Have you checked for more film of the van at the airport, Dave?' asked Brook. Noble's expression tightened.

'Fake plates as you said,' sighed Cooper, looking for the relevant document. 'I sifted through the traffic footage and followed the van as far as the exit on to the A453, where it turned east towards the M1.'

'And after that?'

'Can we have a minute, Dave?' said Noble. Cooper grabbed his mug and stepped out of the incident room.

Brook cocked his head at Noble. 'Problem, John?'

'I don't think Dave can help you.'

Brook raised an eyebrow. 'Mind telling me why?'

'For one thing the traffic film is over a year old,' said

Noble. 'We're not allowed to access ANPR data over twelve months old unless a superintendent signs off *and* it's to do with counter-terrorism.'

'I can speak to Charlton . . .'

'For another, we have an active serial killer at large who's on a timetable.'

Brook pursed his lips. 'And you think I should be devoting more of my energies to catching him.'

'In a word, yes. Look, I know you like your puzzles as much as you hate loose ends, but the Champagne Killer is out there planning his next strike, and when he's ready, two people are going to die.'

'You said yourself he's on a timetable,' said Brook, with as much confidence as he could muster. 'We've got three weeks until the next murder.'

'You know as well as I do that an organised serial killer is prone to escalate between the second and fifth strikes.'

'I do?'

'Well that's what you taught me,' said Noble. 'Remember the high they get from killing, you said. It's like a drug, you said, and to replicate that high they're liable to shorten time gaps between kills, you said. For all we know, he could be preparing to strike tonight.'

Brook was silent for a moment. 'The second and fifth strikes, you said.'

'Not me, *you*.'

'I sound like a damn fine detective.'

'So-so.'

'You've a snowball's chance in hell of getting a usable sample if there's been an aftermath clean,' said Don Crump, biting down on a doughnut. He unloaded a heavy box from the back of his van, checked the contents, then turned to Caskey, who stood beside him staring transfixed at the building. 'Sergeant?'

'Sorry?'

'I *said* there's a snowball's chance in hell of finding bloods after cleaning. Those guys wear hazmats and hurl bleach around like it's going out of style.'

'We're not fishing, Don, we've only got one place to look.' She smiled. 'Now, you're sure you've got enough cotton buds?'

'Cotton buds?' he said, registering her mocking expression. 'We've got forensic tech gags in our locker now, have we?' He set off with his box, waddling towards the house, muttering to himself. 'Well, wind-up merchants who think they're funny deserve a lecture on visible wavelength hyperspectral imaging . . .'

Caskey stared at where the bed had been, picturing the blood that had sprayed in all directions in an arc of roughly six feet from the neck of Jonathan Jemson. Had he not already been on his knees, it could have spurted twice that distance.

After the fatal cut, most of Jemson's blood had pooled under his head where he'd collapsed, face first, half on, half off the bed, wearing an expression of shock. She recalled the bitter bile of satisfaction from that day, derived from the fact that a rapist and would-be murderer had been eliminated in the act, no matter how unlikely the avenging angel. Most of all she remembered the ordeal of the vulnerable young woman, the beautiful Reardon, her world, like her clothes, torn to shreds in one brutal afternoon.

It was a short hop to that terrible night when Georgie had been taken from her, raped and bludgeoned to death in her bed, her own avenging angel arriving home after a double shift, too late to save her.

Caskey drew a calming breath and held up the photographs to compare against Reardon's bedroom, now completely bare. The carpet was no more, but from the SOCO photographs and the blood spatter plan, it was possible to approximate the location of the bloodstains that Brook had mentioned. She walked to the spot about three feet away from the window where the smears of Mrs Thorogood's blood had been transferred.

'Bloodstains here,' she said, noisily putting her feet together on the boards. 'Mrs Thorogood's blood.' She looked across to the window. It was modern uPVC, but instead of a top-opener, it was a double-glazed sash window with chrome locks and fittings. The estate agent who'd let them in had unlocked it, leaving the key with Caskey. 'Why Mrs Thorogood's and not her husband's?'

'No mystery, love,' said Crump, readying what looked like a camera but wasn't. 'Transference is a funny business. Sometimes two people die and both sets of bloods can be transferred on to a shoe or a foot. It doesn't mean that both bloods are going to show a trace on everything they touch.'

'Even if Coulson's shoes were covered in both,' said Caskey.

'The laws of physics don't require Coulson to step in both sets of blood equally. The female victim died first because her wounds were more severe. Hence her blood loss would've been much greater and, crucially, quicker.'

'That makes a difference?'

'Of course,' said Crump. 'By the time Coulson prepares to leave the kitchen, the wife has virtually bled out, while the husband was still in the process.'

'So Mr Thorogood's blood pool was still forming when Coulson left, his shoes covered in the wife's blood.'

'I'd say so. I checked the plan when you rang. The husband's throat was cut from behind, but that was his only major wound. He was disabled by it but bled out more slowly.'

'So Thorogood's torso would have protected Coulson's clothes and shoes from the worst of the blood spray,' nodded Caskey.

'Exactly,' said Crump. 'But having attacked the wife frontally, he had *her* blood all over his clothes, hands *and* shoes within seconds.'

'So more of her blood on him to transfer to other rooms.'

'There you go. You can chart his path all over the property from that contamination. And by the time he reached the daughter's bedroom, what little of the male victim's blood he'd stepped in had already been displaced.'

Caskey nodded, gazing at the blood spatter plan. 'Okay. But if Coulson arrived in Reardon's bedroom, killed Jemson, then walked here to the window,' she said, pointing down at her feet, 'how come there aren't bloody footprints between Jemson's body over by the bed and here?'

Crump looked across at her. 'What do you mean?'

'According to the plan, the area from the bed to the window is free of blood, apart from this one spot where Mrs Thorogood's blood appears. But the stain is ten feet away from the bed.'

'And?'

'And I'm guessing Coulson didn't trampoline over here and leave it.'

Crump walked across to her and looked over her shoulder. 'Easy.' He brandished the glossy photograph of blood smears at her. 'That's not a footprint.'

'What is it?'

'Blood dripping from his clothes? Maybe he knelt down for some reason.'

'Yeah, but how did he get over here?' insisted Caskey. 'He had blood on his shoes. There should be traces of that blood travelling to here even if he's already displaced most of it. Come to think of it, he'd just killed Jemson, so shouldn't he also be leaving traces of Jemson's blood over by the window?'

Crump pulled a face. 'Bit late for all this, isn't it? The guy maxed out and is serving the full tariff in Monster Mansion. DI Ford was happy and you didn't ask any of these questions at the time.'

Caskey reddened. 'I'm asking now.'

Crump shrugged and thought about it for a couple of minutes. 'Simples. He killed Jemson, then took his shoes off.'

'Why?'

'He changed out of his clothes, didn't he?' grinned Crump. 'Maybe he started in here.'

'Coulson stole Mr Thorogood's clothes from the master bedroom, and according to your blood plan, that's where he changed, because there were smears of Jemson's blood in footprints there.'

Crump shrugged. 'Look, it's our job to tell you where and whose the blood is. It's your job to figure out how and why it got there.'

'But—'

'DI Ford didn't think it was significant and he signed off. You saw the blood plan. If you weren't happy, you were welcome to bring it up. Why didn't you?'

Caskey remained silent. Brook was right. Ford's investigation had barely scratched the surface of events that day and she was partially responsible.

'I'm ready,' said Crump. 'Where do you want me?'

'Over here at the window.'

'That's the best she can do,' said Smee.

Brook stared at the artist's impression of the mystery man at Frazer and Nolan's party before pinning it up on a display board. 'McConnell approved?'

'As far as she could remember,' said Smee. 'It was a while ago. We're comparing him to local mugshots. Nothing yet.'

'No need,' said Cooper. 'That's Jason Statham.'

'You know him?' said Brook excitedly, causing a ripple of laughter around the incident room.

'He's an actor,' explained Noble. 'Of sorts.'

'Actually he'd be decent if there's ever a movie,' smirked Banach.

'Brad Pitt and Ryan Gosling can play you and me, Sarge,' said Cooper to Noble.

'And William Shatner for the boss,' Noble added under his breath.

'I heard that,' complained Brook, to more laughter.

'I'm surprised you even know who he is,' said Noble.

'I don't, it was the way you said it.' Brook handed the sketch back. 'Okay, get Jason ready for circulation to the media. What about the party guests?'

'We've reinterviewed everyone,' said Smee. 'Nobody remembers speaking to the guy, though one person did talk to Frazer *about* him. All he remembered was what McConnell told us. The guy was a stray they met while shopping and they invited him out of pity to matchmake with the neighbour.

Unless we get a hit from the composite, it looks like a dead end.'

'Maybe it's time to concentrate on the Gibson murder book,' said Noble. 'It's the freshest kill.'

'But also the most accomplished,' said Brook. 'Frazer and Nolan were his first kills, where he was developing his method and making any mistakes. He either knew them or knew about them. That's where he got the idea.'

'But if this *is* our guy, why kill where he's been seen?' demanded Noble.

'Why not?' said Brook. 'What news on Fry?'

'Still off the reservation. You don't seem too worried.'

'Don't I?' Brook sighed. 'He may not be the Champagne Killer, John, but he has a violent temper and he's out there, desperate and potentially dangerous.'

'And if you're right that he was struggling with his sexuality and he crossed Frazer and Nolan's path . . .'

'Big assumption, John,' replied Brook.

'It's more than an assumption to say he was in the Gibson house.'

'That doesn't give him a plausible motive for their deaths.'

Noble stared at the picture of Matthew Gibson on the photo array. 'Then maybe he had another motive.'

Brook looked thoughtfully at the picture, then across to Noble.

Twenty-Five

'WE KNOW YOU LIED ABOUT DAVID Fry,' said Brook, above the din of a cement mixer manned some thirty yards away by Trimble and his son. Both looked on, in damp and dusty building clothes, their hands and arms stained by cement dust.

'You employed him to decorate your parents' house,' added Noble, leaning in to Gibson to be sure his helpful information was fully appreciated. 'A house you own.'

Gibson's manner, so confident and sneering on their last visit, was more subdued. 'Says who?'

'David Fry.'

Gibson shrugged. 'His word against mine.'

Brook's smile was genuine. This was the part of the job he loved – calmly but relentlessly pulling a suspect's testimony apart and watching their resistance crumble with it. 'We also have Fry's fingerprints on a light switch in your parents' bedroom. He was in the house.'

'Then maybe you should arrest him for murder.'

'We have to find him first,' said Noble. 'He seems to have gone to ground.'

'Have you seen him?' enquired Brook.

361

'Why would I have seen him?' replied Gibson.

'Because you know him. Because you lied. Because he was in your parents' house. You're their landlord. If they didn't let him in, you did.'

Gibson was tight-lipped. 'When can I get my case of champagne back?'

Brook glanced at Noble. 'Do you believe this, John? His parents are gunned down and we can't get a straight answer, never mind the help we ask for.'

'Incredible,' said Noble, shaking his head.

'I don't know anything,' protested Gibson.

'Mr Gibson, David Fry has disappeared,' said Brook. 'A man with whom you had a dispute about money. An ex-soldier with a record of violence and comfortable around guns.'

'We have to wonder why you denied knowing him when in fact he'd worked for you,' said Noble.

'We find that perverse,' added Brook.

'If not downright suspicious.'

Gibson was keeping his cool. 'You think I hired him to kill my parents.'

'Did you?'

'Why would I? I've nothing to gain and plenty to lose.'

'Such as?'

'Such as a tainted house that will be harder to sell, plus the hassle of being harassed by you lot.'

'Where does being deprived of your parents come on that list?' asked Noble.

Gibson blanched. 'Top, of course. Look, hasn't it occurred to you that I could've killed my parents with one hand tied behind my back? I wouldn't need anybody's help to do it and I certainly wouldn't take a bottle of champagne and make them dress up for a night out, for God's sake.'

'You might if they asked you,' suggested Noble.

'So it's an assisted suicide now,' said Gibson, nodding. 'Problem is, Mum and Dad were healthy for their age.'

'But they weren't getting any younger,' argued Brook, glancing across to the Trimbles, smoking cigarettes beside the roaring cement mixer. Trimble Senior discarded his cigarette then tipped the contents of the mixer into a wheelbarrow and turned off the machine. The deathly quiet of the countryside intruded and Trimble made his way over to them, halting a few yards away.

'Everything okay, Matty?'

'Everything's fine, Jimmy,' smiled Gibson, a hand held up to reassure. 'Just a few additional questions.' Trimble looked from Gibson to Brook and back again before trudging slowly back to the half-built barn, his body language betraying a keen ear tilted in their direction.

'Have you finished testing my gun yet?' demanded Gibson, loud enough for Trimble to hear.

'We have,' said Brook, smiling. *Two can play at that game.* 'It hasn't been fired,' he added, his voice carrying across to the barn.

'When can I have it back?'

'Where is David Fry?' shouted Brook.

Gibson's expression changed. 'How the hell should I know?' he replied angrily. Trimble shook out another cigarette. 'Now, I've got work to do . . .'

'But you know who he is,' declared Brook boldly.

'I've told you, no.' Gibson turned his face to Brook and Noble, licking his lips nervously. Noble realised Brook's strategy.

'Then why is his fingerprint—' he shouted.

'Could I use your toilet, Mr Gibson?' demanded Brook, before Noble could complete the sentence.

Gibson held Brook's eyes briefly, then raised a guiding arm. 'This way.'

A moment later, the three men stood in the privacy of Gibson's spacious kitchen.

'Through there on the left,' indicated Gibson.

Brook smiled but didn't move. He glanced at Noble.

'Fry was in your house,' said Noble softly. 'The same David Fry who, while in the army, was brought up on charges for attacking a fellow soldier.'

'We can make the case that the victim of that attack made unwelcome sexual advances towards David Fry,' said Brook. 'Which he rebuffed so violently that his victim was in a coma for days. And this is where we get confused. Why, we ask ourselves, would an openly gay man like you hire someone so demonstrably homophobic to work for him?'

'I've told you,' said Gibson. 'I didn't hire him.'

'That is a lie,' said Brook.

'You can't prove it.'

'For now, it's enough that I know,' said Brook. 'And what's more, I know why.' Gibson narrowed his eyes at this. 'Now, I've given you a chance at discretion, but if I don't get full co-operation and the truth this instant, I'll be forced to go back outside and start asking your partner.'

Gibson stared for several seconds and Brook let him stew in his discomfort. Finally Gibson's head dipped. 'Please don't do that.'

'Then tell us about your affair with Fry.'

Gibson's expression soured. 'Affair, you call it.'

'What would you call it?'

'A moment of madness.' He shook his head, took a deep breath. 'David was . . . is struggling with his sexuality.'

'Struggling in what way?'

'He's gay but he's having a hard time facing up to it.'

'Why?'

'Who knows how people see themselves?' said Gibson. 'But with David's background and his life in the army, being gay was not the easiest option.'

'And he sees his sexual urges as a form of weakness.'

Gibson nodded. 'That's exactly it.'

'A weakness that could be overcome?'

'If he fought it hard enough.'

'But you can't fight nature.'

'No, you can't,' declared Gibson, on safer ground. 'In the *community*, we believe that every queer-basher is trying to smash his own desires to a pulp. The more violent the attack . . .' He left the rest unsaid. 'He was sorry about that poor boy in the army, but others were watching so he had to make a point and hang tough for public consumption.'

'I see. And was he struggling with his *weakness* whilst your parents were away last year?' said Brook.

Gibson closed his eyes in self-loathing. 'I want you to know I love Jimmy with every fibre of my being.'

'Noted,' answered Brook.

'This thing was over in two days and it was strictly NSA, or supposed to be.'

'NSA?' enquired Brook.

'No strings attached,' explained Noble.

'But it hasn't turned out that way.'

'Far from it.' Gibson put a hand over his eyes. 'God, what a mess.'

'We need to know everything,' said Brook.

'Very well. The house was empty, my parents were in Cornwall. Davey had posted a few flyers in the neighbourhood offering decorating services, gardening, that sort of thing. Mum and Dad's house was looking a bit tired and Davey was cheap and needed the money.'

'So you hired him?'

'He spruced up a couple of rooms for me, yes.'

'Go on.'

'Surely you can guess the rest.'

'This is a murder inquiry, Mr Gibson,' said Noble. 'Not a game show.'

Gibson took a deep breath. 'I went to check on progress one day just before Christmas.' He was silent for a moment. 'Jimmy was up in Scotland visiting his family and . . . Davey and I had . . . sexual relations.' He covered his eyes with a hand again. 'I can't believe I was so stupid. In my parents' bed as well,' he added with a twisted sense of pride, glaring at Brook, daring him to judge.

'And then?'

'And then nothing. We went our separate ways.'

'So why was Fry hammering on your parents' door before Christmas?' asked Noble.

'A few days after we had sex, he asked for money. A lot of money.'

'More than you'd agreed for the decorating?'

'Fifteen hundred pounds.'

'And you refused to pay.'

'Yes, I refused to pay.'

'He tried to blackmail you,' said Noble

'Fifteen hundred pounds is hardly blackmail.' Gibson's

smile was crooked. 'I used to be in the business, so I understand the kind of sums that could change hands if you picked up the right mark.'

'So if not blackmail, what would you call it?'

'He just tried it on, that's all.'

'Money for services rendered.'

'And for not sharing our little indiscretion with loved ones.'

'And you said no?'

'Of course I said no,' exclaimed Gibson, indignant. 'I've never paid for sex in my life, and I wasn't about to start.'

'I'm sure we can root around for the irony another time,' said Brook. 'What happened then?'

Gibson shrugged. 'He's married, same as me, so the sword cut both ways. When I said no, he started to bargain, came down to a thousand or he'd tell my parents.'

'But they already knew you were gay.'

'We did it on their bed, Inspector. Have you any idea?'

'Go on.'

'When my parents came back, Davey dropped round. Bless 'em, they gave him three hundred pounds when he told them I'd forgotten to pay him.'

'Did he tell them about your little dalliance?'

'He wouldn't dare,' said Gibson, tight-lipped. 'I paid them back and gave Davey an extra three hundred to get him off my back.'

'And he accepted?'

'What choice did he have?' said Gibson. 'I called his bluff. He had just as much to lose as me. Probably more.'

'Then why pay him anything at all?' asked Noble.

It was Brook who answered. 'Guilt money.'

'Amongst other things,' said Gibson. 'Also I felt sorry for him. He was conflicted. And he really did need the money.'

'Did he threaten you?'

'Not really. He had a short temper, yes, but he didn't know my address, so I slipped him the extra cash before he was minded to find out. And that was that.'

'And now?'

'Now what?'

'Now he's on the run,' explained Brook. 'Location unknown.' Gibson splayed his hands, playing dumb.

'Has he been in touch?' asked Noble.

'He didn't kill my parents,' said Gibson. 'He would have taken the rent money.'

'We know.'

Gibson's face creased in confusion. 'If you know, what the fuck is the point of all this?'

'Are you really that obtuse?' said Brook. 'The point of all this is to bring him in safely. If he feels cornered or threatened, his record shows that he resorts to violence.'

'What's that got to do with me?' demanded Gibson.

'You don't know?' declared Brook.

'Know what?'

'If he didn't kill your parents, then someone else must have,' said Brook. 'For all he knows, *you* killed them, and he knows how it would look if you were to accuse him.'

'His fingerprints are in the house and he has a violent criminal record,' continued Noble. 'He's the ideal patsy and he knows it.'

'And when you denied knowing him, he probably felt you were lining him up to take the fall.'

'For killing Mum and Dad?'

'Why not?' said Brook. 'It would make a lot of sense to him, the way you've behaved.'

'Christ,' said Gibson quietly, thinking it through. 'Poor Davey.'

'And poor whoever gets in his way if we don't pick him up. So I'll ask you again, and I don't want to repeat myself. Has he contacted you within the last twenty-four hours?'

A pause, followed by an almost imperceptible nod. 'He phoned me, said he knew where I lived, said he needed somewhere to lie low. I told him I couldn't help so he asked for more money.'

'Did you give it?'

'A thousand pounds. On condition he didn't show up at my house.'

'Then how did you get the money to him?'

'I met him in the village.'

'Do you know how he got there?' asked Noble.

'He had an old motorbike. A Norton Commando, I think he said. A real antique.'

Noble shook his head at Brook. 'Fry's got nothing with the DVLA.'

'It was pretty old,' confirmed Gibson. 'Looked like it'd been in a shed for a decade.'

'If he turns up or phones . . .'

'He won't.'

'If he does, please tell him to call us, and stress to him that we don't suspect him of your parents' murder.'

Gibson agreed with a nod.

'And it might make things easier if you also tell him that *you* don't suspect him either.'

'There's something else,' said Gibson softly. 'Last year,

when Davey and I . . . We talked about guns.' Brook prompted him with an eyebrow. 'I never saw it, you understand, but he said he had a souvenir in a lock-up in Peartree. A gun he smuggled back from Afghanistan.'

'It wouldn't be a Glock, by any chance, would it?' said Brook.

Gibson stared at the ground. 'A comrade was killed. Davey took his weapon.'

'One last thing,' said Noble. 'Your parents had kept a copy of the *Derby Telegraph*, dated the twenty-fifth of August, which carried an announcement celebrating their wedding anniversary. Did you pay for that?'

'I did,' said Gibson. 'Jimmy's idea. I told him Mum always read the obituaries in the paper, looking for people she knew. We thought it might be nice if she came across something positive for a change. Why?'

Twenty-Six

'I F HE'S GOT A GUN, WE have no choice. Tell Cooper to get Fry's face to all news media, top priority. And make sure the release stresses that he's armed and not to be approached.'

'We're hanging a target on him for Armed Response.'

'What else can we do?' sighed Brook. 'Fry may not be a murderer, but if he's armed, he's dangerous. What about the motorbike?'

'No trace. Nothing licensed to him.'

'And the lock-up?'

'Read and Smee are heading to Peartree to look for the gun.'

Brook nodded. 'Let's hope they find it. Any signal from his mobile yet?'

'No hits on GPS.'

'With all his training, he's unlikely to be careless,' mused Brook. 'Apply for a tap on his home phone, John – quick as you can. If he gets desperate, he may want to speak to his wife at some point.'

'He's a soldier,' said Noble. 'He won't ring her. He'll expect us to be listening.'

'But he might not care if he only wants to say goodbye.'

'And give us a fix on his position? Doesn't make sense. If I was him, I'd be lying low out in the sticks during the day and making my way out of the county by night.'

'You're assuming he wants to get away, John.'

'Well bugger me sideways,' said Crump, peering through the lens.

'What?' said Caskey, kneeling beside him.

'Blood. And better yet, a fingerprint.'

'Brook was right.'

'Coulson must have opened the window for some reason,' said Crump, mimicking the action with both hands. 'And in pulling it up, he placed his hands underneath the frame and left the print on the underside. When the aftermath cleaners came to do their thing, the window was closed and the contact preserved.'

'Sounds viable,' said Caskey, crouching to peer intently at the faint blackened smudge, her face almost touching Crump's jowl. She stood and put her hands on the upper part of the frame. 'Except you'd expect him to leave similar bloody prints when he closed it again.'

'It would've been visible and we would have found it,' said Crump. 'He must've wiped it clean.'

Her expression registered scepticism at the absurdity of Coulson bothering to wipe away a blood-smeared fingerprint in a house drenched in blood. 'Unless you missed it,' she suggested.

Crump greeted the notion with icy disdain. 'Wash your mouth, out, girl. Now if you don't mind, this may take a little time.'

*

As Crump did his work, Caskey left Reardon's bedroom and wandered along the bare hall, past the locked security suite, to the brand-new refurbished kitchen. The hacienda-style double doors had been replaced with something more tasteful, and she pushed through into the virginal snow-white room, spotless and unused.

Everything was different, new, even the flooring, to which Caskey's gaze was drawn, seeking the spot where she'd first laid eyes on the lifeless bodies of Monty and Patricia Thorogood.

Realising that her breathing had quickened, she recalled the surge of envy rushing through her the moment she saw the two of them. Envy for the couple who had died together, one enveloped in the other's arms, walking into infinity locked in a fatal embrace.

How different from the worst night of her life, knife on vein, and lying beyond her vision in stark brushstrokes, Georgia's disfigured, inert beauty, cold and lifeless.

'Do your job, Rachel,' she mumbled, fists clenching, breaking away to the French windows to take in the scrub of the grounds. 'You *will* get past this.' Distant fireworks sprayed their colours into the darkening navy sky, the explosions muted by the double glazing, and she realised the rehearsals were over and Bonfire Night had arrived.

Turning back to the room, her eye wandered to the only familiar artefact from that deadly afternoon – the white phone on the wall. She padded across to it and for no particular reason lifted it to her ear to listen to the dial tone, hand resting on the thermostat. It was working. She replaced it on its cradle and turned to leave then stopped, returning her gaze to the wall, her eyes narrowing.

'All done,' said Crump, spinning her round. 'Now if you don't mind, my missus is expecting me home for a few fireworks and a barbie.'

'Clear print?'

'Crystal,' said Crump.

'I'll need to know whose,' she said, fixing him with her gaze. 'Soonest.'

Crump was tight-lipped. 'What's the rush? The case is closed. It's not like you don't know Coulson was in the victim's bedroom with blood on his hands.'

Caskey was unmoved. 'If it makes you feel any better, I'll come with you while you run it.'

'Why are we only now taking Fry seriously?' demanded Charlton. 'An ex-soldier living round the corner, finger-print found in the Gibson house, and you failed to bring him in?'

'We did try, sir,' replied Brook, not meeting his eyes. 'He made a run for it.'

'That's why we take backup,' snapped the Chief Superintendent.

'It didn't seem to be indicated, sir.'

'Not indicated? With his record of violence, he should have been on the radar from the off.'

'He doesn't fit the profile,' said Brook. 'The Champagne Killer isn't driven by the sort of anger and confusion that drives Fry.'

Charlton's expression turned to ice. 'Does Fry have an alibi?' Brook was silent. 'No. Motive?' Again Brook didn't answer. 'I'll take that as a yes.'

'It's not motive enough to prompt a series.'

'He's connected to Gibson and his parents' house,' said Charlton. 'He knows how to handle guns and he's armed and on the run.'

'It's not him.'

Charlton glared at Brook. 'Then why has he run?'

'Because he's worked out all the reasons you just listed for picking him up, and when Sergeant Noble and I went to interview him, he panicked.'

'And absconded with a weapon.'

'Unconfirmed as yet, but Matthew Gibson claims Fry told him he'd smuggled home a Glock from Afghanistan.' Brook was aware he was banging another nail in Fry's coffin. 'He took it off a dead comrade's body.'

'Armed Response?'

'Alerted.'

'Where are we looking?'

'Gibson lives in Ticknall, and Fry was there yesterday to pick up funds.'

'Which suggests he intends to put some miles between himself and Derby.'

'Maybe,' said Brook. 'He has the resilience and skills to make himself scarce and stay that way.'

'Let's hope we catch him before that happens. Roadblocks around the area?'

'Yes, sir.'

'What else?'

'We're calling in a chopper for first light tomorrow.' Brook's phone vibrated and he held up a hand. 'Okay, John. Seal it off.' He ended the call. 'Fry has a lock-up in Peartree. It's full of ladders and paint but they also found several nine-millimetre ammunition boxes. Empty.'

'Any sign of the gun?'

Brook shook his head.

Back in the incident room, Brook flicked on the kettle as he looked up at Fry's mugshot on the display board. The e-fit of the unknown man at Frazer and Nolan's party sat next to it.

The telephone rang on DC Cooper's desk. 'Caskey for you.'

Brook moved across to pick up the receiver. 'Sergeant?'

'Just out of EMSOU,' said Caskey, sounding breathless.

'You didn't need to ride shotgun this late.'

'I wanted to. And you were right. We found blood on the casement. In fact we got an actual fingerprint. It seems when the cleaners washed everything down, the underside of the window was shielded against the sill.'

'And?'

'We've just got a hit, though they haven't compared the bloods yet.' She paused for effect. 'It wasn't what we expected.'

'Was it Reardon Thorogood's print?'

There was a momentary silence from the other end of the line. 'You knew?'

'Not for sure,' replied Brook. 'But there were no bloody shoe prints leading over to the stain, and Reardon was the only one in the room with bare feet.'

'Right,' conceded Caskey. 'Well, we'll know for sure soon enough. I'm on my way to Nottingham to ask her.'

'No!' said Brook, louder than he'd intended.

There was silence at both ends of the line. Brook glanced up to see Cooper hurriedly looking away.

'Why not?' said Caskey, her voice clipped. 'Don't you trust me?'

'It's not that,' said Brook, casting around for a viable reason to keep Caskey away from Terri. He failed. '*If* we need to speak to her, I want to be there.'

'Why wouldn't we need to speak to her?'

'It's her bedroom, after all. The fingerprint may be nothing.'

'But it has blood on it,' replied Caskey. 'Plus she never mentioned in her statement opening and closing the window.'

'She was under stress and in shock,' argued Brook.

'Maybe, but the blood . . .'

'. . . is probably Jemson's, and if so, its presence on the window is explicable. Look, Sergeant, we don't talk to Reardon until we know whose blood it is, then we frame our questions around that context.'

'Then why send me all the way to the farm? Crumpet could have run the print on his own.'

'It's still your case,' said Brook, trying to sound encouraging. He regretted it immediately.

'If it's my case, why can't I interview Reardon?'

'Because I came up with the print, so now it's my case too. You've done good work today, Rachel,' said Brook. 'We'll pick it up—'

The line went dead. Brook sighed. The newest member of his squad was now thinking he didn't fully trust her. And he wasn't certain she was wrong.

Caskey glared maliciously at the handset before switching it off in case Brook tried to call her back. She flung the tablet on to the passenger seat, glaring resentfully across at Reardon's large stuccoed house, the dark park beyond. A spray of red and green gunpowder cascaded across the blackened sky, briefly illuminating the shadowy exterior.

'This is *my* case,' she muttered, clambering out of the car and training her gaze on the upper storey. There was no discernible light or movement behind the heavy curtains pulled firmly across the windows. 'My shambles, my case.'

She marched across the road to rap on the heavy door, then depressed the intercom button.

'Reardon. It's Rachel Caskey. Open the door, please.' No answer. She tried again. 'I know you're in there, Reardon.' She waved her warrant card at the security camera.

After further, and louder, attempts to gain entry, Caskey headed for the flagged patio that ran around the house to the gloomy rear. Once there, she squinted through the darkness to the upper floor. No sign of life at the windows or the access door to the wrought-iron fire escape. No lights, no movement, not even the tiniest twitch of the curtain from a nervous occupant.

She returned to the front door and held down the intercom. 'Reardon. We need to talk. It's important.' She began to fumble in her pocket, but stopped when the shiny brass latch caught her eye. It was brand new. The locks had been changed.

'Reardon!' she shouted, furious now, pounding on the door, jabbing her thumb down on the intercom button. 'Let me in. I need to speak to you.'

Light rain had begun to fall, and when another explosion reverberated nearby, Caskey stepped away, glaring at the door before striding belligerently back to her car. Jumping into the driver's seat, she slammed the door and, with a screech of tyres, sped away.

Caskey splashed through the puddles at the entrance to the firing range, relieved to see that Freddie wasn't the Firearms

Support Officer on duty – at least she'd be spared the usual banter and intrusive enquiries about her welfare.

Once signed in, she hurried to her locker. Two minutes later, she emerged from the range, jacket pulled tight around her.

Back in the car, she sat behind the wheel, raindrops streaking her hot face, cooling her. As the rain beat harder on the windscreen, the world of pain beyond disappeared from view behind a curtain of water. Screened from the world, Caskey pulled the photograph of Georgia on the platform of the Eiffel Tower from beneath her jacket and pressed on the beads of Blu-Tack at each corner to fix it to the dashboard. Tears filled her eyes and her shoulders began to shake.

'I tried, baby, I really did.' She touched the metal G resting on her breastbone beneath her shirt, then reached under the driver's seat and withdrew a handgun – a Glock 17 – and slipped it into her waistband. 'No way I can make it without you, baby. I'm sorry. You were the best thing that ever happened to me, and I betrayed you.'

Fry woke to the faint double crack of simultaneous shots, long after most fireworks had ceased. Half awake, he rolled over in his lightweight sleeping bag while his unconscious mind identified the weapon. A Glock. Maybe a 17, maybe a 19. He sat upright when the temperature told him he was no longer in Afghanistan. A third crack. Then a fourth. Louder. Nearer.

Already dressed for a speedy evac, he slithered out of his tent, rummaging in a pocket for his night-vision binoculars. Within seconds he'd trained them on the line of houses beyond the trees a quarter of a mile away. A movement caught his eye

– a figure striding purposefully from the end house, pulling on a black balaclava. From a distance, in the dark country night, the house looked like a small boat afloat on the ocean. The figure paused to push two black metal objects into a zipped pocket before sealing them emphatically. It was a pair of guns.

'Fuck,' breathed Fry, lowering the glasses briefly. He resumed his vigil, following the figure, dressed head to toe in black or navy, to the end of the lane. He could see the epaulette strips and radio loops on the jacket, and although he couldn't make out insignia, the distinctive high-vis yellow jacket carried tight under one arm was unmistakable.

'That's a copper,' he breathed, his pulse quickening. A second later, the figure disappeared from view on to the deserted main road running through Ticknall village.

Fry stowed the binoculars, drew out a torch and flicked it briefly over his watch. Gone two in the morning. He had plenty of darkness left to make himself scarce. And even assuming the cops threw up a few roadblocks, he was unlikely to be troubled travelling cross-country any time soon.

It took him a little over a minute to dismantle his lightweight tent, even in the stygian gloom of the overgrown copse. He stowed the tent and sleeping bag in his go bag, slung the straps over his broad shoulders and prepared to yomp across to his bike. But something rooted him to the spot.

The code. A code he'd lived by in Helmand. Never leave anyone behind! Not without knowing, not without seeking proof of life. Even when Private Dunphy's legs had been blown off by an IED, no one suggested an evac, in spite of overwhelming enemy firepower – AKs and 90-mill M79 shells rained down, but no one moved as Doc worked to control the bleeding.

We held our ground until everything that could have been done had been done.

Fry clipped his bag to the back of the Norton, resting against a young tree, then pushed the bike to the house a couple of hundred yards away. He leaned it against the dry-stone wall and drew his Glock from his jacket, checking the clip and easing off the safety before starting his sortie. He saw the first body a second after clearing the gate – a young man lying on his back on the path, dead yet with mouth open as if to speak. Shots to head and heart. A clean kill. No need to check the pulse.

He jogged low towards the house. Peering in through a lighted window he saw two more bodies, and regret pulled on his gut as he gazed at the lifeless couple. Matty and his partner – Jimmy something. Lashed to a pair of chairs. *Dead as Dunphy but a lot less messy.* One to the heart. Man down. He had his proof. There was nothing more to be done.

Staring at Gibson, blood pooling in his upturned mouth, he thought through his options. There weren't many. *You are so fucked, soldier. Did you put me in the frame, Matty? Did you finally get to butt-fuck me?* He put a knuckle to his mouth. His hand was shaking. Coming to a decision, he reached into a pocket, pulled out the wad of money and threw it on the ground, where it scattered over the damp grass.

'A land fit for heroes,' he laughed bitterly, ejecting the clip from his weapon and stowing it in a trouser pocket but keeping the unloaded gun in hand. 'Make men of us. Kill or be killed. But what do we do with the peace, Your Majesty? You bring us home, frazzled and fucked, only to tell us we're violent misfits. The killing ground is where we belong. And that's where I should have died. With

Dunphy. Did you fuck me, Matty? Did you?'

Looking around, he saw the open door by the patio and walked slowly through into the kitchen.

Thirty minutes later, Fry ambled casually out of the kitchen, his jacket unbuttoned, blood on his chin from a last kiss. He carried an unopened bottle of bourbon under one arm and the dregs of another in his hand. He downed the last drop and threw the empty at the half-finished barn, where it shattered loudly, then opened the second bottle and took another hearty swig before screwing the cap back on and stuffing it into one of the voluminous pockets in his combats.

A light fell on him and a neighbouring window opened wide, a middle-aged man leaning out for a view. He stared uncomprehending at the body on the path for a few seconds, then his eyes locked on to Fry. In a trice, Fry dropped to one knee and raised the pistol to the window. Wailing in fear, the neighbour threw himself to the floor.

Fry stood, smiling. 'Keep the home fires burning, citizen,' he shouted, ambling back to the Norton. He slung his rucksack over his shoulders, then leaned in to give the old machine an affectionate pat. 'That's it for you, Graham. You're even more fucked than me.'

Striking out towards the blackness, Fry took up a desultory verse of the Camp Bastion anthem. 'Is this the way to Amarillo . . .'

Brook woke from his slumber at the vibration of his mobile in a trouser pocket. He glanced blearily at the display as he sat up on the tiny sofa in his cottage.

'John!' He licked his dry lips. 'What time is it?'

'You were right.' Noble's voice was tight as a drum and he sounded very far away.

Brook glanced myopically at the clock. 'About what?'

'It wasn't Gibson.'

Twenty-Seven

THE COUNTRYSIDE AIR WAS DAMP and the cold pinched at his nose and ears, though the protective suit and overshoes allowed gusts of body heat to warm his face and neck as he walked. Brook plotted his way past the puddles along the dark lane, illuminated by the remorseless flashing of squad car lights. Windows glowed in every house, framing residents as they watched the grim proceedings unfold, forbidden to leave their homes with a deranged gunman at large.

At the end of the track, an old motorbike leaned against the boundary wall, being examined by DS Morton and a pair of suited scene-of-crime officers.

'Fry,' said Brook, gazing at the bike, his heart sinking. Charlton was going to have a field day over his failure to take the ex-soldier seriously.

'Yep,' said Morton.

Brook turned his gaze to the distant building but got no further than DC Banach, examining a body in the garden. Morton gestured to a taped walkway taking pedestrian traffic around the body and away from potential footprints, already being marked and photographed by a SOCO.

By the light of a single arc light, Brook recognised Sean Trimble, on his back on the gravel path, mouth open, arms out as though preparing for a hug. Rivulets of blood fanned in all directions from the dark hole exploded on to his forehead. Another wound, black as night, showed that a second bullet had smashed into his ribcage.

Banach looked up briefly at his approach. 'Sean Trimble,' she offered superfluously. 'Wrong place, wrong time.'

'Aren't they all,' observed Brook.

'Twenty years old,' she added with an edge of bitterness in her voice.

Brook was briefly held by her show of disgust. 'Anger is an emotion that blinds, Angie. The slower it burns, the easier it is to function.'

She nodded. 'I'm okay.'

Brook nodded to the pale flesh on the ground. 'Higginbottom?'

'Been and gone,' replied Banach. 'No doubt about cause. The two at the house took one in the heart apiece. Sean was heart and head.'

'The classic double tap of the professional,' said Brook. 'What are we thinking?'

'That he was an afterthought,' said Banach, indicating the position of the body. 'On his back, head towards the gate, feet pointing to the house. My guess is he was returning home when he was shot. Fry didn't expect him to be here, which is odd as you'd think he would've been watching the house. There's a smell of beer about him, so he might have nipped out for a drink and come back sooner than expected.'

'Stumbling upon the killer making his escape,' nodded Brook. 'We're checking local pubs?'

'We are.'

Dropping on to his haunches, Brook could smell the beer. Fortunately the body was fresh, untainted by the usual stench of evacuated bowels and bladder. Death had come so suddenly to Sean Trimble that he'd barely had time to feel the fear. And in the cold air, what blood there was had not yet taken up the sweet coppery odour of decay.

'Not much of an escape,' he said, straightening up.

'Sir?'

'His bike's still there.' Brook gestured to the large double garage. 'Gibson's vehicles?'

'Untouched. Next-door neighbour says Fry left on foot, heading cross-country.'

'On foot? How long ago?'

'Maybe two hours. Dog teams are on the way. Chopper, too. They'll have infrared. The RPUs are throwing up more roadblocks.'

'He's not heading for the roads or he would've taken one of Gibson's cars.' Brook looked out into the night, his head moving in a smooth arc around the black horizon, coming to a stop at a wooded copse rising above the flat meadow on a ripple of higher ground. 'When you get a minute, have someone take a look over that vantage point.'

Brook continued on towards the house, past the half-built barn and a brazier still kicking out a glowering heat, past a shattered bottle being photographed and carefully collected for fingerprinting. Dead fireworks lay on the ground. To his surprise, he also noticed several twenty-pound notes on the ground being photographed then carefully bagged by a suited SOCO.

Arriving at the kitchen, he registered the open bottle of champagne and the single flute, nearly empty. Two full glasses of red wine stood beside it.

The victims were already drinking when Fry arrived.

The dazzle of a camera drew him to the murder room, a sparsely furnished lounge with polished parquet flooring and minimalist furnishings that abutted the kitchen. Two leather armchairs had been pushed incongruously into the middle of the room; each supported a corpse.

Like Frazer and Nolan five weeks before, Matthew Gibson and James Trimble were lavishly tied to prevent resistance. The severity of the bindings left just enough play for a touch of hands, hanging limp now. In a departure from the two previous crime scenes, Gibson had blood smeared around his chin and top lip.

'They fought it.'

'Wouldn't you?' said Noble, appearing at Brook's side.

Brook glanced briefly at the DS, deciding that a half-truth would be less distracting. 'Of course.' He returned his unblinking stare to the scene, storing everything in his memory so he could interrogate every detail at a later time.

'One bullet each,' confirmed Noble.

'Two guns?'

'Unknown. But the neighbour only saw one. Fry smashed a bourbon bottle, woke him up as he was leaving.'

'He wasn't woken by the shots?'

'Bonfire Night,' said Noble.

Brook nodded. 'This kill is different, John.'

'Escalation?'

'More than that. He's reached the end and he's chucking in the towel. That's why he's drawing attention.'

'I'll say. As well as the eyewitness and the bike, there are clear fingerprints on the broken bottle, the wine glasses and the champagne bottle. We've even got muddy boot prints on the floor.'

'He's signing off,' sighed Brook.

'Great. Now all we have to do is catch him.'

Brook's brow furrowed. 'This doesn't make sense.'

'Sure it does,' said Noble. 'Fry and Gibson had a thing. Gibson tried to shut him up with money and Fry threw it back in his face before he killed them.'

'But it was Fry who asked for money.'

'Maybe he had a change of heart.'

'Crime of passion?'

'Well the neighbour saw blood around Fry's mouth.' Noble gestured at the blood on Gibson's face.

'Sealed with a kiss of death.' Brook shook his head. 'Then why go to the trouble of tying them both up? He's a crack shot. Why not just shoot them where they stood?'

Noble cast around for an explanation. 'It's a crime of passion. He wants to follow the method but he snapped because he's at the end of his tether. We know that much. Post-traumatic stress. And he has a temper. So maybe Gibson and Trimble professed undying love for each other, and jealousy kicked in and he lost it. *No bubbles for you two. Bang bang.*'

'Jealousy begets disorder and violence, John.'

'Which is reflected in higher levels of disorganisation, as you see. And most normal people would consider shooting someone fairly violent.'

'I suppose,' grumbled Brook, unconvinced. 'Either way I'm not covering myself in glory on this case, am I?' No answer from Noble. 'The victims didn't drink the champagne.'

'There's only a glassful missing. My guess is Gibson and Trimble didn't play ball and refused to drink, so Fry tried pouring it in their mouths. You can smell it on their shirts. He loses his rag, pops them both. It's the end of the line so he has a drink to celebrate and stops worrying about trace.'

'But why kill Matthew's parents?'

'No idea, but there's a clear connection to the family at least.'

'There isn't to Frazer and Nolan.'

'We'll find it. You saw the son?'

Brook nodded. 'Something else off script.'

'It might have brought him to his senses, because he had the neighbour in his sights but didn't fire.'

'Remorse,' replied Brook, rolling the thought around in his head.

'Makes sense,' said Noble. 'He's supposed to be sending couples off to eternity together but has to kill Sean – who dies alone. The guilt snaps him out of his psychosis.'

'And he doesn't steal a car to make a break for it because he's preparing for suicide by cop,' concluded Brook, thinking it through. He shook his head. 'But where's the loss in Fry's life? His wife is alive. Where's the trigger?'

'Dead boyfriend in the army?' suggested Noble. 'Who knows?'

'I don't see it, John. And how did he get control of Trimble and Gibson? The brazier is lit. If they were outside having a bonfire, why would they let Fry march them indoors and restrain them?'

'He had a gun.'

'But no element of surprise. Gibson would have realised

what was coming, especially if Fry was carrying rope. He wouldn't let himself be tied up without having a go.'

'History's full of corpses rooted to the spot as death walks up,' said Noble. 'Everyone's different. And if Fry waited until Sean went out, he might have told Gibson and Trimble that he'd grabbed him up and if they didn't play ball, he'd be dead.'

Brook nodded, impressed. 'You should've run this inquiry on your own, John. I've been a lead weight because of Terri and this Black Oak Farm nonsense. You were right about the escalation and right to give me grief. Where's Caskey?'

'I called, but her phone's turned off.'

Brook was thoughtful. 'She lives in Ripley, doesn't she?'

'I think so.'

'Try again. And failing that, get a squad car round to her place, tell her to get herself here immediately.'

'It's an hour's drive. I think we've got this covered . . .'

'Immediately,' repeated Brook, fixing his gaze at Noble to eliminate any doubt.

Noble took out his phone and held it to his ear. 'Something I should know?'

'Let's get some air,' said Brook, setting off through the kitchen towards the patio. 'Where are we on the canvass?'

'We're waking the whole village. Ticknall's a quiet place, people are likely to notice things.'

'Put the emphasis on catching Fry for now. Make sure everyone's got a description and a Last Seen Wearing. He's smart and may have doubled back to throw us off, though I doubt it.'

'We're a bit short of bodies.'

'Then get as much manpower as Charlton can rustle up from County. What about a local branch?'

'Nearest stations are Swadlincote and Ashby, but there's a village hall we can commandeer for an incident room.'

'Good. Co-ordinate the chopper, RPUs and the dogs from there.'

'Armed Response?' When Brook hesitated, Noble pressed the point home. 'Fry was here. People are dead. He has a gun. If we don't pick him up before daylight, this could get ugly.'

Brook acquiesced with a dip of the eyes. 'He won't run, but get a firing squad here anyway.'

'Let's hope it doesn't come to that.'

'Fry's a misfit who doesn't belong, John. He didn't help himself to a high-powered car and he's no intention of giving himself up. There's only one other option.'

Through the trees, Fry trained his night-vision binoculars on the distant helicopter.

He smiled and took another long pull on the bourbon. No dogs yet. He should be fine until daylight. That was as long as he needed. He downed another large measure of the bourbon and lay back against the crumbling brick wall of the outhouse at the furthest edge of the Calke Abbey estate. He'd torn off the derelict barn's rotting wooden shutter in case he needed to dive for cover from the infrared cameras once the chopper's grid search expanded. Even so, without dog handlers to co-ordinate on the ground, he was safe for a few hours. He took another warming slug.

Sit rep critical. FUBAR. SNAFU. With you soon, Dunphy.

He grinned at the thought of his fallen comrade, at the sense of brotherhood, of common purpose and camaraderie. It warmed him more than bourbon ever could.

'Next time I see you, you'll have your legs back.' He stared glassy-eyed into the darkness. 'And I'll be the man I want to be.'

He took out the unloaded Glock and put it on the ground, then pulled out his smartphone from a pocket of his jacket but didn't turn it on. He didn't want to activate the GPS just yet, but more importantly, he didn't want to drain the power he'd need for a final message to his wife. He just needed a signal. His surprisingly buoyant mood dissipated when he thought of her, so he took another tug on the bottle. Time to think. Time to compose what he wanted to say to his long-suffering Roberta.

With you soon, Dunphy.

Brook and Noble stood in the damp field allowing SOCO to swarm all over the site. They could feel the cold seeping into their bones and Brook felt the urge to go for a stiff three-mile walk to get his temperature up. 'No response?'

'Her phone's still off,' said Noble, ending the call.

'Check if local plod got a response when they knocked on her door.'

Noble stared at Brook. 'What's going on with you and Caskey?'

'Not a blessed thing,' quipped Banach, striding towards them with a tray supporting two steaming hot mugs.

'Something to contribute, Angie?' remarked Brook.

Banach offered the tray. 'Tea and coffee from the locals do?'

Brook accepted his mug and wrapped both hands around the heat, still eyeing the DC.

'You're a lifesaver, Angie,' gushed Noble, taking a hearty sip. 'You couldn't rustle up a bacon—'

'Don't even go there,' rebuked Banach.

'Are you American?' enquired Noble, grinning at Brook for support. It didn't arrive.

'She told you?' said Brook, eyes glued to Banach.

'Rachel?' Banach smiled. 'She didn't need to tell me. A girl just knows.'

'Knows what?' said Noble, looking from one to the other.

'She obviously said something to *you*, though,' said Banach.

'I worked it out,' replied Brook.

'Worked out what?' insisted Noble.

'And there was me picturing you cruising the Gaydar hook-up sites,' she mocked.

'I have literally no idea what you just said,' commented Brook.

'Someone's gay?' queried Noble. Brook and Banach finally broke off to engage him. 'Caskey?' No reply. 'Rachel Caskey's a lesbian?'

'Keep it down, John,' hissed Banach.

'This stays between us three,' said Brook. 'She has a right to privacy.'

'Caskey's a lesbian,' said Noble softly, trying the phrase on for size as though looking for its meaning.

'You've heard of them, then?' quipped Banach.

Noble winked at her. 'Explains why she hasn't hit on me.'

'Jesus,' groaned Banach.

Noble grinned at her. 'What?'

'You think every woman lusts after you?'

'Only the ones with eyes.'

'Jesus,' repeated Banach. 'This is why gay officers are reluctant to come out. If I had my way . . .'

'Is the canvass finished, Angie?' said Brook, draining his mug and holding it out for her in a way that told her she ought to be somewhere else. She placed the tray under it and waited for Noble's mug, giving him a last admonishing glare and placing a finger across her lips as she left.

'A lesbian,' repeated Noble.

'Have you finished your suffragette workshop, John?'

Noble pointed a digit at him. 'So this George you told me about, this dead partner, was a woman.'

'Apparently it's quite common these days,' remarked Brook drily.

'Good for her,' nodded Noble. 'How did you find out? Station gossip?'

'The opposite,' said Brook. 'There wasn't any.'

'Well, there's not enough love in the world . . .'

'That's what Jason Statham said at Frazer and Nolan's party, isn't it?' Brook turned to the horizon, where the pale light of impending dawn was beginning to bruise the sky. 'I know it's hardly news at the moment, but I may have been wrong. Or rather, inadvertently right.'

'About what?'

'When I told Charlton there might be a connection between Black Oak Farm and the Champagne Killer, I did it to head him off.'

'And now?'

'Now I'm starting to think there *is* a link,' said Brook.

'I'm listening.'

'Do you trust my instincts, John?'

Noble hesitated. 'Mostly.'

'Then trust me when I tell you that the day the Thorogoods were murdered at Black Oak Farm, someone saw something they wished they hadn't, and I think it triggered an impulse to kill.'

'*Someone* meaning on the Force,' ventured Noble.

Brook waited for him to catch on.

'Caskey?' Brook raised an eyebrow. 'Because she's a lesbian?'

'Because she's in mourning, John. She's a very troubled young woman who's suffered a traumatic loss.'

'She's a bit twitchy, maybe . . .' Noble paused, still wrapping his head around it. 'Do you have any evidence?'

'Only circumstantial,' conceded Brook. 'She's an AFO, carries handcuffs and could gain access to people's homes with a flash of ID. She fits the profile perfectly.'

'But she *created* the profile,' pointed out Noble.

'And you heard her deliver it from the heart.'

'She did sound like she was talking to a priest, I'll grant you that. A killer in mourning, celebrating the lives of devoted couples, then shooting them simultaneously so they can spend eternity together.' He pulled a face. 'I'm not convinced.'

'Neither am I,' agreed Brook. 'But a glance at her work shows she started going off the rails after Black Oak Farm and she's been struggling ever since.'

'So what did she see?'

'Monty and Patricia Thorogood dead in each other's arms.'

'Something that messy could knock anyone back.'

'Especially if that's the fate she wishes she'd suffered with the love of her life.'

'You realise this is a massive leap.'

'I'm aware of that.'

'Who have you told?'

'Just you.'

'Good. Charlton would have kittens.'

'Do you think?' mocked Brook.

'What do we do?'

'Not much we can do except keep an eye on her.'

'Hard to do if she's AWOL,' nodded Noble. His mouth dropped open in shock and he gestured towards the crime scene. 'Wait a minute. You think . . . ?'

'I think if someone else is the killer, then Fry is the ideal fall guy.'

'But he was here. With a gun.'

'He doesn't fit the profile, John. Killing Gibson like that makes little sense.'

'Then why was he here?'

'He was camping over in that copse,' said Brook, indicating the shoulder of land in the distance. 'I suspect he heard the shots and came to investigate.'

'Why would he do that? He's already a murder suspect.'

'You said it yourself. He's struggling on all fronts. Maybe he's had enough. And, of course, he may have had genuine feelings for Gibson.'

Noble was thoughtful. 'How long have you suspected Caskey?'

'After she came up with the profile, it offered me a glimpse of her suffering,' replied Brook. 'That's when I started to take a real interest in Black Oak Farm.'

'Come on,' said Noble, doubtful. 'You were all over it before then, and it wasn't just about Mullen having his say. There's something you're not telling me.'

Brook took a deep breath. 'Reardon Thorogood is in a relationship with my daughter.'

'You're kidding!'

'I wish I were. They met at university a couple of years ago.'

'Terri's a lesbian too?' said Noble, with a sharp laugh that turned the heads of detectives and scene-of-crime officers alike.

Brook ushered him further into the darkness. 'She's needy and damaged, John. And right now she doesn't know what she is.' The helicopter passed overhead as a van carrying a dog-handling unit pulled up at the end of the lane.

Noble's brow furrowed. 'I thought Reardon Thorogood was once in a relationship with Jonathan Jemson.'

'It doesn't mean a thing. She's another young woman damaged at the hands of men,' replied Brook, prompting Noble with a raised eyebrow. 'And the needy gravitate towards each other.' Noble wasn't getting it, so Brook tried again. 'And Reardon would have been very vulnerable in the days following her parents' murders.'

Noble's eyes widened. 'You think Caskey and Reardon . . .'

Caskey lowered the binoculars. After half an hour, there was still no movement in the flat and the curtains were still drawn. Then again, the sun had barely risen. Shivering, she strode briskly back to the car and started the engine to get warm. After five minutes with the fan on full blast, she turned the engine off and checked her tired eyes in the rear-view mirror. Satisfied that the drops had helped dissipate the red rim of sleep deprivation and tears, she got out of the car and marched across the road to the imposing door, unwilling to wait a moment longer.

When five minutes of pounding and buzzing had gone unanswered, a young man crested the park steps carrying a pushbike. He slid a key into the adjacent door of the software company and glanced across at Caskey, who had suspended her hammering until the man entered the building.

'Morning,' he said, pushing open his door. 'Long time no see.'

Caskey turned to face him. He was one of the computer geeks from the ground floor. 'Yes. Hello.'

'Lost your key?'

Caskey's thin smile was a huge effort. 'Something like that.' He finally wheeled his bike into the building and closed the door on her, and she promptly took up the pounding again. She pressed the buzzer and barked into the intercom, 'Open this door, Reardon, or I'm breaking it down. I mean it.' She waited a few seconds. 'Have it your way then.' She hunched a shoulder and prepared to shove against the sturdy door, but at that moment it opened and a pretty young woman stuck her head through the crack, blinking at the daylight.

'Do you know what time it is? What do you want?' she growled, her voice husky from cigarettes and sleep.

'Who are you?' demanded Caskey, although she recognised her face from previous stakeouts.

'I live here,' said the young woman haughtily. 'Why the hell are you threatening to break down our door?'

'I'm a police officer,' said Caskey, fumbling for her warrant card.

'That doesn't give you the right to break in.'

'You don't know a lot about police powers, do you?'

'I know plenty,' snarled the girl, not easily cowed. 'You were here last night shouting and hammering.'

'So you *were* in.'

'Yes, we were, and thanks to you, Reardon was frightened half to death all night. And if you're really a police officer, you'll know why.'

'I'm sorry about that, but I have to speak to her.'

'About what?'

Caskey hesitated. 'Police business.'

'The murder of her parents?'

Caskey was surprised and unable to guard her reply. 'That's right.'

'Newsflash, lady,' said the young woman. 'That case is closed and the killer is in prison.' Caskey raised an eyebrow. 'Yes, I do know all about it. And if you were ever on the case, you'd know Reardon has barely set foot outside since that day, so what you think she can tell you about anything is beyond me. Why aren't you out looking for her brother?'

'He's out of the country,' replied Caskey.

'You don't know that.'

'Are you going to let me in or not?'

'No,' said the young woman defiantly. 'It's not convenient.'

Caskey set her jaw. 'Step out of the way, please, or I'll arrest you.'

'You wouldn't dare,' she pouted back. 'Did my dad put you up to this?'

Caskey was wrong-footed for a second. 'Your dad?'

'The high-and-mighty Inspector Damen Brook,' sneered the young woman. Caskey's jaw dropped. 'He did, didn't he? He's trying to split me up from Reardon and he doesn't even have the guts to come here himself. I should've known he'd try something like this. All that liberal shit about just wanting me to be happy.'

Caskey stood speechless. Brook's refusal to allow her to speak to Reardon on her own suddenly made a lot more sense. 'I . . .'

'Yeah, you're busted. And you can tell him from me, it

won't work. Reardon and I are in love and there's nothing he can do about it. Now go away.'

The door began to close, but Caskey put her foot in to stop it, her face tight with determination. 'I need to see Reardon,' she said through gritted teeth.

'Well you can't . . .'

Caskey reached for her handcuffs, but a second later the door opened wider and Reardon's pale face appeared next to Brook's daughter.

'Hello, Rachel.'

'Reardon,' said Caskey, quietly.

'It's okay, Terri. I'll speak to DS Caskey.'

'You don't have to,' said Terri, looking into her eyes, her expression softening. 'She's got absolutely no right.'

Reardon's pallid smile countermanded. 'I'll be fine.'

Terri folded her arms to register disapproval before relenting and stepping behind Reardon. 'Okay, but I'm staying right here.'

'You changed the locks,' remarked Caskey.

'Given how things ended, I thought it best,' answered Reardon.

Caskey nodded, slid the key ring from her jacket and held it out. 'The latch key is useless,' she said, a half-smile directed at Terri, 'but I dare say future *lodgers* can get some use out of the others.' Terri glared resentfully back at her.

'Thank you,' said Reardon, taking the keys. 'You said you had police business.'

Caskey eyed Terri. 'On reflection, I think I'll leave my questions for a later time.'

'Good,' said Terri, touching the door on Caskey's foot to prompt a withdrawal. It didn't move.

'My necklace,' said Caskey softly. 'I'd like it back.' Reardon hesitated, then turned. 'Wait!' demanded Caskey. She glanced anxiously at Terri. 'And the other thing. I shouldn't have given it to you.'

Reardon paused, forming her reply. 'No, you shouldn't. That's why I threw it away.' Before Caskey could reply, she jogged up the stairs.

'So you're her ex,' said Terri with a smirk.

Caskey didn't meet her eyes. 'You'll get there.'

'No chance,' said Terri, with a mixture of defiance and pride. 'We're in love.'

'You might be, but Reardon isn't. She's not capable.'

'We're working through her issues,' said Terri haughtily. 'Together.'

'Bully for you,' scowled Caskey.

The descending notes of the staircase announced Reardon's return, and her pale arm extended towards Caskey, a silver necklace with a chunky letter R clutched in her fingers.

'Thank you,' said Caskey, removing her foot from the door and showing the pendant to Terri. 'R for Rachel,' she said, pointing to the letter.

'Skank,' hissed Terri, and slammed the door.

Caskey's savage amusement dissipated and she returned to the car deep in thought, patting herself down for her mobile. It was still on the passenger seat from the previous evening. She turned it on and was assailed by a dozen messages and missed calls from Noble. Instead she flicked at the solitary text from Donald Crump and read the message.

'That's impossible,' she mumbled, sinking back in the driver's seat to think it through. 'Impossible.' She flicked at an icon and Crump picked up on the third ring. 'It's Caskey. Are you sure about the blood?' She listened, eyes blank. 'I see. No, don't worry. Like you said, the case is closed. There's no rush. I'll inform DI Brook and you can send him an updated blood plan in due course.'

She rang off, her expression mutating from confusion to realisation to bitterness. 'You bloody fool, Rachel.'

Twenty-Eight

OUTSIDE TICKNALL COMMUNITY CENTRE LATER that morning, Brook peeled the plastic lid from a Styrofoam cup and sipped at the welcome tea. He warmed his hands on the hot vessel and stared up into the pale winter sun, glad of a clear sky for the helicopter. A major manhunt was under way, and it had been a busy morning co-ordinating roadblocks with the RPUs and organising search teams and dog handlers with the Force Incident Manager, now in the helicopter, criss-crossing the surrounding country-side grid by grid.

Brook loathed the administrative minutiae of such an operation, but on the upside, the involvement of firearms meant that much of the strategic work had been taken out of his hands by specialist officers. Even Charlton was in the field, though thankfully he'd taken himself off to Matthew Gibson's house to inspect the latest crime scene.

Brook extracted his mobile from a pocket to check the signal. It had gone again. He couldn't answer his daughter's text, sent earlier that morning, so he settled for rereading it.

Real classy, Dad. NOT! Please don't send over that skanky bitch to drive a wedge between me and Reardon. We're in love. Deal with it!!!!!!!!

'Skanky bitch,' he repeated, convinced that Terri must be referring to Caskey. Who else would be banging on Reardon's door? And if Caskey had been to Nottingham, against his direct instructions, chances were she knew Terri's identity.

'Theresa May call you?' quipped Noble, nodding at the tablet in his hand.

'It's a bit early for levity, John,' muttered Brook. 'Any developments?'

'Nope. But local radio are all over it. TV, too. We might be about to get swamped, but the RPUs are ready.'

'The media will get in somehow. They always do.'

Caskey's car pulled up and she jumped out, making her way towards Brook and Noble, her face a mixture of emotions – all strong.

'Where've you been?' demanded Brook.

She did her best to smile. 'I got here as fast as I could.'

'You look terrible,' said Noble. 'Where were you?'

'Home,' she said, not meeting their eyes. It seemed to be an effort to speak, but she roused herself, affecting normality. 'My phone was switched off. I didn't realise.'

'We sent a patrol car round,' said Noble, suspiciously. 'They said there was no sign of life.'

She processed the information for a few seconds. 'They must've got the wrong address.' Noble recited her address from memory. 'That's my place all right. Wait, I took a sleeping pill,' she replied with finality, comfortable in her lie.

'And Reardon Thorogood?' said Brook.

'What about her?' Caskey's eyes bored into Brook's, her expression daring him to enquire further.

'Never mind.'

With an attempt at engagement, she added, 'So, David Fry. Is it definite?'

'He was at Gibson's house last night,' said Brook. 'With a gun.'

'He'd tapped Gibson up for more money the previous day,' added Noble.

'Did he get it?'

'A thousand pounds.'

Caskey was puzzled. 'I don't understand. Why kill Gibson and his partner if they paid out?'

'When we see him, we'll ask him,' said Brook.

'And maybe he'll tell us why he dumped the money in Gibson's garden and walked away,' added Noble.

Caskey shook her head. 'Doesn't make sense. Do we really like him for this?'

'He was at the house,' repeated Brook. 'And people died.'

'You don't sound convinced,' said Caskey.

'He's armed and at large, so I don't think my opinion matters very much,' said Brook.

'But the money . . .'

'Fry and Gibson had a brief fling last Christmas,' said Noble. 'Since you've been off the grid, there hasn't been a chance to tell you.'

A bitter smile creased Caskey's top lip. 'Some kind of gay sex killer revenge scenario?' Brook didn't rise to the bait. 'Then why the blackmail scam if it wasn't about the money?'

'Allowed Fry the chance to set up a meet,' said Noble. 'The best we can come up with is that they argued, and Fry decides to kill Gibson and his partner, so he stays close to the house and waits for his chance.'

'And the son is collateral damage,' concluded Caskey. 'But why?'

'Jealousy?' speculated Noble. 'Fear of being outed?'

'Some people can be obsessively secretive about their sexuality,' observed Brook.

'So I gather,' said Caskey, her eyes narrowing. 'And I see how that might tie Fry to Frazer and Nolan. But Gibson's parents?'

'It's academic now,' said Noble. 'Fry was armed and here. ID is cast-iron.'

'Do we have a fix?'

'Not yet. But he's on foot.'

'I went to Gibson's house first,' said Caskey. 'There were two cars untouched in the garage.'

'Better make a note of that, John.'

Caskey scowled at him. 'I mean he's not running, is he?'

'He's conflicted about his sexuality and looking at life behind bars,' answered Brook. 'Throw in post-traumatic stress and self-destruction doesn't seem a bad option.'

A police van hurtled round the corner and screeched dramatically to a halt, a high-powered Volvo pulling up behind. A dozen Authorised Firearms Officers in full gear – baseball caps, ballistic vests – disgorged, their boots crunching on the broken tarmac outside the makeshift incident room. They carried holstered semi-automatic Glocks and X26 Tasers, and several of them cradled high-powered Sig Sauer carbines under their arms.

Caskey raised a lazy arm and called a greeting to the officer jumping out of the passenger seat. He was tall, well-built, face covered by a full beard, bushy and thick. 'Hey, Tink.'

'Rachel,' replied the officer, walking over to her. 'I keep missing you at the range.'

'CID,' she said, as though that was explanation enough. 'I shoot when I can.' She raised a hand to tug at his beard. 'How long have you had this monster?' He grinned without reply. 'If you've got a spare gun and jacket, I'll be happy to tag along.'

He raised an eyebrow at her. 'If it were up to me . . .'

'I know,' smiled Caskey. 'Rules and regs.'

He turned to Brook and offered a large hand. 'DI Brook? Sergeant Tinkerman, Armed Response and Bronze Commander.'

Brook shook his hand. 'You have a good reputation, Sergeant,' he said, aware of Noble's head turning quizzically. 'Alex, isn't it?'

Tinkerman's smile was equally quizzical. 'Ellis,' he corrected.

'Ellis,' nodded Brook. Noble's confusion was reaching critical mass. 'Your work at Black Oak Farm was exemplary.'

Tinkerman was a little nonplussed. 'Here to help,' he responded to fill the silence.

Noble's expression changed and he glanced at Brook, an element of comprehension creeping over his face.

Cooper sprinted across to them, a map flapping in the breeze. 'The helicopter picked up a contact.'

'Where?' said Brook.

'Serpentine Wood. It's only a mile or so, over Calke Abbey way.'

'I know it,' said Noble, fumbling for his keys and hurtling off to fetch the car.

'My team are ready,' said Tinkerman. 'We'll follow you, Inspector. You have jackets?'

Brook shook his head, so Tinkerman whistled to one of his squad and mimed putting on a jacket, pointing at the two CID officers. Two ballistic jackets were handed to Brook.

Caskey meanwhile was already at her vehicle, throwing her coat in the boot of the car. She pulled on a stab vest and fastened it around her upper torso before sliding protective ceramic plates into the specially designed pockets.

Noble drew up and opened the passenger door for Brook. One of the AFOs jogged across from the Volvo with helmets and dropped them on to the back seat.

Tinkerman adjusted a dial on the airwave radio clipped to his epaulette. 'Get us there,' he said to Brook. 'When we make contact, the FIM will take over. Weapon status is already confirmed, so I'm afraid you'll just be bystanders. Make sure you don't get in the way.'

A young woman from his team jogged over with Tinkerman's protective helmet. He removed his baseball cap and put the helmet on over his dark hair. Then he tapped the radio in his ear. 'Firearms channel, guys!' Adjusting his earpiece, he ran through a couple of tests on his way back to the van, then clenched a fist in the air to initiate a rapid departure.

'Sergeant?' Brook called over to him from Noble's car. 'How do these things usually end?'

'Up to the target,' said Tinkerman, a hand over his mic. 'We'll do our best to end it peacefully, but if we have to shoot, we shoot to kill.'

After pulling on a protective helmet, Caskey raced round to the passenger door of the police van.

Tinkerman ushered her in, then stood on the footplate on the passenger side. 'Let's roll.'

'How did you know?' asked Noble, eyes glued to the road, hurtling along deserted country lanes.

'As soon as I saw him, I remembered his name from the Black Oak Farm files.'

'You recognise him?' Noble risked the briefest glance across in a search for understanding.

'I've stared at the artist's impression long enough. The beard and the hair are recent. Take them away and he's a match for the e-fit. Tinkerman is Maureen McConnell's guy from the party.'

'Are you sure?' said Noble.

'Ellis, not Alex. He was at Black Oak Farm, John.'

'So it's not Caskey now.'

'I've no idea, but if it is, she should be manoeuvring David Fry over the trapdoor. Instead she's defending him.'

Noble ducked down, saw the helicopter in the distance. 'What are you going to do?'

'I don't know.'

'He's one of our own. You can't call him out unless you're absolutely certain. Not now, not with an armed killer at large. If you're wrong, Charlton will bury you.'

At the top of a rise a stationary squad car with flashing lights blocked the road and Noble came to a screeching halt, but the Armed Response van powered past and turned down a track, slithering to a halt at the top of a slope in the next meadow. The van emptied rapidly and Tinkerman directed his troops with practised precision.

Brook opened the passenger door to follow. 'Get hold of Cooper. Don't use the radio, use your mobile if you can get a signal. Tell him to find Tinkerman's service record and get a picture to Maureen McConnell. If she recognises him, go through his personnel file.'

'Looking for what?'

'A dead wife.'

*

Fry stared up through the foliage at the black and yellow helicopter hovering above his hiding place.

'This is it, Davey boy,' he muttered, stripping off his camouflage jacket. He tipped the bourbon for a final pull, but the bottle was empty and he flung it into the undergrowth. Opening a flap of his rucksack, he extracted the unloaded gun before shoving it into his waistband, then slipped out his mobile phone from a trouser pocket and turned it on.

To his relief, battery life was decent, but with a tic of dismay, he noticed he had no signal.

'Shitty kit,' he spat, tempted to throw the phone into the undergrowth after the bottle. He looked beyond the trees to higher ground, thinking it through. Settling on a solution, he flicked at an icon, then turned the camera on himself and sucked in a calming breath. He tried to smile.

'It's me, hon. I don't have long.' He took a moment to compose himself. 'It's time you had a fresh start. We've got some wonderful memories but that's all they are. This is for the best and I think you've known for a while.'

He grinned. 'Honey, I'm sorry I ever married you. Not because I don't love you but because I really, really do. It's not been fair on you, the lie I've been living. Guess I don't need to tell you I'm not the man you thought I was, and it's been eating away at both of us for longer than I care to remember, even before I joined up, hoping the army could make a man of me. Maybe you should sue. Might get them to change the slogan at least.' He chuckled at this and wiped away moisture gathering in an eye. 'I want you to know I'm at peace. No more violence, no more struggle, no more hanging tough, jumping on the first wrong word and beating it to a pulp. I'm finished with deceit, hon, with all of it. So forget me and live the life you deserve. Hope it's not too late to find a nice bloke.' He laughed. 'You, I mean. Maybe you can finally have the kids I promised a million years ago.'

His expression hardened. 'And if you're even remotely interested, Inspector Brook, I didn't kill Matthew and I didn't kill his family or his parents. It was one of your own. I don't shoot people, I get shitfaced then smack 'em around to prove what a real man I am.' The chuckling started again but stopped abruptly. 'Staff Sergeant David Fry, 2nd Mercian. Over and out.'

Brook's phone vibrated. He finally had a signal and another text arrived from Terri, sent only ten minutes after the previous one.

WTF, Dad! Seriously??

Brook arrived at Tinkerman and Caskey's position, in the shelter of a clump of trees on high ground looking down into a small wood, above which the helicopter hovered. He pocketed his phone then threw on the helmet and pulled on the protective jacket.

'This is Silver Commander. Holding steady directly above the target,' said a voice on Tinkerman's radio. 'Target hasn't moved. No sit rep on weapons status, over.'

'Bronze Commander. Roger that,' said Tinkerman, before relaying the suspect's location to his team, binoculars glued to his eyes. He sat with finger hovering over the talk button, glasses trained on the small thicket. Fry's army camouflage jacket was clearly visible under the thinning foliage, though he didn't appear to be in it.

'Holly bush,' said Tinkerman, identifying the only verdant

cover since the autumn winds had removed many of the leaves. He could even see the steam rising from Fry's body in the sharp dank air. 'Bronze Commander, target acquired.'

Brook knelt behind Caskey, watching Tinkerman manoeuvre his team into position in a rough circle beneath the helicopter. One by one they radioed their readiness.

'AZ nine in position – eyes on target.'

'AZ ten in position – eyes on target.'

'AZ nine, AZ ten, stand by,' said Tinkerman before glancing up at Brook. 'Five eyes on the target.'

'We want him alive,' said Brook.

'We want the same thing,' said Caskey, taking the binoculars from Tinkerman. Brook noted her use of the word 'we' – the ARU was her home.

They heard a noise behind them and turned to see Charlton running at a crouch towards their position, panting in his heavy wool uniform, shiny buttons hidden beneath his protective vest. Noble was with him and exchanged a quick glance with Brook.

'Where's the target?' breathed the Chief Superintendent when he reached them.

'Directly under the helicopter,' said Brook.

'We have him surrounded,' said Tinkerman.

'So what are we waiting for?' demanded Charlton.

'Giving him time to review his options, sir,' said Tinkerman. 'Right now, he's considering everything under the sun, including staying put or going out in a blaze of glory. He's trapped so he's no danger to the public – giving him time to fully register the futility of his position might prevent loss of life in the long run.'

'So we wait,' said Charlton as though it was his idea.

Tinkerman didn't bother to reply.

'He could've taken a vehicle at the Gibson house, sir,' said Caskey.

Charlton nodded, the implication not lost on him. 'Can we communicate?'

'He has a mobile phone,' said Brook.

'We should try—'

'We're not negotiating here,' interrupted Tinkerman. 'He has no options. When we're ready to tell him what to do, there's a loudspeaker in the chopper.'

'Let me go down there,' said Brook. 'I might be able to talk him into a surrender.'

'We don't give him a hostage, Inspector,' said Tinkerman. 'He's armed. No one goes down there. No exceptions. We keep it simple, make it easier for him to decide.'

Fry scoured the higher ground with his field glasses in the hope of locating whoever was in charge. The glint of sunlight on a shiny button drew his eye and he found what he was looking for. A man in a fancy uniform, Brook crouching low next to him.

'Inspector Brook,' he said, training his gaze on him. 'Just the man I was looking for.'

With a deep breath, he dropped his field glasses and broke cover, arms extended as though about to be crucified, his shirt out of his trousers covering the unloaded weapon in his waistband. He began to climb up the shallow bank towards Brook's position on the ridge. It wasn't easy – the grass was lush and damp, and instead of watching his footing, he kept his head turned to monitor the phone in his right hand, his thumb poised to send the recorded message to his wife as soon as he had a viable signal.

*

'Bronze Commander. Target is on the move. Repeat, target is on the move. Direction RVP. Repeat, RVP. Over.'

Tinkerman repeated the message for those behind him and pressed the radio to his mouth, staring down the hill. 'I have him.'

'RVP?' muttered Brook.

'Approaching RVP,' said Tinkerman, ignoring him. 'Do you have eyes? Bronze, over.' Half a dozen AFOs confirmed they had the target in view.

'Rendezvous point,' explained Caskey, pointing to the ground beneath her. 'Right here.'

'He's coming this way?' said Charlton, straining to see.

Caskey stared at Brook, a strange smile drifting across her face. 'I liked your daughter. She stood her corner.'

Brook's reply was terse. 'We're doing this now?'

'Might not get another chance.' Her expression darkened. 'Get her home and don't let her out of your sight. The monsters are everywhere.' She smiled, then moved dramatically away from cover, standing to face David Fry down the hill and taking a few quick steps towards him.

'Rachel,' barked Tinkerman, and then, into his radio, 'Sergeant Caskey. Get back here. Take cover.' Caskey pulled her radio earpiece out, allowing it to dangle down on to her protective vest.

'What are you doing?' shouted Charlton. 'Get back here, Sergeant. That's an order.'

'Silver Commander, this is Bronze,' Tinkerman barked into his radio. 'Make contact, over.'

The loudspeaker on the helicopter came to life, the message slow and clear. 'David, get on the ground. Face down. Spread

414

your arms. Do it now, David. Get on the ground . . .'

After a pause to stare at the helicopter, Fry spotted Caskey and took another step up the hill. The helicopter repeated the message, but Fry wasn't stopping.

Caskey mirrored Fry's pose, arms outstretched. 'I'm unarmed,' she shouted. To confirm this, she began to remove her protective jacket as she inched forward, ignoring the various entreaties from behind to stand down. The message from the helicopter continued to repeat, but to no avail.

'We need to put him on the ground,' said Brook.

'Think I don't know that,' shouted Tinkerman.

'Get on the ground, David, or they'll fire,' called Caskey, continuing her slow descent towards Fry, some forty yards away. She dropped her protective jacket on the damp grass.

'I can't hear you,' shouted Fry above the noise of the helicopter. He was smiling but appeared perplexed by Caskey's disregard for protocol. The turbulence from the helicopter flattened the chunky grass and ruffled his shirt. 'Hiding behind a woman, Brook,' he bellowed. 'I'm surprised at you.' He snaked his eyes towards the phone. Still no signal.

'Get on the ground, David, or they'll shoot,' shouted Caskey.

'I still can't hear you,' said Fry, feet feeling their way slowly up the hill.

'What's that in his hand?' said Tinkerman over the radio, eyes glued to his binoculars, as the smiling Fry again moved his head to check the display. 'He's got something in his right hand.'

Brook wrenched the binoculars from Tinkerman and trained them on Fry's hand. 'It's a phone.' He leaned over to grab Tinkerman's radio, but the AFO wrestled it back. 'It's not a gun, damn it. It's a phone. Tell them.'

'He's a soldier,' said Tinkerman, snatching back the binoculars. 'He could have a concealed weapon or even some rough-and-ready IED. What the hell is Caskey doing?'

'She's lost her mind,' said Charlton. 'And if she gets through this in one piece, that's not all she'll lose.' The sound of a second helicopter arriving turned their heads. It was a Sky News chopper.

'Oh, brilliant,' said Tinkerman.

'How the hell . . . ?' began Charlton.

Tinkerman turned to Brook. 'What's going on? She's one of yours.'

Brook looked grimly back at him. 'She's damaged, Sergeant. You understand grief, don't you?'

'What does that mean?'

'It means we've got a suicide competition on our hands,' replied Brook, getting to his feet and heading down the slope after Caskey.

'Brook! Get back here, damn you,' screeched Charlton, not moving from his cover.

'Put down the phone and get on the ground,' Brook shouted at Fry.

'Inspector,' called Fry above the whirr of the rotor blades, nodding to the sky. 'Just in time for the evening news.'

'Get back, Inspector,' shouted Caskey when she saw him. 'I've got this. You're out of your element.'

'On the contrary, Rachel,' called Brook. 'Self-destruction is my speciality.'

'What?'

'She won't be there, Rachel,' he said.

'Who?'

'Georgia.'

Caskey hesitated. 'She won't be where?'

'Where you're going. She didn't wait for you. She's gone. She's not anywhere, Rachel. She's dead, and the only place she lives is in your head and in your heart. And if you die today, she's gone for ever.'

Further down the slope, Fry laughed. 'You starting a cult, Brook? Count me in.'

'Drop the phone and get on the ground,' bellowed Brook. 'It doesn't need to end this way.'

'Can't do it,' said Fry, taking another step.

'But ... I ...' Caskey turned back up the hill, staring at Brook, her face drained of all colour, pleading for meaning.

'I know,' said Brook. 'You could have saved her. Well now you can.'

Caskey's shoulders slumped as though she were a puppet whose strings had been cut, and she collapsed to her knees.

'He's right, kiddo,' called Fry. 'Go home. It's big boy rules today.'

'David, throw the phone away and lie on the ground,' shouted Brook.

'Not gonna happen,' said Fry.

'Put down your weapon and get on the ground,' boomed the police helicopter speakers.

'It's a phone,' Brook shouted to the sky, then turned to Tinkerman. 'Stand your team down, for God's sake. I'll bring him in.'

Fry took another step and smiled at the stirring of a signal on his mobile. He depressed his thumb to send the message just as a gust from the news helicopter blades rippled at his shirt, exposing the handle of the gun in his waistband.

'Gun sighted, over,' crackled urgently over the firearms

channel in Tinkerman's ear, followed seconds later by several sharp reports as the semicircle of AFOs dotted about the ridge opened fire.

'No!' screamed Brook.

The smile on Fry's face tightened a notch as he looked down at the explosion of muscle and rib above his heart. The phone fell from his hand, smashing on a rock, and he dropped to his knees. His breathing became jagged, resembling laughter almost, and after what seemed like minutes but was only seconds, he fell face down on to the ground.

With you, Dunphy.

Twenty-Nine

WITH NOBLE STILL ABSENT, BROOK sat in the incident room running through what he was going to say in the briefing that morning, especially as Charlton had threatened an appearance to shake hands and slap backs. As far as he was concerned, an armed and dangerous serial killer had been taken down with minimal fuss and without further harm to the public. And even though Fry's weapon was later found to be empty, the shooting board were unlikely to find against officers who had perceived a threat and fired. In Charlton's eyes, the fact that Fry had effectively committed suicide seemed only to confirm the profile of an organised and motivated serial killer who, when cornered, preferred to take the easy way out.

'The *Telegraph* press office say Matthew Gibson took out a personal ad of his own at the same time as his parents' anniversary,' said Cooper. 'It went in the same week.'

'Something else he didn't tell us,' said Brook.

'What did it say?' asked Banach.

'"I love you, Jimmy",' replied Cooper.

'To the point at least,' remarked Banach.

At that moment Charlton marched into the room, beaming broadly. 'All here?'

'DS Noble is still giving his statement on the shooting,' said Brook.

'And yours?'

'An hour ago.'

Charlton nodded. 'Good. Everything by the book for when the IPCC and Professional Standards take a gander. You're cleared for duty?'

Brook nodded. 'I didn't fire a weapon.'

'What about Sergeant Caskey?' ventured Banach.

Charlton glanced testily across at Brook. 'Clearly your SIO hasn't had a chance to inform you, but Sergeant Caskey is on indefinite suspension pending psychological evaluation and a full investigation into her conduct.'

Having been appraised of events at Calke Abbey, none of the assembled detectives expressed surprise.

'Bit harsh suspending someone for *not* shooting a suspect, sir,' ventured Banach.

'Angie,' warned Brook.

'Sergeant Caskey was an experienced AFO, Constable,' said Charlton. 'She knew the protocols better than anyone yet she put herself in danger, and by extension the rest of the unit.'

'And by the time the shrink is done with her, she'll be lucky if she's allowed to shoot ducks at the fair,' chipped in Morton.

'Very colourful, Sergeant,' said Charlton, his smile tight.

'Well if I were in Armed Response, I wouldn't be chuffed to see her roll up to an armed siege,' said Cooper. Read, Morton and Smee nodded their agreement.

'Anyway, Sergeant Caskey's failure of judgement apart, I just popped in to congratulate you all on a good result.' Charlton glanced at Brook. 'Inspector, if you could thrash out the main bullet points of a statement and get it to Media Liaison by four so they can draw up a script. We face the cameras at six.'

'Sir,' said Brook. 'I suggest we hold off on the full epilogue until ballistics matches Fry's gun to the seven victims.'

'I don't mind throwing in the usual caveats, but there's no doubt we have our killer,' boomed Charlton. 'And the people of Derby need to know that.'

'But he tested negative for GSR at this morning's post-mortem,' said Brook.

'Then he wore gloves,' said Charlton.

'There weren't any in his kit,' pointed out Banach.

'So he dumped them on his travels,' retorted Charlton, irritated now. 'What is this?'

'You saw last night's footage on the news?' asked Brook.

'I saw an armed and suicidal suspect advancing on police officers . . .'

'I mean Fry's farewell message to his wife. And to me.'

'Catnip to what passes for newsrooms these days,' said Charlton. 'Doubtless the not-so-merry widow now has a few thousand pounds to put towards the funeral. What of it?'

'Fry denied killing Matthew Gibson and his family.'

Charlton unfurled his most sarcastic tone. 'Suspect Denies Guilt Shock!' A few awkward smiles broke out amongst the gathered officers but were just as swiftly stifled.

'*It was one of your own.*' Brook paused before voicing the unpalatable. 'He accused a police officer of the Ticknall murders. Sir.'

'I hope you took that with as big a pinch of salt as I did.'

'Of course,' lied Brook. 'But if we rush to judgement and ballistics doesn't come through, a statement announcing Fry as the Champagne Killer may look hasty. Or worse, disingenuous.'

'Are you serious?' exclaimed Charlton.

'I just want to be sure,' said Brook. 'We don't want to be accused of a cover-up.'

'What possible grounds can Fry have for accusing a police officer?'

'He was camped near Gibson's house last night, and we found night-sight binoculars in his kit, sir,' said Banach.

'Which means he could have observed anyone approaching or leaving the property.'

'A police officer?' Charlton's voice was soft and menacing. 'Utter rubbish, and I suggest you don't speak of it again. The eyewitness evidence against Fry is overwhelming.'

Noble walked into the incident room, easing the tension slightly. He made immediate eye contact with Brook and followed up with a curt nod.

'Fry's guilt is circumstantial,' said Brook, with more confidence. 'The sensible thing would be to wait for ballistics.'

'We're issuing a statement, Brook, and that's an end to it.'

'Sir, Fry—'

'What are you doing, Brook?' demanded Charlton, his voice flat and hard.

'Trying to get the truth, sir.'

'We have a good result, thanks to you and your team, and all the evidence points to Fry. He was seen at the Gibson house with a gun and three people were shot dead there. How much clearer do you need it?'

'Clear enough that I know his gun was used at all three crime scenes, including Ticknall.'

'But we only recovered one weapon from Fry,' said Morton. 'Two guns were used in Breadsall and Boulton Moor.'

'Something else that doesn't add up,' said Brook.

'I suppose he could've dumped the second gun while he was legging it,' said Morton. 'There's plenty of acreage between Ticknall and Serpentine Wood to lose one of the murder weapons.'

'And Fry's an ex-soldier,' pointed out Smee. 'He could've had a dozen guns in that lock-up for all we know and dumped *both* murder weapons last night. The Glock we recovered from him doesn't even have to match and he could still be the Champagne Killer.'

Charlton spread his arms triumphantly and grinned at Brook. 'Wise words, detectives.'

'Then we find those weapons and test them as well,' said Brook.

'Find them?' said Charlton. 'DS Morton's right. They could be anywhere.'

'Fry's route from Gibson's house was fairly tightly defined, sir,' said Noble. 'It shouldn't be a huge problem with the right gear.'

'I don't believe this,' said Charlton. After a few seconds' thought, he took a sharp intake of breath. 'Very well. I'll mark time in front of the media tonight, and when Fry's gun is found to be the murder weapon, *you* can make the statement to the press, Inspector. But be clear on this. I am *not* blowing the budget looking for phantom guns across the Derbyshire countryside.' He sighed irritably and looked at his watch. 'I've got a meeting.'

'One more thing, sir!' Brook nodded to Noble, who flicked on the projector and dimmed the lights. 'We've identified the unknown suspect from Frazer and Nolan's engagement party.' When his computer was booted up, Noble tapped a few keys to split-screen the photograph of the partially obscured partygoer with a head shot from an ID card. 'Sergeant Ellis Tinkerman, Bronze Commander from yesterday's shooting.'

There was a shocked silence until Charlton managed to speak. 'Sergeant Tinkerman? From Armed Response?'

'The same.'

'One of the officers who shot David Fry.' Charlton's voice was almost inaudible, such was his anger and disbelief. 'You confirmed the ID?'

'Another partygoer, Maureen McConnell, spent time talking to him,' said Noble. 'As you saw yesterday, Tinkerman has grown his hair and a beard since then, but we showed his photograph to McConnell. ID is a hundred per cent.'

Charlton was stern, considering his response. 'He went to a party given by Frazer and Nolan.'

'Yes, sir.'

'Did he know them?'

'Very slightly. He met them in Derby. They felt sorry for him and invited him to their party.'

'What do you mean, felt sorry for him?'

'Tinkerman's wife died eighteen months ago. He was grieving.'

'So they invited him to a gay party.'

'It was just a party,' said Brook.

Charlton was quiet, searching for the right words. 'There's no mystery here. Obviously Sergeant Tinkerman went to the party under a misapprehension and was embarrassed about it when he found out. Yes, he should've spoken out when Frazer and Nolan were killed, but he didn't, and for reasons I think any red-blooded male would understand. Is that all you've got?'

'There's also the profile, sir.'

'The one that said the killer was a professional shooter,' snapped Charlton. 'Like David Fry.'

'Fry may have been a decent shot, sir, but his record of violence counts against him here.'

'How so?'

'The crime-scene management at the first two killings. Fry didn't have the training to subdue victims without resorting to physical violence. He was a disorganised individual, not plausible enough to gain entry to a victim's home without arousing suspicion and resistance.'

'And come to think of it, his finances were wafer-thin,' added Morton. 'Bank account running on fumes, no credit card, no regular income.'

'Since when do you have to be well-off to commit murder?' Charlton scoffed.

'From the moment you decide to take sixty-pound bottles of vintage champagne to your kills,' declared Brook.

'Fry didn't own a pair of handcuffs either,' said Noble.

'You've searched his house?' asked Charlton.

'This morning,' said Smee.

'The lock-up, too,' said Noble. 'We found nothing incriminating. No handcuffs, no champagne, no research materials . . .'

'Research materials?'

'Notes showing the victims' names and addresses, surrounding streets, physical entry points, details of their movements and habits, copies of the *Derby Telegraph* with personal announcements marked.' Brook paused. 'Fry knew Matthew Gibson intimately and his parents slightly but we couldn't find a single link to Frazer and Nolan. And he had no credible motive for *any* of the killings.'

'Also he didn't own a car,' said Banach. 'Getting to Breadsall would be problematic.'

'What about the motorbike?' said Charlton, more thoughtful now.

'That barely got him to Ticknall,' said Morton.

'It got him to Ticknall; it could've got him to Breadsall,' barked Charlton. 'As for motive, Fry and Matthew Gibson had an affair . . .'

'I don't deny a case can be made,' insisted Brook. 'But if Fry had an issue with Gibson, why kill six other people?'

'You heard the last message to his wife,' argued Charlton. 'He was ashamed of his sexuality. He killed Gibson and his partner so no one would know he was gay. Sean Trimble got in the way. Gibson's parents may have found out, so they had to die too.'

'But then why bother to stage the killings?' argued Banach.

Charlton was silent for a moment. He interlocked his fingers as though in prayer. 'You have a motive for Sergeant Tinkerman?'

'In my opinion, the crime scenes and the method show that the Champagne Killer is motivated by life-changing grief,' said Brook.

'According to his personnel file, Tinkerman took his wife's death hard,' added Noble. 'He had time off, and counselling, and stood himself down from the ARU for six weeks.'

'Grief could affect anyone like that,' argued Charlton.

'Of course, but for some, it can become an obsession,' said Brook. 'Tinkerman was stricken. So stricken that maybe he wished he'd died beside his wife.'

'And when he meets Frazer and Nolan, he gets the idea,' said Noble. 'He sees how happy they are and decides to kill them so they can never be parted.'

'It goes well,' said Brook. 'In fact he's so pleased, he scours the personal columns of the *Derby Telegraph* looking for more couples to send off to eternal bliss.'

Charlton shook his head. 'He wouldn't wait so long to start killing. There had to be some kind of trigger.'

'Black Oak Farm, sir,' said Brook.

'DI Ford's case?'

'Tinkerman was in charge of the Armed Response Unit that day,' said Brook. 'He and Sergeant Caskey found the Thorogoods dead in each other's arms. That planted the seed. When Frazer and Nolan invited him to their home, he saw what he had to do.'

'Killing them was no way to repay their hospitality,' scoffed Charlton.

'In a strange way, he thought it was,' said Noble.

'It was his gift,' said Brook. 'Like you or I might give champagne.'

'And once the idea had taken root, it wouldn't be a stretch to plan and carry out further attacks, especially with his expertise in home invasion and pacification,' said Noble. 'All he needed were the right victims.'

Charlton stood, making for the door. 'Well it's been interesting, at least. Shame you don't have any hard evidence.'

Cooper raised an uncertain hand. 'The *Telegraph* press office emailed us this morning, sir. A month ago, they gave out details of Matthew Gibson's name and credit card payment for two personal announcements for an edition in August. The request came from someone purporting to be from the County Constabulary press office in Ripley.'

'Where Armed Response is based,' said Brook.

'And a credit card leads to an address,' chipped in Noble.

'Two addresses,' said Banach. 'Gibson owned his mother and father's house. He may have followed him there.'

Charlton stared, unable to conjure a response, so Brook pressed the point home. 'Sir, we need a search warrant for Tinkerman's home, any vehicles he owns and his locker at the shooting range in Ripley. If we can scare up some of those research materials we talked about . . .'

'Unless you can tie Tinkerman to that phone request, the answer is no,' replied Charlton.

'Sir?'

'Really, Brook. Do you honestly think I'm going to authorise a warrant application to search the home of a respected police officer on such flimsy circumstantial evidence?'

'Have I ever let you down before, sir?'

'Too often to calculate.'

'Sir . . .'

'Stop,' ordered Charlton. 'I'm not immune to your persuasive powers, but I am *not* about to expose myself in that way. The Federation would go ballistic.'

'Sir, we've had two separate killings in five days,' said Noble. 'The Champagne Killer is escalating and there's no telling how soon—'

'Sergeant Tinkerman has been stood down from duty,' said Charlton. 'He has no access to the ARU armoury until the board hears his evidence on the Fry shooting. The Exhibits

Officer has taken possession of all guns from yesterday's—'

'He didn't use an official weapon, sir,' said Brook.

'Impossible,' agreed Morton. 'Every carbine, every Taser and every handgun has a strictly enforced paper trail. Weapons are signed out and back in again every day, whether it's for practice or armed duty. He must have picked up a couple of decomms.'

'A couple of what?'

'Decommissioned weapons,' said Noble. 'When a force has surplus or obsolete firearms, they're either destroyed, transferred to another division or sold. There's a lot of scope for weapons to go missing.'

'It's a problem in Nottingham,' agreed Morton. 'Even worse in the PSNI.'

'This isn't Northern Ireland, Sergeant,' chided Charlton.

'Rob's right,' said Brook. 'If—'

'Enough,' barked Charlton, looking at his watch again. 'I don't want to discuss this any further. Brook, I suggest you expedite the ballistics exam of Fry's weapon and the bullets recovered from Ticknall. Once they provide a link to the other murders, we can all get on with our lives and pretend this conversation never happened.'

'And if they don't?'

'Then you have one card to play,' said Charlton. 'If Tinkerman was at Frazer and Nolan's party, you have every right to bring him in and ask him the question.'

'Thank you, sir,' said Brook, glancing at Noble.

'I know that look, Brook. Do not take that as an invitation to start accusing a respected police officer. Tread very, very carefully, and I do *not* want to hear any whispers about your suspicions outside this room until the ballistics comparison is in.' Charlton glared at the assembled detectives to make his meaning clear. 'From anyone.'

Thirty

Wednesday 9 November

'MAKE SURE HE HAS HIS rep with him,' said Charlton.
'We'll suggest it,' smiled Brook. 'But he'll be expecting another go around the houses about the Fry shooting, and bringing his rep into it will put him on his guard.'

'I want him on his guard,' said Charlton.

'Then we'll suggest it strongly.'

'Fine. But you're not to ask him about the Fry shooting directly, do you hear?' Brook nodded. 'I assume Tinkerman has no idea you're interviewing him.'

'That's the plan, sir.'

'Then be clear about offering the rep,' insisted Charlton. 'He might claim later that you blindsided him.'

'I will be blindsiding him,' remarked Brook.

'No you won't, you'll ask him about the party and his acquaintance with Frazer and Nolan and that's it.'

'And one or two matters arising,' put in Noble.

'Such as?' demanded Charlton.

'If we mention Frazer and Nolan, surely we can introduce

431

the profile of their killer,' said Noble.

'Strictly in the abstract sense,' added Brook. 'Sir.'

Brook's reassuring smile had the opposite effect, and Charlton eyed them both doubtfully. 'Maybe I should sit in.'

'Is that wise?' Brook stared evenly at the Chief Super, willing him to recall his disastrous contribution to a suspect's interrogation the year before, and his subsequent embarrassment, so he wouldn't have to bring it up himself.

'Perhaps I'll just watch on the monitor.'

Brook smiled broadly. 'Your call, sir.'

Tinkerman looked up in surprise when Brook and Noble entered, the latter carrying hot drinks. 'Inspector?' he said with a grin. 'You're taking over as Post Incident Manager?'

Brook's smile was tight and professional, as were the introductions for the tape.

'Your rep's not here,' observed Brook. 'Do you want us to postpone?'

'I've done all my debriefs,' said Tinkerman, his affability fading. 'I assumed this was just a handshake and a carry-on-with-the-good-work back slap. You were there, Brook. Fry had a gun. It was a righteous shoot.' He shrugged. 'If it's about Caskey and her little stunt, she didn't learn that routine from me.'

'This isn't about Caskey.'

'Then what? Some media bullshit?' said Tinkerman, his mood souring. 'If so, they didn't get it from me. I don't talk to hacks.'

Brook glanced at Noble, who placed a selection of photographs on the table – a pair of crime-scene photos of Frazer and Nolan, their corpses side by side in their Breadsall home, next to post-mortem photographs of the dead men.

Tinkerman stared without expression, his dark eyes darting from picture to picture as Brook and Noble watched for a tell. When faced with an image of a life taken, a killer would often push the photographs dismissively away in a subconscious admission of guilt and revulsion. Or look quickly then turn his face away.

Tinkerman did neither, instead engaging Brook with a nonchalant shrug. 'You want a comment on marksmanship, I'll need a range.'

'No more than ten feet,' said Noble.

Tinkerman weighed it up. 'Indoor shot? Not difficult, especially if the vics are stationary. One in the heart, right?'

'Right.'

'Quick at least.'

'Do you recognise the victims?' ventured Brook.

Tinkerman paused. 'Sure. Fry's first kill. The gay couple in Breadsall about six weeks ago.'

'Do you remember their names?'

Tinkerman shook his head slowly. 'Can't say I do.'

'What about this man?' said Brook, laying down two more photographs.

Tinkerman pulled the picture closer – Sean Trimble, lying on his back on the gravel path. 'Is this the Ticknall scene? It's a more skilful shot.'

'How so?' said Noble.

'It's a night shot, moving target. Heart and head. Classic. But the heart's the stopper. The head shot is backup, usually from close range when the target is down. Go for the heart. You miss, you do major damage. Miss the head shot and your target could still be live. And the skull's pretty tough if you hit at the wrong angle. The bullet can easily glance off.'

'Impressive,' mumbled Noble.

'Basics,' grinned Tinkerman. 'Any AFO will tell you the same.'

'So you went for Fry's heart?' said Brook.

Tinkerman stiffened. 'You know damn well I did.'

'A fine shot.' No reply from Tinkerman. 'Do you ever miss, Sergeant?'

'Never,' said Tinkerman. 'I'm in the range three times a week.'

'What about this victim?' said Noble, tapping the photograph.

'His name is Sean Trimble,' said Brook.

'Okay,' said Tinkerman, a wary note creeping into his voice. 'Soldier boy knew his stuff.' He shrugged. 'Infantry, right. Look, I'm sorry Fry's dead. He fought for his country, but it was him or me. Or one of my team. I've done my psych evaluation and I'm fine with it. Can I go now?'

'The first victims, Frazer and Nolan, died together,' said Brook. 'But Sean died alone.'

'Most of us will,' said Tinkerman. 'We just have to get on with it, don't we?'

Brook smiled. 'Yes, we do.'

'The thing is, ballistics failed to match Fry's gun to any of the recent shootings,' said Noble. 'Not the one at Ticknall, or Frazer and Nolan in Breadsall, or Mr and Mrs Gibson in Boulton Moor.'

Tinkerman stroked his thick beard and nodded. 'You think he had a second weapon and dumped it after the shoot. Makes sense. A pro would have a backup.'

'That's what we figured,' said Noble, who placed the

photograph of the mystery partygoer on the table, alongside the e-fit produced from Maureen McConnell's description.

Tinkerman stared at both, his colour rising.

'You've grown your hair and a bushy new beard,' said Noble. 'But that's you at a party thrown by Stephen Frazer and Iain Nolan, the first victims of the Champagne Killer. The woman you spoke to there, Maureen, identified you.'

'Oh God.' Tinkerman put his head in his hands and loosed off a groan. He pulled his hands through his beard and away, coming to a decision. 'It's not what it looks like.'

'What does it look like?' said Noble.

'After Alison . . .' Tinkerman managed to engage their eyes. 'My wife. She died.'

'We know. It's on your personnel file. Along with a record of your visits to a bereavement counsellor.'

'That was over a year ago. I loved my wife. I still do. I was grief-stricken. We were planning to start a family.'

'Hit you hard, no doubt,' said Noble.

'I don't mind admitting it,' said Tinkerman. 'Or that it took me a while to get over it. Haven't you ever lost someone close to you? I mean, so close that they've become a part of your very being, so that you exist together or not at all.' He glanced down at the picture. 'I realise I should have said something when they were murdered, but . . .'

'You were embarrassed.'

He nodded. 'Don't get me wrong. I've got nothing against gay people. Stephen and Iain were lovely guys, very considerate and thoughtful . . .'

'But if your team found out . . .'

'Exactly. I was at a low ebb, and when they invited me to the party, I just needed some company. I knew it was a mistake as soon as I got there. A couple of the guys in my squad wouldn't have understood. At the very least, I'd be the butt of station gossip for the rest of my days, and I wasn't mentally strong enough for that kind of attention just then. I have to lead, Brook. You must know about that, about being in control. I have to know the guys trust me. I'm not proud, but it's not like I had any information to give.'

'So you kept silent.'

He lowered his head. 'This can't be happening.' He gestured at the photographs. 'Why is this relevant to anything?'

'I think I should remind you that you're entitled to have your rep here to look out for your interests.'

'But I've done nothing wrong.' Brook and Noble were silent, letting him work it out for himself, giving Charlton no cause for complaint. 'Jesus Christ. You think I'm this serial killer?'

'Are you?'

'No! Why would I kill those people?'

'You tell us.'

'I didn't do it.'

'Not even Sean Trimble?' said Brook, pushing his photograph back towards Tinkerman.

'He was shot dead after the killer had murdered his father and his partner,' said Noble.

'At least they died together,' said Brook. 'Like the Thorogoods at Black Oak Farm.'

'Black Oak Farm?' said Tinkerman, his brow furrowing.

'Nasty business, that,' said Brook.

Tinkerman stared. 'I remember. I was there.'

'Two people dying in each other's arms,' said Brook. 'That's the way to go, isn't it?'

Tinkerman smiled bitterly. 'You think I killed them as well?'

'Far from it,' said Brook. 'But I think you admired the way they died.'

Tinkerman's smile froze on his lips. 'Am I under arrest?'

'No, Sergeant,' said Brook. 'We're just having a friendly chat, in strictest confidence, of course. This goes no further.'

Tinkerman scraped back his chair and glared at him. 'Then I'm out of here.'

'What do you think?' asked Noble, outside the interview room.

Brook considered. 'He was very convincing.'

'You noticed?'

'But then all organised serials are. They rehearse the end-game a million times in their heads until they're word-perfect.'

'The grief is still raw,' added Noble. Brook nodded doubt-fully. 'Something wrong?'

'His reaction to Sean Trimble.'

'Well thank you for treading carefully,' complained Charlton, marching towards them.

'We didn't accuse him, sir,' said Noble. 'He opened that door on his own.'

'Just the same, I'd like you to make the call to the Chief Constable. Explain yourselves.'

'That won't be necessary,' said Brook. 'Tinkerman won't be taking out a grievance. We were talking in confidence.'

'You sound very sure.'

'He's not going to hide his connection to Frazer and Nolan for so long then start blabbing to his rep. We don't have a scrap of evidence and he knows that, so unless we make the first move, he's going to wait and see.'

'I don't know,' said Charlton.

'Besides,' continued Brook, 'it's not him.'

Charlton stared. 'I'm glad to hear it,' he said cautiously. 'How do you know?'

'Sean Trimble was our pressure point,' said Noble. 'He didn't deserve to die alone. It wasn't part of the grand plan and the killer would feel remorse.'

'But Tinkerman showed us nothing,' said Brook. 'Not a flicker of regret.'

'What were you expecting?'

'Once an organised serial killer has started to escalate, it's the beginning of the end,' said Brook. 'They're coming to terms, preparing themselves for it to be over.'

'And when the game is done,' said Noble, 'the only thing left to do is tell the world about the beautiful work of art they've created, and why.'

'So unless he's suffering from an extreme form of dissociative disorder, Tinkerman isn't our man or he would've crumbled and told us everything.'

'Well,' said Charlton, nodding. 'Good. Assuming you don't want to interrogate every AFO in the county, I'd better see about retracing Fry's route from Ticknall and finding his other weapons . . .'

Banach burst into the incident room. 'Inspector, your daughter's here.'

'My daughter?' Brook's look of confusion gave way to concern when he saw Banach's grave expression. 'What?'

Brook stood outside the unremarkable row of terraced houses in Ripley. A flash of headlights from a parked police car caught his eye and he trotted over to the driver's side, a detective from

County lowering the window to acknowledge him. 'Inspector Brook.'

'DS York,' said Brook, remembering the name thanks to Noble's recent prompt.

'My DC's watching the back. She's definitely in there. Tell me when you want to drop the flag.'

'Would you mind if we went in to get her,' said Brook. 'I'd like to keep it low-key.'

'You realise you're on our turf,' said York.

Brook smiled. 'Of course. But she's one of our own.'

'And armed . . .'

'If the balloon goes up, you can come in hard and heavy,' said Brook. After a few seconds, York nodded. 'We appreciate it.'

Brook gestured at colleagues and approached the garden gate as Banach, Smee and Read followed Noble from the other direction.

Noble was finishing a call. 'That was Cooper,' he said. 'Caskey was off duty during Frazer and Nolan as well as Gibson's parents.'

'And AWOL for the Ticknall shootings,' added Brook.

'You don't really believe she's capable?' said Banach.

'Everybody's capable, Angie,' said Brook.

'It's not in her,' insisted Banach. 'Trust me.'

'You saw the security film from Reardon's flat,' said Noble. 'She was waving a gun around, trying to break in.'

'And just a few days ago she tried to get herself killed at an armed stand-off,' said Brook. 'That's a classic sign-off from an escalating serial killer.'

'Her partner was murdered,' said Banach. 'She's got issues.'

'Or she was feeling guilty about the death of Sean Trimble,' said Noble.

'Enough.' Brook gestured at the house. 'Let's get this done. We'll unpick everything at the station.'

'I still think we should have the heavy mob go in first,' said Noble. 'She's armed, remember, and a crack shot.'

'We do that and she's liable to start shooting,' said Brook, rapping on the door. 'She's reconciled, trust me. We try reason first.'

The door opened and Caskey's tired eyes creased into a smile. She seemed smaller than Brook remembered, diminished, leaning against the door jamb of her nondescript terraced house, dressed in white T-shirt and jeans torn at one knee, hair scraped away from her make-up-free face.

'Inspector Brook. John. Angie. What a nice surprise. Have you come to clear me for duty?' She smiled at their hard expressions. 'I guess not. At least you didn't bring a rubber suit.'

'You'll get a fair hearing, Rachel,' said Banach, trying to load sympathy into her voice. 'It's a professional process.'

'And if only I'd been the same, right?'

'Let's not do this on the doorstep,' said Brook.

'Course. Come in and get comfortable.' Caskey turned and padded barefoot along the uncarpeted hall towards the stark kitchen, the footsteps of her three colleagues pounding on the boards behind her. Brook looked in on the tiny lounge as they passed. It contained a dog-eared armchair facing a three-bar electric fire. No lamps, no other furnishings and no TV. Nothing except a well-thumbed picture of an attractive young blonde woman grinning from a platform of the Eiffel Tower, Blu-Tacked roughly to the grubby wallpaper of the chimney breast.

Banach widened her eyes at Brook and Noble when she saw the bareness of the room.

'Cup of tea?' asked Caskey, waving an arm at the tiny kitchen table with three old-fashioned wooden chairs around it. No one sat.

'We don't . . .'

'Why not?' said Brook, ignoring Noble's admonishing glance. 'We have time.'

'Good,' grinned Caskey, flicking on the kettle. She turned to see her colleagues staring at the barren room. 'Bet you've not seen a place this comfortable since your last crack-den bust.'

'I've seen worse,' said Brook, his voice clipped and tight. Caskey seemed at peace – often the way once a fate was sealed. The anxiety of carrying a secret was too much for many, and unloading that burden brought release, even levity.

He watched her wash three unmatched cups and drop a tea bag in each, then look up at her stone-faced audience as she poured hot water into the mugs. 'Sorry. No milk or sugar.'

'What's that?' said Brook, nodding at a pile of papers on the table.

'A transcript of your interview with Luke Coulson,' said Caskey.

Something in her voice caught Brook's attention. He picked up the sheaf of papers and shoved them into his coat pocket. 'You're off the case, remember.'

She glared back at him, head held high before the hint of a smile creased her lips. 'Vaguely.'

'I'm going to ask you a question, Sergeant,' said Brook. 'And I want an honest answer.'

'Ask away. I'm a professional. Or at least I was before Black Oak Farm, right?'

Brook kept it simple. 'Do you have any illegal handguns in your possession?'

Caskey leaned back against the hob and folded her bare arms across her chest. 'Reardon took her sweet time telling you, then?'

'Answer the question, please.'

Caskey's breathing seemed to quicken and her eyes glazed. 'I'm finished, aren't I?' This time Banach had no words of consolation or encouragement for her.

'Sergeant, if we have to search your house, we will. We have a warrant.'

'I wasn't going to do what you think I was,' said Caskey.

'And what's that?'

'Blow my brains out in front of her. I'd never do that. Not after what you said about keeping my Georgie alive. In here.' She banged a fist against her ribcage, then her head. 'And in here.'

'I'm glad to hear it,' said Brook coldly. 'Do you need me to repeat—'

'I have a Glock 17.'

'Just the one?'

Caskey hesitated. 'Yes.'

'Can we have it, please?'

Caskey stared at him, then padded to the armchair in the lounge, her eyes drawn to the photograph on the chimney breast. Brook nodded for Noble to follow. She indicated the armchair cushion and Noble lifted it to reveal the Glock. He extracted a plastic evidence bag, pulled it over his hand then picked up the gun, folding the bag around the weapon and sealing it. He checked the safety through the plastic, then escorted Caskey back to the kitchen, not letting go of her arm. Banach moved behind her to snap on the cuffs.

'Is it loaded?' asked Brook. Caskey shook her head. 'Where?'

She nodded to a kitchen unit, and Banach slid out a drawer and dropped another evidence bag over a ten-round magazine of 9mm bullets. She showed it to Brook.

'Any more ammunition?' Caskey shook her head again. 'Where did you acquire this weapon?'

'Armed Response raided a pub in Gillingham when I was stationed in Kent. It was after my Georgie . . .' She lowered her head, took a deep breath. 'Intel told us the landlord was dealing in decommissioned PSNI weapons. When I entered the premises, I got separated from colleagues and ended up in a room with several weapons on display on a table.'

'And you liberated one for your personal use.'

'Georgie had just been killed,' explained Caskey.

'So it was for your protection,' said Noble. She nodded.

'Not self-destruction,' suggested Brook.

She glared at him. 'I'm here, aren't I?'

'And you're sure it was just the one handgun you stole.'

Caskey stared evenly back. 'How do you steal what's already been stolen?'

'Did you *take* a second handgun?' insisted Brook.

'You have a very low opinion of me, don't you?' said Caskey.

'I'm fighting it,' said Brook. 'Answer the question.' Caskey lowered her eyes and nodded. 'Where is it?'

'I threw it in the river.'

'Why?'

She stared at him, then decided on a more conservative course. 'No comment.'

'Was it another Glock?' asked Noble. No answer. 'Was it another—'

'Yes.'

'Where is it?' said Brook, soft and slow. 'Really.'

Caskey looked beyond him, her head up. 'I told you. In the river.'

'Show her the warrant, John.' Noble held it in front of Caskey's face. 'Where were you on the night of November the fifth when we couldn't reach you?' asked Brook.

'I was here.'

'Before that,' said Noble.

'Ask your daughter.'

'So you went to Reardon Thorogood's house,' nodded Brook. 'What happened?'

'She wouldn't open the door.'

'Was she there?'

'I thought so. She usually is. I decided to leave it, and came home and sat up with Georgie.'

'Where?'

'In the lounge, where you saw her.'

'A local squad car came looking for you,' said Noble. 'They knocked on the door.'

She shrugged. 'The lights were off. They got no answer. They went away.'

'So in fact you could have been anywhere,' said Brook.

'I was here.'

'And the next morning, November the sixth?'

'I returned to Reardon's,' said Caskey. 'Early. We had questions to ask her, remember?'

'Only this time you took your gun.'

She looked at Brook. 'Yes.'

444

'Reardon's front door has a security camera,' said Brook. 'You've been inside her apartment. You must have known you were being filmed.'

'I didn't care.'

'So why did you take a weapon with you?'

'To make sure I got in.'

'Were you intending to kill someone?'

Caskey was shocked. 'No.'

'Yourself? Reardon? My daughter?'

'No, I told you,' exclaimed Caskey. 'Why on earth would I kill your daughter?'

'I don't know,' said Brook. 'But you had a conversation with Reardon and my daughter and left. A few minutes later, you returned with the gun in your hand and started hammering on the door, screaming and shouting. Why?'

'I needed to speak to Reardon again,' said Caskey.

'You'd just spoken to her,' said Brook. 'Against my direct order.'

'Because you didn't want me finding out that she was shacked up with your kid.' Caskey turned to Banach and Noble, but their expressions registered nothing. They already knew.

'My daughter's relationship with Reardon Thorogood is incidental,' said Brook. 'Yours, however, is not. Why did you take the gun? Reardon was terrified.'

'Tough,' sneered Caskey.

'What was the plan? Who were you going to kill?'

'I wasn't going to kill anyone. Reardon made a fool out of me and I wanted to pay her back.'

'Like you tried to pay her back by crashing her car.'

Caskey took a deep breath, closed her eyes. 'After the

murder of her parents, Reardon and I started seeing each other. I know I shouldn't have got involved with a victim, but I couldn't help myself. She needed me and I needed . . . somebody. I'm not proud and I didn't plan it that way, it just happened.'

'And the crash?'

'Sometimes I'd stay over at her flat in Nottingham. That day I was with her in the car. It was her first time venturing outdoors since the attack.'

'Were you driving?'

'No, Reardon was. She was getting better, you see. Wearing make-up, going out.' Her face hardened. 'I'd helped her get that far. I mean, really helped her.'

'And you thought everything was rosy.'

'We were in love. Or so I thought. After Georgie . . .' Her expression soured. 'There we were, driving along, and suddenly I can hear Reardon saying the words, but I can't quite take them in. "I'm better now," she says. "We've taken this as far as we can. I was vulnerable after my parents died, Rachel, but now I want to try and stand on my own two feet." Fucking bitch.'

'You were angry.'

'You have no idea. After all I'd given her, betraying my Georgie like that, I just wanted us both to be dead.'

'Dead together,' said Brook. She nodded. 'The way you wished it could have been with Georgie. The way Reardon's parents died.'

Caskey narrowed her eyes at him. 'I suppose. I know it was stupid, but I was in shock. I waited until she got some speed up, then grabbed the wheel and steered the car into a wall.'

'And that brought you to your senses.'

'I guess.'

'And for the sake of your career, you made Reardon promise not to involve you in the accident report,' said Brook. Caskey confirmed with a dip of the eyelids. 'In return for you accepting the relationship was over.'

'Yes.'

'But you didn't accept it, did you?'

'I accept it now,' she said sourly. 'I was a fool and I deserve everything that's coming to me. As for Reardon . . .'

'What?'

Caskey stared at Brook. 'Never mind.'

Thirty-One

BROOK ESCORTED CASKEY TO THE car and manoeuvred her into the back seat while Noble and Banach summoned Read and Smee to organise a thorough search of the house with DC York and uniformed officers from County. When they returned to the car, Noble started the engine.

'They'll let us know if they find the second gun,' said Noble.

'You're wasting your time,' said Caskey. 'I don't have it. I told you.'

'We have trust issues, Sergeant,' said Brook, disappointment seeping from his pores.

'Did your daughter tell you about Reardon and me?'

'I worked it out,' said Brook.

'And the film from Reardon's security camera?' No reply from Brook. 'Let me guess. Reardon didn't want to say anything about the gun, but your daughter persuaded her.'

'I don't think you should say any more until you speak to your rep,' said Brook.

'Why are we here?' said Caskey, craning her neck as they turned into the car park serving Butterley Hall.

'The search warrant covers all premises,' said Noble. 'That

448

includes your locker at St Mary's and the one at the firing range.'

Caskey shrugged nonchalantly. 'Knock yourselves out.'

Noble jumped out of the car to extract Caskey from the back seat and the party made their way towards the underground shooting range.

'Do you mind?' said Caskey, at the top of the steps, waving her cuffed hands behind her. 'I was a good copper once and they know me here.'

Brook shook his head at Noble, who escorted her downstairs to the entrance, still cuffed. Sergeant Preston looked up in recognition, then dismay.

'Hi, Freddie,' said Caskey.

'Sorry to hear your news, love. You know you're not allowed to shoot until further notice.'

Caskey smiled humourlessly and turned to reveal her cuffed hands. 'I'm afraid it's a lot worse than that, Freddie.'

Noble handed over a copy of the warrant. 'We need access to DS Caskey's locker. We won't be long.'

Preston read the warrant, then logged the party in, and they set off past the armoury towards the locker room.

'I don't have my locker key,' said Caskey.

'You have a master?' enquired Noble. Preston nodded and fumbled for his keys, springing up from his booth to join them.

Brook's phone began to vibrate. 'Dave.' He followed the others but realised that the call from Cooper was breaking up the further he penetrated the underground chamber, so he backtracked to the entrance. 'Just a minute, Dave,' he said, catching Noble's eye and gesturing for them to continue. He stood on the bottom step to speak to Cooper. 'Go ahead.'

*

'How could you, Rachel?' said Banach, as they walked.

'How could I what?' demanded Caskey. 'Reardon?'

'We can start with that,' said Banach.

'You think I preyed on her?'

'Her parents had just been butchered and she'd been sexually assaulted, for God's sake. She was vulnerable.'

Caskey's eyes glazed over. 'She was beautiful. And needy. I couldn't help myself.'

'Even though you knew it was wrong?'

'The heart wants what the heart wants, Angie. What can you do?'

'It's tantamount to abuse.'

'I know what I did, Constable,' snarled Caskey. 'But I was in love.'

'In love?' exclaimed Banach. 'Rachel, seven people are dead.'

Caskey looked askance at her. 'What's that got to do with it?'

'There's an email from Crumpet with an updated blood plan for Black Oak Farm,' said Cooper. 'He's already spoken to Caskey about it, so I thought you'd want to know.'

'What does it say about the fingerprint on the window frame?' asked Brook, gazing blankly at the booth behind the Perspex screen. Steam rose from a welcoming mug of hot tea, and his mouth watered.

'The blood was Patricia Thorogood's . . .'

Brook began to drift out of the conversation as the circled paragraphs on a dog-eared copy of the *Derby Telegraph* began to register. He stared at the trite little rhymes, composed to convey undying love to a partner, the hand holding his mobile gradually lowered from his ear. Then his eye was drawn to a photograph of a middle-aged woman smiling from a wheelchair, a black ribbon across one quarter of the frame. A younger Sergeant Preston stood behind her, clutching the handles.

A second later, Brook was in full flight across the rubber matting, pushing violently into the locker room. Caskey, Banach and Noble were standing together in front of an open locker. All three were rooted to the spot, staring beyond Brook. The door closed behind him and he turned. Sergeant Preston stood in front of another open locker, two bottles of champagne visible between his legs. He brandished a gun in each hand, calm and unruffled, holding them steady. He flicked a wrist at Brook to move him away from the door.

'It's over, Sergeant,' said Brook, looking down the barrel of one of the Glocks.

Preston smiled. Brook saw relief there. 'I know. I'm glad.'

'His name was Sean Trimble,' said Noble.

Preston's expression soured. 'I'm sorry about the boy. I thought he'd gone out.'

'Well he came back,' said Noble.

'And died alone,' added Brook.

'I know what that's like,' said Preston. 'My Janet . . . I'm sorry. I truly am.' He broke off as Brook tried to edge closer. 'Don't think my left hand is any less good than my right, Inspector,' he barked, regripping the Glock to show he meant business.

Brook put his hands out to acknowledge Preston's prowess, trying to gauge the distance between them. Seven yards, maybe eight. He eased a few inches to his right, then glanced at Noble. The DS didn't react, but Brook could see from a slight move to his left that he understood. If they could widen Preston's field of vision, one of them might catch him off guard.

'What about Sean's father and his partner, Freddie?' said Brook.

'That went well,' said Preston. 'They struggled a bit because they didn't understand at first, but I think they realised when the end came and they appreciated it. Now they're together for ever. They'll never have to suffer what I've suffered.'

'You found Gibson through the personal columns.'

'Well done,' said Preston. 'He put an announcement in the paper for his parents' anniversary. I liked what I read and thought I'd pay them a visit, but when I cased the Ticknall house I only saw Gibson and his partner. I thought I'd made a mistake, but that morning I followed him to the house in Boulton Moor, and that's when I saw Edith and Albert. I watched them as they went for a walk across the fields. They were the perfect couple for me to help – happy, but I could see Albert was failing and pain was on its way. Edith was lovely. I didn't want her going through what I did with Janet, and she was pleased to go with her Albert.' Preston smiled. 'It was a beautiful moment when they passed together.'

'And Frazer and Nolan?'

'Get me talking,' said Preston, smiling. 'Very good. You!' he said to Noble, thrusting his gun at him. 'Over there with the Inspector. Move.'

Reluctantly Noble stepped across to Brook.

'You too.' He gestured at Banach.

'No,' said Banach, edging closer to Caskey.

'There's no time,' said Preston, aiming at her. 'Get over there.'

452

'DC Banach has a small child, Sergeant,' said Brook.

'I'm not in this to kill colleagues,' said Preston, a pained expression on his face. He smiled at Caskey. 'Except those like Rachel who want to go. All those anguished looks at that girl in your locker. She was very beautiful.'

'Thank you,' smiled Caskey. 'She was.'

'I've watched you, love,' said Preston. 'The desolation, the pain. It never goes away, does it?'

'Never,' said Caskey. 'It defines me.'

'Me too,' nodded Preston. 'Looking at you was like looking in a mirror. I wish you'd felt able to tell me what happened to her. I'm sorry I've let you suffer for so long when I could've helped you. But it's over and now I can set you free.'

'Death isn't freedom,' said Brook. 'Freedom is a construct of the mind. A living, thinking mind.'

'You!' Preston gestured to Banach. 'On my desk, the framed photograph. I want it. And don't be long or I'll kill this lad here.'

'I'm not leaving,' said Banach.

'It's okay, Angie,' said Caskey, nudging her away. 'I'll be fine.'

Brook nodded for her to go, his expression telling her not to come back. Reluctantly Banach dragged herself to the door and, after a final look back, stepped out.

'You must feel really tough, ordering people around with a gun in your hand,' sneered Noble.

Preston was unruffled. 'It helps.'

'So what happens when you get your wife's picture?' asked Brook.

'Like you said, Inspector. It's over. Ideally I would've have preferred to send Ellis and Rachel on their way together.

They've both suffered enough, and if their loved ones haven't waited, at least they'd have each other for company.'

'Oh how lovely,' mocked Brook. 'Did you have a piece of music in mind?'

'Ditch the sarcasm, smart-arse,' said Preston, raising the gun towards Brook's head. 'Rachel and me understand about pain.' He smiled regretfully at her. 'Sorry, love. Looks like you'll have to put up with me on the journey instead.'

Caskey nodded. 'That's okay, Freddie. We should be going.'

'As soon as my Janet gets here.'

'So you're an expert on pain,' said Brook, to keep him talking.

'People tell me things, yes,' said Preston.

'AFOs?'

'This is where they wind down,' nodded Preston. 'Where they waste the bad guys they're not allowed to shoot during the day. I'm like their priest. They tell me the stuff they've seen in the field. And at home. The things that hurt them.'

'About love and loss?' said Brook, smirking.

'You wouldn't understand. Tink – Sergeant Tinkerman – was a broken man when his Alison passed. Nothing I said made any difference.' Preston smiled bitterly. 'Well it doesn't, does it? Words are no substitute for a soulmate's embrace. But he tried so hard to put it behind him.'

'He succeeded,' said Brook. 'People move on.'

Preston smiled pityingly. 'Some do. Not Tink. A year ago he told me about the couple in Findern who died in each other's arms. That really touched me. He told me how much he envied them, and that's when I got the idea that I could really help people. Devoted couples who would rather die than suffer what I went through.'

'And he told you about Frazer and Nolan's party?'

'He did.' Preston laughed. 'Swore me to secrecy. Well, a lot of the guys wouldn't have understood. But I did. Love conquers all. Gay or straight, it doesn't matter to me.'

'So you're an equal-opportunities serial killer,' sneered Brook.

Preston's expression hardened. 'Have you got a death wish, Inspector?'

'He has,' declared Noble. 'Ignore everything he says. He wants you to shoot him.'

'Is that right?' smiled Preston. 'Then be careful what you wish for, matey.'

'I'm not your mate, I'm your superior officer.'

'None of that matters now.' Preston looked at the door. 'Where's your colleague? She should be back by now.'

'She's not coming,' said Brook.

'What do you mean?'

'I told her to raise the alarm.'

Preston glared at Brook. 'How did you do that?'

'I'm a telepath,' replied Brook.

'So what am I thinking right now?' growled Preston, gripping the Glocks tighter. Brook didn't answer. 'You heard me say I'd shoot this lad if there were any tricks?' He aimed one of the guns at Noble, but Brook stepped across his line of sight.

'I'm afraid I can't allow that,' he said. 'Out you go, John.'

'You've got a fucking nerve,' said Preston, becoming agitated. 'Get back where you were.'

'No,' said Brook. 'Go for the door, John. I'll cover you.'

'Why do you always do this?' demanded Noble.

'Out!' commanded Brook. 'That's an order.'

'See?' said Noble. 'Death wish.' Using Brook as a shield, he slipped out through the door before Preston could react.

Preston was becoming agitated. 'I want Janet,' he shouted. 'Bring me my Janet.'

'Why don't you blow your sorry brains out and go find her?' said Brook.

Preston's brow knitted in consternation. 'The lad's right. You want me to kill you.'

'I want you to put the guns down,' said Brook. 'This nonsense has gone far enough.'

'I don't like you, Brook.'

'Back of the queue,' snapped Brook. He stepped adroitly in front of Caskey. 'You're next, Sergeant.'

'No!' shouted Caskey, moving from behind him. 'I'm staying.'

Preston found his grin again. 'Looks like you're outvoted, Inspector.'

Brook moved back in front of Caskey, clamping his hands on her. 'Stay there. You're leaving.'

'No,' said Caskey, struggling. 'I'm not afraid to die.'

'Georgia won't be waiting, Rachel,' said Brook.

'I'm willing to take a chance.'

'Get away from her,' said Preston.

'Shut up, Sergeant,' said Brook. 'That's an order.'

'An order?' grinned Preston. 'Rachel and me are way past all that.'

Suddenly Brook stopped struggling with Caskey and turned to face Preston, resigned. 'You're right. Why am I bothering? You're better off dead. Both of you.'

Caskey moved away, and Preston immediately raised a gun to her heart and waggled the other at Brook. 'You can leave now, Inspector.'

Brook nodded. 'Just a thought,' he said. 'But what will your Janet say when you turn up in the afterlife with an attractive younger woman by your side?'

Preston's guns were lowered a notch and he stared at Caskey. 'My Janet? How dare you even speak her name.'

'You're right,' smiled Brook. 'I'm sure she'll be fine about it.'

'Don't listen to him, Freddie.'

Preston's breathing became laboured. 'Sorry, love. He's right. She wouldn't understand.' With no more ado, he jammed one gun under his own chin and took aim at Brook's heart with the other. 'At least I can do some good here.'

'That's the spirit,' said Brook, raising his hands. 'Don't you want the photograph?'

Preston shook his head. 'I remember every detail, every line on her face, every hair on her head. And next time I see her, she'll be good as new, like she was before the cancer.'

'No glass of bubbles before we go?' enquired Brook.

'It's not chilled,' quipped Preston, taking a deep breath and finding Brook's eyes. To his confusion, the Inspector was smiling. 'On my way, beautiful,' he said as he squeezed both triggers. The dual explosion reverberated around the underground chamber like an atomic bomb.

While he was still able, Brook watched the top of Preston's head blow away, his brains spraying out in all directions like a pan of hot jam thrown into the air.

A millisecond later, he was struck in the eye by blood as the second bullet slammed into the diving Caskey, throwing her

457

backwards. She'd taken the full force of it in the chest, and her body, recoiling from the blast, pinned Brook to the ground.

He screamed in anguish but, temporarily deafened, could hear not a note. Acrid smoke and the flash of the discharge blinded him to everything but an ejected shell casing spinning in the air as it fell to earth.

As the shock waves died, the world was silent and Brook could believe he was dead. He liked it. It was peaceful, and a strange calm washed through him. Then, in what seemed to be slow motion, people began running through the door towards him. Brook recognised Noble through his one good eye. Banach, too. The pair hauled Caskey's prostrate form by the arms and legs out into the range, where the oxygen was untainted.

Brook sat dazed on the floor of the locker room, his left eye stinging and sightless. He put his hand up and felt the unmistakable texture of warm blood. Noble rushed back in and helped him to his feet, and together they stumbled unsteadily through the carpet of blood and brains.

Clasping a handkerchief to his eye, Brook saw firearms instructors and uniformed officers gathering around Caskey as Banach forced oxygen into the stricken detective's mouth through her own. Someone caught the keys from Noble and unfastened the cuffs on her wrists. Brook could see Banach shouting in between each kiss of life, but he heard not a sound. Then, from nowhere, a man appeared with an oxygen mask, which Banach duly put over Caskey's face before clutching at her wrist to find a pulse. Noble was examining Brook's clothing, trying to satisfy himself that he hadn't been hit.

'I'm okay, I'm okay,' screamed Brook, and he fancied he heard his words as a distant squeak. He got to his knees and forced himself closer to Caskey, her blood still in his eye. Suddenly the sound of panic rushed in and he heard Banach screeching, 'I've got a pulse.'

He made a grab for Caskey's other hand and she opened a glazed eye and fixed it on him. He squeezed her hand for want of something better to do, and reassured her with a smile. He could see her trying to mouth something at him through the mask.

'What?' he said, pushing his ear towards her mouth. With great difficulty she pulled the mask aside. 'No,' said Brook, trying to put it back. She clenched a fist to keep it from covering her face. 'What is it? Shut up,' shouted Brook. 'Quiet, she's trying to speak.'

Against the background hum of the fans, he listened intently. Caskey licked her lips. 'Protection . . . for . . . Reardon.'

'Reardon's safe,' said Brook, smiling at her slackened face. 'Now put the mask back on.'

Caskey blinked twice at him and licked her lips before her eyes closed and she lost consciousness.

A second later, paramedics appeared, running a stretcher between them. They spent a couple of minutes examining and preparing Caskey before lifting her expertly on to the trolley and bolting up the stairs with their burden. The range emptied as officers hurried after them.

'Sir?' beseeched Banach. Brook waved a weary hand and Banach leapt into the ambulance as it pulled away at speed.

Some eight hours later, Brook drove away from the Royal Derby Hospital, the roads slick with winter rains and pulped leaves. He was in a daze, with little idea of the time; all he registered were the white lines of the A52 hurtling towards him like bullets fired in the night. Three words echoed around his head. *Protection for Reardon. Protection for Reardon.*

When he reached his cottage in Hartington, he flicked on the kettle and slumped at the kitchen table, putting his aching head in his hands. His vibrating mobile brought him round.

'How is she?' said Noble.

'Still in surgery,' answered Brook.

'She's a fighter,' said Noble.

Brook grimaced. 'Why do people always say that?'

'Because most people cling on to life until their fingers bleed.'

'There must be those who just say, fine, let's get it over with.'

'You mean like you.'

'I mean like Caskey. She dived in front of me, John. Why would she do that? She barely knows me, and what she knows she doesn't like.'

'You heard Preston. She's in pain. She had a death wish too.'

Brook sighed. 'I don't have a death wish, John.'

'I was there, remember. You wanted Preston to shoot you instead.'

'That's different. I'm her boss, I have a duty to protect my people.'

Noble shook his head. 'If you say so. What did Charlton say?'

'I ducked out when he arrived.'

'Wise move. So what now?'

'Now? We work the case, collect the evidence on Preston and tie it up in a neat bundle so not even Charlton can lay the blame on David Fry.'

'That won't bring him back,' said Noble.

'No.' Brook poured hot water into a mug.

'Someone else with a death wish.'

'Thank you, John,' grumbled Brook. 'I've got the message.'

'You see the email from Crumpet?'

'Cooper was telling me about it before I saw the newspaper on Preston's desk. It's a revised blood plan for Black Oak Farm.'

'Important?'

Brook was thoughtful. 'I'll let you know.'

Brook sipped at his tea while he read Crump's email. After a moment's thought he retrieved all the Black Oak Farm documents from the office and isolated Reardon's statement about events in her bedroom on the fateful day. Nothing appeared to explain her mother's blood on the window.

From his coat he pulled the transcript of Luke Coulson's interview in Wakefield Prison, recovered from Caskey. He read to where Coulson dealt with the killing of Jonathan Jemson in Reardon's bedroom. Again nothing. No possible way Patricia Thorogood's blood could have been on that window, if both statements were to be trusted.

He flicked through the rest of the transcript, pausing on a page disfigured by handwritten notes in Rachel Caskey's hand. At some point before her arrest, Caskey had triple-underlined a couple of sentences in which Coulson described the sensation that had overwhelmed him beside the bodies of Monty and Patricia Thorogood. *When I leaned over, I felt their souls leave their bodies. It's like they went right through me to go up to Jesus.* Beside it she had written *Bollocks*, and in capital letters in the margin, *TIMELINE?*

Brook pondered this, but finding no inspiration, pulled a pile of SOCO photographs towards him. It was the black-and-white pile photocopied by Terri for Reardon. He thumbed past shots of Reardon's parents in the death pose that had so affected Caskey and Tinkerman, as well as Coulson, followed by the two photographs of the blood smears near the bedroom window. As before, the black-and-white photographs were too indistinct so he picked up the colour pictures and skimmed past the images of Patricia and Monty Thorogood and Jonathan Jemson to retrieve the corresponding shots.

The bloodstains were so insignificant. Yet somehow Brook knew they were important, because of the location at the window. He replaced the two separate piles on the table and took a sip of tea before yawning heavily. It was gone midnight and he was completely spent. He drained his tea and walked towards the stairs, but froze like a statue for several seconds before racing back to the table, scrabbling for the scene-of-crime photographs and flicking through both piles, a rising sense of excitement and trepidation overwhelming him as he stared at the picture of the dangling phone in the kitchen.

Thirty-Two

'Y OU JUST MISSED HER,' SAID REARDON.

Brook climbed the final stair to the spacious landing, the low winter sun streaming through the skylight. Reardon Thorogood held the door open for him and he stepped through into the attractive apartment. When she closed the door behind him, he could see that she looked different. Make-up for a start. And her clothes were more striking than the shapeless things he was used to seeing her in.

'Do you know when she'll be back?'

'She took Sargent out for his morning gallop,' said Reardon, smiling. 'He's a bit of a handful. They should be in the park if you need her right away.'

'I don't mind waiting. If that's okay.'

'Of course. Tea?'

'Thank you.' Brook sat on the sofa while Reardon went through to the kitchen and turned on the kettle. 'You look well,' he called after her.

'Thank you,' she shouted back before coming to the doorway. 'After our chat, I thought long and hard about what you said. You were right. Hiding indoors like this isn't living.

463

So I'm making an effort.' She smiled sweetly at him. 'Thanks to you.'

Brook nodded. 'Have you heard the news?'

Reardon's expression changed to shock. 'We saw it on TV last night. I feel terrible. We couldn't believe it. I didn't want to report Rachel, but Terri insisted. Well, she did have a gun. How is she?'

'She died this morning.'

'Oh my God.' Reardon threw a hand to her mouth. 'I'm so sorry. Rachel was a nice person. She had her problems, I know.' She shook her head. 'Terrible. Just terrible.'

'She won't be troubling you again, if that's what you were worried about?'

Reardon stared. 'I wasn't. You look tired. This thing with Rachel must have been distressing.' She nipped back into the kitchen when the kettle clicked and returned with two mugs of tea. Brook took his mug to the fire escape door. 'May I?'

'Of course.'

He opened the door on to the sharp, cold morning. Sunlight streamed in. Reardon picked up her cigarettes and stepped on to the wrought-iron staircase, lighting up with a sigh of pleasure.

'So will you venture out into the great outdoors again?'

'We're going out to the Peaks this lunchtime,' said Reardon. 'Give Sargent a proper workout and maybe go to a pub. I can't wait.'

'Is that when you'll tell Terri she's outgrown her usefulness?'

Reardon studied Brook. 'That's very hurtful. And untrue.'

'You're right,' said Brook, taking a sip of tea. 'Technically it'll be the second time you've had to cast her aside. She was useful when you first met at university. You were able to pump her for information about me, about when I took my leave, who were the other DIs in the division.'

Reardon was taken aback. 'Why on earth would I do that?'

'Because your farm is on the Derby border with County and, given what you and Jonathan Jemson were planning, you thought it wise to kill your parents when someone like DI Ford was on call.'

Her face went white. 'That's a terrible thing to say.'

'Immodest as well, I shouldn't wonder,' replied Brook. 'It must have come as a shock to be confronted with a detective as skilful as Rachel Caskey. Fortunately she was emotionally vulnerable, otherwise she might have seen through the way you threw yourself at her to distract her from the investigation.'

'I think you've been working too hard, Inspector,' said Reardon.

'I'm certain I have,' laughed Brook. 'That's because you've been very clever. I'm impressed. Not least with your acting skills.'

'Acting skills?'

'Must have been a tricky balancing act, playing the victim, getting people like Rachel and Terri to devote themselves to supporting you, all the time wanting to get on with your life and spend your inheritance. Then, when you'd rid yourself of DS Caskey and were emerging from your cocoon, Terri told you about the letter I'd received and you had to drag yourself back to the world of drab clothes and unwashed hair to play the traumatised victim a little longer. That must have been galling.'

'I think you should leave, Inspector.'

'But you haven't heard my news.'

'I don't want to hear, thank you . . .'

'Your brother's dead.'

Reardon took a sharp intake of breath and gazed at him. 'Oh my God. How?'

Brook smiled. 'I don't know yet. But if I were a betting man, I'd wager he had his throat cut from behind when he was least expecting it. Like your father.'

'So you . . .' began Reardon, before stopping herself.

'No, we haven't found his body,' said Brook. 'Yet.' Reardon's eyes filled with tears. 'But we will, now that we're looking for it. His cottage garden is first on the list. I noticed you haven't instructed the estate to sell it yet. Not had a chance to relocate him?'

The tears began to fall. 'You horrible man. How can you say such terrible, terrible things? My parents . . .'

'. . . were in your way. All the things you laid at Ray's door – the envy, the mockery of their tastes, the resentment at them wasting their money on enjoying themselves – they all came from you, not Ray. That was why you decided to kill your family and frame your brother into the bargain. From its complexity, a plan a long time in the making, I should think. The resentment you must have harboured. Was Ray your mum and dad's favourite? Did they really deny him money when he needed it, or did they give it willingly?'

Reardon dried her eyes and took a pull on her cigarette. 'I think I need to sit down.' She pushed past Brook and draped her shapely form on the sofa. 'Just as I was starting to make progress.'

'Stop it,' said Brook. 'You killed your family in cold blood and used sex to get what you wanted, even enduring a beating from JJ if it meant being able to get your hands on the money. And it worked a treat. Having taken such punishment, nobody could seriously think you murdered your family for profit, especially if the line of inheritance was blurred. Such a neat touch, the estate being tied up the way it was. But you were prepared to wait. You'd waited years, after all. How are the lawyers doing, by the way?'

Reardon took a huge belt of smoke, her hand shaking.

'I've upset you,' said Brook. 'Do you want me to leave, or would it be wiser to let me talk and find out how much I know?'

She stared back, then held her chin up defiantly. 'If you really want to indulge in this sick fantasy, I'd better hear it all before Terri comes back and has to listen to your poison. Who else knows about this crap you're spouting?'

'Nobody. Unless I find Ray's body, I have no evidence.'

'And until then?' No answer. Reardon smiled at him. 'Then how will you make your case, Inspector? Are you expecting a confession for the tape you're no doubt running?'

Brook opened his coat so she could see his shirt tight against his torso. 'Not my style, even if the tape were admissible.'

'Then how are you going to frame me? You won't find anything to implicate me concerning Ray, assuming he really is dead.'

'He's dead, no question. Apart from the location of his corpse, the only detail escaping me is whether it was you or JJ that killed him.'

'And what does your instinct tell you?'

Brook considered. 'I haven't made up my mind yet, but it was your greed, your decision to act before there was nothing left. Your plan. Recruiting Jemson was easy, an old boyfriend, down on his luck. And was he ever the perfect choice. I'm guessing he didn't take much persuading to accept money and sexual favours to come on board.' Reardon raised an eyebrow at this. 'Better yet, he brought the perfect fall guy with him. Or one of them, at least.'

'One of them?' she enquired.

'You needed two fall guys,' said Brook. 'One to take the blame for the murders and one to take the hit for the planning, because no one would accept Coulson, or even JJ, as a criminal mastermind. No, that had to be Ray, your *scheming* brother. But Coulson was the key. He had a whole raft of reasons to come to the farm, and, even more important, he had some kind of motive to kill your father.'

'Inspector, before that day, I hadn't spoken to Luke since we left school,' snarled Reardon.

'I believe you. But you didn't need to. You already knew everything you needed to know. You remembered his obsession with you at school, and, of course, you'd seen him from a distance stalking you, watching you, yearning for you. Your father saw him too and chased him off. He probably mentioned it but you shrugged it off as nothing and pretended you didn't know who Coulson was. But you did. In fact, you encouraged him, fed his fantasies. Not so that he knew, of course. He probably thought that seeing you wandering around your bedroom in your underwear was just a lucky break, that you were an innocent, chaste beauty, oblivious to the ugliness in the world.

'No, Luke was easy,' continued Brook. 'Your brother, however, was a different proposition. He had to disappear. For ever. So you killed him the week before the attack on the farm to get him out of the way. You left it late because having him drop out of sight sooner would be risky. Your parents might notice, for one thing. But once you were ready, it wouldn't be difficult. I suspect you called round to his cottage one night, caught him off guard. That would be simplest. The hard part would be making it look like he was still alive for that week, but once you'd pinned your parents' murder on him, that would take care of itself. If Ray really was planning to kill his parents and his sister, it would be perfectly natural for him to be out of circulation.'

'You've decided that I killed Ray, then?'

'On balance, I think so. He wouldn't suspect a thing. You call round one night, he turns his back, you slit his throat. Either way, JJ would have to be close to bury the body, dismantle his phone, remove his passport and his wallet so he could max out his credit cards, all of which played to your back story about his debts and love of money as well as making it look like he was planning to disappear.

'The trick with the Porsche was especially good.' Reardon narrowed her eyes. 'Yes, I worked it out, though I gather from your expression that Sergeant Caskey didn't mention that. I'm glad. I did wonder whether she might be desperate enough to offer up a few titbits from the investigation to tempt you into taking her back.'

'I really don't know what you're talking about, Inspector.'

'Shame, because it was a masterstroke. JJ steals a big enough van for the two of you to transport the Porsche to East Midlands Airport, make it look like Ray's done a runner. Of course, it helped that Ford had Coulson all wrapped up as the killer and wasn't too interested in digging for the truth. Even more that you'd done a number on his DS. You realised after the attacks that Caskey was the better detective, so you sprang into action, and after the death of her partner, Caskey was unprepared for your . . .' Brook hesitated, unsure of the right words.

Reardon lit another cigarette. 'Seductive wiles?'

'Just so. I can only imagine how you steamed into her, playing the hapless victim, betrayed by men, needy and defenceless. I'm sure she fell hard.'

'You flatter me,' said Reardon.

'I don't think so. From what I've seen, she would have done anything for you.'

'Anything?'

'I don't think she buried evidence, no, but it was enough that she was distracted from key aspects of the crime, like the hunt for Ray. After a few months, once the fuss had died down, you dumped her. As I'm sure you were planning to dump Terri as soon as you felt safe.'

'This is fascinating,' said Reardon. 'I hope you'll be finished by the time she gets back. She won't take kindly to you saying such mean things to me, jeopardising all the progress I've made.'

'I'll try to be quick,' said Brook, glancing at his watch. 'But I don't want to sell your achievement short. It's breathtaking in its complexity.'

'I can't wait to hear how brilliant I've been.'

'Don't pat yourself on the back too soon,' said Brook, his face hardening. 'There were flaws.' Reardon raised an eyebrow. 'Sargent for one.'

'My dog? What about him?'

'It troubled me that he survived,' said Brook. 'Not that I wanted him dead, but I did wonder why a pair of cold-hearted criminals would take the trouble to drug him rather than poison him. Much simpler, and no chance the dog might wake.'

'Maybe JJ and Luke were animal lovers.'

'No, JJ was under strict instruction from you. At this point

Luke knew nothing about the attack or he wouldn't have gone along with it. He knew the dog, of course, from his long hours watching you from afar. But it was Jemson who brought the drugged meat, Jemson who carried the plan of the house and the list of valuables drawn up by Ray.'

'I thought you said Ray was a fall guy,' she scoffed.

'Another lovely touch. After you killed him, you rifled through his cottage looking for the combination of the safe as well as ways to implicate him in the crime. Ray had drawn up the plan of the house for the security firm and a list of valuables for an insurance policy he intended to take out on his parents' behalf. But with the right spin from you, they could equally be construed as a map for burglars and a shopping list of choice items, most of which you removed from the safe ahead of time in case JJ got greedy. I have duplicate copies from the insurance company at the station if you want to see them.' Reardon's eyes glazed over and she stubbed out her cigarette as though she wished the ashtray was Brook's face.

'And so the attack began,' said Brook, pleased to see her rattled. 'Or so it would seem. You'd already disabled the security system and wiped the film the night before, following Jemson's instructions – a little expertise he brought to the operation that you didn't have to fake. And around midday, the pair of them entered the farm.'

'Fascinating.'

'From here I'm ad-libbing,' said Brook. 'I'm guessing Jemson sent Luke to look for valuables around the house while he went straight to your bedroom to tear off your clothes. If I'd been JJ, I would have told Luke your parents were away so he wouldn't suspect a thing. I'd have given him the plan, too. After all, it's important that he finds his way back to the bedroom so he can have his wicked way with the defenceless victim and leave his DNA for the police. But when he gets to the kitchen, he finds your mother dead and your father dead or dying, the floor awash with their blood.'

'Luke Coulson killed my parents,' said Reardon, her eyes boring into Brook's.

'No he didn't.'

'The jury at his trial would disagree with you.'

'That's because they didn't have all the facts,' said Brook. 'You see, you'd already killed them at least half an hour before Luke and JJ broke in.'

'What? Are you mad?'

'Your father was attacked from behind, Reardon. Luke couldn't have surprised him like that. A complete stranger walking unannounced into his home. He would have been facing him, challenging him.' Brook shook his head. 'You cut his throat from behind, disabling him so he couldn't protect your mother, then you stabbed her over and over. An attack so cold-blooded, so brutal that no one could possibly suspect a family member. Or maybe it was insurance in case you were caught, the ferocity of the attack speaking to some imaginary abuse from your past. I don't know.'

'You're forgetting something, Inspector,' said Reardon. 'I saw the files Terri brought me. The post-mortem findings said my parents were killed between twelve and one p.m. I couldn't possibly have murdered them or it would be on the security film.'

'That was brilliant,' said Brook. 'I wish I could take credit for figuring it out, but Rachel Caskey was there before me. Oh yes, she knew. She worked it out. That's why she came for you. To confront you.'

'She had a gun,' snarled Reardon. 'I was petrified. Ask your daughter.'

'I can't excuse her actions, but by then she was an emotional wreck. And as she's dead, I'll assume the gun was to force some answers out of you and then, I hope, put you under arrest.'

'We'll never know, will we?' smiled Reardon.

Brook was sombre. 'Not for sure, no. But as she fought for life, she realised you might get away with it, so she gave me a nudge.'

'A nudge?'

'I've just come from the farm, Reardon.' He shook his head in admiration. 'Brilliant. You murder your parents around half past eleven, then turn on the kitchen's under-floor heating. The thermostat's right next to the phone. The heat kept them just warm enough to delay estimated time of death by half an hour, an hour at the most.

'The really clever bit was turning the heating off in full view of the security cameras that you yourself had just rebooted. You enter the kitchen ostensibly to check whether your parents are alive then you try to call for help. You check if the landline works, knowing very well that it won't, then lean your head and arm against the wall, apparently in distress, while surreptitiously returning the thermostat's setting to zero. But earlier, when Luke arrived, the heat would have been blasting out. When he found your parents dying, he did the decent thing, checking for signs of life, covering his clothes and shoes in blood in the process. But in so doing, he noticed the heat pouring off their bodies; he told me he thought it was their souls leaving to go to heaven.'

'Luke's an idiot.'

'You don't really believe that, do you?'

'I was at school with the cretin. Why wouldn't I believe it?'

'Because he was smart enough to work out that you were the killer, Reardon. Oh, I'm sure in the run-up, JJ was saying Ray this and Ray that, but Luke knew you'd done it.' Reardon was tight-lipped. 'But then you already know that, because he turned the tables on you, and by the end, *he* was using *you.*'

'What the hell are you talking about?'

'He played your game, Reardon, and he played it well. You needed Luke's silence and he agreed. What's more, he did it in full view of the security cameras. And to seal the deal, he looked up at the camera and gave us a motive for his attack on your father. Pretty quick thinking under the circumstances.'

'You don't know what you're talking about.'

'Don't I? When I went to see him at Wakefield Prison, he kept trying to lead me away from the truth, kept saying Ray was clever and wasn't coming back. He must have guessed Ray was dead but he kept up the pretence, kept your secret, because he loves you. And the price for his silence was simple. He wanted a promise of your love and devotion, and in return he'd happily spend the rest of his days in prison, comforted by your words and knowing that you needed him.

'You gave him that promise right before he let you go. A secret whisper in your ear. "Tell me you'll love me for ever, Reardon, and I'll take the blame." Your reply, we know. "Of course I will."'

'If you've seen that footage,' said Reardon softly, 'you must have observed how scared I was. Luke had a knife, for fuck's sake. I was terrified – literally shaking – when I ran into him.'

'I don't doubt it,' said Brook. 'You were improvising. Luke was a loose cannon. He hadn't done what you and JJ expected, so you were flying blind. And you were right to be scared. He didn't co-operate when it came to the bedroom department. He's not like JJ, driven by greed and lust. When JJ tried to initiate a rape, showing Luke how it was done, he got carried away and made it look too real, and when he started beating you, Luke didn't hesitate to kill JJ in defence of the only thing he'd ever loved.'

Brook took a pause to get his breath back. 'All you wanted was a sample of Luke's DNA on you to complete the narrative, but Luke loves *you,* not your body. A pure love you simply couldn't understand. So with JJ dead and the plan in trouble, you had to think quickly because – let's face it – you hadn't done all that work just to be thwarted at the last hurdle.

'While JJ bled out, you had to come up with another sequence of events. JJ was dead so he could stand in as the killer and Ray's co-conspirator. Nobody knew about your renewed relationship – it was a secret. So far, so good. Then you had to genuinely summon up your courage and go out into the house to turn on the cameras and run through your grieving-daughter performance, knowing Luke was running around with a knife. But you were more than up to the task. You even remembered to keep saying Ray's name to camera to back up your statement that he'd spent the night at the farm.

'In the end it worked out pretty well. Luke played ball and made a run for it and you went to get help, apparently distraught. In fact Luke saved you a job.'

'What was that?' enquired Reardon, sullen now.

'You'd already decided to kill Jemson when things quietened down.'

'And why would I kill JJ?' asked Reardon, affecting indifference.

'Because he was unreliable. You could never fully trust him, and with his drinking, you couldn't be sure he wouldn't start bragging. No, JJ had to go. You'd already hidden the prepaid phone in his flat so it would be found when he turned up dead. You'd bought two phones and filled them with texts you dreamt up purporting to show Ray and JJ planning the attack. The other phone – Ray's – you discarded, but we'd only need one phone to show the interaction between them. At some point in the near future, when Jemson was found dead in his flat, the whole sordid plan would be laid out for us. How Jemson conspired with Ray to kill your family and leave Luke Coulson to take the blame. Naturally DI Ford would assume Ray had come back to silence Jemson. It was brilliant, apart from one thing.'

'Enthral me,' said Reardon.

'You kept signing the texts with Ray's name. Two pre-paid phones used only for communicating with the other, and for some reason Ray felt the need to keep reminding Jemson who he was talking to. It didn't ring true. That's what got me wondering about Ray. Where was he? Abroad, as the car at the airport seemed to imply? Doubtful. So if he was alive and in the country on the day of the attack, he had to either be at the farm making sure the plan was successful *or* somewhere miles away getting himself a cast-iron alibi. He couldn't be in both places, but it didn't make sense that he was in neither.'

'You're almost out of time, Inspector. Terri will be back in a minute.'

Brook held out his hands. 'That's it apart from one further slip-up. After you'd killed your parents, you stripped in the kitchen and put your bloodstained clothes and shoes into a plastic bag. You returned to the bedroom naked to shower and wash the blood out of your hair. Your hair was still wet on the security film. You lit the tea lights around the bath, then texted a friend as though you hadn't got a care in the world and waited for JJ to arrive and tear off your clothes. But before he got there, you went to open the window to put the bag of clothes outside for collection and later disposal, presumably by JJ after the pair of you had cut Coulson's throat . . .'

'Sounds sensible.'

'It was. Only the bag must have had a slight leak and your mother's blood ended up staining the carpet near the window, enough to be noted on the blood plan. Worse, you got some on your hand as well, and when you opened the window, you left a fingerprint on the underside in your mother's blood.

'If your narrative were to hang together, such a stain would be impossible, because you didn't "discover" your parents' bodies until *after* you were sexually assaulted. The security cameras show that you never returned to your bedroom after you went to the kitchen, so you couldn't possibly have transferred your mother's blood to the window. That proves that the narrative with you as victim was a lie. Then, when Luke let you go, you ran away, skirting the reach of the cameras, collected the bag yourself and, on the way to get help, found a suitable place to hide it until later. Risky, but then you were improvising.' Brook smiled.

'What's so funny?'

'The fact that it was my daughter who gave you away. Unintentionally, of course.'

'I'm listening.'

'The photocopied files she stole. I was looking at them last night.'

'What about them?'

'The colour photographs that SOCO took are in chronological order of events at the farm, but as *we* saw them. The wrong order, as it turns out.'

'I don't understand.'

'The black-and-white shots that Terri gave you were in a different sequence after you looked at them. The right sequence. Without thinking, you reordered them placing the photographs of bloodstains from your bag of clothes *before* Jemson's death, because that's when it happened. SOCO placed them after Jemson's death, thinking the stains had been transferred from Luke Coulson's clothing or shoes after he cut JJ's throat. When I realised what you'd done, I knew.'

There was silence for a few moments and their eyes locked, Reardon looking coolly back at him before standing. She moved towards the open fire escape.

'Finished?' she asked, turning. Brook shrugged. 'What kind of sick mind comes up with a story like that?'

'I have a tendency to think the worst of people, I confess.' His features hardened. 'But I'm not often wrong.'

'But if you've seen the security film,' she said, 'you must know I'm the victim here.'

'No, you're a greedy, self-centred, cold-hearted bitch.'

Reardon stared, unmoved. 'So what now?'

'Now?' Brook was impassive. 'I tell the whole story to Terri and take her away from here, kicking and screaming if necessary.'

'You're not arresting me.'

'Without Ray's body, I have no evidence. Luke won't give you up. He kept his bloodstained clothes in the Range Rover to support your story when he could've thrown them away at any point along the M1. In fact, before I left him, he even asked me to reassure you that you were safe. How's that for love and loyalty? There's always the fingerprint, but that's suggestive at best. It wouldn't be hard to make the case that you picked up your mother's blood from Luke's clothes when he killed Jemson.'

'No,' said Reardon, thoughtfully. 'It wouldn't.' She smiled. 'Well, if that's all, I think you should leave.'

'Fine,' said Brook, buttoning up his jacket. 'But don't relax just yet. A forensics team is taking an in-depth look at Ray's cottage and garden using ground-penetrating radar.'

Reardon shrugged. 'Part of me hopes you do find him. Then we'll know that he is at peace and that JJ is a murderer as well as a rapist who got his just deserts.'

'Odd then that your testimony placed Ray at the scene the night before the attack.'

'It's been over a year,' smiled Reardon, her head held high. 'If you can pinpoint Ray's death to the week before I was attacked, I'll put the handcuffs on myself. You've got nothing.' She indicated the door. 'Now if you don't mind, I've got a relationship to end.'

Brook was sombre, defeat dulling his eyes. He played his final card. 'You're forgetting one thing.'

'And what's that?'

'I know what you did. And if you paid even the slightest attention to what Terri said about me, you'll realise I won't rest until I bring you to justice.'

Reardon was silent for a moment. She lit another cigarette and stood framed against the brilliant sunshine pouring through the fire escape doors.

'You're right,' she said, tossing her cigarette to the metal platform after just one drag. She stepped briefly into the kitchen and emerged with a gun. 'I can never be safe if someone knows.'

'Caskey's second gun,' said Brook, closing his eyes in self-reproach. *'Protection for Reardon.'*

'What?'

'She tried to tell me, but I missed it. So that's why she was armed when she came to confront you.'

Reardon laughed. 'It's not been your finest hour, has it, Inspector?' Brook took a step towards her, but like lightning she flicked off the safety catch and pointed the gun at him. 'Don't imagine Rachel didn't show me how to use this.'

Brook stopped in his tracks. 'You think you can shoot me and get away with it?'

'Me? Shoot you?' retorted Reardon, shocked. 'God, no! I'm a timid little mouse, remember. But while you've been showing off, I've been constructing another narrative. About how you stormed in here looking for Terri, hoping to prise her away from my loving arms, unable to stand the thought of your beautiful, damaged little baby falling into bed with a perverted lesbian.'

'Anybody who knows me will know that's rubbish.'

'On the contrary, like it or not, people who know you will define you by your mental illness.' She grinned.

Brook narrowed his eyes. 'My God, what kind of monster are you?'

'The thorough kind,' she crowed. 'Terri told me all about it. Your breakdown, your instability. I gather it's well docu-mented. As is the way you dote on your daughter. You'd stop at nothing to protect her, even sending one of your own detectives to try and break up our relationship. Sadly, the late lamented Sergeant Caskey isn't around to confirm or deny it, but luckily it's all on the security film Terri so helpfully told you about.

'And then there are the messages on Terri's phone that show you tried to split us up. That's why you came here today, to have one last go. When Terri refused, you got angry and threatened me, so Terri grabbed the gun that I'd foolishly accepted from your dead colleague for self-defence. She shot and killed you and then, realising what she'd done to her own father, turned the gun on herself.' Reardon aimed the gun at Brook's heart. 'What do you think?'

'I don't think it will play,' said Brook softly. 'But put one between my eyes if you're feeling confident.'

'Your eyes?' Reardon shook her head. 'You didn't know Rachel very well, did you? The skull is tough. A professional goes for the heart.' She pointed the gun at the aforementioned organ, but lowered the barrel a second later at the noise of a door slamming and a dog barking. 'And here's the tragic daughter, right on cue.'

She lifted the gun again and fired, hitting Brook full in the chest. He stood, wincing in shock and pain, clutching his hand to his heart before falling to his knees. For a second he stared in disbelief at the blood on his hand, then he fell face forward on to the bare floor with a thud.

'In here, Terri,' screamed Reardon. 'Help me!'

The door burst open and she raised the gun to the two burly officers at the threshold. Crouched on one knee, in full protective gear, they trained their guns on her in turn.

'Put the gun down! Get on the floor,' came the shout, at ear-splitting volume, again and again, until Reardon dropped the weapon in shock at her feet. The two marksmen ran towards her, bundling her to the ground and throwing her on to her stomach. She was cuffed in a trice, then hauled to her feet. An Alsatian appeared and reared up on its hind legs, restrained by a dog handler.

'He attacked me,' she screamed.

Noble ran into the apartment, eyes flicking round urgently. 'Inspector!' he shouted, locating Brook's body, face down on the floor. In a second, he was on him, pawing at his shoulder. 'Inspector.'

'He attacked me,' repeated Reardon, tears welling. 'I had no choice.'

'Get her out of here,' screamed Noble, tugging on Brook's shoulder to roll him over. Brook's face was creased in pain, eyes closed.

Morton ran through the door.

'Inspector! Oh Jesus. Rob, call an ambulance.'

A noise of escaping breath from the floor and Brook opened his eyes, sucking in fresh oxygen. 'Ow!' he grimaced, as Noble looked at him in astonishment. Gingerly he clambered to his feet, rummaging in his breast pocket to pull out a ceramic plate sporting a shallow crater where the bullet had struck.

'You bastard,' screamed Reardon, struggling against the burly officer holding her. 'You were dead. I saw blood.'

Brook dipped a hand into a pocket of his jacket, then held up his fingers for her to see. 'Ketchup,' he said, wincing as he rubbed his chest with his other hand.

Noble gestured at the AFO, who guided Reardon roughly towards the stairs, screaming and cursing all the way.

'Ruined my jacket,' observed Brook.

Noble's face was like thunder. 'I'll buy you one made this century.' Brook gave him a sidelong glance. 'Don't bother. You deserve it. Did you know she had a gun?' Brook looked away. 'Did you?'

'Caskey gave it to her for protection.'

'Yet you marched in here, defenceless,' shouted Noble. 'You wanted her to shoot, didn't you?'

'We had no proof, John,' pleaded Brook. 'I had to force her hand.'

'And get yourself killed?'

'I put the ceramic plate over my heart, didn't I?'

'You took a hell of a gamble.'

'Not really,' said Brook, making for the door, still grimacing.

'What if she'd fired at your head?'

'After what happened to her partner, Caskey was always going to teach Reardon how to shoot.'

'Bet your life?' frowned Noble.

'I was right, wasn't I?' said Brook, trying to smile through the pain.

'Don't ever do that again.' Noble punched him hard where he'd just taken the impact of the bullet, then stalked away shaking his head, leaving Brook rubbing his ribs in pain.

Recovering his breath, he saw Tinkerman emerging from his sweep of the apartment. 'Lovers' tiff?' asked the AFO, removing his helmet.

'Professional disagreement,' said Brook.

'The place is clear.'

'Thank you, Sergeant.'

'Here to help,' he replied, not cracking a smile.

'No hard feelings?'

Tinkerman sniffed. 'Let's just say you owe me one.'

*

Terri jumped from the patrol car as Reardon appeared, still struggling against her bonds. Banach held her back as two officers thrust Reardon into the wagon.

'Reardon,' called Terri, waving her arms, trying to get to her. She broke away and ran to prevent the door's closure. 'What's happening?' she screamed. 'Where are they taking you?'

Reardon's face hardened. 'You stupid little cunt. Why couldn't you keep away? Everything was going great until you dragged your fucking father into this.'

Terri's hand fell from the door and she burst into tears as it was unceremoniously closed. Brook emerged from the building clutching his chest. His shoulders slumped when he saw her distress and he went to enfold her in his arms, but she thumped him in the ribs and stomped away sobbing.

'I hate you,' she cried. Sargent barked and pulled on his leash, trying to get to her.

Brook grimaced. 'Getting shot really hurts.' As soon as the words were out of his mouth, he was remorseful. 'I shouldn't have said that.'

'You can apologise to Caskey in person,' said Noble.

'What?'

'Cooper says she came round an hour ago. Looks like she's going to make it.'

'Great news,' nodded Brook, the hint of a smile fading when he saw the distraught Terri burying her face in the dog's neck.

Noble clapped a hand on Brook's shoulder, making him wince again. 'Don't worry. So will Terri.'

Brook thought about it for a few seconds, then headed towards his daughter.

496